The Colonel

A Novel

By Michael L. Rea

www. workshopforwriters.com

Other works by this author include:
Fiction
Justice
The Raven Stone
Non-Fiction
Connected-Remaining Human in a Networked World

Other books available through Workshop for Writer:

Christ at the Center by Janet E. Rea
Old Bones by Greg Picard and Wendy Picard Gorham

For My Children,
Jonathan, Katie and Julia

What gain has the worker from all his toil? I have seen the business that God has given to the children of man to be busy with. He has made everything beautiful in its time. Also, he has put eternity into man's heart, yet so that he cannot find out what God has done from the beginning to end. I perceived that there is nothing better for them than to be joyful and to do good as long as they live; also that everyone should eat and drink and take pleasure in all his toil-this is God's gift to man.
Ecclesiastes 3:9-13

(Quotes are from the book of Eccleisastes, Holy Bible, English Standard Version, Crossway Bibles, 2007)

The Colonel

Authors Preface

This is a work of historical fiction, although, this may seem a contradiction in terms. Historical is often assumed to mean having to do with factual events and real people. Fiction on the other hand implies that the work has nothing to do with what are real facts. What, then, could be meant by historical fiction? The simplest answer might be that although this is a work of fiction, there may be some truth to be found in the pages that follow.

One of the greatest authors of historical fiction is Alexandre Dumas, author of *The Three Musketeers* and *The Count of Monte Cristo*, as well as a long list of other works. The author of this work owes a debt of gratitude to the writings of Dumas for they provided him with hours of pleasure in his youth and have no doubt contributed greatly to his own inspiration. One of the great attributes of Dumas' writing is that the reader is often left wondering if the work is fact or fiction. So many of the characters are real people from history, and Dumas worked tirelessly in researching events to give his stories an authentic nature, thus they were both historical and fiction. Who hasn't wondered whether the *Musketeers* weren't, in fact, hiding beneath the scaffold at the time of the execution of Charles I, plotting his rescue, as portrayed in *Twenty Years After*.

The Colonel is a work of fiction. Many of the characters are actual people who lived at the time of the story, which is intended to provide some historical authenticity. However, the detailed events, the plot and dialogue are purely fictional and are not intended to be taken as anything else. Should the reader begin to imagine that the events are real shall only serve to provide the author with some satisfaction in knowing that he has been successful in creating a story that leaves the reader with an impression of truth.

It is no coincidence that the surname of the main character of *The Colonel* and that of the author are in fact the same. This is simply because they are connected by birth, although separated by six generations. This also is in keeping with Dumas' work, since many believe that the character of D'Artagnon or perhaps Athos, in *The Three Musketeers*, may have been an allusion to the author's father.

The story of The Colonel takes place at the time of the Peninsular Wars and much attention is given to the 27th of Foot Regiment that was endearingly referred to as the Inniskillings by the people of Fermanagh County, Northern Ireland, and by the soldiers who served in the regiment. The largest market town of the county was Enniskillen, which makes the name of the regiment a near homonym. The author is indebted to Gareth Glover, author of *An Eloquent Soldier* and Mary Beacock Fryer, author of *Our Young Soldier*. These two works give a detailed description of the life of a solider in the Inniskillings during the Peninsular Wars. They chronicle the lives of Lieutenants Charles Crowe and Francis Simcoe, both officers in the regiment. Both of these works proved to be invaluable in the development of this story.

At the time of the publication of this work, the author has been unable to confirm any record of a Thomas Rea ever having served as a Colonel in the Inniskillings. However, he has visited Victoria County, Ontario, Canada where residents still refer to Thomas Rea as "The Colonel" some 170 years after his death and there remains a sword in the local museum of Lindsey, Ontario, which is said to have been used by the same Thomas Rea at the Battle of Waterloo. This mystery frames the plotline for this story, whether it is plausible or not is entirely up to the reader to decide.

As a work of historical fiction, the author has done exhaustive research into the events and people of the time period described, but as is always the case, there might possibly be some slight errors in the historical accounts, for which the author humbly apologizes in advance. As far as the characters go, if any sort of disparaging description is made of any real persons, please understand it was unintentional.

The Inniskillings suffered greater losses than any other British regiment at Waterloo. Two thirds of the regiment suffered casualties and they were instrumental in holding the center of Lord Wellington's line. This work has no other intent than to respectfully pay the Inniskillings with the highest honor for their steadfast courage.

If you enjoy this work, and I trust that you will, you will be pleased to know that work on the sequel is already underway. Look for an excerpt at the end of this work.

The Colonel

Table of Contents

The Colonel

Chapter One

1 There is a time for everything,
and a season for every activity under heaven:

(1843)

The sun was setting beyond the horizon as the deepening shadows stretched across the landscape and the last glimpse of light caught the extreme edge of the leafy treetops. Thomas was sitting alone, watching those last moments of daylight fading, bringing to an end, once again, to that brief interval of time which was the finite measuring rod of his existence. With every repeated advent of night, he was reminded of his temporal life, which was ever waning and hastening to its conclusion. And like so many previous moments, he found himself in contemplation, examining his life, trying to comprehend its full measure.

It is appointed to each man a time to die. It is what makes every man impotent, completely and utterly in submission to the will of the Creator. Therefore each man must consider how he will spend his appointed days, and to what end. How will his life be measured?

The land he now looked upon was not just any land. It was his land, 700 acres of the richest farmland in the county. He had labored to cut it from the wilderness with his own hands with the help of his sons. It had provided many joys and many hardships, and he was now connected to it, but he realized that possessing it was only an illusion. Long after he was gone, it would still be there. If for a moment in time, it created a false sense of wealth and security, that to was an illusion, a vanity.

(1777)

He was born Thomas Rea, in the year of our Lord, 1777, in the small village of Owenskerry, located in Fermanagh County,

Northern Ireland. He was the oldest of ten children born to James and Anne Rea. His father was a farmer, proprietor of his own land, not rich, but not a slave to poverty either. The Rea family had first come to Fermanagh County in the early 1600s as a part of the mass migration of Scotts which came over to establish the protestant influence desirous of King James. They were no longer Scotts, but Ulsterman, a name derived from the ancient Gaelic people of the region.

It was a simple beginning for Thomas, growing up on the farm with his siblings, lending a hand to his father, learning how to care for the land and the rewards of hard labor that come with the harvest. As he grew into a young man, however, he began to get the itch for adventure, that longing that wells up inside the heart of every young man when he comes of age. He couldn't really explain it. It was a desire to leave his home and make his own way in the world, to discover what life had to offer, to seek his fortune, regardless of the risk and peril.

(1794)

Six months to the day from his seventeenth birthday, he left home, turning his back on all he had ever known, and striding forward into the great unknown of his life journey ahead. He left, carrying only what he could hold on his back, and what little funds he had been able to save in his pocket. There had been a little trepidation in his step and a thread of uncertainty weaving its way through his thoughts, but there was also the excitement and the anticipation of what might come.

Young men, before they have entirely left their youth and entered into the life of responsibility that comes with adulthood, deceive themselves into thinking they have life all thought out. Rarely can any reasonable thinking person persuade them differently, and thus it was with Thomas. Despite the pleas of his mother and the arguments of his father, he would not yield his determination. He could still remember the words of his father, "Anne, we must let him go. He must make his own way. In any case, he will know that he will always have a place here." With the words still ringing in his ears, Thomas had left, not looking back. It was not that he didn't love his parents or his siblings. He loved them all. But, he was feeling suffocated, and he couldn't let go of the urge to strike out on his own.

He was only a few days on the road before he began to wonder if he had made a horrible mistake. Despite having visited several villages, there were no prospects of finding work, or learning a trade. He had exhausted his funds and he knew he would soon be feeling the pangs of hunger. He was left with little choice. He would have to go to the closest market town. As a result he came full circle and returned to Enniskillen, located on Lough Erne and the main trade center of Fermanagh County. It was only ten miles from his boyhood home.

Fermanagh had been the site of many frays between the local clan of Maguires and the O'Donnells of Donegal. The town of Enniskillen was on an island in the middle of a straight between the upper and lower Lough (lake) Erne. It had risen during the reign of King James, and in the early years there had been a castle that sat on the south west corner, separated from the opposite shore by a draw bridge. That castle had long since been destroyed and a new one had been erected on the north end of the island by the Coles. The name of the town had originally been from the Irish Inis Caithlen, or isle of Kehlen. Tradition told of a Kehlen the wife of Balor, a chief of pirates that had infested the waters off the Irish coastline to the west. By the late 18th century, Enniskillen had grown into a prosperous community.

Thomas had been to Enniskillen several times, with his father. He had hoped to avoid settling there, not because there was anything unappealing about the town, but just because it was all too familiar. When striking out on one's own, to have the first stopping point be one that he had already been to many times, seemed to be a failure of sorts. This disappointment soon waned, when within the first day of arriving he was able to secure a position as an apprentice to a local blacksmith.

The Colonel

Although he was not paid any wages, it provided board, and a room above the shop. For now that was enough.

A smithy was responsible not only for the local community metal works, but also skilled in leather work, construction and repair of farm implements as well as the design of horse tack. In a community like Enniskillen, where there was a constant stream of visitors and tradesmen, there was no shortage of work. The smithy was kept very busy given that his shop was just across the draw bridge next to the Gaol. As a result, John Kennedy, not having any sons of his own, was pleased to take a young man under his wings, put him to work and show him the trade.

For the first few months, Thomas did little more than keep the fire stoked, secure supplies, deliver products and make sure the shop was orderly and clean. He made the most of the opportunity to watch every movement of the smith, taking in each aspect of his technique and skill. It was not long before Mr. Kennedy noticed his natural aptitude for the craft, and slowly but surely he began to pass on to the young apprentice, every method and trick he had learned through years of practice.

(1797)

For two long years Thomas continued to work without wages, as he grew both in knowledge and in stature. On his twentieth birthday he stood six foot three, and the constant use of the striker and tongs had chiseled a muscular form that rivaled any among the young men of Enniskillen. With his strawberry blonde hair blowing in the convection currents created by the furnace, sparks flying from the hammer with each strike and perspiration glistening off his muscular frame, he was an imposing form to anyone who visited the shop. He had long since been earning more than his keep and so as a birthday present, Mr. Kennedy agreed to start paying Thomas a wage, a small percentage of the shops earnings which made him feel, for the first time, a sort of independence given that he now had a consistent wage.

Despite this favor shown to him, Thomas still had a longing for adventure. He knew it was a large world and he wanted to see more of it. In the back of his mind he kept thinking that as soon as he was able to save enough funds, he would be off to discover new places, to find his fortune. However, as fate would have it, his plans to leave Enniskillen were soon forgotten due to an unforeseen change in his circumstances.

A few weeks after he had received his birthday present, the shop was visited by old customer; a farmer by the name of William Copeland. He hailed from Lisbellaw, a small village just five miles to the east of Enniskillen. He required a special repair on the harness and shaft of a wagon that had been damaged in some sort of accident. What made this visit unique was that he was not alone.

As Thomas inspected the damage to the wagon his attention was immediately drawn to the two individuals occupying the bench seat. One, the wife of the farmer, had brilliant red hair pulled back into a bun, and green eyes that glistened like emeralds in the afternoon sun. The other, was a younger version of the first, clearly her daughter, only, her hair was not tied back, but instead flowed in tight curls down around her shoulders. She was about two or three years Thomas' junior and so strikingly beautiful that it was all he could do to keep from staring. He attempted to keep his mind and eyes on his work, but he couldn't help but glance up from time to time. When he came to the realization that the object of his attention had become aware of his distraction, he blushed with embarrassment. Out of the corner of his eye he saw a slight smile on the lips of the one who was causing his discomfort.

He turned to hide his countenance and returned to the problem at hand. Not only was the shaft of the wagon badly damaged, but the rim of one of the wheels had pulled away and was in need of repair as well. One of the horses' harnesses was also badly damaged and at closer inspection he noticed that the horse it was attached to was scratched and bruised and there was blood on the lower front left leg.

"Do you think you can repair it young man?" Mr. Copeland asked.

"Sure, it can be repaired. But, it will take a couple of days. I have a carriage in back which you can use to get you home, but I would not recommend going anywhere today. I'm afraid that one of your horses here has a badly bruised leg, and needs some rest and healing."

"The harness gave way and the horse stumbled into a ditch, a very nasty piece of luck. Well, Annie," as he turned to his wife, "I'm afraid we will have to spend the night. Young man, do you know of place where we might be put up for the night?" as he helped his wife down from the wagon.

Thomas was quick to step to the other side of the wagon, "may I help you down miss?" he offered to the young lady.

She smiled as she placed her hand in his and stepped from the wagon, dropping like a feather and landing lightly to earth; evidence that she had made the same maneuver many times before. "Thank you," she whispered as she rose to her full height and stood with her face just a few inches below his.

"You're welcome, uh, I mean my pleasure," Thomas stammered trying to regain the composure he lost the moment her hand had touched his.

"I see you have met my daughter Alice, my second oldest. Alice this is...what was your name again?"

"Thomas...Thomas Rea."

"Ah, yes Thomas. He's going to be kind enough to fix our wagon. Now what about lodging for myself and my family?"

"Yes, there is an inn just up the street on your right. The *King's Arms,* you can't miss it, right at the corner of Pudding Lane, across from the market. The proprietor is a pleasant sort and I am sure he can put you up. I will see to your horses. You can go on ahead. I will check on you a bit later to see how you're getting on."

"Very well, young man, thank you for your help."

Thomas unhitched the horses from the wagon and then led them to a nearby stable. He then reexamined the wagon and began dismantling the damages pieces. After setting everything aside, he returned to the task he had been working on when Mr. Copeland had interrupted. It was getting late in the day, and he needed to finish working the metal which already had been heating in the fire. It would take most of the next day, and then some, to complete the work for Mr. Copeland, therefore, it did no good to start on it that evening. Mr. Kennedy was gone, left to help a farmer with some fence mending and would not be back for a couple of days. He would have to do the work himself.

Just as it was getting dark, he set aside his tools, straightened up a bit, and then went to the water basin to wash. After believing himself to be presentable, he stowed his leather apron and left the shop, heading up the street toward the *King's Arms.* As he entered the front door of inn, he could see the Copelands sitting at a table near the fire. They were just being served their dinner. He walked toward the table, with just a little hesitation in his step.

"Ah, Mr. Rea, what's the word on our wagon?"

"Good evening Mr. Copeland, Ma'am, Miss," as he turned to each of the individuals at the table in turn. He paused slightly looking at Alice causing her to blush slightly. "I have boarded your horses, they should be fine. As I said earlier, it will take me better than a days work to completely repair the shaft and harness. If you need to return home to Lisbellaw, I can loan you a curricle that will serve to get you home. I can deliver your wagon in a couple of days. The curricle is certainly sufficient for you and your family, but I am afraid your goods will have to remain with the wagon." Just then the innkeeper's daughter arrived with their dinner.

"I suppose that will have to do," Mr. Copeland hesitated, "we were just about to have some dinner. Would you like to join us?"

"I...I would not want to impose."

"There would be no imposition. In fact we would enjoy the company. That is if you are able to provide us a little dinner conversation. Perhaps you could tell us a little about yourself. How did you come to be a smithy?"

Thomas hesitated slightly, but then slid down into an open chair. He glanced at the innkeeper's daughter and thought he caught a look of consternation. Then he looked at Alice and felt reassured that he had made the wise choice. "I'm not actually from around here," he started. "I was born in the village of Owenskerry, my father a farmer, like yourself. I came here a three years ago looking for work, and Mr. Kennedy, the owner of the shop, was kind enough to take me on as an apprentice."

"I don't understand, you left your farm and your family, to come here on your own," Mrs. Copeland asked. "You can't be more than one and twenty."

"Well, yes. You see, I wanted to...well sort of make my own way, if you know what I mean."

"Yes, yes, of course young man. How very courageous. But do you like being a smith?" Mr. Copeland asked.

"Yes, I suppose I do. That is to say that it is okay for now. A few months ago Mr. Kennedy made me the offer of a decent wage in the shop and we are kept very busy. It's a steady wage. However, I must admit that I'd like to see more of the world."

"Ah the dream of every young man, to see the world, to find adventure," Mr. Copeland winked at his wife.

Thomas thought he could see a little empathy in Alice's eyes, "Father, you don't need to embarrass him." She tried come to his rescue.

"It's okay. I realize it is a bit of a dream. It's just that I know there is more of the world to see, than just what is here in Enniskillen."

"But what about your parents" Mrs. Copeland intervened, "what do they think about all this?"

Thomas felt a little under the magnifying glass and the mention of his parents gave him the opportunity to change the direction of the conversation and to talk about his family. He explained that he was the oldest of ten children, but only nine were now alive, his youngest sister having died of scarlet fever when she was only five. As he talked, Mrs. Copeland kept interrupting, asking questions. He did the best he could to provide a picture of what his childhood was like, while at the same time properly characterizing his siblings. Alice remained quiet, but clearly attentive to every word.

After they had completed their dinner and as the conversation was starting to wane, Mrs. Copeland announced that it was time to retire, in her sort of abrupt manner. She rose from her chair and gave a look to Alice that clearly was the signal for her daughter to follow. Thomas rose from his seat, said his goodbyes and then excused himself.

Two days later, Thomas delivered the wagon to the farm before midday. Mr. Copeland invited him to stay for lunch before heading back to Enniskillen and he was quick to accept, given the prospects of spending more time in the presence of the beautiful Alice. From that moment on he knew that she was going to become his wife. Over the next six months he took every opportunity to visit the farm. There was nothing secretive about their courtship, in fact Mr. Copeland and Thomas had become friends. It seemed as though the farmer was quite content to allow Thomas to court his daughter.

At one point Mr. Copeland invited him to join the Orange Order. (The Orange Order was a protestant league formed after the Battle of Boyne, won by the army of William of Orange) He, of course, could not refuse, given that he wanted to remain on good terms with the father, so that he could continue to court the daughter. He was unaware that this decision would prove to have far reaching implications for the rest of his life. Besides serving as a political organization in support of Protestant succession, the Orange also acted to recruit young men for enlistment into the British military.

(1798)

The following year, 1798, the Irish Rebellion began. A group of Protestant and Catholics joined together for the first time to try and overthrow the British rule in Ireland. The members of the Orange Order, the most loyal of the Protestants, were pressed to join with the British forces sent to squelch the rebellion. Although not particularly politically inclined, Thomas saw it as an opportunity for advancement, or at least a chance to impress his soon to be father-in-law, so after being encouraged by Mr. Copeland, he enlisted. He and Alice had been courting for nearly a year, and she was quite disheartened to hear that he would be going off to war. With that naïve confidence of indestructibility that every young man possesses, he tried to assure her that he would be fine and when he returned, they would be married.

His first experience as a soldier brought Thomas face to face with the brutality of war and the tragedy that often accompanies it. On June 12, the rebels led by Henry Munro were cornered at Ballynahinch. The British forces were too great, and the rebels were squashed beneath the onslaught of the more powerful, and better equipped British army. Toward the end of the battle, Thomas found himself a part of a minor skirmish in which the rebels had become surrounded, and were attempting to offer up one last desperate defense. At the center of the foray was a woman. She was protected on either side by her brother and a friend. To her credit, she was a skilled combatant, and her fortitude was unmatched. However, before long, it became clear that the effort of the rebels was in vain, and they had little hope of escape, much less victory.

Courage gave way to prudence and the rebels chose to accept their fate, surrendering to the soldiers of the Orange Order. The Orange accepted their surrender, believing it served no purpose to continue. Shortly after the defeated had laid down their arms, the 22nd Dragoons arrived on the scene, insisting there would be no surrender. The Orange Order attempted to offer resistance, but the 22nd would have none of it. The prisoners were immediately set upon by the dragoons, sword in hand. Thomas watched in horror the scene that unfolded. It seemed only a matter of moments for the slaughter to come to an end. Appalled and disillusioned at the attack upon the defenseless rebels, he rushed to the side of the woman who lay beside her dead brother, her life blood ebbing from her body from wounds that would prove to be fatal. He held her head in his lap trying to offer some comfort, realizing she was not long for the world.

She looked up into his eyes, "have you done this?" she asked. "Alas, betrayed and destroyed by my own countrymen."

"No Miss, please do not presume that I could participate in such a devilish act. It was not your countrymen who have betrayed your confidence, but those who claim to be your lord and master from across the water. You have fought bravely, but the end is near, an unjust end as a result of an unmerciful and dishonorable foe. Forgive me brave one, for my inability to intervene on your behalf."

"Fear not, friend, God knows thy heart and if He does not judge you guilty, then neither do I. My life is His. It has never been for man to determine whether one should live or die, it is only for God to determine. Only…" with this her breathing became labored, and it was clear the end was near. "Only, would you do me one thing?"

"Of course, anything," Thomas felt the tears begin to well in his eyes.

"Would you remember me…and should you greet my parents, would you tell them I was not afraid? Tell them I died doing what I thought was right."

"Yes, but I do not know your name."

"Betsy Gray…" and with this last utterance she gave up the ghost.

Thomas laid her gently to earth, "don't you fear Betsy Gray, I will remember." Tears welled up in his eyes. It seemed a senseless thing. She was so young, and had so much to live for. She should not have died, not this way. He would never forget.

Chapter Two

[2] a time to be born and a time to die,
a time to plant and a time to uproot,

The rebellion was only to last a few months and Thomas was soon on his way home. As he had promised, when he returned to Enniskillen, he immediately proposed to Alice. There was no hesitation in her reply and they were given the blessing of both of their parents.

The experience of the rebellion had left Thomas somewhat melancholy. He was in love with Alice, and he was pleased that they were getting married, but the episode at Ballynahinch had left its mark on him and he had difficulty shaking the dark cloud that now hung over him. He wanted to explain it to Alice, but he never could find the words, nor was he certain that he should say anything about it. He did not want to cause her grief just as she was anticipating their wedding day.

Alice, for her part, recognized the sullen spirit of her beloved. She realized he had been changed somehow, but she did not know why. Every time she tried to inquire, he just seemed to push her away. He continued to affirm his love for her, but it didn't ease her concern that he had somehow distanced himself from her, from everyone. She could sense he was troubled and felt helpless to do anything about it.

(1799)

They were married in the Cleenish Parish Church, just a couple miles south of Inniskillen and Lisbellaw. The Parish rector was Rev. Hugh Howard. The rector's daughter Isabella was a childhood friend of Alice and served as the maid of honor. Stewart Pogue, Thomas' closest friend from childhood served as the best man. It was a simple wedding, attended by both families and a few friends and neighbors. Alice had a natural elegance about her and she made a beautiful bride. Thomas was able to put aside his demons for the moment and relish in the joy of his new wife.

Thomas' parents invited him and his new bride to return home to Owenskerry, but Alice had no brothers and so they chose instead to stay in Lisbellaw, enabling them to help with her parent's farm. Thomas put his talents to work and opened a blacksmith shop in the village. The two slept in a small room over the shop. It wasn't much, but the two newlyweds were quite content.

Stewart and Thomas' brother William helped the young couple rebuild a home on the edge of the Copeland farm, it took them nearly a year. It had been the original farm house built by Alice's great-grandparents and through the years had fallen into disrepair. The foundation was solid, but it was small. Additional bedrooms were added to the back of the house, in anticipation of the family the two hoped to raise. A new roof was also needed. With the help of her friend, Bella, Alice set to work cleaning and painting the interior.

Thomas applied himself to his work to ease the memories of the rebellion. Meanwhile, Alice was more than aware that her young husband was now haunted by the ghosts of war. She did not know exactly how to comfort her young husband, but she kept trusting that time would heal all wounds.

Bella Howard was a very attractive young girl, just one year younger than Alice. She had flaxen hair and dark eyes that seemed to look right through a person. She had always had her eye on Stewart Pogue, but he seemed to be completely unaware of her attentions. However, after the wedding, something changed. For the first time, it seemed, he began to take notice. He was apprehensive and unsure which made his first approaches appear coarse and awkward. Bella handled his floundering attempts with grace, giving in to her own ambitions, but remaining patient and understanding.

Alice attempted to aide the young romantics in anyway she could, but the match appeared to be doomed from the start, since the Reverend Howard would have none of it. He was first cousin to the Second Baron of Erne by marriage, and a farm boy could hardly be his daughter's equal. The only reason he had allowed Bella to continue her friendship with Alice, was due to the latter's grace and commanding presence, which caused the rector to forget her station.

Besides his prejudice against Stewart, the Reverend had much greater expectations for his daughter's marriage prospects. The Baron of Erne's youngest son, Robert Crichton was just a few years older than Bella, her second cousin by marriage and in his mind would make an excellent match. Bella on the other hand despised Master Crichton and thought him to be spoiled and a bit of a scoundrel. She was not alone in this opinion, of which the rector was completely oblivious.

Most attributed the lack of character in the young Crichton was due to the fact that his mother had died giving birth to him. This tragic end of the mother resulted in the father remaining emotionally detached from the poor child during the whole of his upbringing. Later, when the boy was grown, the father attempted to ease his own guilt in having neglected his son by providing the young man with anything he pleased, creating the now spoiled adult. This defect in character was quite obvious to Bella and she was sure that she could never love such a person. Fortunately for her, her cousin seemed completely unaware of her existence, and no promise of marriage had ever been made, nor did it seem to be forthcoming.

Alice was pleased to discover that Stewart had finally taken an interest in Bella. Nothing would delight her more than to have her two closest friends marry. As a result, she made every effort to bring the two of them together. This began by her insisting that Stewart attend church with them in Cleenish each Sunday. This was then followed by the occasional invitation to both of them for dinner in their new home. Stewart was kind of shy, and required a great deal of prodding. Bella was clearly in love with him, but for her part, she remained patient, waiting and hoping that he could summon up the courage. Fortunately, the rector remained completely unaware of Alice's attempts at matchmaking.

(1800)

On a warm sunny Sunday afternoon in September, the four friends met after church for a picnic near the Upper Lough Erne. It was a beautiful day and Alice saw it as a perfect opportunity to kindle the fires of romance. She kept trying to break the ice, attempting to draw Stewart out, but his quiet demeanor made it nearly impossible. Recognizing her friend's frustration and realizing her friend's motivation, Bella took the lead in the conversation, trying to keep it superficial so as not to embarrass her suitor in front of their friends.

"Did you hear the news," Bella announced. "Lord Crichton is to remarry. Can you imagine, after being a widower for 23 years he has decided to take himself a second wife, at his age."

"I hadn't heard," Alice replied. "How old is he?"

"Nearly seventy, I think," Bella said with a smirk.

"And who is he marrying?" Thomas asked, joining in.

"That's the best part. His new bride is barely twenty five years of age. I think she's the daughter of the Earl of Bristol, or something of the sort. It's ridiculous."

"Twenty five, are you sure?" Alice said surprised.

"That's what father said. Can you believe it? Cousin Robert must be fit to be tied. Imagine; his new stepmother is barely a year older than he is. Oh, how I wish I could have been there when he received the news."

"Maybe this will encourage him to find himself a wife," Alice chided. "You better watch yourself Bella, Cousin Robert may come to pay you a visit."

"He can stay right where he is," Bella retorted.

"Who is this Robert?" Stewart asked, with a slight tone of concern.

"Oh, didn't you know," Alice started before Bella could say anything. "Robert is Bella's cousin. Her father has been hoping that he would make a match for Bella for some time now."

This caused the color in Bella's cheeks to redden slightly. "Don't listen to her Stewart. Robert doesn't have the least interest in the daughter of a rector. He would not even pay me one moment of his attentions. He is too occupied with spending his father's fortune to even give me a thought."

"What about you Bella, would you be pleased to marry the son of a Baron?" Stewart asked. Alice's ploy had obviously struck him to the heart.

"I could never marry Robert," Bella insisted. "He is incorrigible and a cad. My father is completely blinded by wealth and ambition. I could no more marry Robert Chrichton than I could... well it could never happen...it will never happen."

"It would be something though Bella, living at Crom Castle. Can you just imagine?"

"That's enough Alice. I know your just teasing. Besides we don't want to give Stewart the wrong idea," she winked as she said it, trying to appear calm and in control.

Alice thought Bella was driving her point home a little strongly, but by his continence it was clear that Stewart was getting the message. She was pleased with herself, it appeared that she had been successful in stirring up a little jealousy in Stewart, he was clearly uncomfortable.

"I...don't know exactly what you mean, Alice. What wrong idea? It seems as if Bella has a mind of her own and will do as she pleases."

"Easy Stewart," Thomas intervened, coming to his friend's defense. "I think the ladies are merely playing, trying to make you a little jealous I suppose."

"What makes you think that?" Alice said with a mischievous smile.

"Don't pay any attention, Stewart. Besides, if Alice is so impressed by Crom Castle, she won't mind being my companion at the wedding."

"Are you serious?" Alice questioned somewhat in shock.

"Why not? Father and I are expected to attend and I don't think they will mind if I bring a friend."

"Bella, I'm the wife of a smithy, daughter of a farmer, I have no business being at such an affair and you know it."

"You could wear one of my dresses and you would look quite proper. No one there would know you, nor would they be the wiser. I could introduce you as my friend and the granddaughter of the Bishop of Elphin, or something, they would never know the difference."

"But...what about your father?"

"Oh, he won't care. Besides he likes you. He seems to think you were born into the wrong station to begin with. He still can't figure out why you married Thomas here, he thought you could have done better."

"Hey, what's this?" Thomas tried to fain that he was hurt by this remark.

"Sorry, Thomas, nothing personal," Bella quickly apologized.

"What do you think Thomas, should I do it?" as she looked toward him.

"Well, despite the rector's low opinion of me, I have always thought very highly of you and I think you would fit right in at Crom." He was trying to be funny, but it did not seem as if the others caught his attempt at sarcasm. "Besides," he continued, "what's the worst they could do, kick you out on the street."

"Don't be silly," Bella assured. "They would do no such thing. The worst thing that could happen is that they would choose not to invite father and I back for the next affair, which may never happen again in my lifetime anyway. Besides, I can't imagine going by myself with just father. I would be bored stiff."

"I know what you're thinking. You're just worried that you'll get cornered by Cousin Robert and you need me there for protection." Alice could not avoid one last temptation to tease.

"So you're going alone, I mean without any male companions?" Stewart clearly did not understand the implications of his question.

Thomas jumped in, "No Stewart, you and I will have to find something else to occupy us. This adventure is for the ladies alone. Besides, you don't think the rector would want you tagging along."

With this Stewart blushed, "no I guess your right. I think the last thing he would want was to see me again."

Bella could tell that Stewart was embarrassed, "don't worry Stewart, father will come around. You'll see, he just needs to get to know you better. And don't you go worrying about Cousin Robert. The last I heard was that the Baron was trying to arrange something between him and the granddaughter of Richard Hardinge of Belle Isle."

"That would be a pretty match, considering she is barely eight years old," Alice chimed in.

"I don't see why that would stop the Baron, that would make her only 15 years younger that her mother-in-law to be. That hardly seems unreasonable." With this observation they all laughed out loud, Stewart included.

Bella jumped to her feet, "come on Mr. Pogue. How would you like to accompany me on a walk along the lough?"

Thomas started to get up, but thought better of it when he caught a little shake of the head by Alice. "You go on ahead," she said to the couple. "Thomas and I will clean up here a bit. We'll be able to catch up later."

"Oh Alice, I did not mean to leave this for you," pointing to the luncheon faire.

"Don't be silly Bella, you and Stewart go on ahead. Thomas and I will be along shortly."

Thomas and Alice did make it appear as if they were cleaning up a bit, while Bella and Stewart went on down to the lake alone. After a few moments Alice took Thomas by the hand and together they followed their friends at a safe distance, close enough to have a proper view, but far enough back to allow for a private and discreet conversation undisturbed and unheard.

It remained a pleasant afternoon, and the friends were all disappointed when it came to an end and they had to depart. Alice seemed quite pleased with herself during the ride home in the curricle and Thomas left her to her own thoughts, unwilling to pry into the machinations of a female mind that was preoccupied with the complicated and intricate plot of matchmaking

A few weeks later, Alice accompanied Bella and her father to Crom Castle for the wedding between the Baron and his child bride. Crom sat on a huge estate overlooking the southernmost part of upper Lough Erne. It was fifteen miles as the crow flies from Cleenish, the better part of a day's ride by coach. Upon arriving they were met by Lord Crichton, who, upon introductions, gave Alice a questionable look, but said nothing. They were directed to rooms in the West Wing, where they were allowed to refresh themselves before dinner.

Leaving Bella alone in their room, Alice decided to explore the west wing. There was a pleasant sitting room where she found a quiet place to relax perched in front of a large bay window which looked out upon a green. She was deep in her own thoughts, imagining what it was like to live in such place, completely unaware of the presence of the young woman who had silently approached from behind her chair.

"Hello, who might you be?" the stranger asked.

Alice was completely caught off guard. She gave a jump and nearly fell from her chair before regaining her balance. She stood abruptly and faced her inquisitor. "I...I'm Alice," she said stumbling over the words, and gave a slight nod of the head, not sure what to do.

"Alice? Oh yes, you must be Bella's friend, Alice Rea, I believe."

"Yes ma'..am, er miss," she stuttered.

"Please to meet you Alice, I am Lady Mary Hervey, soon to be Bella's cousin once removed."

29

"Please to meet you milady," she greeted as she gave a slight courtesy. Lady Hervey looked a little older than her 25 years, perhaps Bella had it wrong, or maybe it was the way she wore her hair tied up in back. She was not particularly pretty, not unattractive, merely plain. However she had a sort of elegance about her and a continence which portrayed an air of confidence and poise. This tended to make up for her lacking in the typical physical attributes associated with prettiness.

"Please call me Mary. I hope you will consider us friends."

"Yes, thank you mi...Mary."

"Did you have a pleasant trip, I trust? Where is Bella? I have been so looking forward to meeting her."

"Our trip was quite pleasant, thank you. Bella is resting in the bedroom just there. I am sure she would be happy to meet you." Alice started to take a step toward the bedroom.

"No, please do not disturb her on my account, let her rest. There will be time later. Perhaps you would not mind keeping me company here, please sit with me a moment."

"I would be pleased to do so, Mary." She was not pleased at all. She did not want to sit and talk with her, what was she going to say? They had nothing in common. She wished Bella were here.

"Rea? I don't believe I know any Reas. Is your family from here about?"

"Rea is actually my married name, and yes I am from Fermanagh County, near Enniskillen. Bella and I have known each other...well nearly our entire lives." She tried to avoid any reference to her family that might give her away.

"You're married, and so young. I had no idea. I suppose then you might be able to provide me with some counsel, considering the present circumstances have determined that I am about to enter into matrimonial bliss and all."

"Oh, I don't know M...Mary. I have only been married a very short time. There is still much for me to learn, I am afraid my counsel might be somewhat presumptuous and lacking any real prudence." Alice was starting to grow a little more comfortable. Lady Hervey was actually quite amiable and she was quickly growing fond of her.

"But you are married, and I assume you love your husband?"

"Oh yes, with all of my heart. I could not imagine a life without him."

"This is a special thing, love between a man and a woman. I would desire to know such love."

"So...you don't love Lord Crichton? I mean to say, do you love each other?"

The Lady paused briefly, clearly thinking hard about her answer. "Shall we say, there are no pretenses between the Lord and myself. I suppose you think it kind of strange, a woman of...well of my youth marrying Lord Crichton. I'm quite aware of what people may think. However, I am not unaware of my limitations...I am not pretty, and although I am young, a girl of twenty five may not have too many more opportunities placed in front of her. And after all, Lord Crichton is a very kind and generous man. I believe he will be good to me, and I think I can make him a devoted wife. Just the same, I can just imagine what people must think."

Alice could tell that her ladyship was in turmoil over her upcoming nuptials. She kept reaching for the words, something that would put her at ease. "Do not worry, Mary, I am sure that everyone only thinks the best of you, and can only hope for your happiness. And if they don't...well it doesn't really matter what they think. What really matters is what you think and feel. If your heart is telling you that what you are doing is right, that is all that is important. And as for whether you are pretty or not...well from the first moment I saw you I was struck by your elegance and poise, something that is of far greater value than mere prettiness. Lord Crichton is a very fortunate man, and I hope he comes to appreciate his good fortune in finding such a bride."

"How kind you are. Do you really mean to say that you can understand my position? Is it possible to make sense of a girl my age marrying a man nearly three times her age. It would mean so much for me to know that you don't think ill of me for entering into this marital contract, for a contract it is."

"I have no right to act the part of your judge. We are not always in control of life's circumstances. In fact, it would more likely be the other way around. All that we can hope to do is to demonstrate fortitude in the face of tragedy and grace and dignity in the face of disappointment. I think if we look closely we will find both here, fortitude and grace. Not that your situation is tragic," Alice tried to cover her mistake. "You must know what you're doing. You don't impress me as someone who would enter into marriage lightly, without contemplation. And if Lord Crichton is as you say, kind and gentle, well then you could do much worse in the choosing of a husband."

"These are encouraging sentiments indeed. I can see why my soon to be cousin is fond of you and considers you her friend. I would hope in time that you would consider me in the same light, a friend."

"There is no reason to fear on this account, the honor would be far more mine." Alice was beginning to feel a little guilty. She really admired Lady Mary, and did not want to deceive her. She was beginning to think that she should tell her the truth.

"How do you like Castle Crom, Alice?"

"It is beautiful, Mary, and placed in such a beautiful setting here above Lough Erne. I would enjoy an opportunity to explore the grounds."

"And so you shall, and what's more I hope this will not be your only visit. I shall be pleased if you and Bella would come and visit me often."

At that moment Bella emerged from the hallway that led to their room.

"Ah, Bella, come and meet her Ladyship," Alice greeted rising to her feet, while at the same time giving Bella a look of slight consternation.

Lady Hervey rose to her feet as Bella approached. Bella curtsied. "Hello milady, I am very pleased to meet you. Congratulations on your upcoming marriage."

"Please, cousin, none of this formality. Call me Mary. I can't tell you how pleased I am to finally meet you. I do hope that we are going to be fast friends. And look at you, so very pretty, just as his Lordship described. May I call you Bella?"

Bella started to blush. "Yes of course, I would be honored."

"Please sit with us a moment. Alice and I were just getting acquainted."

Just then, a footman arrived from the far hall. "Dinner is served madam."

"Thank you Williams," Lady Mary replied. "I am so sorry. I guess I didn't know the time. You two must both be starved. Shall we proceed to the dining room?

The footman led the way, followed by Lady Mary and Bella walking shoulder to shoulder. Alice trailed slightly allowing the two others to become acquainted as they walked. She couldn't help to be impressed by the distance from their apartment to dining hall. Had she tried to find her way on her own she would have surely been lost.

The dining room was grand and unlike anything she had ever seen or experienced. Everything glittered and glowed in the light of the two chandeliers hanging from the ceiling. The table was elegantly set in silver and porcelain in a manner that she was completely unfamiliar. It intimidated her, she was not sure how to behave. She watched Bella's every movement as each course was being served. Whatever Bella did, she did the exact same thing, all the time trying to appear inconspicuous.

The Lord of the manor sat at one end of the long dining table, with his bride to be on the complete opposite end. Lady Mary had arranged to have Bella sit to her right and Alice to her left. This provided Alice with some comfort since she had already grown at ease with her ladyship. On each side of the table were seated several guests who had come for the wedding, most of whom were distant relatives of some nature. The only exceptions seemed to be Alice and the vicar of the local abbey, who no doubt was performing the ceremony. To the right of the Baron was his eldest son Abraham, heir to Castle Crom and the baronetage of Erne. To his left was his middle son, Captain John Crichton of the 6th Inniskilling Dragoons and his wife Jane.

To Alice's left was a rather large, middle aged woman, a distant cousin of Lord Crichton. She was fairly pleasant, although she was easily given to a form of hysterics any time anyone offered anything that was the least bit jovial. When she laughed it was with such energy and commotion that Alice was afraid that she would upset the entire table setting placed in front of her due to the convulsions of her well endowed chest. Although distracting and unnerving, it provided her a sort of strange easiness, knowing that any momentary mishap in proper etiquette by her would, more than likely, go completely unnoticed by the rest of the guests.

The chair to Bella's right sat unoccupied through the first course, only to be filled by the tardy, and somewhat disheveled Robert Crichton. Lord Crichton was clearly displeased with his son for failing to appear punctually and in good form, but refrained from calling attention to it in front of his guests. Besides what appeared to be an intentional lack of decorum-for there was no offer of apology-the young Crichton appeared to be rather put off that he was expected to be in attendance at all. Having been placed in close proximity to, what was obvious to all, the most attractive and unattached young lady in the room, made little difference to his continence of clear contempt for the whole proceeding.

Alice thought it strange that Robert Crichton should bare a similarity in appearance to Thomas. He was of the same height and build, with the same strawberry blond hair, and the same sort of sharp nose. He had a mustache, and shortly cropped beard which made it a little difficult to tell if he was similar in the trace of his jaw line as well. Looking more closely, she could see a difference in the eyes. They were rather vacant and unfeeling. It made her feel cold, and it caused her some discomfort that she had, if only for a moment, made any comparison between this stranger and her loving husband.

It soon became clear to her why Bella could never love such a man. He was clearly self absorbed and arrogant. She couldn't see any possibility of the two of them ever being together, which made Stewart's position seem all the more secure. Looking in the direction of Bella's father, she tried to imagine how he could have ever wished for his daughter to marry such a man as this.

Robert seemed to have very little to say to anybody, and appeared somewhat oblivious to everyone in the room. So it came as a complete surprise when he turned and addressed himself to Bella, interrupting a somewhat amiable conversation between her and her soon to be cousin.

"Well, Cousin Bella, have you failed to attach yourself to a husband," he said loud enough so that everyone at the table could hear, causing a few heads to turn. Alice thought he was being more than impertinent, and it was quite clear that he had too much of the spirit in him.

"No, Cousin, I have not," Bella responded as discreetly as she could, given the circumstance. Lady Mary clearly wanted to come to her aid, but was at a loss for words.

"Well don't fret cousin," he continued with the same vulgarity, "I am sure you could follow the example of my soon to be mother here and find an old worn out baron who would be flattered by your attentions."

"You have said enough Robert! Be still or leave us." Lord Crichton shouted from across the table.

"You're right father," Robert replied sarcastically. "I'm quite sure there is nothing more that can be said." With this he rose from his chair and sullenly left the room, leaving everyone in a state of dismay.

Lady Mary was able to maintain her composure throughout this rude display. "I'm terribly sorry, Bella, I can't excuse Robert's behavior, he has treated you very badly."

"And you as well Mary," Bella replied. "Don't fault yourself. I have known him much longer than you, and I am quite accustomed to his ways. I can not allow myself to be offended by the comments directed toward me, because I neither admire nor respect the source. However, I am sorry that you should have to carry such a burden on the eve of your wedding. I trust you will not take his disparaging remarks to heart."

"No, rest easy there, I think it best that we put the whole incident behind us. In some instances it is better to have a poor memory."

"Yes, I agree, I think it wise that you both put it aside." Alice added. "Let's not let it ruin this otherwise beautiful evening, nor tomorrow's joyous affair."

"Agreed," Bella said in support.

The remainder of dinner went without incident. Bella and Mary seemed to be getting on extremely well. After dinner, Mary invited them both for a turn in the garden. It was a beautiful evening, the summer sun was just setting behind the hills and the air was pleasantly cool. Alice enjoyed being in the open air. Despite its grandeur, she felt as if the walls of Crom had begun to close in about them. They continued their conversations until it was time to retire. On occasion, Mary would pose questions to Alice about Thomas. Fortunately, she was able to deflect anything that might reveal their station, and instead spent the time talking about how Thomas was a very handsome young man, very kind and loving, avoiding any real details about their lives. When Mary would start to get too detailed in her questions, Bella would interrupt and change the subject entirely. Alice felt a little guilty about this deception. She had grown in her fondness and respect of Mary and she did not want to lie to her.

The next day they all gathered at Crom church for the wedding. It was a simple affair with a highly restricted guest list. It was clear that Lord Crichton had no desire to make the event a spectacle. Alice felt a little sorry for the young bride. It was difficult for her to get past the injustice. Despite her ladyship's resolve and consent to this arrangement, Alice couldn't help but think that the bride was settling.

When it came time to say goodbye, Lady Mary made it very clear to both Bella and Alice that she would love to have them come again for a visit. They both agreed, although Alice could not conceive of continuing the ruse. It was best to allow Mary to enjoy the moment, but she was determined to tell her the truth should they ever meet again.

The ride home in the coach was very quiet. Bella and Alice were both lost in their thoughts. The rector would occasionally make some remark concerning Crom Castle or Lord Chrichton, but neither of the young ladies were paying any attention to him. For her part, Alice was looking forward to getting home and seeing Thomas again. It had only been a couple days, but she was homesick. Castle Crom had been delightful, but she had felt somewhat out of place.

Chapter Three

³ a time to kill and a time to heal,
a time to tear down and a time to build,

(1800)

The fall slowly turned to winter and the days became shorter. Alice was soon to realize that she was pregnant. Despite this joyous news, she was not diverted from continued attempts to try and bring Stewart and Bella together. Bella needed little encouragement, but Stewart was nearly hopeless. She was beginning to wonder if she would have to do the proposal of marriage on his behalf.

Early in the spring, just after the completion of their home, Thomas and Alice were blessed to receive into the world their first son. In honor of the child's two grandfathers he was christened James William Rea. If Thomas was still feeling any of the effects of his military action during the rebellion, it was soon forgotten. He was soon himself again, relishing in his son and the joys of fatherhood. A year and a half later, James was joined by a younger brother, William. And still Stewart had made no hints of a proposal to Bella.

(1802)

Even as William was being rocked in his cradle, rumors were circulating concerning the aggression in Europe of the French emperor Napolean. The Inniskilling (27th Regiment of Foot) had returned from the battle of Alexandria and were seeking new recruits. The Inniskilling were originally formed as a militia in Enniskillen in 1689 to fight against the Catholic King James II. They had already achieved a proud history and it had long been the desire of every young man of Ulster to join the regiment. Thomas was no exception. Despite his adverse experience in the Irish Rebellion, he still felt the yearning to join his fellow comrades. But with two young boys to care for, he resisted this urge and tried to turn a deaf ear to the pleas of his fellow Ulstermen. It was of no avail. Stewart kept badgering him until he finally relented.

Alice was not naïve to her husband's desires. She had long since realized the inevitability of Thomas returning to service. She could see the look in his eyes. There was very little she could do. She was filled with the fear and uncertainty of the possibility that if he left, he may never return, while at the same time she realized that if she didn't let him go, she might lose him as well. She was helpless.

When Thomas finally came to speak to her, she was already prepared for what was to come. "Alice," he began. "I know you have heard the rumors about Napolean and the call put out by the Inniskillings. I have been thinking...perhaps for a long time... that I should join. Now, before you get all emotional and tell me what I should or shouldn't do, please know that I have thought about this a very long time. This is not a frivolous decision. This is something I need to do, something I have to do."

She wondered why men always phrased it like this, 'something I have to do', as if they don't really have a choice, when in fact they do. She knew that the decision had already been made, and there was little she could do about it. "I understand. I have always known this was coming. For nearly four years I have been your wife, shared your bed, and there is very little that you do that surprises me anymore. I don't like it. I don't understand it, but I would never stand in your way. But you remember this one thing Thomas Rea, if you go, you had better come back or I will never forgive you. I love you with all of my soul, but you must realize that if you are killed in some God forsaken foreign land, it will break my heart."

With that she threw herself into his arms, hoping that he could not see the tears in her eyes. She had to let him go, if she didn't, she was sure to regret it. Thomas held her for the longest time, trying to provide her some kind of assurance. He knew the risk of war, but he had to go. Somehow he knew that he would come home again. She really didn't need to worry.

39

"Don't worry Alice. I'll come home again, I promise," he whispered in her ear. Then he kissed her.

A few days later Bella appeared at the door sobbing. Alice put her arm around her friend, ushered her in and guided her to a chair.

"What is it Bella? What's wrong?" she asked, already guessing the answer.

"Did you know that Stewart and Thomas have gone and joined the Inniskillings? They are going off to war."

"Yes, Bella, Thomas told me a few days ago."

"But, Alice, Stewart has given me no promise...no pledge of marriage. What am I supposed to do? Does he expect me to just wait around here forever, pining for him?"

"I don't know, Bella, what did he say?"

"He said he can't expect me to wait, it wouldn't be fair."

"But does he want you to wait?" Alice asked, trying to comfort her friend.

"I don't know, I think so. If only he would just speak to me, tell me what he really thinks."

"I'm afraid that's asking a lot. It just isn't Stewart's way. Tell me this, did he say he would write."

"Yes, he said he would write...and he did say he loves me..." Bella started to sob again.

"Well there you go, he loves you. He wants you to wait for him. You'll see they'll be home before we know it. Now, now don't cry." Alice put her arm around Bella and held her close.

"I...I suppose your right," Bella said between sobs. "They will come home, they have to. I can't live without him...", the tears started flowing again.

(1803)

The time came for Thomas and Stewart to leave. The new recruits were being sent to Sicily. After his defeat at Alexandria, Napoleon had remained quiet for a time, and Britain and France were at peace. However, Napoleon used the opportunity to rebuild the French army and after it became known, Britain declared war against the French, and thus the Napoleonic wars began. The 1st Battalion of the Inniskillings, 27th Regiment of Foot, had been quartered in Sicily since Alexandria, and the new recruits were being sent to join the regiment. They sailed from Cork to Portsmouth where they remained quartered waiting for transport. Late in October, they boarded the newly re-commissioned H.M.S. Indefatigable, which was captained by Graham Moore.

Thomas had never been aboard ship before, and although the journey was relatively calm and without incident, he spent the first couple of days trying to find his sea legs. Stewart seemed to be less affected by the unsteady deck beneath their feet, which only served to heighten the discomfort that Thomas was feeling.

"What's the matter, Thomas?" Stewart asked, approaching him from behind as he stood leaning over the ships railing. "The sea doesn't seem to agree with you."

"I signed on to be a soldier, not a sailor," he responded, despite the fact that he was not particularly interested in chatting.

"Yeah, you do look a little green. Maybe this will help," handing Thomas something wrapped in paper.

"What's this?" he started to unwrap it.

"A peppermint, the ship's steward gave it to me. He said it would help."

Although he did not feel much like eating anything, Thomas placed it in his mouth. It did seem to provide some comfort, but it didn't keep him from spending most of the remainder of the voyage at the rail. The time passed very slowly on the ship, with very little for the soldiers to do. It was a relief when they finally heard the signal "land ho!" as they approached the island of Sicily. It was unclear as to what their role would be in Italy, but anything would be better than remaining aboard ship.

The British garrison was housed at Messina on the northeast corner of the island. For the new recruits, the next several weeks were spent in intensive training. The British army was a disciplined lot, and the Inniskillings were more the rule than the exception. Thomas and Stewart were equal to the task. It was not long before their asset to the battalion was realized. Stewart was an exceptional marksman with the flintlock. Thomas on the other hand was unequaled with a saber or the bayonet, most likely due to years of labor as a smithy. By the time the training was completed, they had gained the respect of the entire outfit, with perhaps the only exception being the Sergeant-Major Roger McHugh. The Sergeant-Major was rarely impressed by anything or anyone. It was his responsibility to shape the new recruits into a disciplined fighting unit, and he was not about to give them the satisfaction of believing that their progress had been acceptable.

(1804-5)

Although a long way from home, the winter in Sicily was rather pleasant, easing their longing for home. The year 1804 proved to be somewhat inconsequential for the 27th. Napoleon had declared France an empire with himself as an emperor in May of that year, but there was little promise of war actually reaching the island of Sicily. The French were no match for the British at sea and Napoleon seemed content to keep is strategies focused on the continent. As the coalition of allies was formed, most of the fighting was restricted to Bavaria and the borders of Russia. In March of 1805, Napoleon declared himself the Emperor of Italy, which seemed to offer the prospect that the Inniskillings would soon be called on. The men of the Inniskillings began to grow tense with the anticipation that war was on the horizon. Daily they continued their routine of drills, and the drudgery continued. Winter came and still it remained quiet.

There is nothing more difficult for a soldier, than to remain idle while comrades are engaged in conflicts miles away. As weeks grew into months, the lack of activity caused even the most disciplined soldier to become agitated. Some were affected more than others. Such was the case for Private John Cullen. He was a large burly Irishman with brilliant red hair. When he walked through a doorway, there was very little room for the light to pass through on either side. His temperament was ideally suited to the color of his hair. His imposing figure caused most of his compatriots to steer clear when he was in their presence. However, the constancy of the boredom that now embraced the entire regiment was beginning to cause Cullen's patience to wear thin. It was soon clear that he was looking for a fight, and it mattered little whether it was friend or foe.

It was unfortunate that the victim to fall prey to this unstable giant would turn out to be one private James O'Neil, a young man of slight build, who had yet to reach his twentieth year. It was one of those strange moments of fate which determined that this unwary tadpole would just happen to be passing by as Private Cullen turned in his direction carrying a freshly poured cup of tea. The resulting collision caused the greater part of the beverage to cover the front of the sark of the already tightly wound ruffian. Cullen's initial surprise caused him to swing his arm sending a bewildered O'Neil clear across the room.

It is moments like these that discernment should rule over emotion, but this was not the case for the immature O'Neil. "What d'ya do that for ya oaf," he shouted, realizing too late that keeping silent would have been more prudent.

"You stupid, impudent whelp! Look what you did to my shirt. I think it is about time for me to teach you a lesson you will never forget." With that Cullen began to roll up the sleeves of his shirt.

It was clear that this was not going to end well. O'Neil was clearly no match for Cullen, and given the level of rage of the massive man, it seemed likely that the young man might be in mortal danger. This realization left Thomas, who was sitting nearby at the time, little choice.

"Leave it alone Cullen," Thomas interjected. "O'Neil didn't mean anything. It was an accident, and that was all."

"You stay out of it Rea, this has nothing to do with you," as he threw aside a chair which O'Neil had positioned himself behind. "I'm going to give this boy a beating he won't soon forget."

"I said leave him alone," Thomas shouted a little more firmly as he jumped from his seat and stood between the antagonist and his intended victim.

It was clear that Cullen was out for blood and even though Thomas provided a much more arduous opponent, he was not about to be dissuaded. He immediately threw himself upon Thomas with all the force he could muster. Thomas was equal to the task, and fully prepared for the assault. He stepped aside deftly allowing the undisciplined Cullen to fall to the floor. Failing to secure his prey, the astounded and embarrassed man leaped to his feet ready for a second attempt. This time he proceeded with a little more caution. Instead of charging forward, he slowly stalked Thomas, moving within arms length with the hopes of being able to land a blow. His left jab was deflected by Thomas and then he swung wildly with his right, but Thomas was able to duck and step aside untouched once again.

"Easy, now Cullen, we should be able to settle this without having to come to blows," Thomas was attempting to bring some calm to the situation, but it was clearly an effort spent in vain.

"Stand still, you rogue. I'm going to teach you a lesson for sticking your nose where it's not welcome."

With that Cullen attempted a third assault and then a fourth. It was clear to everyone in the room that Thomas was much too quick. With every swing and miss, he was able to side step, while leaving a solid blow to the midsection of the out of control Cullen. Again and again, the giant came at Thomas, and each time he avoided injury, while inflicting a well placed blow of his own. As the giant began to grow weary, it appeared that his rage was also waning. But he would not quit. Thomas realized he would have to put an end to it. One more time he drew his opponent in, only this time instead of stepping aside, he stood his ground and deflected the blows and then immediately threw himself into the other man with his whole weight landing blows with both fists to the jaw, causing Cullen to stumble backward, falling to the ground. For a moment the conquered man just sat in stunned silence. He then just lay back on the floor. The fight had gone out of him and he was defeated.

Thomas stood over Cullen and then reached out his hand, pulling him back to his feet. "I'm sorry, John, but I just couldn't let you kill O'Neil. Trust me. You would have regretted it later."

Cullen gave a little grin, and then winced in pain as he rubbed his sore jaw. "I suppose you're right. I guess I just let my temper get the best of me."

"Save it for the Frogs," Stewart said as he patted Cullen on the back, while smiling at his friend.

"Yeah, save it for the Frogs," Thomas agreed.

"I just wish we would get a chance at them Frenchies," Cullen sighed. "I'm tired of all this waiting around."

"Don't worry John, our time will come," Stewart said reassuringly. "It can't be long now. Old Boney has made himself emperor of Italy with his brother the king, and I'm sure it won't be long before we're asked to put him in his place."

"Aye, of course you're right," Cullen agreed, wiping the blood from his mouth. "In any case I'm glad Thomas is on our side. I can't say I have been bested by very many men, but I was bested today."

As it turned out, Stewart was correct. A few weeks later they began to receive reports that they would be soon called into action. The allied forces had been defeated at the battle of Austerlitz. As a result Napolean's first division moved to take control of southern Italy. King Ferdinand had set up his defense of the kingdom of Naples and the Sicilies at Campo Tenese, however he was soon overrun by the French and had to withdraw to Sicily. Despite the retreat of Ferdinand, the Neapolitan army remained entrenched at Calabria and Gaeta and a lengthy siege ensued.

The Colonel

(1806)

Early in June, British forces under the command of Major-General John Stuart were to sail from Messina to the beach near Calabria and engage the French army. Altogether there were more than 5,000 British troops, 750 of whom were the Inniskillings, who along with a combined battalion of other companies were put under the leadership of Colonel Lowry Cole. In the all the first battalion had more than 1200 soldiers, including 48 officers.

Thomas and Stewart both remained calm and stoic as preparations were being made. Neither of them said a word, deep in their own thoughts as they boarded ship. Cullen, on the other hand, was strutting around like a bull in heat, prancing and boasting nonsense. Private O'Neil was the benefactor of most of Cullen's remarks. Ever since their altercation, Cullen had taken it upon himself to bring O'Neil under his wing. It was not exactly clear if this was because he had actually grown fond of O'Neil, or if he just felt guilty for nearly killing him.

"You stay close to me, O'Neil and I will teach you something about how to deal with these Frogs," Cullen insisted. "We will teach them a thing or two, and they won't soon forget their dealings with the Inniskillings."

O'Neil didn't say a word in return. It was clear that he was a little nervous about the prospects of war. He simply followed in the shadow of the giant, who had been his enemy and now was his protector.

"Now don't you get ahead of yourself, Cullen," Stewart stated while giving Thomas a little wink. "The last thing we need is for you to go charging out of control into the line of fire of those Frenchies."

"Don't you worry about me, Pogue, there is not a Frog born who could get the better of John Cullen. I wager, when they see me coming, they will turn and run with their tail between their legs."

"They no doubt will turn and run, but you remember to keep your head down, or you might feel the sting of a Frenchie's wayward musket ball against your thick skull. Not that there is Frog alive who is able to hit what they aim at. It's just that your head makes an inviting target, it being so big and all."

Private Cullen began to turn red, as it was clear that he was not amused. "You watch your mouth Pogue, or I will have to shut it up."

Thomas gave a little chuckle at this exchange. "Take it easy John, Stewart didn't mean anything by it. He was just trying to make light of the situation. You know, to ease the tension and all."

"If you say so Thomas," Cullen returned, "but if it weren't for you, I think my fist would have left a mark on Pogue's chin a long time ago."

"Ah, come on Cullen, I didn't mean anything by it," Stewart was beginning to think it was not a good idea to make enemies just as they were about to go into battle. "I tell you what, why don't we make a little wager. What d'ya say we see who does in more Frogs, you or me?"

"That's a wager I'll take, and you'll wish you hadn't."

The voyage from Messina took three days. They landed at the Gulf of Sant'Eufemia and then marched inland toward the plain of Maida. Upon landing, light companies from each of the regiments were assigned to the Advanced Guard under the command of Colonel James Kempt. This included a company from the 1/27th. Thomas, Stewart, John Cullen and James O'Neil were all assigned to this company. By combining these companies, the Advanced Guard was brought to one thousand strong, one fifth of the entire British force. The remaining forces were divided into the first, second and third brigades, each composed of approximately 1,250 men.

The only French force in Calabria, six thousand strong, marched south to meet the British army. On July 4th, the two armies came together, the French on high ground and the British on low. As the French marched toward the river, the British forces marched parallel to their path in hopes of intercepting them. By the time the Advanced Guard met the enemy, General

The Colonel

Stuart became aware that his forces were outnumbered and outgunned, but it was too late to turn back. After a few minor skirmishes, the French made a direct assault on the nearest British line, the Advanced Guard. Although outnumbered nearly two to one, the Guard held their line. At 150 yards the French sent a volley into the British line, but the Advanced Guard held their fire, standing firm. In the middle of the foray were the friends from Enniskillen.

"Hold your fire gentleman," Thomas could hear the cry from Sergeant-Major McHugh. "Wait till you can see the whites of their eyes." The French were firing from high ground and most of their volleys passed overhead, confirming Stewart's description of their lack of marksmanship. The sound was like a thousand bees, and just as Stewart had instructed, the Inniskillings kept their heads low. Although some lost their bonnets, they all remained unscathed. When the smoke cleared the French had advanced to within 80 yards. "Fire," the cry rang out as the Guard returned fire just as the French were unleashing their second volley. The French had abandoned their traditional column and were attempting to form line, but they were poorly organized and poorly trained.

Lead was flying all around and Thomas could sense that at least some of the musket balls had met their mark. There were cries in the mayhem from those who had been wounded and now lay bleeding. The Inniskillings stood tall, not budging from their line. Still the French came on. At twenty yards the French attempted to reload, but they were too slow in contrast to their better trained enemy. Half of the guard had held back their fire in the first volley, and now before the French could get within bayonet range let fly their lead projectiles at point blank range. The company of the Irish Fusiliers was right at the center, and their skill as marksmen showed. When the smoke cleared, there were French soldiers dead and dying all along the line.

Now was the time for John Cullen to act. "Follow me boys," he shouted, just as the shout of charge was heard all down the line. The entire company charged forward, bayonets at the

48

ready. Thomas and Stewart were trailing just behind as Cullen met the first line of resistance. It is hard to imagine what went through the minds of the French soldiers who were still standing when they saw this giant of a man emerge from the haze of the musket fire. Cullen was unrelenting in his attack and a half dozen Frenchmen had met their maker, before they knew what had hit them. To their credit, Thomas and Stewart inflicted their own assault with similar success. In a matter of moments, John Cullen was made out to be a prophet, as the entire center of the French line crumbled and those who remained on their feet began to turn and run. The Advanced Guard charged ahead, giving chase, routing the enemy. The First, Second and Third Brigades realizing the success of the Advanced Guard, threw themselves at the remainder of the French forces. Surprisingly the entire battle lasted barely a quarter hour. The British had gained an early advantage and turned it into a convincing victory.

As the 3rd Brigade continued to chase the French into the hills, the Advanced Guard was called to regroup. Turning to look at each other, the three friends exchanged congratulatory glances. Then Thomas noticed that Cullen had a look of concern spread across his face.

"Where's O'Neil?" Cullen asked looking around.

"He was right behind us," Stewart assured. "I'm sure he was."

Cullen turned and began running back toward the river, to the place where the conflict had begun. Thomas and Stewart trailed behind. As they got to the bottom of the hill they found Cullen kneeling beside their fallen comrade. O'Neil had been hit by a musket ball and was bleeding heavily from his chest.

"O'Neil, what happened?" Cullen was crying out. "I told you to keep your head down. I told you to stay behind me. What happened?"

"Sorry, I guess those Frenchies...can hit what they aim at after all." O'Neil struggled to speak, gasping between each phrase. "But we sure did show them Frogs...didn't we John."

"We sure did kid," Cullen was trying to hold back the tears. "They... they won't be bothering with us again."

"The Inniskillings stood...tall." And with that Private O'Neil breathed his last.

"They sure did kid. The Inniskillings stood tall." Cullen brushed the tears from his eyes.

Thomas knelt down beside O'Neil and then gently put his hand over his face, closing his eyes. "He was a brave lad, John. Don't blame yourself. It was not for you to determine his fate. Only God knows the appointed time. Only God knows..." He placed his hand on his friends shoulder, trying to offer solace.

Stewart stood quietly looking on. Thomas thought he could hear him whisper, "Go with God, young friend."

Chapter Four

⁴ a time to weep and a time to laugh,
a time to mourn and a time to dance,

(1806)

The Battle of Maida was decidedly won by the British forces. As fate would have it, James O'Neil was one of only forty five British soldiers to die in the initial battle. On the other hand the French suffered 480 killed in action, 870 were wounded and another 750 were taken prisoner. Those who survived, fled, and were chased south by the 3ʳᵈ Brigade. In the days ahead several more French companies surrendered.

The afternoon of the Battle of Maida, Thomas, Stewart and John found themselves mourning the loss of their young friend and trying to console each other. The victory was sure, but seemed a bit hollow in the absence of their comrade. The Inniskillings had set up camp on the beach and the enlisted took their turn bathing in the surf, washing the remnants of the battle from both their bodies and their minds.

"Come on Cullen, join us for a swim. The ocean will do you good, lift your spirits and all," Stewart encouraged.

"Yeah, John, nothing will come from moping about," Thomas agreed. "The salt water will do you good."

"I suppose your right. Perhaps it will help to clear the mind." Together they stripped off their uniforms and ran into the surf.

Thomas dove head first into water. The salt water actually felt good against his skin. His whole body ached from the exertion of the battle. The water was cool and refreshing and as he swam beneath the surface, it provided a momentary diversion, if ever so brief, from the reality of what had just happened. O'Neil was not the only soldier to die that day. Death was a part of war and it wasn't difficult to resolve this natural end. However, at the end of the day, he still found him self questioning where there was a purpose to it all.

He emerged from below the surface and stood in water shoulder deep. Not far away Stewart and a few other members of their company were attempting to tackle Cullen and push him down into the water, but the giant of a man would have none of it. One by one he picked up each man as if they were a child and flung them into the water. It was a comical sight and caused Thomas to laugh. Just as it seemed as if they were all giving up, a general alarm sounded in the camp.

"What is it Tom?" Stewart called out.

"It's an alarm. I believe it's a call to arms," Thomas replied.

"I don't believe it. Have those damned Frenchies returned just in time to interrupt our bath. Haven't they had enough?" Cullen shouted in irritation.

Without hesitation the entire company emerged from the water and began running toward the encampment. As each man reached his tent, he took up his arms, and proceeded to assembly. As the brigade fell in line, they turned and looked in astonishment at the company of Inniskillings. The rapidity of which they had left their bathing and taken up arms had not allowed the time required to gain their uniforms. As a result the entire company was now standing in formation with out a stitch of clothing on.

The surrounding companies began to hoot and holler, but the Inniskilling stood tall and at the ready, as if nothing was amiss. Someone from the ranks of the 1/35th shouted, "Hey, look at the skins." Another started to chant, "Three cheers for the Skins! Hip hooray!"

As it turned out, the general alarm had been sounded accidentally. No one was ever able to determine what had prompted the bugler to sound out. Regardless, from that day forward the entire Inniskilling Regiment would be known with favor as the "Skins".

After the Battle of Maida, the Inniskillings remained garrisoned at Messina. Despite the decisive victory, the British

General Stuart did not take advantage and press the French to leave Calabria and Naples. As a result, the Neapolitan army eventually fell at Gaeta and the French under Joseph Bonepart regained control of Southern Italy. This required that Ferdinand remain in defense in Sicily. Once again the Inniskillings were asked to sit and wait for orders.

In early August Sergeant-Major McHugh approached Thomas and Stewart. "Gentleman I have been asked to return to Ireland to seek new recruits. It seems that a Third Battalion of Inniskillings is being formed and I have been ordered to return and oversee the training of the new recruits. I have also been instructed to take a few men with me to help with the recruitment. The Third will be temporarily garrisoned at Enniskillen while the recruitment and training takes place. Given that you are both from Enniskillen, I took the liberty to volunteer you both."

"How long will we be detached from the First?" Stewart asked.

"It could be as much as a year, who can tell. I wouldn't fret though. It doesn't appear that there will be any action here any time soon. The allies seem to be content to leave Italy to Boney, and instead are focused on efforts in the north."

"Stew, it has been two years since we have seen home," Thomas suggested. "If we're not needed here, I can't see waiting around to see if old Boney is going to attack this forgotten island."

"Yeah, you're right. It would be good to see home. Of course you're going to have to tell Cullen. I have a feeling he is not going to be too pleased to see us go."

"Well, that settles it then," McHugh said. "We leave on the tide first thing in the morning on the H.M.S. Lively. Pack your gear."

"Yes, Sergeant," they responded in unison.

The sun had not risen as Thomas sat quietly in the bow of the launch. The oars rhythmically rose and fell, pushing them closer to the H.M.S. Lively. It was hard for him to believe that they were on their way home. James and William were now six and four years of age respectively. They must have changed a great deal since he saw them last. And Alice, what has it been like for her raising their two boys alone? Enlisting in the Inniskillings always seemed the right thing to do, but he'd never anticipated what it would be like to remain separated from his family for months on end. He had been mindful to write every couple of weeks, but the post was slow, and it was sometimes months before he would hear from her, and then it would be several letters at once. He held the most recent letter in the chest pocket of his red coat. He had read it so many times, he had it memorized.

July 12th, 1806

> *Dearest Thomas,*
>
> *I long for the day when we will be reunited again. Each morning I call out to God on your behalf, not that I am afraid for your life, for I know that you will come home to me, but instead I beseech the Lord to not allow you to forget your wife, who waits alone. Do you remember me? Can you see my face? With each day my love for you grows stronger. I do not regret your decision to enlist. It is the measure of the man you are, the man I love. I am not joyous over our separation, but neither am I grieved. You are in the hands of our Maker, I can not despair.*
> *Our boys grow bigger before my very eye. They are the mirror image of their father. Each day I talk to them about you, telling them of your courage and strength. Each night they say their prayers and convey to God their love for you. They miss you greatly and look forward to your homecoming. They are very proud of you.*

*When will we see each other again, I do not
know. I sit at the window looking down the lane.
Each time I see someone approaching I believe it to
be you. Alas, it has not been, and so I remain yours,
waiting still.*

*Take care my love. Hurry home to me.
Your Loving Wife,
Alice*

*P.S. Tell Stewart that there is one who still
waits for him.*

The voyage home was going to be a long one. Thomas was
still not very fond of ocean voyages, but even more than that, he
was suddenly feeling homesick. Alice was right to pray for him.
In reality, her image was slowly beginning to fade from his
minds eye. It wasn't that he loved her any less, but time and
distance had begun to work on his memory. He could still see
her, but it was as if she were in a fog, fading back into the
recesses of his mind. He loved her still. The distance had not
diminished this. It was now, as he was headed home, he realized
how much he missed her. How he longed to hold her in his arms
and tell her just how much he loved her.

For most of the voyage Thomas remained melancholy and
reflective. Stewart left him to his thoughts, mistaking his solemn
demeanor for seasickness. He appreciated the quiet; he had
never been one for openly expressing his emotions, and he
didn't feel any need to involve his friend. Each day he spent
quietly gazing out at the ocean; trying to imagine what James
and William would now look like. Finally they drew near to
Plymouth, and his spirits began to rise. The journey was nearly
at an end. It was a short crossing to Belfast.

In Belfast they boarded a coach that would take them
home to Enniskillen. The coach had to pass near Lisbellaw. As
they drew near the village, Thomas felt suddenly delighted by

the familiarity of the surroundings. It was mid-afternoon, the sun was shining and he was home. At once, he signaled for the coachman to stop.

"This is where I get off," Thomas announced as the coach came to rest.

"Wha, what's that," McHugh spouted as he suddenly came awake from a leisurely nap. "Where are we? Have we arrived?"

"Not exactly Sergeant. Just over that ridge there," pointing to the south, "is my home and family. I'm going to get out here. I will catch up to the two of you in Enniskillen, tomorrow morning, after I have had a chance to say hello to my wife and sons. I'll meet you at the *King's Inn*. Stewart knows where I mean."

"But we are supposed to report to the castle barracks. The colonel in command of the Third is awaiting our arrival. He will be expecting us...together!"

"Ah, relax Sergeant-Major," Stewart came to Thomas' defense. "A few more hours won't matter. We can say we were delayed on the road. Who's to say any different. Come now, Thomas has not seen his wife and children in over two years."

"I...I suppose it will be alright. Okay, Thomas, but you better be at the *King's Inn* first thing in the morning."

"Don't worry McHugh, I'll be there," as he stepped down out of the coach. He paused for a moment and then he leaned back and whispered low so that only Stewart could hear. "Stewart I meant to tell you, Alice said to tell you that Bella is still waiting."

He could see Stewart had turned slightly blushed as the coach departed, and he smiled at the thought. It was kind of cruel to drop this message on his friend just as they were parting. He had intended to tell him earlier, but the time had never seemed quite right.

As Thomas walked toward home, he took note of every smell, and every sound. The afternoon sun was pleasantly peaking through the partly cloudy sky. It made him feel as if all of heaven were smiling on him, welcoming him home. As he turned down the final lane, he could see his home in the distance, nestled in amongst a couple maple trees.

Alice was sitting on the front steps, repairing the hem in her best dress. Her two boys were playing nearby, attempting to corner a small garter snake that had emerged from the long grass. In the distance she could see someone coming down the road. She couldn't make out who it was. The late afternoon sun was directly in her eyes. She watched for a moment, wondering who it could be. Then she saw what she thought was a little streak of red as the sun caught movement of the strangers arm. "It was red, wasn't it," she thought. "It's a red coat, a soldier." All of sudden she jumped to her feet and began walking down the lane, then running. Her two sons tried to follow, but their little legs could not match the quickening stride of their mother.

Her heart was pounding. She could hardly believe her eyes. It had seemed so long, and yet she had waited patiently. She knew he would return to her, she had no doubt. However, the certainty in her mind did not ease the pain of absence she felt in her heart. Oh how she missed him. With each passing day the longing to hear his voice grew greater, the need to be held in his arms and cared for, sat like a yoke upon her shoulders. And yet she had never given up hope, for good reason, because here he was, returned home.

With her last stride she leaped into his arms, her own arms hugging his shoulders as she pulled him close. "Was it real? Was he really home?" were the thoughts that raced through her mind as her cheek brushed his. She kissed him, long and hard, not wanting the dream to end. "It was him, he is real", she thought to herself.

"Thomas, it is you. You are real, you have come home to me," she whispered in his ear. "Just as I said you would."

"Yes darling Alice, it is I, your wayward husband and I have come home, just as you believed."

"But how? Why now? You didn't write you were coming."

"It was kind of sudden, there was no time."

Just then the two little boys had caught up to there mother. "Mommy, who is it?" little William asked.

"Don't you remember Willie, this is your father? Your father has come home."

Thomas bent down to the level of his two young sons. "Hello Willie, Hello Jamie," he said as he ran his hands through their strawberry blonde locks. "Look at you two, your all grown up. Don't you remember me?"

"Father, I remember," James said as he wrapped his arms around his father's neck.

Meanwhile William was holding onto his mother's dress, not too sure of what to make of the whole scene. He had only been two years old when Thomas had left, and clearly he had little or no memory of it.

"Go on Willie," Alice coaxed. "Give your father a proper greeting. He won't hurt you."

Thomas reached down for his youngest son and picked him up with one arm as he stood upright. He then reached out and pulled Alice to his side. She embraced the two of them together.

She smiled up at Thomas, "so what brings you home?" They began walking back toward the house.

"Stewart and I have been sent here to recruit enlistees for a third brigade of the Inniskillings. We've come here with Sergeant-Major McHugh. The Third will be garrisoned and trained at the Castle. I have to report there tomorrow morning."

"Tomorrow morning, so soon," Alice could not hide her disappointment as she stopped dead in her tracks after having only walked a few yards.

Thomas turned and looked her in the eyes, "I'm sorry Alice, but I can't be delayed. Besides it will be okay. I'm sure there will be plenty opportunities to sneak away. We'll be able to see plenty of each other."

"But for how long? I mean, how long will you be in Ireland?"

"There is no way of knowing for sure, weeks, months, maybe even a year. We'll just have to take it a day at a time. We are still at war with the French. I suppose we are here to raise the Third to support the rest of our regiment against Napoleon."

"Well, I will just have to be content with having you home. We will not talk of leaving until we know for sure. We will just have to make good use of the time we have," Alice said as she again placed her arm around her husbands waste. Together they walked back to the house, Thomas holding little William in one arm and Alice in the other as James trailed behind.

As Alice set to work preparing the evening meal, Thomas sat watching her every movement. He found it disturbing to think that he had begun to forget what she looked like. She was a beautiful woman, full of grace and dignity, despite her moderate station. As he watched her, he began to commit to memory every line of her form, from the smooth curve of her neck as it sloped to her shoulders, to her slightly upturned button nose. He would not forget again. She literally danced around the room, going from one task to another with ease, while avoiding the entanglement of her two young sons who were constantly at her feet.

Thomas' heart swelled with pride, as he realized the fortitude that his wife had been able to muster while raising their two boys on her own. He realized how unfair he had been in leaving with the Inniskillings; believing that his decision to enlist was his own, alone. He had felt an obligation of loyalty to his countryman, but had neglected to understand the cost to his family. Alice had never complained, and even supported his decision, but he knew down deep that she had done so with fear and trembling.

He could not help but think of the fate of poor O'Neil. It was strange that fate would take someone so young. One stray musket ball and his life had ended. It reminded Thomas of his own mortality. There were no assurances that he would survive his tour with the Inniskillings. Every man in the brigade was at risk each time they entered into battle. Here he was, returned home, but for the first time he was afraid. Not really afraid of dying, but instead he was filled with fear for his family. What would Alice do if he did not return home? What would happen to his two young sons? It was unsettling to contemplate.

Out of the corner of her eye, Alice noticed Thomas watching her, deep in thought. She glided across the room and proceeded to sit down in his lap, leaning her head back upon his shoulder. "What are you thinking about Tom?" she whispered.

He smiled at her, looking deep into her emerald eyes. "I was just thinking about how much I love you, how much I have missed you, and how proud I am of you."

"Proud? In what way are you proud of me?"

"I'm just amazed at how you have been able to raise Jamie and Willie all on your own. And I suppose I am feeling a little guilty for having left you to it. It wasn't fair."

"Now don't you go feeling sorry for me Thomas Rea! We're doing just fine. You needn't worry. All you need to remember is just how much we love you and that we will always be here waiting for you when you come home."

"Do you really love me Alice? I mean, do you still love me?"

"With all my heart," as she hugged his neck and kissed him on the cheek. "There is not another man in this world that I could love more."

He kissed her, and then held her close. He inhaled deeply, breathing her in, trying to imprint upon his mind every scent, every touch.

"Mommy, I'm hungry," William interrupted their embrace.

"Go on Alice, we can't let this little guy go hungry," as Alice jumped up from his lap.

"Alright, Willie, you help momma get everything to the table, so we can eat," Alice directed.

Thomas sat back in chair. He felt happy, almost giddy. He never wanted to lose this moment.

Early the next morning Thomas stood gazing out the front window. It was still dark, but there was a soft glow just beyond the hills indicating the approach of dawn. He was glad to be home, even if it meant spending most of his time at the castle barracks. It was good to be back in Ireland again. He hadn't realized how much he would miss it. It now seemed strange that he had ever wanted to leave. Now he wished he would never have to leave again, but he no longer had a choice. For now he would have to remain with the Inniskillings.

As he stood watching the sunrise he felt two slender arms wrap around his waste and then the slight pressure of a hug.

"Do you have to leave," Alice whispered in his ear.

"I am afraid so," he whispered back. "I am probably over due now. I must meet Stewart and McHugh for breakfast. I promised them I wouldn't be late."

"It seems you just got here, and now you must leave again."

"It's okay. There will be other moments like these. Once I get settled, I will see about securing some leave from the colonel." He turned around to face her and then took her cheeks in his hands and gently kissed her. "I must go. Say goodbye to the boys for me. Tell them I will be back soon."

"I will. What should I say to Bella? I mean, do you think Stewart wants to see her?"

"Oh, I am sure there is no doubt of that. He hasn't said it out right, but I think he has been pining for her ever since we left. I think he was relieved to find that she isn't already married."

"She has not even as much as looked at another man. And you can tell him so. And while you're at it, you tell him for me, that he better propose to her soon, or I will find a way to make his life miserable."

Thomas knew she was more than capable of carrying out such a threat. "I'll tell him," he smiled slyly as he said it. "Now I really must go."

She put her arms around his neck and kissed him one last time. "Okay. Goodbye Darling. Come back soon."

Thomas grabbed his gear and stepped out into the early morning light. He started walking down the lane at as rapid a pace has he could manage without actually running. He did not look back. He knew that Alice would be watching from the door and that she would be crying. It was good to be home.

The sun had been up a full hour when he finally stepped through the front door of the *King's Inn*. Seargent McHugh and Stewart were already busily downing their breakfast. McHugh clearly looked relieved when he saw Thomas.

"It's about time you've arrived. We were just about ready to go looking for you."

"Speak for your self McHugh," Stewart interrupted between bites. "I had no intention of going anywhere. I told you not to worry, Thomas would not let us down," he winked at Thomas as he said it.

"Yeah, yeah, I know what you said. I'm just saying he cut it a little close."

"Relax McHugh. There is no way that whoever is in charge at the barracks could have an expectation of our arrival time." He promptly plopped down in the nearest chair and began to dive into what was left of their breakfast. "A few minutes...more...won't matter one way...or another," he managed to get out between bites." He then proceeded to get the attention of the barmaid and asked for a cup of tea.

"I suppose your right, but I'm only giving you a quarter hour and then we are on our way," the sergeant-major replied.

"Who is in command of the Third?" Stewart asked.

"A lieutenant-colonel Maclean, that's all I know. Upon its commissioning the Third was garrisoned at Edinburgh, but it has been since broken up and a majority of the original recruits redistributed amongst the First and Second. The officers were sent here to gain more recruits, but my understanding is that none of them have had much experience and have never seen any action. We are here to help them with the recruiting and assist the officers in the training the new lads. The officers have just recently arrived in Enniskillen, and there are new recruits expected from Belfast any day."

"You mean the recruits haven't even arrived yet?" Stewart asked. "Then what is the hurry?"

"We were supposed to report as soon as we arrive, and not ask a bunch of questions and that's what I intend to do. Now get your things together, we should have already been on our way."

Thomas and Stewart knew better than to press the matter any further. McHugh was only a few years their senior, but he had a way about him that made him seem a lot older. When pressed, he could be rather ill-tempered, true to his Irish nature. They had both learned the limits to which they could test him without feeling the full force of his wrath. He was a good sergeant and a good companion to have in battle, which allowed them to overlook any of his faults, minor as they were.

The three of them left the *King's Inn* and started down the main street of Enniskillen toward the castle. The village was on an island and was bounded by water on all sides, with the castle sitting on the edge of the north end. After gaining entrance to the barracks they were led to the office of the officer in command.

"Sergeant-Major Roger McHugh reporting from the 1st Brigade of the 27th as ordered," McHugh saluted as he spoke. "And this here is Private Rea and Private Pogue, also of the 1st."

The colonel remained in his chair and gave a half hearted salute in the direction of McHugh. "Yes Sergeant-Major I have been expecting you. I am Lieutenant-Colonel MacLean. I understand you are here to give us a bit of a hand with the new recruits. Not that we really need the help, but we will take it just the same." He didn't seem to be overjoyed at their presence.

"Yes sir. We are merely here to assist in any way we can."

"Yes, yes sergeant, I meant no disrespect. I suppose you are right from the battlefield then?"

"Yes sir, Maida."

"That must have been some sight seeing those Frenchies turn tail and run. I heard that you gave them quite a shellacking."

"Yes sir, if you say so sir."

"Relax sergeant, I am just making conversation. Well anyway, we should see a batch of recruits arrive from Belfast in two days, on Monday. In the mean time the three of you can make yourself at home in the enlisted barracks. Quartermaster Taylor here will show you to your quarters."

"Thank you sir," McHugh said with one final salute. McHugh was all military, through and through, but it seemed to leave little impression on MacLean.

As they were leaving the room, "By the way gentlemen, Private Rea and Pogue, I believe are your names."

"Yes sir," Thomas and Stewart returned in unison.

"You were given this assignment due to your exploits at Maida and I have been instructed to offer you a promotion, so from now on you will be referred to as Corporal Rea and Corporal Pogue."

"Yes sir, thank you sir," again in unison. They both saluted and then turned and led McHugh out of the room.

As they exited Stewart turned and whispered to McHugh, "What did he mean by exploits?"

"Oh, I might have mentioned something to Colonel Kempt about how the two of you along with Cullen nearly took on the entire French brigade by yourselves and came through without a scratch."

"Wait a second," Thomas whispered in turn, "I thought you said you volunteered us for this duty, you never said anything about a promotion."

"I may have stretched the truth a bit, but what does it matter you're here... Corporal Rea." He smiled slightly as he turned and followed the quartermaster.

"That beat's all," Thomas said turning to Stewart. "What do you make of that?"

"I don't presume to understand the sergeant, and I don't suppose I ever will," Stewart said and he fell in line and started to follow. Thomas shook his head and did the same.

Chapter Five

*5 A time to scatter stones and a time to gather them,
a time to embrace and a time to refrain.*

Alice and her two young sons made it a habit to attend church in Lisbellaw with her parents. However, on this Sunday, she left the boys with her parents and hitched up the horse drawn cart and went on her own to Cleenish Parish Church. It had been a few weeks since she had been able to see Bella, and on this particular Sunday, she had some especially good news to report.

Bella was standing at the front entrance of the church as Alice arrived and she immediately left her father's side to greet her friend.

"Alice, it's so nice of you to come," she greeted as she helped to tie up the horse. "I had no idea you would be here today. What a pleasant surprise, but where are the boys?"

"Hello, Bella. It's good to see you as well," she said as she stepped down out of the horse cart and proceeded to give her friend a hug. "I left the boys with their grandparents. I thought perhaps we could spend the afternoon together, just the two of us. That is if you don't have any plans."

"Splendid. I think father was planning to visit the Kelly's this afternoon and you have provided me with the perfect alibi for excusing myself."

They locked arms and made their way into the chapel. Bella had her predetermined space on the front left pew and Alice slid into the seat beside her. The service seemed to drag on forever. The rector was not much of an orator and even if he had been, Alice was a little more than distracted. She kept trying to think of the right words to tell Bella that Stewart had come home. She knew that once Bella was made aware, she would immediately be swept up in the momentary elation that comes from having ones hope renewed. She didn't want to deny her friend this joy, nor did she want to see her get hurt. By the time the closing prayer had ended, she'd decided to just come right out and tell her the news. There was no need to prolong it any longer. Besides if she didn't tell her at the first opportunity, it would only serve to make Bella upset.

Bella's father said his goodbyes to the members of his flock and then made one last attempt to persuade his daughter to join him for his visit with the Kellys just down the road.

"Father, I can't leave Alice to visit with the Kellys, especially since she has come all this way to spend the afternoon with me."

"But, she could come with us, I'm sure the Kellys wouldn't mind another person for lunch."

"Oh no, Mr. Howard, I couldn't," Alice was quick to respond. "I wouldn't want to impose. You go ahead by yourself. Bella and I have to catch up and you wouldn't want a couple of chattering hens tagging along."

"Well okay, I suppose you're right," It was clear that he felt a bit defeated, but he wasn't about to keep on pressing the point.

"Yes, Father, we will be alright. You have a wonderful time at the Kelly's. Alice and I will get along just fine."

Reverend Howard turned and strode off down the lane. Bella and Alice watched for a few moments and then turned and started for the parsonage.

"Bella," Alice began as they walked arm in arm. "I have some news that I hope will be of a pleasant nature for you."

"What is it?"

"Stewart and Thomas are home from Sicily. They arrived two days ago."

"What, what do you mean two days ago. Where...where are they? I mean where's Thomas, why isn't he here. And Stewart why hasn't he come to see me? Has he forgotten me? Is something wrong?"

"Calm yourself Bella. There's nothing wrong. It's just that they're not really free to visit. They are still in service, but they have been allowed to return to Enniskillen to gain new recruits. They are garrisoned at the Castle Barracks."

"But can't they get away?"

"I'm afraid not, well... at least not yet. Thomas was able to sneak away for a moment, but even that was just for a few hours. I was as surprised as you are now. I had no idea they were coming home."

"But did you see Stewart, he is well...does he...," Bella could not seem to get the words out.

"No, I didn't see him, but Thomas assures me that he is well. As for...well I'm sure he is looking forward to seeing you at the earliest possible moment."

"But why can't we go see them...today, now?"

"Now! Bella, I don't know if they are free to see anyone. Besides, you really need to slow down a bit, patience."

"But what would it hurt to go and see? What is the worst that could happen, we would be turned away and we would merely have spent a pleasant afternoon riding in the cart."

"Well, I must admit I would like to see Thomas, if even for a moment. I suppose it wouldn't hurt to try. But you have to promise me that you won't get your hopes up. I don't want to have to ride all the way home with you sobbing all the way."

Bella smiled, "I promise, no crying, no matter what."

Bella went into the parsonage to pack a lunch. Alice left her for moment and returned to where she had left the horse and cart. By the time she watered the horse and drove around to the front of the parsonage, Bella was already stumbling out of the front door. A moment later and they were on their way. It was a pleasant afternoon, the sun was shining, and there was no hint of any weather. September had been very wet, but with the arrival of October they had had several stretches of dry, cool weather. Both ladies were properly attired and the sun overhead provided them with warmth.

The Colonel

Enniskillen was just four miles to the north and less than an hour away by horse cart. When they arrived they drove straight through the village without stopping. Alice was more than aware that Bella was growing more anxious the nearer they approached their objective. When they arrived at the castle, she tied the horse up to a hitching post and the two walked directly to the front gate. There was a single guard.

"Excuse me sir," Alice began.

"Private Rankin ma'am," the soldier quickly corrected.

"Yes, Private Rankin, I was wondering if you could get a message to Private Thomas Rea for me. You see, I'm Mrs. Rea, and we were wondering...that is my friend and I were wondering if we could see him for a moment."

"I think you must mean Corporal Rea ma'am. If you make your inquiry over there I'm sure someone can direct you to your husband. I would take you myself, but I am afraid we are bit undermanned at the moment, and I am not allowed to leave my post."

Without hesitation, Bella and Alice walked across the open courtyard to the barracks. When they reached the main entrance they were not exactly sure how to proceed. They weren't sure they would be welcome in the barracks. They were about to step through the door when a young man, who couldn't be more than eighteen years of age, emerged abruptly, almost knocking the two of them down.

"I'm sorry misses," he said as he stepped to the side. "I didn't see you there."

"Young man, would you happen to know where Corporal Rea is?"

"Yes, right inside, I will get him for you," and with that he promptly disappeared.

A moment later Thomas appeared at the door with Stewart close behind peering over his shoulder.

"Alice, Bella, what are the two of you doing here?"

"It was a beautiful day, and we just thought we would take the cart over and check in on you, to see how you're doing."

68

"Hello Bella," Stewart greeted as he stepped by Thomas. "It is very good to see you."

Alice looked at Thomas and then at their friends. "Perhaps we could all go for a walk; that is if you're not busy."

"No, as a matter of fact, it has been rather quiet. It turns out that the Barracks are nearly empty. It seems that the recruitment has barely begun and it may be a few days before the greenhorns begin arriving. I don't see any reason why we can't take a turn around the village."

Alice took Thomas by the arm as they passed through the front gate. As they started down the main street of town, she slowed her pace and held firm to his arm to keep him with her. She looked up at him and then at Bella and Stewart a few paces in front.

"Let them lead," She whispered. "Shall we give them some space?"

Thomas winked, "ever the matchmaker I see."

"I'm sorry we just showed up unannounced Thomas. Bella was beside herself and there was just no dissuading her. You know how she is."

"I know. It's okay. I'm actually glad you're here. There is nothing really happening here. Had I known it would be like this, I might have asked for some leave. It is good that you came. It definitely breaks up the monotony of idleness."

"Oh, so I am just a mere diversion from the monotony," Alice tried to sound offended.

"Now don't get your Irish ire up. I didn't mean anything by it. I'm just glad you're here, that's all," he smiled as he said it realizing she wasn't really angry.

The two couples spent the rest of the afternoon, walking and talking and lounging on the green next to the canal. As the sun came low in the sky it was time for the girls to leave. Thomas was not about to allow them to stay any longer, risking the possibility that Alice would be returning home in the dark. They said their goodbyes and Alice and Bella began the journey home."

"Well, how was your afternoon," Alice asked.

"He still loves me Alice. He still loves me." Nothing more needed to be said.

* * * * *

Over the next several weeks the Third Battalion grew as recruits arrived from all directions. Thomas and Stewart were each placed in command of platoons and Sergeant McHugh was given command of their company. These responsibilities were beyond their rank, but given the Third was a new Battalion and they were the only three to have actually seen any action, it seemed a logical assignment. Once a routine was established, given that he was married, Thomas was allowed to sleep out of barracks two nights a week. This allowed him the freedom to spend plenty of time with his family.

In October, after having received the permission of the Lieutenant Colonel, Stewart proposed marriage to Bella. The British army had a standing rule that allowed as many as a dozen men in any company the right to marry, and as a Corporal, Stewart had as much right as any, there was no objection.

Bella, for her part, was beside herself with excitement and anticipation. She would not hear of delaying the date of their marriage for any length of time, so they decided to make it a Christmas wedding. Soldiers who were at home, were often given leave during the holiday to spend time with family, and so it was, allowing Bella and Stewart ample opportunity to enjoy a honeymoon. Alice for her part was aglow with joy of knowing that her friend had finally realized the blessing of marriage. Although, some might have thought the glow was due to the fact that she was pregnant with her third child.

Meanwhile, during the winter months, Napolean's forces were restricted to fighting in Poland, Prussia and Danzig. The call to action of the Third Inniskillings did not appear to be imminent. Stewart and Thomas were not disappointed, given the demands of their respective families. Sergeant McHugh seemed to be the only one who was despondent over their inactivity.

With each passing day he became more and more irritable. Thomas and Stewart had the wisdom to stay out of his way. However, the new recruits were not as fortunate and often felt the wrath of the Sergeant-Major.

By the spring of 1807, Napolean had returned to Paris and was making preparations for the invasion of Spain. In February the 3rd Battalion was relocated to a make-shift barracks in Omagh, in neighboring county Tyrone. This of course was much to the disappointment of Bella whose marital bliss had barely lasted two months before she was saying goodbye to her new husband. There was no way to know how long they would be in Omagh, but it seemed to imply that the Third was about to be deployed to the continent. Shortly after their departure, Bella discovered that she was pregnant, a surprise that provided her with some measure of solace in the absence of her husband.

While in Omagh, the Third continued to welcome new recruits into the ranks. The battalion had now grown to more than 500 strong. It was hoped that continued recruitment would bring that number to nearly 900 by the time they embarked. Since the Third was a new battalion, many of the officers were relatively inexperienced. Most officers secured their rank by purchase, especially during peace time. An ensign might cost L400 and a lieutenancy L550. The ranks of sergeant and corporal were reserved for officers promoted from the rank and file. For an enlisted man to achieve the rank of lieutenant or higher would require a significant act of valor in the field.

McHugh, Thomas and Stewart were all assigned to the first company under the command of Major William Brydges Neynoe of Castle Neynoe, in County Sligo. He was a seasoned commander and since McHugh hailed from Sligo, the sergeant-major was more than pleased to be under his command. McHugh lead the second platoon, with Ensign John Betty his second, and Thomas and Stewart as squad leaders. The first platoon was lead by Lieutenant Charles Crawford, with Ensign William Fortescue his second. At this time the Third was composed of six companies with the hopes of raising four more.

The Colonel

Each morning was spent in parade drill, followed by musket drill. The British foot soldier was expected to be able to load and fire three rounds in a minute. This meant priming the pan, dropping the paper charge, ramming it down, and returning the ram rod back to its rings, all with the greatest efficiency, under the most stressful conditions. Thomas was particularly adept in the use of the musket and had learned early on to stick the ram rod down into the ground instead of returning it to the rings which allowed him to regularly complete four rounds in a minute.

In the afternoon each company would work long hours at trying to master the formation of the square. This was an important defensive maneuver used when in the open and was critical to the survival of the company in the heat of battle. As a result, the drill was practiced daily, repetitiously so that it became second nature to every member of the company.

Sergeant McHugh's platoon was often assigned the youngest and greenest recruits to assimilate into the company, since he was the only non-commissioned platoon leader, and because he had seen plenty of action. He often passed the chore of nursing these lads along to Thomas and Stewart, his most trusted squad leaders.

As Thomas stood looking into the eyes of the newest members of his squad, he couldn't help notice the mix of enthusiasm and naïveté, evidence of their youth. He was now approaching thirty, and it caused him to smile and reminisce that it was not too long ago that he was filled we these same romantic imaginations. There were two young men that particularly caught his attention on this morning. They had each arrived the afternoon before, and now stood smiling up at him as if they did not have a care in the world. It wouldn't take long to remove those smiles, and only a little while longer to replace their dreams with the reality of the doldrums of a soldier's life.

The first was Alexander Dunlop, barely 21 years of age, from the village of Aughavea. He was five feet seven inches tall, with brown hair and grey eyes. His face was round, his complexion swarthy, and he had enlisted with the hopes of becoming a career soldier. The second was Adam Dolmage, just having attained his 20th birthday, he was much taller, over six feet, with blond hair and blue eyes. He didn't have the typical look of an Irishman, and had a bit of an unusual accent. He had journeyed north from Rathkeale, near Adare; his ancestors were of German descent, refugees during the reign of Queen Anne.

Looking at these two young men, Thomas was immediately reminded of poor O'Neil, lying dead at Maida. He too had been filled with dreams of glory, with little thought given to the risks of war. Young men tend to have an air of invulnerability about them. Despite choosing to become a soldier, there was little consideration given to the possibility that death might be waiting for them just around the bend. If it was in his power, Thomas was determined to do everything he could to insure that these young men would one day return home. He would work them and the rest of the platoon to the point of breaking them, shaping them into the best soldiers the Inniskillings had seen. Their naïve dreams would soon be replaced by fortitude and if they took to heart his training, they might return home someday. Over the following weeks, he grew in his fondness for Dunlop and Dolmage. They were adept students, with a natural physical prowess. It was soon clear that they were going to make excellent soldiers, worthy of the ranks of the Inniskilling.

The drudgery of the constant drilling was broken when Thomas was granted leave to attend to Alice as she gave birth to her third son, Thomas Junior. It was May 1, 1807. The distance from Omagh to Lisbella could be easily covered in half a day by horseback and when Thomas' brother-in-law came to deliver the news, he wasted no time in returning home.

The Sergeant-Major was a task master, and like his comrades, Thomas and Stewart, he drove his platoon hard, pushing each soldier to the limit and maintaining strict discipline and order. Day after day they continued to drill honing their skills and growing together as a company, functioning as one mind with one purpose. By the time summer came there was a growing confidence in the ranks and a strong sense of readiness for whatever lay ahead, but still they waited. Instead of leaving for the continent, in July they were ordered to return to the barracks at Enniskillen Castle. Both Thomas and Stewart were relieved, the one wishing to be close to home to care for his young infant son, the other full of excited and anticipation of his first child.

The fall came and the Inniskillings had once again settled in at Enniskillen. In early November, Bella gave birth to a son, James. There was never a father more proud than Stewart Pogue. It was all Thomas could do to help his friend keep his mind on the work at hand, the training of new recruits as they arrived. By this time the Third had grown to 600 and had settled in for the winter, with little prospects of going to war anytime soon.

* * * * *

(1808)

Winter turned to Spring and all was well. Jamey and Willie were now eight and six respectively and they enjoyed doting on their little brother who was about to turn one. Thomas was pleased to be near home with plenty of opportunities to pay visits to his new son. And if that did not fill his heart enough, he had much to look forward to since Alice was anticipating another child in May.

The daily routine of morning and afternoon drills had become mundane for many, but there were new recruits arriving every week. Thomas felt a certain level of contentment. He genuinely enjoyed training the young recruits, and it was beneficial to be so close to home near his family. This personal joy was soon to turn to tragedy when his father-in-law made an unexpected visit to the barracks.

Early in April, just as morning drills were just about to commence, Stewart approached, "Thomas, you must return home at once," he said with a high degree of tension and urgency in his voice.

"What do you mean Stewart?" he said in disbelief. "I don't have leave. Why must I go home what has happened..." his voice trembled slightly. He could sense something was wrong.

Stewart hesitated slightly, "... Mr. Copeland is at the gate, I'm afraid he has brought some bad news... horrible news," his head turned downward as he said it.

"What's the matter... what is it? Did something happen to Alice...," he asked anxiously.

"Yes," Stewart could only shake is head up and down. The words were there, but he couldn't seem to get them out. "Poor Alice, her baby has come, a little early I think...I'm so sorry, it seems the child has not survived the stress of birth. The baby is dead."

Thomas could not believe his ears, "What do you mean dead...? How can this be? I just saw Alice, Sunday past. She seemed fine, perfectly healthy... It was a girl then?" he asked.

"Yes a baby girl...I'm so sorry...you need to go home. Alice needs you. With the Colonel away, I have already spoken to Major Neynoe and he has extended you leave, you can take as much time as you need. In fact he has offered his horse, so that you might make the journey in short order. The sergeant-major and I have things under control here. Now go..." (Colonel MacLean had left for London earlier in the week. Some believed it was to receive their orders to depart to the peninsula.)

Thomas could not think straight, everything was in a daze. How could his baby girl be dead? It was unthinkable. What could have happened? Suddenly his thoughts shifted to his poor wife. "Oh poor Alice, what must she be going through," he thought to himself. He found the major's horse already saddled and waiting for him when he arrived at the gate. He leaped into the saddle, pausing only a moment to greet his father-in-law; he struck off at a gallop. There would be time for explanations later. Right now he had to get home to Alice.

The Colonel

The five miles passed like a blur. When he arrived at the house, Mrs. Copeland was on the porch. She was holding little Thomas in her lap and his other two boys were playing in the yard. She didn't say a word to him as he stepped onto the porch. She just nodded in the direction of the door. As he entered he saw Alice, sitting up in the bed. Next to the bed was a cradle, and in the cradle a small form was lying, wrapped in a blanket, there was no movement. The noise of his footsteps crossing the floor caused Alice to look up at him as he approached, there were tears streaming down her cheeks.

"Oh, Thomas, I am so sorry...I...," she was sobbing and barely able to speak. "I...I don't know what happen. The doctor said she was just too weak. I...don't know what went wrong. I can't believe it...I don't understand. Why would God let this happen?"

Thomas knelt next to the cradle, with one hand he took hold of Alice's hand, and with the other he lightly rocked the cradle. There lay his daughter, a daughter he would never know. He turned to his wife, "It's not your fault Alice. There is no one to blame. We.re not the first to lose a child, it doesn't make any sense, but there was nothing you could have done."

"If...if only...oh Thomas, it's a girl. We so much wanted a little girl. I'm so sorry."

By this time, Thomas could feel the tears welling in his eyes. He pulled Alice close, "It's okay Alice. It wasn't your fault. Only God knows the day and the hour."

They held each other, sharing in their grief. There was nothing more to say, nothing that would provide any comfort. After some time had passed, they both turned as they heard the patter of little footsteps. Jamie, Willie tried to give their parents a hug in the midst of their grief. Thomas pulled the youngest into his arms and gave him a hug.

At the door were Mr. and Mrs. Copeland still holding little Thomas. "Now come on Thomas, take the children outside. Let mother and I take care of things here," Mr. Copeland instructed.

They would prepare the body for burial and make arrangements with the local parish priest.

The funeral for baby Alice was held at the graveyard of the Lisbellaw Parish Church and was attended by the Rea and Copeland families, and there were also a few from the first company of the 3/27th, including McHugh, Pogue, Dunlop and Dolmage. Bella remained close to her friend, doing what she could to ease her pain and grief. Thomas was given three weeks leave to be with his wife and children.

* * * * *

Colonel Maclean remained absent and when Thomas returned to the barracks, there was still no word as to when the Inniskillings would be called into action. In his absence new recruits had arrived along with a couple of newly commissioned officers. Ensign Francis Simcoe had been assigned to Major Neynoe's company as a second. He was a tall handsome lad, having barely reached his seventeenth birthday. Not only was he high born, but he had a significant military pedigree. His grandfather had served as a Captain in the British navy and his father had served as a Major General in the army. His father, John Graves Simcoe was wounded severely at the battle of Brandywine. He later would serve as a colonial administrator in upper Ontario, Canada. Francis grew up in Canada, and then followed in his father's footsteps and was educated and Eton College in England.

Thomas took an immediate liking to the young Simcoe, even though thirteen years younger, he was his superior in rank. The young man seemed to have a natural humility to him, a trait not always common to those high born. The subalterns would often eat together at dinner and this often prompted friendships and alliances to form. Simcoe, John Betty, William Fortescue, and Thomas Craddock were all a part of the inner circle of the first company to which Stewart and Thomas were attached. Each night they would sit and talk about their lives prior to joining the military, as well as their hopes and dreams for the future.

It seemed Francis was destined for a life-long military career. He felt an obligation to carry on the family tradition, given that he was the only surviving son of his father, who had just recently passed from this world. Thomas enjoyed hearing the stories of his fellow officers, since most of them had lived a life unfamiliar to him. He was particularly intrigued by Simcoe's descriptions of Upper Canada. It was still an untamed wilderness, and full of adventure and opportunity. It seemed a place he would like to visit sometime.

[All of Ontario and Quebec had been a single province until 1791 when it was divided. Everything to the west of Montreal in the upper river basin would become English speaking and be referred to as Upper Canada, while the remaining Quebec would be French speaking and referred to as Lower Canada. Today Upper Canada would be known as southern Ontario. The capital of Upper Canada was Newark, today Niagra.]

"Who knows Thomas, perhaps the Inniskillings will be sent to Canada before long. There doesn't seem to be any need of us here," Stewart suggested.

"What do you think of that, Simcoe? Do you think you would like to return to Canada while in the service of the Inniskillings?" Thomas asked.

"I don't know that I'd ever considered it," the young man returned. "I suppose anything is possible. Colonel Maclean has not returned yet, and there doesn't seem to be any indication that we will be fighting the Frenchies anytime soon. I'm sure they would have use for us in Canada, given the unpredictability of the savage natives."

"I'm not sure we are prepared for Indian warfare," Betty interjected. "We might need to alter our training a bit."

"Frenchies or Indians, it doesn't matter much to me. Once they see the Inniskillings, they will turn tail and run," Stewart boasted.

"I doubt that would be the case," Simcoe said. "The tribes of Canada can be fearless and ruthless. They shouldn't be taken lightly. If we are called to Canada, you can be sure that we would be put to the test. They don't really observe the rules of war. They have no qualms about hiding in the bush and shooting you in the back as you pass. And then to add insult, they remove your scalp as you lay dying, as a trophy of their conquest."

"Sounds bloody uncivilized," Betty said as he cringed. "Do they really do that?"

"Yes they do. My father used to tell me some gruesome stories as I was growing up. I suppose he was trying to prepare me for the worst."

"Did you ever encounter any Indians?" Thomas asked.

"Occasionally there would be a few who would wander into Newark. They seemed to be friendly enough, but they always had a menacing look about them. I tended to stay clear of them. I was just a boy after all."

Thomas smiled. At seventeen, Simcoe wasn't much more than a boy now. Despite his physical stature-he was over six feet tall-he still had that boyish look about him. It was unclear whether he had even started shaving. He had a confidence about him, mostly due to his station, but Thomas wondered how he would handle the stress of battle.

As April was waning, Colonel Maclean was still absent and Major Neynoe remained in command. The Inniskillings had still not reached a full compliment and so the Major decided to send McHugh back to his home county of Sligo to gain more recruits. He took Ensign Betty with him leaving Thomas and Stewart in charge of the platoon. With Neynoe commanding the Battalion, Humphreys was put in charge of the first company with Lt. Crawford his second. Simcoe and Fortescue had the other platoon.

Two Weeks later, McHugh returned with 100 new recruits. They immediately set to the task of assimilating these new recruits into the battalion. Already rumors were circulating that they would soon be marching toward Cork to seek transport to the continent. The battalion had now grown to nearly a thousand soldiers and had been divided into the standard ten companies. Ensign Simcoe had always aspired to be a part of the Grenadiers and therefore transferred companies. Lieutenant John Pring was the acting commander of the Grenadiers with Captain John Tucker in absence. With the assimilation of the newest recruits requiring some reorganization, Simcoe requested that private Dolmage as well as Thomas and Stewart to be allowed to join the Grenadiers, as well. The request was granted.

[The Grenadiers was made up of soldiers of the greatest stature, typically measuring well above six feet tall. This was an elite company, as was the Light Company, the skirmishers. Grenadiers needed to be large in stature in order to provide a push in the front line of battle. Thomas, Stewart and Adam Dolmage were well suited to this task. The Grenadiers we easily recognizable in parade, due to their bear skin hats.]

The atmosphere of the drills became more intense and with a revived level of enthusiasm. They were now filled with anticipation that they would soon be facing real action. Given the urgency of the situation, all leaves were scarce and so both Stewart and Thomas found it difficult to visit their families. Within a week of receiving the new recruits, it was announced that they would be leaving for Cork on the morning of May 30th. Cork was on the southern coast of Ireland and it would take several days to make the trip. Word had been received that Napolean had swept through Spain and was making for Portugal. The British army which was now under the command of Sir John Moore, was currently supporting the efforts of their new allies the Spanish and Portuguese. Sir Arthur Wellesley was appointed Lieutenant General on April 25th and was instructed to take an expeditionary force to Portugal, support Sir John Moore, and intercept the French and push them back out of Spain.

Chapter Six

A time to search and time to give up,
a time to keep and a time to throw away.

(1808)

Thomas bent down low and placed a kiss on the forehead of his youngest son and namesake, who was still sleeping in the early morning hours. Alice stood at the door watching her husband as he moved through the room, saying goodbye to his three young sons. It would be some time before they would see their father again. He had to return to the barracks this morning in order to help with the final preparations for departure. The regiment would be leaving early the next morning.

The two stepped out the front door into the early dawn, the sun was just beginning to be peak above the eastern horizon. They stood quiet for a moment, watching as the trees and then the fields caught the morning light. There were no clouds and it promised to be beautiful day.

Thomas broke the silence, "I'd best be getting on Alice, reveille will have already sounded and I will be expected."

"I know, I'm content," Alice said as she turned to face him. "These past months have been more than I could have hoped for. God has been gracious." She put her arms around him and embraced him one last time.

He looked down into her eyes and then kissed her gently. "Do not fret my love, I will return home again."

"When will the regiment depart?"

"At first light."

"Look for us Thomas. Your sons and I will be there to see you off."

"I will find you." He then let go of her and climbed into the saddle of the mount he had borrowed from Ensign Fortescue. He applied his heels and he was off with a jolt. As he reached the bend in the road, he turned to look back. Alice was still standing at the front door. He waved and then resumed his journey toward the barracks.

* * * * *

It was still dark on the morning of May 30th as Thomas and Stewart moved through the company of Grenadiers, rousing each one and bringing them awake. Reveille hadn't yet sounded, but they had been instructed to rise an hour an half earlier than normal to complete the preparations for departure. It was going to be several days march to Cork and it was hoped they would get off just after dawn.

Thomas was filled with mixed emotions. He was excited to know they were finally going to join the war on the peninsula, but he had enjoyed these past months; having been able to spend time with his family and watching his young sons grow. In his heart he was hoping that the campaign would be short lived and that General Wellesley would lead them to a quick and decisive victory.

Once the men were dressed and ready, Thomas made a brief inspection of every member of the company to make sure everything was in order. Once they were deemed ready, one of the officers would make a final inspection. In this case the responsibility had been given to young Ensign Simcoe.

Simcoe was an ambitious young officer. He had aspired to be a part of the grenadiers from the start, recognizing it for a company that would give him plenty of opportunity to make a good impression and perhaps a chance for advancement. Despite only being seventeen years of age, he had already been making inquiries to determine whether there was a chance he could purchase a lieutenancy. Thomas saw this as a little bit of youthful haughtiness that could prove to be his undoing. However, he couldn't help but like the lad. He had a very pleasant demeanor and was very courteous to the rank and file, unlike many of the other officers in the regiment. He found it probable that he would find it a difficult task to keep the young man out of trouble in battle.

When Simcoe arrived to inspect the company he decided to have every soldier fire his musket without ball, to ensure that everything was in working order, and there were no gummed barrels and that the flints were good. Thomas thought this was a little extreme, and perhaps a little showy in front of the other companies, but ordered the soldiers to comply. Stewart looked at him a just smiled.

"It seems the young officer is trying awfully hard to make a good impression," Stewart whispered.

"Yeah, I think we might have to keep an eye on this one," Thomas whispered back between rounds of musket fire."

As the dawn erupted in bright sunshine the Inniskillings began marching out the front gate of the Castle Barracks, taking a path that would lead them right down the main street of Enniskillen. The residents of the town were at their doors, cheering the regiment as they passed. The grenadiers were the last company to pass. They were followed by the baggage carriages and then the battalion wives.

Each company was allowed to bring four or five wives that would provide domestic care. Bella and Alice could have traveled with the battalion, but James Pogue and little Thomas had not yet reached their second birthdays. Since both families were properly provided for, it was decided that it would be best for all if they remained at home.

Marching a column of a thousand soldiers and equipment was slow going and by midday they had only gone as far as Lisbellaw. As the regiment passed across the bridge on the west edge of the village, Thomas and Stewart caught sight of their wives standing on the roadside waving as they passed. They stepped out of line momentarily and strode over to their families. Ensign Simcoe noticed their departure from the line and started to say something and then thought better of it. The two gave their wives one last kiss goodbye. Bella was crying.

The Colonel

"Easy now Bella, I will be home again before you know it," Stewart tried to console.

Thomas reached down at patted his oldest son on the head. "You're the man of the house while I'm gone, Jamey. Look after your mother for me."

"Yes Father."

The two rejoined their company and continued on their march. Jamey and Willie ran alongside the column for a time, stopping only when they heard their mother calling them back.

The column continued its march east, stopping for the night at Maguire's Bridge, having covered only ten miles the first day. On the second day they traveled south passing through Butler and stopping for the night at Cavan, traveling twice the distance covered on the first day. After two days more they found themselves at Kells.

As they passed from one village to another, Thomas became more and more aware of the poverty that gripped the people of Ireland. He and Alice had been fortunate to have had parents who were freeholders, owners of their own farms, and in a sense, masters of their own prospects. However, most of the Irish Catholics were peasant farmers, subject to the whims of the wealthy land owners. This had been the reason for the rebellion of 1798, and despite having supported the Loyalists, Thomas was now having second thoughts. He had grown in his general empathy for the impoverished Irish people; no doubt influenced by his memory Betsy Gray. It was if he was seeing the poverty for the first time and as the Inniskillings moved south, it left him dispirited.

By the fourth of June the regiment had reached Leixslip, just to the west of Dublin. Two days later on the sixth, after a very long march they arrived in Curragh Camp, just ten miles east of Cork, their place of embarkation. They were the first regiment to arrive at Curragh, but they were soon to be joined by several other regiments that would also be making the journey to Spain. In all there would be 10,000 troops gathered under the leadership of General David Baird. These troops would be joined with those of Sir John Moore and together would be given the task of removing the French from Spain.

The 3/27th had, by this time, become a highly disciplined lot. The members of the rank and file were all volunteers, proud of the heritage of the regiment and respectful of duty. This was not always the case with other British soldiers. When confronted with the prospects of meeting an enemy with superior numbers, the British army was not opposed to drafting some unfortunate souls who had no real means of resisting. They remained in Curragh for several weeks and the idleness proved to be ample opportunity for the less disciplined soldier to consider desertion as an option.

On the morning of July 5th Thomas and Stewart were out for a stroll through Curragh Camp when they came upon the encampment of the 23rd. The regiment had been assembled and the officers were all present.

"What goes on here?" Stewart whispered to a corporal standing nearby.

The corporal only turned his head slightly to make an identification of the inquirer. "Deserters, and ye best be still."

It was a ghastly sight. A half dozen or so soldiers had been tied to a small stand of alder trees. A firing squad had been summoned and now stood armed and ready. There was only one penalty for desertion; death. The marshal gave the order and twenty or so muskets rang out at the same time, spewing forth a large cloud of smoke as they fired. The bodies of the convicted sagged, still bound to the trees that held them. One young man was crying out in pain. Death had not come quickly for this one poor lad. The marksman had failed to hit their target and he now writhed in pain, blood flowing freely from wounds on either leg. The twenty to thirty seconds required to reload would seem like an eternity to someone suffering so. Without hesitation, the marshal drew his pistol, went up to the unfortunate soul and brought an end to his suffering with a ball in the head.

Thomas turned away in disgust at the sight. He understood the need for discipline in the ranks, it could mean the difference between victory and defeat; and defeat meant the loss of many lives. Desertion, if gone unpunished, could result in complete anarchy and chaos going into battle. Despite comprehending the need for these barbarous forms of justice, he could not help think of the senselessness of it all. This young man was now dead and there was no going back. It seemed such a waste. It is unlikely that he would have ever been of any use in battle anyway. It is far better for his comrades to know that he could not be depended upon at this time, instead of finding it out in the foray, when it might cost them their lives. Still, killing him didn't really remedy the situation. Had he deserted he would be absent from the battle, just the same as had been determined by his execution.

Thomas was well aware that he was growing older and it was probably why he pondered these things far than when he was younger. He was becoming more the philosopher and less the soldier with each passing day. It didn't deter his courage and determination, but instead caused him to be more disciplined and focused on the task of ensuring the success of his company. His feelings of responsibility for the young men under his command ran deep.

The next few weeks were spent in drill; day in and day out the same routine. Thomas was driven by the urgency. He would do his part to ensure that the grenadiers were fully prepared for whatever lay ahead. They would live up to the expectation of being the best company in the regiment.

Late in July the regiment moved to Middleton, a little nearer to the cove of Cork. There was a mixture of excitement and anxiety flowing through the camp. It was clear that they would soon be departing for the peninsula. Finally in September they received their orders. On the 25th they departed Cork on the transport vessel *Tyne.*

Thomas was glad that the journey would be a short one. Transporting 10,000 troops on 60 ships was no easy task and every inch below decks was occupied, crowded and cramped. He didn't like to be aboard ship, and these conditions made it even worse. As he stood on the aft deck, he looked back at Cork. He knew that it would be a long time before he would see the shores of Ireland again. He wondered what Alice was doing at that very moment. He could see her face, her beautiful green eyes and capricious smile; it was almost as if she were standing right before him. He missed her.

"Thinking about home?" Stewart asked as he came up from behind, as if reading Thomas' mind.

"As a matter fact, yes. Don't you miss it? I mean don't you miss Bella and James?"

"Yes, I must admit, it is not like before. It's not easy to leave when you know you have family at home waiting for your return. When we were in Sicily I was always looking forward to the adventure, whatever it might be. Now, all that I ever think about is what I left behind." He clutched his chest where his fingers found a locket he had strung around his neck. In it was a small lock of Bella's hair.

"It's the same for me. When we first joined the Inniskillings, it seemed a romantic idea, adventurous, but now none of those things seem to matter. I think that when this whole thing with Boney is over, I will hang it up and leave the service."

"Well then I better make sure you get home again. Alice would never let me hear the end of it if I were to let you get killed." Stewart put his hand on his friends shoulder and smiled.

Thomas smiled back, "I'm not about to face Bella with bad news, so you had better keep your head down." He smiled as well. Together they looked out over the ocean, the port of Cork shrinking on the horizon.

It took five days to get to Falmouth, where they remained for ten days. On October 8, they sailed for the peninsula and on October 13th, they laid anchor in Bilbao, Spain. However, instead of disembarking, they left Bilbao and sailed to Corunna to the west. It was here that they hoped to meet up with Sir John Moore's army and together push the French back out of Spain before winter set in. Moore was inland at Salamanaca and they were to rendezvous at Valladolid, some fifty miles away.

The Colonel

However, they were once again delayed in disembarkation by the locals, and when they finally landed there was no transport provision to aid them in their journey inland. As a result, they were not ready to leave Corunna until late in November. Without any forewarning, the 27th and 31st regiments were ordered to sail to Lisbon, this meant they would not be present when Baird and Moore finally joined forces.

   With Baird's brigade delayed in Corunna and without further support, Moore was unable to make any headway. As a result, in December he was forced to withdraw back to Corunna. Unfortunately, transport ships were not ready to rescue the weary soldiers upon their arrival. Moore was forced to turn and fight. The French General Soult was determined to cut off the British retreat. Although the British rose to the occasion and beat back Soult and his army, Sir John Moore was killed in action and General Baird was wounded severely.

   The French then turned their attentions to Portugal and it seemed the 27th would soon be called into action.

Chapter Seven

7 a time to tear and a time to mend,
a time to be silent and a time to speak.

(1809)

The 27th remained in barracks in Lisbon throughout the winter. The French had yet to make an appearance. At the end of February they were ordered to board ship once again and sail south to Cadiz. Just as they were leaving Thomas received a post from Alice. The mail had been intermittent at best and any news from home was like sweet nectar to a starving man. Once they set sail, he found a quiet spot up on deck and began reading.

February 15th, 1809

Dearest Thomas,

How long the days seem when you are not here beside me. I miss you greatly and pray daily for you safe return. May God be gracious to me.

I have wonderful news to share with you. Four days ago I gave birth to our fifth child, a girl. She has your eyes and a hint of strawberry blond hair. I have named her Jane, after your sister, I hope you approve. God is good. In His wisdom he has eased my mourning and turned it once again into joy.

She is beautiful and a delight to her brothers. Jamey has been a great help, watching out for his younger brothers while I care for the baby. You would be very proud of him.

Bella has not been by since the baby has been born. She is expecting her own new arrival any day now. She is hoping for a girl as well, and I pray that

God will grant her this wish. I must admit that this is a bit selfish, since I am really wishing for a playmate for our Janey.

We hear very little news of the war and so I can only imagine what your life is like. Your last letter indicated that you had not yet met the enemy. I must confess that this is good news to me. I know the duty of the soldier takes him into danger, but I pray that these moments are infrequent for you.

Your sons are growing daily, looking more and more like the image of their father. Young Thomas is now talking up a storm. He is very inquisitive, asking questions about every little thing. His older brothers remain very patient with him. They all miss you very much and talk about you daily. They are very proud of their father.

We all look forward to the day you return to us. Keep safe, and pass our greetings along to Stewart.

Your loving wife,

Alice

Thomas folded the letter neatly and placed in the pocket of his jacket. He would read it again several times over the next few days. He could read between the lines, Alice wanted him to come home, to give up his life as a soldier. He was inclined to do just that, but he had a job to do and he would see it through to the end.

Once they arrived in Cadiz and were settled in their lodgings, he wrote Alice a reply. He tried to offer assuring words that he was safe and not in any immediate danger. He also wrote of how he hoped that the war would soon be over and then he would soon be home. Regardless of how he attempted to phrase it, he felt it would be inadequate in bringing Alice the comfort he wished for her.

Two weeks later Stewart received a letter from Bella indicating that he too was a new father and just as all had hoped, it was a girl. Bella named her Anne after her mother. Bella was beside herself with joy.

Alice was to get her wish, for the 27th remained detached from the main army and in a month sailed back to Portugal, having again avoided any contact with the enemy. With the loss of Sir John Moore and the injury to Sir David Baird the British forces were in need of a new leader. Sir Arthur Wellesley recently returned from an inquest in England, was appointed the new commanding officer of the British Army on the peninsula.

* * * * *

At the end of April, Alice received a surprising invitation. Lord and Lady Hardinge of Belle Isle requested her presence along with that of Jane at a luncheon to be held in honor of the visiting Lady Crichton of Crom Castle. It seemed Lady Mary had recently heard of the births of Janey and Annie and wished to pay them a visit. Realizing the young baby's would not be able to travel to Crom, she arranged for a meeting to take place at Belle Isle, much to the pleasure of the hosts.

Alice could not believe her eyes as she read over the invitation. She felt it strange that Lady Crichton would choose to entertain a farmer's daughter. Bella, after all, was sort of family, but Alice was not deserving. She couldn't imagine what she had done to gain so much attention from her Ladyship. She would go of course, she could not refuse and Bella's presence would make it tolerable.

"What would she say? What was she going to wear?" was all she could think about.

It was pretty clear why the Lord of Belle Isle had agreed to such an arrangement. There were still rumors circulating that their granddaughter was promised to Robert Crichton, despite the fact that she was still only a teenager. There were no sons in the Hardinge family and she was an only child, her mother dying in childbirth. The family had just recently received the devastating news that the girl's father, Lieutenant Ralph Hardinge, had been killed at Corunna. Without any other male heirs, even amongst distant relations, it meant that whoever married young Anne Hardinge would take Belle Isle as a part of the dowery. This was more than appealing to Lord Crichton who was still looking for a bride for his son Robert.

When the day arrived, Alice had made arrangements for her mother to look after the boys. Lord Hardinge had sent a carriage which had stopped in Cleenish first to pick up Bella and Annie. By mid-morning it arrived to pick up Alice and Janey. As Alice stepped into the carriage she could sense Bella's excitement.

"Hello Bella," she greeted. "I suppose you're overjoyed at the prospects of our day?"

"Surely you're not going to tell me that you're not the least bit excited yourself, Alice. It's not every day that you get invited to Belle Isle."

"No, I can't say I have ever been invited to Belle Isle. And I'm not exactly sure why I have been invited this time. I find it strange that Lady Mary has taken such an interest in me."

"You under appreciate yourself Alice. Despite your circumstances, you still carry the air of a lady of respectability. Beyond that you are pleasant and indiscriminate in showing charity to all."

Alice blushed a little. "This I would expect from you, for we have been friends for as long as I can remember, but it seems a strange thing that a Lady who knew me for only a few days would show me such favor."

"I think you protest a little too much. The truth is, you just don't like to put on airs. It makes you feel a little anxious, I think. Put your mind at ease. I don't think Lady Mary cares about such things. So just be yourself and enjoy the day. In any case, I think these two little ones will be the center of attention," she said indicating the two babies.

"I suppose your right. I will try not to think about it, and just have a good time. I do like Lady Mary and I am looking forward to seeing Belle Isle. And I must admit that I am a little curious about this young girl who is promised to Mr. Robert Crichton, poor thing. She must be nearly grown by now."

"Her name is Ann, and I would have to agree that the prospect of her marriage to Robert Crichton is unfortunate circumstances indeed, and she deserves our sympathy on more than one account."

"More than one account, whatever do you mean?" Alice asked.

"Perhaps you didn't hear that several months ago she lost her father. He was a lieutenant under the command of Sir John Moore, and was killed at Corunna."

"...I see. You're quite right, she shall get our sympathy regardless. Poor girl, indeed, very poor girl..." Alice paused for a moment as a thought crossed her mind concerning the safety of Thomas.

As if thinking the same thing Bella suddenly burst out, "Stupid war! Why must we endure such things?"

"Quite right. Meaningless, meaningless, just as the great king once said," Alice said. And then, as if reading her friend's thoughts, "Don't worry Bella, Thomas and Stewart will come home. God will keep them safe."

Bella turned to face Alice, her eyes tearing slightly, "I know Alice. I just wish it would be sooner rather than later. This waiting is interminable."

Alice changed the subject altogether, and asked how Annie was doing. Bella adored her new daughter and it didn't take much to prod her into telling stories about every moment of every day of Annie's short existence. This was more than enough to fill the remaining time of the trip to Belle Isle.

As they drew near to Belle Isle, Alice's excitement began to grow. The castle was situated beautifully in a little park. It was a large residence with a tall tower on one end. The spring flowers were already in bloom making for a very picturesque scene. It was not as large as Crom, but still very impressive in its own right.

As the Carriage pulled to the front of the house, they discovered their hosts were already standing out front to greet them. Lady Mary was the first in line as they stepped down from the carriage carrying their delicate packages. Behind her stood an older couple who Alice took to be the Lord and Lady of the house. The gentleman was quite distinguished, though advanced in years. He had lost a good deal of hair on top, but his features were sharp and handsome and he had a slight mustache that complimented his pleasant smile. The lady, although gray haired, show an elegance and grace befitting her station.

"Welcome to Belle Isle," Lord Hardinge greeted, speaking for all. "We are so pleased you could come. You must be a little tired from your journey please come inside and take refreshment with us."

By this time both Annie and Janey had woken from their morning naps and were beginning to squirm a little, and so it made it a little difficult to make any attempts at a proper courtesy, but Bella and Alice made the attempt in any case, abbreviated though it was.

"Now, now none of that formality here," Lady Hardinge said gently. "You go inside and get yourselves settled. Please make yourself at home and let us know whatever you or the little ones might need.

As they walked to the house, Lady Mary took hold of Bella's arm and escorted her into the house. "Come follow us, Alice," she said over her shoulder.

Alice did as she was instructed and followed the two through the foyer and into a small sitting room that looked out onto a nice little patio. Mr. and Mrs. Hardinge left them alone.

"I thought it might be best for you to take a bit of rest here in private for a little while," Lady Mary explained. She seemed to be quite at home. "We'll not be missed, they will call us when lunch is ready." She then sat down next to Bella on a small couch. "Do you think I might hold her?" she asked, indicating Annie.

"Of course your Ladyship, but she is getting a little fidgety."

"Please, call me Mary," as she took the baby in her arms. "She is very beautiful...adorable. Thank you for coming. When I heard the news, I just had to come and see for myself. You have both been blessed."

As she was talking a young woman entered the room dressed in black. Despite her somber appearance, Alice was immediately taken back. She looked older than her fifteen years. She was beautiful, with dark hair and striking steel blue eyes. She was tall and moved through the room with confidence and ease. She was smiling pleasantly, with a sparkle in her eye.

"Hello Ann," Lady Mary welcomed the newcomer. "Ladies this is Ann Hardinge. Ann this is Bella ... and Alice Rea, friends of mine."

"Yes, hello," she gave a slight courtesy. "I am pleased to meet you both, I have heard a great deal about you, from Mary and I have been looking forward to making your acquaintance." She sat down in a chair near Alice, who was still holding Janey.

"And this," Mary held up the baby in her arms, "is Annie. And there next to you, is Jane. Aren't they just adorable?"

"Surely they are," Ann said as she peered over Alice's shoulder at Jane.

"Would you like to hold her?" Alice offered.

"May I?"

"Of course," Alice turned and laid Jane in Anne's arms.

"Ann, we were so sorry to hear about your father. Please accept our greatest sympathies. You must have been devastated," Bella offered her sympathies.

"Thank you, you're very kind. I was...perhaps still am a bit devastated. I loved my father very much, and since I never knew my mother, he has been the whole world to me. Well that is except Grandma and Grandpa of course. We were quite close...," there was a moment of silence, no one sure quite what to say. "What about you? I understand that you have husbands in the army. Are they well?"

"Yes, they are both corporals in the Inniskillings, and at last report they are well and far from danger. It seems they have been able to avoid the enemy up until now," Alice responded.

"Safe for now, but we too live with the fear of the future, not knowing the outcome, constantly beseeching heaven to watch out for those we love. Wondering and waiting," Bella added.

"They are in God's hands, only He can determine our days," Mary interjected, "now, enough of this gloomy talk. We are not here to talk of war and death, but to celebrate life, the very life I now hold in my arms."

"You are right Mary," Ann agreed. "There is a time to laugh and a time to cry, and I think this is the former." She held Janey up so that her feet set lightly on her lap, and then began to make faces, trying to get the baby to smile. Janey responded with cooing and giggles.

Alice had already begun to feel warmth for Ann, not just sympathy, but a genuine admiration. She liked how at ease she was with the baby, and how Janey immediately took to her. She was not only a beautiful young woman, but had a very pleasant way about her. She showed an unnatural maturity for her age and there was no indication of pretense. Even though her attire suggested someone in mourning, she was not melancholy, but instead she was alive and enthusiastic.

Before long, a butler entered the room to announce that lunch was ready. They were escorted to a nice day room that looked out on the lawn. It was brightly lit with large bay windows extending from floor to ceiling. Lord and Lady Hardinge were awaiting their arrival. The table smartly decorated with centerpieces of spring bloom. Alice thought it strange that she actually felt comfortable in her surroundings. Although this level of opulence was not a part of her natural experience, her visit to Crom had prepared her and she found herself quite at ease in this second venture into society.

Lady Mary tended to dominate the conversation, asking a number of questions about Bella's and Alice's young sons. It was clear that she found some level of vicarious pleasure from hearing about the life experiences of the young mothers. She scolded her friends for failing to visit her at Crom and made them promise that they would make the journey with the boys, before the summer was at an end. Reluctantly, both Bella and Alice accepted her invitation.

"Sir," Alice addressing Richard Hardinge, "I noticed a striking portrait of a distinguished man and woman in the entry way when we came in. Might you explain who they are?"

"Those are my parents," Mary Hardinge responded before her husband had an opportunity, "General Ralph Gore and Katherine Conolly Gore. My father, who was the Earl of Ross, built Belle Isle. He died in the winter of 1802. Sadly his only son, my half-brother had preceded him in death and so Belle Isle passed to me. I have a cousin who could have taken possession, but he is now a Governor in India. And now with the loss of our son at Corunna, Belle Isle is once again without heir."

"And what about Ann here?" Bella asked, "Is she not the heir?"

"It's possible. Since there are no other heirs making claims, she might inherit, if she were to marry well."

To marry well could really mean only one thing. Her husband would have to be of a noble family of property, and it would mean that Belle Isle would be joined to a larger estate. Alice knew what this meant and of whom they were all thinking.

Ann blushed slightly, no doubt aware that the topic of conversation was about to make her to focal point. "Now grandma, there is no need for us to be talking about my marriage prospects, I have not even been out yet. Besides, I don't expect that you will be going anywhere anytime soon. It will be a long while before I would ever contemplate taking possession of Belle Isle."

"Tis true," Bella affirmed, "but when the time comes, I think you will have many worthy suitors Ann. You are a very bright and attractive young lady and I have no doubt you shall have many prospects. Don't you think so Alice?"

"Indeed I do. You are very beautiful and with qualities of person that would be very attractive even without the benefit of Belle Isle. I think this provides you with the great advantage of being highly discriminating in your prospects."

"You are both very kind," Ann blushing again, "but as I have just stated, I see no reason to be neither anxious nor impetuous."

"No one is suggesting that you need be hasty my dear," Lady Hardinge assured, "but it is not impetuous to at least consider your options."

"What of young Chricton, Lady Mary?" Richard Hardinge asked without warning. Everyone had been thinking of it, but no one had expected the question to be asked out loud. "I understand that he has not yet found a suitable wife."

"Grandfather, really," Ann tried to deflect the question. "I don't think that Lady Mary should be compromised, to suit your curiosity."

"It is okay Ann," Lady Mary assured. "I am not compromised, however, I am also somewhat at a loss, since young Robert (remember that Robert was actually only two years her junior), does not confide in me concerning his affairs, least of all his prospects of marriage. I am afraid the question would have to be directed to him, although I think his father would disagree. It seems the Baron is of the opinion, that the father, not the son, should have the last say on this account."

"And what say you two?" Lord Hardinge would not let it drop, "do you think that young Robert Chricton would make a good match for our dear Ann?" He looked directly at Alice as if almost demanding a response.

Alice didn't really want to be a part of this conversation, but it appeared everyone was waiting to hear what she had to say, with perhaps the exception of the young lady in question. "Well I'm afraid I cannot say for sure. I only met him the once and it was a brief encounter at first. He is attractive," this at least was not a lie, "but I'm not sure that I am able to speak of his character or person," this was a half-truth. "I suppose I'm of the conviction that the young lady in question should form her own opinion, when given a chance."

Ann turned to face Alice directly and offered a wry smile. It was a way of showing her appreciation for offering such a delicate and discrete response. "I think Alice is quite wise and perceptive, and in any case I do not see why this needs to be settled here, or why I have become the center of this conversation. Surely there are other things we could talk about."

Although Lord Hardinge had not made any progress on the matter, he was discerning enough to know that he should not press the matter any further. Mercifully the conversation changed, the subject would not be broached again.

Later that afternoon, Ann offered to watch the babies as they were napping and so the three friends took a walk through the park surrounding the great house. It was a beautiful spring day, and it made for a very pleasant stroll. Bella and Mary walked arm in arm as Alice trailed a few steps behind. She rarely had moments of solitude anymore, with three little boys and a new baby girl always demanding her attention, there was never a moment for herself. She walked quietly, deep in thought, wondering what Thomas was doing at that moment. It seemed frivolous that she would be spending a leisurely afternoon on the estate of Belle Isle, with hardly a care in the world, while at that same moment Thomas could be experiencing any number of hardships, even be engaged in battle, her completely unaware. It bothered her, not just that he was in danger, but that these different circumstances were tainted by injustice. She was feeling a little guilty.

"What are you thinking about Alice, you have been very quiet," Lady Mary finally broke through her moment of solitude. They had come upon a shady spot beneath a huge elm tree. There were a couple of benches neatly set, which encouraged them to sit and take some relief from the warmth of the sun.

"Nothing really," Alice tried to hide her mind. "I'm just enjoying the beauty of the day, counting my blessings." It was a little white lie, but she felt it was prudent. There was no reason to ruin Bella's day with worry and stress. She seemed to be having such a good time.

"Yes you are blessed, Alice," Mary said. "In many ways I envy you, your beautiful children and your brave and handsome husband."

"Envy me? That seems unlikely Milady, given that you are the mistress of Crom Castle, and I, a poor farm girl. Besides how do you know that Thomas is handsome, you have never met him?"

"Yes envious, I have no children to care for, my husband has grown old, and although he loves me and provides for me, my days are quite dull. Not that I am complaining, mind you, but it would be nice, if just for a moment, if I felt needed, that someone depended upon me. As for your husband, I'm sure his beauty pales in comparison with yours, however, Bella tells me that he is quite striking and even bears some resemblance to our Robert."

"He is handsome at that, if I may boast," Alice confirmed. "As far as his resemblance to Robert, it is on the surface alone. His heart is as noble as any Duke's and his temper even, so that I have never known a cross word from his lips, or any form of disparaging remark intended for the unfortunate. Although not by birth, he is a gentleman in every sense of the word."

"Your words betray your deep love for him, and I admire you for it. However, I also hear a hint of disdain for Robert in your voice. Would I be right to presume that you question my step son's character?"

"I'm sorry Mary, I didn't intend to mean anything by it. I have only met Robert once, and I dare say he did not leave me with a positive impression. I was only suggesting, despite his position by birth, he does not compare favorably with my Thomas."

"And what about you Bella," Lady Mary turned toward her, "what do you think of Robert."

"For my part, I have had much more opportunity to observe the man in question than my dear friend here. I have

100

never known him to show the slightest interest in behaving as a gentleman should. I fear the Baron has coddled his youngest son, which has done him a great disservice."

"Your discernment does you well, both of you," Mary affirmed. "I must admit that I too have a question about Robert's character. It has left me anxious for young Ann. I have grown quite fond of the young girl in the short time I have known her. I realize that she is still very young, and nothing may come of it, but the Baron seems quite fixated on making this match. I do not think Robert is disserving of her."

"I would have to agree," Alice said, speaking more forthright. "Ann seems a delightful young lady, and although she has heart and has already had the opportunity to show her fortitude in difficult circumstances, it would be an unfair match in her interests."

"I empathize entirely," Bella added. "There was a time when my father was bent on making a match between Robert and myself. I count my blessings that he finally relented and released me to marry Stewart. No amount of wealth would have consoled me had I been imprisoned in such a marriage."

"I'm afraid there would be little that we can do for the lady in question. She seems of generous heart toward her grandmother, and would likely do whatever is necessary to preserve Belle Isle."

The three sat quietly for a moment, each in contemplation of the plight of their young friend. Alice felt a sort of relief, realizing, for the first time, the advantage enjoyed by those who did not carry the burden of expectation of position. Ann was not free, not it any real sense. Her life was not her own.

Chapter Eight

*[8] A time to love and a time to hate,
a time for war and a time for peace.*

As they had promised, Bella and Alice made a visit to Crom Castle in August. They were hesitant to bring all of the children, but Lady Mary had insisted and so they relented. As it turned out, their hostess had planned a number of outings for the children that took advantage of the pleasant summer weather and the extensive park surrounding the Castle. Jamey and Willie particularly enjoyed fishing at the edge of Lough Erne. The visit went without mishap, and the children had a wonderful time. Just the same, Alice was pleased to return home again. Upon arriving she was delighted to receive a post from Thomas.

August 15, 1809

Dearest Alice,

We are now returned to Lisbon. We hear that General Wellesey and the main force has had a number of recent successes against the French in Spain. He has now returned to Portugal to wait on the enemy. As of yet the 27th has yet to see any action.

The Inniskillings are now a part of the 4th Division, and we just recently received the good news that General Galbraith Lowry has been given our command. He is the second son of the 1st Earl of Enniskillen and you might imagine the news was more than pleasing to the men of the 27th.

I know that our failure to engage the enemy up to this point would be pleasant news to your ears, however, I sometimes find myself wondering what we are doing here, and what place I have in all of this. It appears that Wellesley has us along only to cover his retreats. The more he succeeds, the less likely we will see any action. Our young lieutenant of the grenadiers is quite anxious on this point. I fear that I will have to keep an eye on him, as his ambitions put him at risk.

It goes without saying, how much I miss you and our children. Give them my love and an extra special kiss for our daughter of whom I have not yet had the pleasure of meeting. If we continue to remain in Lisbon for any length of time, I may ask Colonel Maclean for leave. Although, I must be careful not to give you false hope, for our future remains very uncertain.

Stewart sends his love to Bella. Trust and know that we are now safe and in God's hands.

Love,
Thomas

Thomas was correct about the uncertainty of the future. A few weeks later the 4th Division was ordered to leave Lisbon and march inland to Bardajoz, a strategic town just across the border into Spain. There they would set up defensives and provide relief to Wellesey's army, many of whom were weary from having recently engaged the enemy at Talaveras.

Like his lieutenant Thomas was growing weary of marching from one place to another, with very little to show for it, except the wear and tear on his boots. The members of the 27th were healthy and in fighting form, but there was still little sign of the enemy on their horizon. Once in Bardajoz, they remained encamped, at the ready. They continued to spend their days training and maintaining some reasonable routine, but it was clear that the rank and file were beginning to grow restless.

Before the onset of winter the entire army was ordered back to Lisbon. By this time, General Wellesey was now Lord Wellington. He had already returned to his headquarters and the army was merely following their commander. The 4th Division was the last to leave Bardajoz and thus the last to arrive in Lisbon. It was quite clear that Wellington had no intention of leaving Lisbon before winter was over and so Thomas and Stewart both took advantage and asked for leave. With the exception of Stewart's honeymoon, and the occasional night away from the barracks, neither Thomas nor Stewart had taken any leave since first joining the 27th and were overdue. Maclean saw no reason to deny them and so on December 15th they were able to catch passage on a frigate that was returning to Portsmouth.

Once in Portsmouth, it took a couple days before they were to catch passage on a small merchant vessel headed for Dublin. Late in the afternoon on the 24th of December they arrived by mail coach in Lisbellaw.

It was a brisk day, but clear. The sun was sinking toward the horizon as Stewart and Thomas walked up the lane toward Thomas' house. They were weary from the journey, but lighthearted to be at home. Thomas looked skyward and mused to himself that it was very unlikely that they would have a white Christmas.

"Tomorrow is Christmas, and I don't have any presents for the Children," He said aloud.

"I think you're about as good a Christmas present as they could hope to get," Stewart assured him, giving a little smile. There is nothing like getting surprised on Christmas Eve."

"I suppose you're right, Stew...It sure is good to be back home in Ireland. It seems as if it has been such a long time...Little Janey and Annie must be almost 9 months old by now."

"Nine months, and we've missed it all...," Stewart lamented.

"Yes we have."

As they arrived to the house they could hear the chatter of children playing and laughing inside. Thomas opened the latch on the door and swung it open with a thud causing everyone in the room to stop and look. One by one their startled looks turned to joy as they realized what or who had just entered the room.

"Father!" Willie was the first to jump to his feet and run to greet his father. Jamey was not far behind. Alice just remained frozen to the place where she was standing with little Thomas holding on to skirt. A few feet away Janey sat playing on the floor, looking a little disappointed that her brothers would abandon her.

"Well don't you beat all," Alice was finally able to speak. "Thomas, Stewart...what do you mean surprising us like this and on Christmas Eve and all."

Thomas did not respond. He just walked over to her and hugged her and then kissed her.

"Hello, Alice, Merry Christmas," he whispered in her ear.

"Oh Thomas, it is so good to have you home, what a surprise." She hugged his neck for what seemed to be minutes, not wanting to let go, for fear that it was all a dream.

Thomas reached down and picked up the baby who was still sitting in the middle of the floor. "And who is this?" he asked as he held her up so he could see her face.

"It's Janey!" he heard a little voice at his feet.

Thomas holding the baby in one arm, reached down and picked up little Thomas with his open arm. "And who is this big boy?" he asked.

"I'm Thomas, don't you 'member," he responded.

"Hmmm...I hate to break up this family reunion, but I really must be getting on to my own family," Stewart interrupted.

"Hello Stewart, welcome home," Alice stepped toward him and gave him a light kiss on the cheek.

"Right, sorry Stew, I almost forgot about you," Thomas smiled as he said it. "Jamey, do you think you could help Uncle Stewart harness the horse and the cart. He's going to borrow it to get home tonight."

"Sure, Father," Jamey said. "Come on, Uncle Stewart, I'll show ya!" The two started toward the door.

"Stewart, before you go…tell Bella that you are all invited for Christmas dinner tomorrow, at my parents. We'll celebrate your homecoming together."

"Sure Alice, we'll be there."

Thomas had sat down in the nearest chair, partly because he was weary, but partly because he was in awe of the little girl he still held in his arms. She was beautiful, she already had locks of auburn hair and her eyes were brilliant green, just like her mother. Willie and little Thomas were both talking a mile a minute, trying to get his attention, but he barely heard them. He could only think of Stewart's words, "we have missed it all." It wasn't right for a father to be separated from his family for so long. For the first time, Thomas was beginning to question whether he should have ever joined the Inniskilling? As he looked in Janey's eyes, he could sense that she was apprehensive, that she didn't know who he was. This frightened him. It was difficult to realize that his own daughter did not know him.

He began to feel anxious about his duty as a soldier. He had always known the risk to himself, but in this moment he could not help wonder what it would be like for Janey to grow up without knowing her father. This could not happen. "It would not happen," he said to himself.

Alice was standing behind him, and as she bent down she placed her arms around his neck and set her chin upon his right shoulder. "What do you think of our little angel?" she whispered.

"She's beautiful, just like her mother," he answered as he turned his head slightly and kissed her on the cheek. He then looked back at Janey, "she hardly seems real to me. She doesn't know me, nor I her."

"In time, Thomas, you must be patient." Just then Janey realized the close proximity of her mother and she reached for her, cooing as she did so. Although he hated to do so, he handed her into her mother's arms.

The remainder of the day, he spent sharing about their adventures in Portugal, and the trip home. It was true that they had not engaged the enemy as of yet, but he still had plenty of stories to tell about the soldiers he traveled with, their personal histories and unique personalities. He tried to imitate young Dolmage's German accent, and told of his difficulty in drills when forming the square, as if he couldn't remember his left from his right. He also talked about the young lieutenant who was always ranting that he couldn't wait to the meet the enemy even though he was barely nineteen and had never seen a hint of action in battle. Willie and Jamey were particularly humored when he told of the time they had to transport the baggage on barges across the bay at Lisbon and how it had been poorly secured, causing a portion of it to let loose knocking six of his fellow soldiers, including the lieutenant into the water, leaving Thomas and Stewart the only dry ones on board.

As the evening wore on, Alice insisted that it was time for bed. The boys, not wanting to risk anything with Santa Claus, made no objection, hugged their father good night and slipped off to bed. Janey had long since fallen asleep and so Thomas picked her up and carried her to her bed. As he placed her gently in her bed and pulled her blanket across her, he just stood looking at her sleeping silently. He could not move. It was as if he was trying to soak in a lifetime of such moments in that one instance. He remained there several minutes watching his daughter. He could hear Alice's movements in the other room, making preparations for the next morning.

Without thinking, barely conscious of his own actions, he stripped off his uniform and climbed beneath the covers of his own bed. He just lay there staring at the ceiling, watching the flicker of candle light from the other room. As he lay there in the quiet, he could hear Janey breathing in the bed a few feet away. He must have dozed off, for he didn't remember hearing Alice in the room and then suddenly she was there in bed next to him. She placed her arm around him and whispered, "It's so good to have you home."

"It's good to be home," he whispered so softly, he wasn't even sure she heard it. And then he fell asleep.

The next day was full of activity. Alice had left treats of nuts and candy in the stockings hung by the fire, and the boys had opened the presents left for them beneath the tree. After breakfast, they all braved the cold weather and paid a visit to Mr. and Mrs. Copeland, down the lane. Alice had a younger sister, Maggie, who was still unmarried and living at home. She was always pleased to have her nephews and niece come for a visit. She played games with the children, while Alice and Thomas visited with her parents. Around noontime, Alice's sister Mary and husband arrived. Mary was five years younger than Alice, and had married John Trimble, a rector at Enniskillen Parish church. Mary was expecting her first child in the spring. Not long after, Stewart and Bella arrived. It was a large gathering for such a modest farm house, but no one seemed to mind the crowded conditions.

It was a joyful celebration with the surprise homecoming of the two soldiers. No one was more delighted than Bella, who was beaming throughout the entire day. Alice was no less cheerful, but she tended to keep her emotions somewhat contained in comparison to her friend. As the afternoon waned, she took a moment to sit and relax and simply take in all of the commotion around her. Thomas was preoccupied with Janey, almost to the point of neglecting his three sons. Fortunately, Maggie was more than pleased to occupy the boys. As she sat and watched, Alice could only think in her heart of how grateful she was for this blessing. She was at peace, completely content in the moment, as if nothing else in the world mattered beyond what was happening right there in front of her. It was the best Christmas present she could have ever received.

The next two weeks passed by much too quickly and soon it was time for Stewart and Thomas to return to the Inniskilllings. The goodbyes, as always, were very difficult. As was her habit, Bella could not stop crying, despite Stewart's attempts to reassure her that everything would be alright and they would be home again soon. Alice gave Thomas a long embrace, not wanting to let him go. He too tried to offer words of consolation, but she could see concern in his eyes; there was something troubling him. He smiled as he said his goodbyes, but she could sense that it was somewhat forced. It was not simply that he appeared sad about their impending separation, it was more than that. For the first time she could see fear in his eyes and it left her shaken.

"Goodbye, my love," she said softly and she hugged him one more time. "Return to me."

"Goodbye, Alice," Thomas returned. "Take care of yourself. God willing, we will be home again soon." He placed one last kiss on the forehead of Janey, as she was held in the arms of her Aunt Maggie. He then bent down and gave little Thomas a hug. As he stood up he brushed the hair of Willie and Jamey with his hands. "You two look after your mother, and your little brother and sister. I am counting on you."

"We will Father," they both sang out in unison.

"Give those Frenchies a whippin' Uncle Stew...," Jamey said turning toward Stewart and Bella.

"You can count on it Jamey boy," Stewart returned. "And you can bet we will be home before next Christmas."

Stewart and Thomas started down the road, with Jamey and Willie trailing behind. The boys followed them to the end of the lane before turning back. Thomas turned one last time to wave goodbye. Alice was still standing where he had left her, now holding Janey in her arms and with little Thomas clinging to her leg. "Goodbye Alice," he said to himself. "May God grant me the fortune to return to you once more."

Chapter Nine

[9] Two are better than one,
Because they have a good return for their work.

(1810)

It took Thomas and Stewart sixteen days to return to Lisbon. They were delayed in Portsmouth for three days because the weather was making it impossible for any ships to leave port. When they finally arrived in Lisbon, they were surprised to find that the 4th Division had been ordered to leave Lisbon and to march north to Coimbra. When they reported to the adjutant's office in Lisbon, they were handed a letter which provided them with instructions. The letter was from Colonel Maclean and simply said, "Remain in Lisbon at the disposal of General Wellesley. Be prepared to leave at any moment to carry communications from command to the 4th Division in Coimbra."

It was not until the first week of February that they were finally given their orders. They were to leave for Coimbra on horseback, carrying a sealed message for General Cole. The distance to be traveled was 140 miles. On horseback, this would take five days, significantly less than the two weeks it took the 4th to march. When they arrived, they were greeted by their comrades with enthusiasm. Most of the Inniskillings were Irish and therefore relished any news from home. Besides the instructions for General Cole, Thomas and Stewart had also been entrusted with the post addressed to soldiers of the 4th. This made the two of them highly popular with the entire division. As of yet, they had not encountered the enemy and any break from the monotony of the day to day march and drill was welcomed by all.

It turned out that the orders delivered to General Cole determined the division would once again be on the march. This time they would go west to Guarda. It was clear that the French army would enter Portugal from the North and therefore General Wellesley was positioning his army to create a defensive line stretching east to west all the way to the sea. Surprisingly the French did not come. This might have been due to the fact that they were poorly supplied or were waiting reinforcements. Whatever the reason, the British Army with support from the Spanish and Portuguese sat in wait of the enemy. This waiting stretched all the way into the summer.

In July Thomas was given the charge of escorting Lieutenant Simcoe back to Lisbon. Simcoe had been ill of health and it was believed it would be better if he convalesced far from the impending battle. Thomas was also carrying dispatches from Wellington. He returned to Guarda two weeks later only to discover that the French had still not attacked. Wellington knew that he was outnumbered and could not rely on his Spanish and Portuguese allies to provide ample support, and so he continued to play a cat and mouse game with General Messena, who was commanding the French forces.

In August, Wellington remained encamped around Guarda, with the bulk of his main force present, the 4th Division included. By early September, he decided to march and withdraw to the West in hopes of enticing Messena to follow. Lieutenant Simcoe returned to the grenadiers just in time to join in the march west. He was fully recovered and was excited at the prospects of finally seeing some action. The entire regiment was now at the ready, anticipating that a battle was imminent. The Inniskillings had now been on the Peninsula for more than two years, and as of yet, had not seen a whisker of the enemy.

Each morning Simcoe inspected the grenadiers with scrutiny and precision. He was forever trying to make an impression. Even though he had not reached the age of twenty, he had hoped to have received his captaincy by this time and the command of the grenadiers. However, he had been turned down and the grenadiers remained under the command of Captain Pring. This made the young officer all the more zealous of gaining his promotion by any means. He had confided to Thomas on their journey to Lisbon that he had even entertained volunteering for a forlorn venture (it had long been believed that an officer surviving a forlorn venture would be in line for immediate promotion). Thomas thought this a very frivolous idea, since such an ambition was not a risk the young officer would take on his own. In fact the entire company would be at risk. He continued to assure young Simcoe that his time would come, and he need only remain patience. Experience had made it clear that openings for command positions were becoming more frequent, if not in the Inniskillings, it was true in the other battalions. Simcoe was comforted by this, but he was still troubled that he might have to leave the grenadiers to gain his promotion and this was not satisfying to him.

As the British army moved westward, Massena and the French took the bait and began to move in a parallel line, hoping to cut off what appeared to be a retreat. Wellington had done his homework and realized that his best option was to make a defense on the cliffs of Bussaco, just a few miles to the north of Coimbra. The British army now stood at 51,000 and having placed his army in a position to defend the high ground, Wellington was optimistic of the result.

The 4th Division was asked to defend the northern most flank from a cliff top that overlooked uneven and broken ground. As the grenadiers took their position, Thomas gave a look over to Simcoe. It was clear that the young officer was excited to the point of being giddy. He didn't have to look far to see that this enthusiasm was quite contagious amongst the rank and file of the grenadiers. For his part, Thomas remained stoic. It was clear that he would have to keep an eye on his young friend, to be sure he didn't act carelessly in the heat of battle. Despite having been given the responsibility of leading men into battle, the young officer had never seen the true horror that can accompany the fray.

On the evening of the 26th of September the British soldiers were bivouacked in their respective positions waiting the night and the enemy. Wellington had instructed that no one was to light a fire, knowing full well that the enemy would make good use of their giving away their positions. Across the way they could see the night fires of their enemy. It was a reminder of the sheer weight of the numbers of their opposition. Despite having the advantage of high ground, there was no thought given to the possibility of an easy victory.

By six o'clock of the morning of the 27th, the sun had risen, but was still unseen due to a heavy fog blanketing the entire valley beneath the cliffs. The French saw the fog as an opportunity for surprise. Massena believed that he could circle around behind the British forces to the south, attacking from the rear, taking away the advantage of the high ground, and catching the enemy by surprise. He gave this task to General Reynier, who had at his disposal 14,000 French troops. Wellington was not caught off guard, having left the largest portion of his army to the south where he knew he was most vulnerable. Reynier began the attack before the fog had lifted and before he could see the enemy, or be seen. However, he made a slight miscalculation in approach and found himself caught between the 1st and 3rd Divisions who easily repulsed the attack and sent the French scurrying down the hill. A second French assault met with no greater success and was again repelled by the better positioned and high disciplined British forces. A third assault, a little further to the north, again met with the same result.

Meanwhile, all of this was happening while the Inniskillings remained fit and ready on the cliff top. The fog was so thick that it was impossible for the grenadiers of the 3/27th to see anything. As each French assault occurred, the sounds of battle moved closer and closer to their position and still they waited. They stood patiently, looking out into the fog, expecting that at any moment they would see the blue coats of their adversary emerge from the mist, but it never happened. They never came. By the time the fog lifted, the battle was over and the French were in retreat.

Thomas looked out over the valley to the south with horror. Dead and wounded, mostly French, were everywhere.

The Colonel

There were cries of agony of those who were suffering in the pain of their wounds, many mortal. Even though they were perched safely on the cliff, some distance away from the battle, he could see blood staining the ground everywhere he looked. He turned and looked into the eyes of Simcoe. Gone was the sparkle of enthusiasm of a young man going to battle for the first time. His eyes were now dark, his continence sullen. Perhaps, for the very first time, he was now looking into the face of death and it stung. Once again the 3/27th had avoided any contact with the enemy, but this time they didn't avoid witnessing the carnage.

"Well it looks as if we have been left out of it again," Stewart said, as he and Thomas stood side by side looking out over the decimation in the valley below.

"Tis true Stew," Thomas replied. "It seems fate is determined to keep us at arm's length from the enemy. Even so, I fear the battle has left our comrades a bit shaken," nodding toward the grenadiers who remained in line, gazing out over the battlefield.

"Yes...I see the pain reflected in their eyes," Stewart agreed. "It's not fitting, the first time they see any action and it is from a distance. It would have been better that they shouldn't have seen any battle at all, than to see only the result, without having been intimately involved. I'm afraid this will leave a bitter taste that will not soon go away."

"I am of the same opinion. I don't think they will forget this moment anytime soon..." Thomas reflected in silence. In the distance the faint groans and cries could still be heard from those who had fallen. "I think it would be less than beneficial for our friends here to have this scene playing over in their minds the next time we should face our enemy."

"Agreed...but it will be no easy task to rid them of it. I'm afraid it has left quite an impression." Stewart placed his hand on Thomas' shoulder and spoke a little softer. "...But we will do our best."

The French suffered 6,400 dead and wounded, the British less than 650. Massena made a horrible miscalculation, one he would not soon repeat. Wellington would not wait to see what Massena's counter offensive would be. As it turned out, the fog had served to benefit the British more than the French. Realizing he was still outnumbered, Wellington was not going to give Massena the opportunity to make amends, so the entire British army slipped away in the night, before the French had time to rebound.

In the days that followed, it became clear to Thomas, the real object of his commanding general. If he hadn't been fully convinced of the wisdom of General Wellington before, he was now. The defense of the cliffs of Busacco was only a ruse, a faint. Wellington knew that he was outnumbered by the French and he needed more time, both to call on reinforcements and to create better defensive positions. While the British army engaged the French, the engineers had been employed to build defensive lines stretching east to west, directly to the North of Lisbon, the French's intended target. While the French were licking their wounds, the entire British army, 50,000 strong, was able to retreat to positions behind these defensive barriers. With heavy artillery in place, it was here that Wellington would make his stand.

Massena had to follow, the entire Portuguese army remained to the north, winter was approaching and the French were badly in need of supplies. There only hope was to press through the British lines and take Lisbon. There Massena would be able to secure the resources he desperately needed. Wellington was about to spring his trap.

The Inniskillings made their encampment near Sobral. On the morning of October 11th Thomas awoke to the sound of musket fire. As he emerged from his tent, he found soldiers scrambling in all directions. There seemed to be no rhyme or reason to it, they were stumbling over each other, running in all directions. He stood his ground, peering through the morning mist, trying to discern what was happening. He could hear musket fire to his right, but the mist and trees were blocking his view. Stewart appeared at his right shoulder.

"What do you make of it Thomas?" His friend asked.

"I can't be sure, from the direction and distance. I would say the outer perimeter sentinels have encountered the enemy."

Just then a young soldier bumped into Thomas, he looked up realizing his error. "Sorry sir. I didn't see you there."

"Where are you off to soldier?" Thomas asked calmly.

"It's the entire bloody French army! They surprised us in our sleep, caught us completely unaware."

"Easy soldier," Thomas held him by the tunic. "Keep your composure. I hardly think it is the entire French army. More likely it is some scouting party or perhaps a vanguard. Now go find Colonel Maclean and apprise him of the situation."

As he said it he heard the cry of Lieutenant Simcoe, "Grenadiers to me!"

By the time Thomas could reach the side of his lieutenant, most of the company had already been assembled. "Where is Captain Pring?" Thomas enquired.

"He is on the other side of camp, a meeting with the Colonel I believe."

Thomas could see it in his eyes. He was about to do something foolhardy.

"Begging your pardon Lieutenant, but I hope you're not thinking of charging out into that mist without orders. There is no telling what you will find out there."

"What do you suggest?"

"Form line and then proceed slowly. The Frenchies are not known for their marksmanship. When we have sight of the enemy, we will have the advantage. There is no need to run to them, if they are attacking, they will come to us and before they know what hits them, we will have released two volleys into their midst."

"See to it then Corporal Rea. There is little time to waste."

As the grenadiers formed line, other companies of the 3/27th followed suit. As they moved forward toward the fray, they encountered soldiers running in the opposite direction, undisciplined and lacking any leadership. As the Inniskillings emerged from the trees, they caught sight of the French uniforms through the mist not more than 100 yards away. It was time for all the training to pay off. The Inniskillings let go the first volley before the French were able to react. Several blue coats fell to the ground. The first row knelt as the second row stood and fired another volley, only seconds after the first. This was repeated several times, and with each cycle, the lines moved forward. The French were not very well organized and began to falter. Within minutes the first line of the French were joined by others, but by this time the Inniskillings had formed a solid line of defense that would cover the retreat of those who had made first contact with the enemy and were now in retreat. The attack by the French had stalled.

Moments later they heard the orders to retreat. Thomas had been right, it was only a vanguard. However, General Lowry didn't want to take the chance that Messinas main forces were close behind. Despite having gained the advantage, the Inniskillings were ordered to withdraw, cautiously, just slow enough to cover the retreat of the rest of the 4th Division.

They made their retreat to the fortified Monte Agraco. Once again they had the upper ground. As the grenadiers reassembled in their new defenses, they took a moment to make an accounting of their ranks. There were two soldiers that had received slight flesh wounds, but no one had been lost. There first encounter with the enemy and everyone could be accounted for.

The French vanguard didn't follow. It was three days before Massena arrived in Sobral with the main force. Not wanting to make the same mistake he had made at Busacco, the French general hesitated this time. Only a small French division remained encamped at the base of Monte Agraco. Massena kept his main force back. The grenadiers made several skirmishes down the ridge. The goal was to strike and retreat, partly to get an idea of the positions of the enemy and partly to try and goad them in making an attack up the ridge. Despite these irritating encounters, the French remained at a distance, not wanting to come within range of the British guns on Mount Agraco. Realizing that Massena could not make any headway without reinforcements and supplies, he decided to remove to Santarem. The 4th Division remained encamped at Sobral waiting for further instructions.

Thomas received a letter from Alice, it was the first mail they had received in over two months. He stole away from his fellow soldiers and found a quiet place beneath a willow tree on top of a rise. It was near dusk and he could see the light of the fires of the encampment in the shadows below.

October 11th, 1810

Dear Thomas,

Autumn has arrived in Ireland. It has been very rainy for several days now, but it has not robbed me of my joy. One week ago I gave birth to our second daughter. I have named her Margaret after my sister. She is a beautiful little girl, you would be very proud.

This no doubt causes you much surprise, since I have never informed of you of the impending birth. I am sorry I have kept this from you, but I had always hoped that you would return home so that I could tell you in person. It is now nine months since we have seen each other, and with each passing day my heart feels heavier in your absence. When will you come home to me?

Each morning I pray that God will keep you safe, and grant me one more chance to see you home again. I sit here now with our five children at my feet, and I realize how little time they have had to know their father. Will you be home soon?

Jamey has grown tall, like is father and Willie is not far behind. Little Thomas follows his older brothers, constantly irritating them with his incessant

*questions. Janey is now walking; she has grown so
much you would hardly know her.*

    *We are all well. God has been good, and by his
grace we will all be together again, husband and wife,
father and children.*

    Take care, my love.
    Alice

Thomas carefully folded the letter and placed it in the pocket on the inside of his coat, next to his heart. He smiled as he thought about his new daughter. It was a surprise, and also a disappointment. He wanted to be there, to see her, to hold her in arms. He should be there, not just for Margaret, but also for Janey. It should have been him holding her hand as she took her first steps. Could duty to King and country be more important than duty to his wife and children? It was a paradox, how could duty and honor mean sacrificing duty and honor.

Despite the news about Margaret, the letter left him feeling melancholy. It was not like any other letter he had received from Alice. She had always expressed her love, and her hope for his return, but this was different. There seemed to be despair or perhaps fear, written between the lines. It pained him to know that Alice was unhappy. He missed her deeply. He wanted to be there and hold her in his arms and tell her that everyone thing would be alright.

He sat for a moment watching the darkness creep across the landscaped as the sun disappeared behind the mountains beyond. It would soon be dark, another day having passed into night. And then the night would pass, and the sun would rise again bringing a new day. He used to enjoy watching the dawn. It was hopeful, a beginning, a part of life; but not anymore. For the soldier the dawn of each new day meant the possibility of meeting the enemy, and for some this would mean pain or death, and for others sorrow. It was no longer hopeful.

The Colonel

Fortunately for the 27th, it would be several months before they would experience casualties. The French and British forces continued to play cat and mouse with each other as Massena and Wellington tried to outwit each other. The grenadiers were involved in some minor skirmishes, but they remained relatively unscathed. Wellington had managed to secure some minor victories, but the 27th had not been involved. At the same time, the French had been able to drive the Spanish from the fortress city of Badajoz. It was be given to the 4th Division the task of laying siege to the city and regaining possession of it. This would prove to be both difficult and costly.

The 4th Division, under General Cole, was given the task of attacking the fortress of Saint Cristobal, overlooking the river guarding the bridge that provided entrance to the city. The bridge was heavily fortified and would have to be cleared to allow passage. As a result a part of the 27th had been chosen as working party to the clear the bridge under the leadership of Captain Pring, leaving the grenadiers in the capable hands of Lieutenant Charles Levinge. Before they could make any attempts on the fortress of Saint Cristobal, word was received that Marshal Soult was marching with a large force toward Badajoz to provide relief. Timing was becoming critical. General Beresford took the 2nd Division and the right brigade of the 4th Division to intercept Soult before he reached the city. General Cole took a portion of the 4th which included one wing of the 27th under the command of Colonel Maclean across the bridge to defend against any French attempting to leave the city. Major Birmingham took the other wing of the 27th and with the remainder of the 4th attempted to take Saint Cristabol.

The fort was well defended and the British guns were poor specimens and could not make any impact on the defensive walls. If the British were to have any impact they would have to deal with the battery that guarded the fort. Major Birmingham was too optimistic in his approach, and attacked with the full force of the 500 soldiers at his disposal. Before they came within 150 yards of their target, cannon rained down upon them in rapid succession. The major was struck by exploding mortar and knocked from his horse. Lieutenant Levinge was also wounded in the early melee.

The sound of the cannon was deafening, and it was as if the earth was exploding on all sides all at once. Thomas could barely see anything through the smoke and debris. The Inniskillings had not been in action comparable to this since arriving on the Peninsula. His concern was growing. It was more than fear; he was overwhelmed by a flood of uncertainty. He had seen Birmingham fall from his horse and he knew that without leadership the battalion would soon be in chaos. To his credit young Simcoe had stepped to the forefront when Levinge was wounded in the leg. He had kept his calm and was doing all he could to rally the grenadiers. The entire battalion tried to regroup, taking what little cover they could in the rocky terrain.

"We can't remain here," Simcoe yelled above the roar of the battle. "We'll be ripped to shreds by those cannon, we must move forward."

It was clear that there was no quit in the Simcoe, and in this case Thomas was in agreement. If there was any chance of gaining the advantage, it would have to be now. "Agreed," Thomas shouted. "We must go now."

It appeared that Major Johnstone had taken command of the battalion in place of the injured Birmingham. He immediately dispatched two companies to take out the battery, which by some fortune they were able to accomplish, although at considerable loss. This slowed the barrage of cannon fire. The remainder of the attacking force saw their opportunity.

Without hesitation, recognizing that the circumstances had suddenly changed in their favor, Simcoe leapt to his feet and yelled, "follow me boys."

Thomas and Stewart were right on his heels. As they neared the fortification, they were set on by a French cavalry unit, followed by five hundred foot soldiers, emerging from the haze. They were caught in the open and badly outnumbered.

"Form square!" the call went up from the young Lieutenant.

The Colonel

All those months of training, day in and day out, the same drill over and over, had finally come to fruition. Within seconds the battalion had formed square; the first row of fusiliers on their knees, followed by a second standing. As the French approached, the cavalry held back, not wanting to be the first to taste the British musket. As the French column approached within a hundred yards the cry of "fire" rang out. Those in the front of the French column fell to the ground. They advanced and again a volley was sent by the fusiliers.

This was when the British soldier was at his best, the French could not match the efficiency displayed by the British line. Still the French came. After the third volley, the cavalry suddenly broke forward in a rush. It was clear they had only been waiting for the two opponents to draw close.

"Prepare for cavalry!" Simcoe yelled.

The grenadiers in unison affixed their bayonets and held their line as a fourth volley from the fusiliers cut through the cavalry from close range. There was a huge clash of weapons as horse and man became entangled in a writhing mass of energy and will. It was a tremendous struggle with each combatant trying to gain the advantage.

Thomas had been brushed aside by a passing charger, whose rider narrowly missed taking off the top of Thomas' head with his saber. Thomas rolled to the ground and then was up again swinging the butt of his musket with all his might, dislodging the rider from his horse. Saber and bayonet clashed together as the two soldiers faced each other, with death at the door of the defeated. Thomas' physical strength and stature were more than a match for his opponent and he soon gained the advantage and dispatched his victim. He immediately looked around to surmise the situation, only to discover young Simcoe in mortal danger with a French soldier standing over the young officer, intent on making an end of him. Thomas drew his sword and jumped to his rescue, catching the Frenchman unaware, and sending him to his Maker, before he was aware of what had befallen him.

Simcoe jumped to his feet, gave Thomas a nod of thanks and then shouted for the grenadiers to reform the line. The cavalry attack had been withstood, but it had allowed for the French foot soldiers to reach the fray. The Inniskillings tried to respond in defense, and for a moment it looked as if they would be able to hold their ground, when all of a sudden the square began to fold inward. The grenadiers continued to push back, but their numbers had been depleted by a fifth and it seemed hopeless.

When it seemed the battle had completely turned and they were about to lose all, a familiar cry was heard. "FAUGH!" It was the cry of the Inniskillings come out of the smoke and dust from somewhere beyond.

Thomas looked over his shoulder, only to catch a glimpse of a familiar red beard. It was Sergeant McHugh and the light brigade, followed closely by Captain Pring and the remainder of the grenadiers who had been assigned to guard the bridge. Within seconds, the reinforcements were on the enemy with a violent clash. Again the cry of "FAUGH!" rang out, this time returned from those who had already been engaged. McHugh, Pring and those that followed fought with voracity, tearing through the enemy as if they were made of paper. Within moments the 27th regained control of the battlefield, and the French began to wilt.

Without warning cannon fire erupted again. It seemed they had only been quiet to protect against the chance of hitting their own soldiers. Now that the battle had turned, they could remain quiet no longer.

The call came out from Major Johnstone to retreat. The grenadiers obeyed, but not without hesitation. They had come so close, and having gained they advantage they wanted to make one final attempt at taking the fort; they would not could another chance. Johnstone let prudence rule his own passions. The battalion had already suffered to greatly, and if it had not been for the surprise support of the light brigade, all might have been loss. He could not risk any further attack. It would have to wait to another day.

This Inniskillings withdrew, and mourned their losses. After more than two years little more than light skirmishes, for the first time, they met with severe losses. There had been more than 200 casualties from their battalion. It turned out that Major Birmingham's injuries were fatal. Lieutenant Levinge's injuries were slight, however, Captain Pring, their rescuer, had suffered a serious wound, and although he would recover, it would be unlikely that he would return to command the grenadiers. With both Levinge and Pring removed from action, it meant that command of the grenadiers would now fall to young Lieutenant Simcoe.

Thomas and Stewart had once again come through uninjured, thanks to the timely arrival of their old friend McHugh. That evening the three friends, along with privates Dolmage and Dunlop, shared a fire together.

"You pulled us out of the fire today Sergeant-Major," Stewart said as he stirred the fire.

"I agree. You and Captain Pring happened along at just the right time," Thomas added.

"We couldn't very well let you blokes have all of the fun," McHugh said with a smirk. "We were just waiting for you to soften those Frenchies up a bit. It's a shame about Major Birmingham though. It seems we should have been a little more punctual. I liked the Major, he was a good man."

"That he was," Thomas agreed. "He was a brave and honorable man, although, I think a bit to bold in his actions today."

"You think he was a little too optimistic?" Private Dolmage asked.

"Only, because we lacked the guns. Those bloody Portuguese cannons were not going to make a dent on the enemy's defenses. To take down their battery was too costly and as it turns out we have nothing to show for it."

"It was a bloody day," Dolmage said has he hung his head.

"Don't hang your head laddie, today's defeat will turn into tomorrow's victory," he attempted to console.

"How are Pring and Levinge doing?" McHugh asked. "Will they survive?"

"The surgeon has treated their wounds and they are both resting," Thomas explained. "They will recover, however it will be some time before they will be fit for action. I'm afraid we will not be able to depend upon them any time soon."

"I suppose this means that young Simcoe will inherit the grenadiers?" McHugh asked. "I imagine he is quite eager, in spite of the circumstances. Do you think he is ready for command?"

Thomas reflected a moment before responding. "It's true, he is a bit eager, and perhaps a little foolhardy at times, but he showed himself well today. In the heat of the battle, he maintained his calm, and fortitude. He has the respect of the lads and they will follow him anywhere."

"In any case, Thomas and I will have our hands full keeping him out of trouble. We have already had two company commanders go down, we're not about to suffer another."

"Did you hear that Colonel MacLean was wounded defending the bridge," Dunlop interjected.

"He will recover as well," McHugh added. "This day will not be remembered fondly by the Inniskillings."

"Aye," the others agreed in unison.

"To the Inniskillings," Stewart said holding his cup aloft. "May they soon forget this day and may tomorrow bring victory again."

"To the Inniskillings," repeated by everyone, holding there cups aloft. "Faugh!"

Chapter Ten

[10] If one falls down, his friend can help him up,
But pity the man who falls and has no one to help him up!

(1811)

The attempted siege of Saint Cristobal had been costly. Besides their wing commander, there had been more than 200 casualties, 19 from the company of grenadiers. It was the first time since arriving on the peninsula that the Inniskillings had suffered such a loss. Not only was this vexing, but it was also all in vain. By early June, Badajoz was abandoned. Any further attempts of siege were deemed to be too costly, so for the time being, it would be set aside, until the proper siege equipment could be assembled and larger artillery could be obtained. Even then, it would require a larger army than was presently assembled. The 4th Division was order to remove itself to Elvas, just across the border into Portugal.

After a short stay in Elvas, which allowed those with minor wounds to heal, the 4th began moving along the border between Portugal and Spain. Periodically there would be minor skirmishes, but the Grenadiers remained intact, without injury. For the next two months, they marched, remaining in small villages for only a few days at time. It was clear that Wellington was trying to keep the French confused. By the end of September, Colonel MacLean had recovered from his wound at Badajoz, and rejoined the regiment. This had a very positive affect on the moral of the Inniskillings.

As they marched from village to village, Thomas was deeply moved by the destruction and devastation. Many homes had been damaged or destroyed entirely. Even the village churches had felt the effects. The few buildings left intact, were overcrowded with the refugees. Many of the locals were homeless, poor and often hungry. It was a disconcerting sight, knowing that winter would soon be upon them, making conditions even worse.

On the 5th of October, they were settled in the small village of Nave de Haver. Most of the buildings in the village had been badly damaged or destroyed and for the past several days they had endured a torrential rain storm. On this day however, the sun made its appearance and it seemed the whole village was out and about, enjoying the momentary respite from the stormy weather.

Thomas, Stewart and Private Dolmage were enjoying refreshment at a small cantina near the center of the village, which had somehow managed to escape being damaged. In the square, not thirty yards away, some boys were playing with a ball. Thomas was particularly distracted by the boys. They were about ten or eleven, the same age as James. It made him homesick. He began to think back to when he last saw his sons, and tried to imagine what they might look like now. He wondered about how much they would have grown.

While he was reminiscing, the ball got loose from one of the boys and rolled under the table where the three soldiers were sitting. The young boy started to retrieve it and then hesitated, not sure what to do, not wanting to offend the soldiers. Dolmage reached for the ball, then stood and proceeded to lightly kick the ball along the ground, playing keep away from the boy. The boy's friends then tried to take the ball from Dolmage as he tried to ward them off. Thomas and Stewart decided to join in with the fun. The boys took it as a challenge to try and get their ball back from the soldiers. This went on for several minutes, the ball exchanging sides several times, as men and boys stood on opposite teams, each trying to gain the advantage. The soldiers were bigger and stronger, but the young boys outnumbered them and were blessed with, seemingly, unlimited energy. After playing for nearly an hour, the three soldiers were exhausted and collapsed in defeat, much to the delight of their adversaries.

The Colonel

Thomas, who was now sitting on the ground, turned to the boy closest to him and asked in somewhat broken Portguese, "como e seu nome?"

"Afonso, sehnor," the young boy responded.

Thomas took a shilling from his pocket and tossed it to the boy, "obrigado, Afonso," he said.

The boy looked at the coin and then at his friends, and with a big grin shouted, "obrigado, sehnor. Muito obrigado!"

The three soldiers stood, dusted themselves off, and started walking back to their encampment, laughing and joking the entire way. The game with the boys had been a nice diversion from the war, and a reminder of what was waiting for them at home.

*****

Autumn slowly turned into winter and the weather turned wet and cold. Daily marches were slowed by the mire created on the road by incessant rains. Wagon and cannon would often become bogged down, which sometimes took hours to dislodge. All of this began to take its toll on the soldiers of the British army. The supply ships from home had become infrequent and uniforms were becoming worn and in desperate need of repair or replacement. This, combined with the lack of decent lodgings, were cause for a depressed morale. As November rolled into December, the low morale was brought lower as an influenza swept through the ranks.

Although Thomas remained in good health, Stewart was not so fortunate. His normal jovial countenance was brought low by the discomfort of his ailment. He was in agony, and there seemed little relief. Several days of fever and a respiratory infection left him in a weakened state. Thomas remained in vigilance by the bedside of his friend, trying to bring any comfort that he could, but the disease would have to run its course. Due to the level of infliction on the regiment, the commander ordered to have the sick removed to Lisbon, both to isolate them

128

from the healthy, and to provide them with better medical care and a safer environment in which to convalesce.

Thomas was anxious for his friend, but there was little he could do. One fifth of the regiment had been incapacitated and Colonel Maclean could not risk it getting worse. He saw to his friend's comfort and then stood watching as he was carried away down the road in a wagon. Long after the wagon had disappeared in the distance, Thomas remained gazing into the distance. He was feeling homesick again, longing for the green hills of Ireland. Stewart was his connection to home, a daily reminder of all that he had left behind, and now he was gone. He wished his friend the best, hoping that their separation would be a brief one.

He'd hoped to put in a request for leave, but it was clear that no leaves would be given this Christmas. With so many in the regiment who had fallen ill, there was no way that Maclean would grant any leaves. As a result Thomas didn't even make an attempt.

The weather continued to remain wet and cold. The morale of the Inniskillings continued to sink lower. It was one thing for them to be far from home, enduring the cold and hardship in threadbare uniforms, but quite another to sit and wait, not knowing when they would next meet the enemy. Many were disheartened, and Thomas began to hear grumblings amongst the rank and file, "What are we doing here? We have not seen the enemy in days? Let's bring the fight to those Frenchies and be done with? Why must we sit and wait? What purpose is there in it?"

Thomas had to admit that he was feeling much the same. It was difficult to always ascertain the strategy of their leaders. It appeared that Wellington was content to take a defensive posture, even though it seemed that his intent was to drive the French back out of Spain. Instead the French continued to remain in Spain and here they sat defending the borders of Portugal. Adding this discontentment was the fact that the Portuguese and Spanish soldiers seemed to have little heart for fighting and defending their homeland. It was clear that Napolean needed to be stopped, or he might one day cross the water to Britain, but it was difficult to understand why the British soldier understood this urgency more than those of the peninsula.

Things remained quiet for the next few weeks. Two days before Christmas, Thomas decided to ask if he could journey to Lisbon to check on the recovery of Stewart. He persuaded Maclean that it would be good for morale. Not only would he be able to encourage those who were in the hospital that their comrades were still thinking of them, but he would also be able to return with what he hoped would be good news of the recovery and imminent return to the regiment. Maclean begrudgingly agreed, and also allowed Thomas to take Private Dolmage along as a campanion.

The two set out before sunrise on Christmas Eve morning. The air was brisk and cold, but the sky was clear, which promised a dry and therefore relatively comfortable journey. They rode there mounts hard, resting when required and stopping at noon in a small village where they took refreshment. As they traveled there was little opportunity for conversation leaving Thomas alone with his thoughts.

It was approaching ten years since he and Stewart had first joined the Inniskillings. Sicily, and the battle of Maida seemed to have been an eternity ago. He could still see private O'Neil held in the arms of Cullen. 'Poor lad,' he thought to himself. He looked over at Dolmage who was riding at his side. In many ways he was like O'Neil, especially in his youthful naiveté. He felt a responsibility for him, wanting to be sure that he one day was able to return home.

They arrived in Lisbon just as the sun was setting. Dolmage wanted to find a place where they could take lodgings, but Thomas was anxious to see his friend and so they made an inquiry as to the location of the hospital. It turned out the injured and ailing British soldiers were being housed in a small church that had been renovated and made into an infirmary.

The two were met at the door by a young private guarding the entrance.

"Can I help you gentlemen?" the private asked as they approached.

"We're here to see our comrades, soldiers from the 4th Division," Dolmage blurted out before Thomas had a chance to speak.

"Anybody, in particular?" the guard asked.

"Yes, as matter of fact, Corporal Stewart Pogue." Thomas replied.

"Let me see…" the guard was leafing through a list in front of him. "…Ah yes, here it is Pogue, Stewart…sorry, he's not here."

"What do you mean he's not here? Where is he?" Thomas asked, the anxiety clear in his voice. "Is he okay?"

"I'm sorry, but it says here he was sent home on leave."

"Leave, what do you mean leave? Who granted him leave?"

"Why, Captain Thompson, of course. He is the acting adjutant and in command here. He was given authority to grant any wounded soldier who was recovered to return home on leave for the holidays."

"But Pogue, wasn't wounded, he was only sick," Dolmage said with a note of exasperation.

"The British army evidently doesn't make such distinctions. In any case, he was recovered and therefore was sent home. It says here he has leave until the tenth of January."

"Do you know if he in fact left Lisbon?" Thomas asked.

"I'm afraid you will half to check at the adjutants' office for a record of travel orders, but I believe a ship left for home, a little more than a week ago with those who were granted leave."

"Where is this adjutant's office?" Thomas asked a bit gruffly.

"Just down the street here, on the right hand side. You can't miss it. However, I suggest you wait until morning. I'm certain the Captain would not want to be disturbed this evening."

Thomas had nothing more to say. He was about to the bite the private's head off, but prudence got the better of him and he just stood fuming.

Dolmage realized they were not getting anywhere. "Do you know of a place where we might take lodgings?" he asked.

"Sure, just back down the street is a hotel. They will take care of you there, with all the comings and goings of our soldiers, it could make a claim as a barrack."

"Thanks. Come on Thomas, there is nothing we can do about it tonight. We will check with the adjutant tomorrow. Let's get something to eat, and then a bed for the night."

Thomas nodded solemnly. He was still a bit irritated. They had come all this way so he could check in on Stewart, and then of all things, he was not even here. He was not sure what made him more resentful, the fact that Stewart was not here and they had wasted the trip, or that Stewart had actually been granted leave. On the one hand he was glad that his friend was fully recovered, but on the other hand he was just a little envious. This made him feel a little guilty which only added to his irritation. He tried to put all aside. If nothing else, he and Dolmage would have the pleasure of spending the night in more comfort than they were accustomed to. The trip might still prove to be profitable.

The next morning they visited the adjutant office first thing. They were met by a young ensign who introduced himself as the assistant to the adjutant. They inquired after Stewart.

"Yes, I do remember a Corporal Pogue," the ensign informed him. "He was a nice sort of chap, very well mannered. Very well indeed..." he paused as he started rifling through his desk. "It seems he left something here...now where did I put it...ah yes here it is." He produced an envelope that had been buried beneath a stack of papers on the desk. "He thought someone might come to inquire after him. He asked me to hold this here and deliver to the person in question. Are one of you, Thomas Rea?"

"He is," Dolmage answered, again failing to allow Thomas to speak for himself.

"Well there you go. This must be for you then," handing the envelope over to Thomas.

Thomas held it in his hand for just a moment, and then slid open the flap. It was a note addressed to him.

December 15, 1811

Dear Thomas,

I am of the opinion that you will come to Lisbon to check up on me. I am confident in this, for had our situations been reversed, I would have done the same. I am sorry I will not be here to greet you when you arrive, but circumstances have happened that our beyond our control. It seems the good Captain Thompson has seen fit to grant me leave, even though I was never wounded. He seems a sort of cheery fellow and perhaps it gave him some pleasure to do so. In any case, with Christmas fast arriving, I could not refuse this opportunity to return home to my Bella. I feel a bit guilty going without you, but I am sure you would have done the same had you been in my shoes.

In any case, I leave for Portsmouth and dawn two days hence. If all goes well I should make it home by Christmas. They tell me I have leave until the 10th of January. You may expect my return then.

Farewell brother, I will convey your love to Alice and the young ones. Take care while I am gone. Do not do anything foolish, for I will not be there to guard your back. Convey my best wishes to Dolmage and Lieutenant Simcoe, as well as the rest of the Grenadiers.

God Bless. Your Friend,

Stewart

Thomas handed the letter over to Dolmage and then stood watching him as he read it. There was no use being upset with Stewart. He had been quite right. Thomas would have done the same thing. His resentment was subsiding. At least Stewart would be able to be an encouragement to Alice and he would have plenty to share when he returned.

"Well that's that," Dolmage said after he had finished reading. "I suppose the only thing left to do is to see if there are any from our regiment who might still be here and after that to return to the encampment."

Thomas nodded without giving comment. They spent the rest of the day visiting those who had convalescing in the hospital and then making preparations to leave the next morning. It turned out that there was a half-dozen soldiers from the 4th that were fully recovered and were fit to return to duty. As a result, they would not be returning empty handed.

*****

(December 25, 1811)

The sun was just beginning peek over the eastern horizon as he crossed over the bridge. He could just see the top of the steeple of the Cleenish Parish church. It would not be long now before he was home. His heart was pounding, in part because he was now nearly running, but also in part because of his excitement over seeing his family again. He could picture Bella and the look on her face when he came through the door. How surprised she would be. James would have just turned four, and Anne was two and half. He was nearly beside himself with the anticipation of holding them in his arms. It would not be much longer.

As he drew near enough to see the house through the trees, he noticed a wisp of smoke lazily rising from the chimney. The fire had already been lit in the fireplace. His jog suddenly turned into a sprint. He could wait no longer. In less than a minute he was bursting through the front door, while simultaneously yelling, "Merry Christmas!"

Bella was sitting at the kitchen table. She gave such a start that she nearly fell out of her chair. James and Annie were so surprised that they ran to their mother to hide in the folds of her skirt.

"Stew...," Bella stammered, trying to catch her breath, while at the same time reaching for the table to maintain her balance. "Stewart. I don't believe it. Where did you come from? What are you doing here?" She managed to gather herself enough to rise to her feet.

Stewart didn't attempt to explain. In a flash he was across the room, grabbing Bella in his arms and swinging her around such that her feet literally came off the floor. "It's me Bella, my love. Your husband, come home from the war, just in time to wish you a merry Christmas."

The two children, who had been left to fend for themselves with their mother completely swept off her feet, now looked in startled amazement as the husband and wife embraced. Bella held on for the longest time not wishing to let go, afraid that it was only a dream. The children, now at her feet, began to chatter. They wanted some reassurance that all was right. Bella let go of Stewart and reached down and stroke their hair, letting them know she had not forgotten them.

"It's alright children, it's you father. Look here, it's your father come home from the war," she first looked at them and then back at Stewart. "I don't quite understand," she said, gathering her wits. "How did you get here? Where have you come from? Why didn't you let us know you were coming? The last thing you wrote is that you were ill. Oh, how I prayed for you, how I feared for you. And yet here you are?"

"Hush, Bella. If you give me a moment to catch my breath I will explain." Even as he said it, Stewart bent down to greet his children. "Hello, James, my how you have grown. And Annie, I can't believe how big you've gotten. It seems just a moment ago, when I held you in my arms."

James summoned up enough courage to give his father a hug, but Annie remained clutching to her mother's skirt, not sure what to make of this stranger who had suddenly appeared on Christmas morn.

"What about Thomas? Did he come with you?" Bella asked.

Stewart shook his head. "No, I am afraid not. It's true, I was very sick. So much so, that they sent me to recover in Lisbon, away from the front. When I had fully recovered, the adjutant in charge gave me leave to return home. I couldn't turn it down, although it meant leaving Thomas behind with the Inniskillings. I still feel a bit guilty, but I just couldn't take the chance. I had to leave right away, there wasn't even enough time let Thomas know."

"Poor Alice," Bella said. "She will be so disappointed."

"I am afraid disappointed won't be the half of it. I promised her I would look after Thomas and yet here I am and there he is. She is going to tan my hide. I don't look forward to facing her. Thomas had better keep his head down while I am gone, or I will never hear the end of it."

"But for how long... how long are you here?" Bella almost hated to ask.

"Not long, I'm afraid. I am due back on the 10th of January. We'll just have to make the best of what time we have."

"Yes, of course," Bella's continence changed slightly. "I guess it can't be helped, but I wish you could stay longer." She paused for a moment, not sure what to say next. "Well enough of this talk about coming and going. It's Christmas, and we are going to make it the best Christmas ever."

In many ways it was the best Christmas Stewart could ever remember. He began to realize just how much he had missed his family and just how much he was giving up to remain so far away. James was now four and Stewart had only been home a few short months in those four years. And for Annie it was even worse, she was two and half and had no idea who this strange man was. He had wanted to come home, but now for the first time he began to question whether he ever wanted to return to the regiment. As soon as the question entered his mind, he dismissed it. Even if he wanted to remain, it was out of the question. The army would not release him and even more importantly his honor would not release him from his obligation to Thomas and the rest of the grenadiers.

The next day they visited Alice and her children. Alice greeted Stewart with genuine affection and she appeared to be happy that he was home. Every once in a while, he would catch her eye and he would see the sorrow there. This was worse than if she would have been angry with him. He could sense how desperately she wanted to see Thomas, to be with him, and yet there was nothing Stewart could do. He would go back, and the next time he returned, he would have Thomas with him. He had no desire to face Alice as she was now, ever again. And if it was in his power, even if it meant his own life, he would never let any harm come to Thomas.

*****

It had been several days since Thomas and Dolmage had returned from Lisbon. He had been in the doldrums ever since. He had been greatly disappointed that he had missed seeing his friend, but he was even more disappointed in not having been allowed to return home. He missed Alice and the children terribly.

The weather continued to be wet and cold which only added to his depression and to that of the soldiers around him. With each passing day, the tension grew, and tempers became fragile. Every once and awhile a fight would break out in camp. It was his duty to step in and break it up, but he was of the inclination to let the individuals work in out on their own. If anything, he almost felt the urge to join in, anything to provide a diversion from the monotonous gloom and dreariness.

The Colonel

There were reports that the troops of the 3rd Division had gone mad as they stormed the town of Ciudad Rodrigo. Evidently the siege had been a long one and just like the rest of the British army, the soldiers of the 3rd had reached their breaking point. Upon breaching the defenses of the town, the soldiers began looting and destroying everything in their path. The officers tried to maintain order, but the rank and file were uncontrollable. After months of hardship and the loss of comrades they not only wanted victory, but they wanted revenge.

As Thomas heard the reports, he grew concerned. Was it possible that the members of the 4th could also succumb to such uncivilized, even barbaric behavior? He could sense they too were approaching their breaking point. And then the relief came.

As promised, Stewart returned on the 10th of January. He arrived driving the lead wagon of a train carrying supplies. As he stepped down from the bench, Thomas ran up to him and gave him a big hug.

"It's about time you got here you lug," Thomas said in greeting. "I was beginning to wonder if you had decided to remain in Ireland."

Stewart smiled. "Not that it hadn't crossed my mind. Hello, Thomas. It's good to see you. Good to see you are well. Hello, Adam, hoped you haven't missed me too much," he said to private Dolmage as he shook his hand."

"Hello, Corporal Pogue. Good to have you back. What is all this?" Dolmage said in reference to the wagons now being unloaded.

"Well, I was able to gain passage on one of the supply ships from Portsmouth. It seems that the army finally came through and has sent us our new uniforms, complete with new boots. A sort of belated Christmas present I think."

There were already some shouts of joy going up from the crowd of soldiers that had now enveloped the wagons. The supplies had long been delayed, and most had given up hope that they would ever arrive.

"How are things at home?" Thomas asked. "How are Alice and the chidren?"

"Everyone is fine Thomas, put your mind at ease on that account. They all miss you terribly and send you their love. Alice was quite cordial to me, but down deep I could tell she was incensed that I had not brought you home with me. I don't think I ever want to see that look again."

As they were catching up, Lieutenant Simcoe approached. "Well I see our wayfarer has returned to us."

"Yes sir, Lieutenant," Stewart said as he shook Simcoe's hand. "I couldn't wait to get back to the men, Sir. Any news about that captaincy?"

Thomas shook his head, trying to get Stewart's attention, but to no avail.

Simcoe turned and walked away, mumbling beneath his breath, "good to have you home Pogue."

Stewart raised his hands in the air, "What? What did I say?"

"He didn't get the captaincy, you fool. He has been stewing about it for weeks," Thomas explained. "You sure know how to put your foot in it."

"I'm sorry, how was I to know? I thought for sure he would have been promoted by now."

"It seems he lacks the necessary maturity," Dolmage said with a little sting in his voice.

"Easy, Adam." Thomas said calmly. "We all wanted Simcoe to get his promotion. He is a good man and a capable leader, but the truth is he hasn't reached one and twenty. Despite the opening in the grenadiers, it was unlikely that anyone back in London would have seen it our way."

"Does this mean we have a new commander of the grenadiers?" Stewart asked.

"It has been promised, but there has been no assignment. For now Simcoe will have to be content with be the acting captain," Thomas answered.

The Colonel

"And that suits me fine," Dolmage added. "He will be a fine captain, acting or not."

Stewart put his hand on the shoulder of the young private. "That's right Adam. And we will follow him anywhere, even to the gates of Hell." Then he smiled at Thomas, who could only smile back.

Chapter Eleven

Generations come and generations go,
But the earth remains forever.

(1812)

It's amazing how a new uniform and a pair of boots can raise the moral of an entire regiment. One moment they were depressed and on the brink of mutiny and the next they were hopeful and anxious to meet the enemy. It's hard to comprehend whether the effect is due simply to the physical comfort, or whether it is deeper than that, having something to do with a sense of pride.

The supplies came at just the right moment. The next day the 4th Division was commanded to march along the Mondego River toward Almeida. By the first of February they had arrived at the small village of Villa de Agua. During the march, rumors began to circulate that they were going to return to Badajoz. It seemed, despite previous setbacks, Wellington was determined to gain this strategic fortification. However, his intentions were not immediately obvious as the British divisions kept on the move, a faint that kept the French guessing.

The rumors came to fruition when, early in March, the 4th was ordered to Badajoz. Previously they had been given the task of attacking San Cristabol on the North, but this time they joined forces with the 3rd Division and approached the city from the south. By the 21st of March they were in position just to the west of the Rivillas River. There were two small forts just a half mile south of the battlements of the city which served as lookouts and minor defenses. One of the battalions from the 3rd was given the responsibility of taking the fort on the east. This was important to Wellington's strategy, believing that the British could use this rise to install a battery which could hammer the southern battlements and create a breach in the southern defenses of the city.

The 4th were entrenched beneath the fort, in a ravine that ran to the southeast corner of the city. From here they deflected minor French sorties and made preparations for the offensive. The weather was dreary as rain continued to fall, making a muddy mess of the encampment. The temperatures were pleasant, but the continued overcast skies and falling rain caused the visibility to be poor.

At ten o'clock in the evening of the 25th, Thomas emerged from his tent to the sound of musket fire. Against the blackened sky he could see the flash of musket and cannon on the hill to the east. The attempt to take the fort had begun. The entire camp came awake and made ready for battle, anticipating they might be called to support the 3rd. The call never came. Thomas and Stewart along with a half dozen grenadiers were sent on reconnaissance to determine whether the soldiers of the 3rd were successful in their attempt. They were given orders to stay out of sight and to not engage the enemy. They were merely to observe and report, nothing more.

Thomas led the soldiers along the ravine northward, keeping in the shadows so they couldn't be seen from the battlements of the city. When they were within a quarter mile of the city, they turned east toward the fort that was now under attack. Since the 3rd Division was attacking from the south, Thomas was counting on the preoccupation of the French soldiers inside the fort, leaving this small scouting party to approach from the west unnoticed. There was enough foliage on the western slope of the hill to provide enough cover for them to approach within 100 yards of the western wall. Here they remained, watching for any evidence of the progress of the battle. The sky remained dark and the rain continued to fall in torrents. Although it provided some cover for the attackers, it also made the approach muddy and slow. The flashes of musket fire continued on both sides for a couple hours. Remaining in hiding, beneath a huge elm tree that provided some protection from the rain, the grenadiers sat huddled in silence, watching the fort for the smallest sign of activity.

"What do think Thomas?" Stewart finally broke the silence. "Have we gained any advantage?"

"It's too hard to tell. I can barely see anything through this rain. All I know for sure is that no one has given in at this point." The flash of musket fire continued on both sides.

"I just wish I knew what was happening, or whether we could provide any help."

Looking around at the group Thomas smiled. "We are only eight Stewart, and even though we might be as good as double that number, I hardly think we would be able to provide even the slightest dent in the wall of yonder fort. Besides, we have our orders, watch and report nothing more."

At that very moment, the musket fire became increasingly more frequent, and it appeared that the British line has breached the southern wall. Their little company stood as one, remaining at the edge of their cover, staring intently out into the rain.

"Corporal Rea, look there," Dolmage said pointing to a small opening in the western wall.

Thomas had already detected the movement. It seemed that a dozen or so French soldiers were climbing through a small window and dropping to the ground. "Down!" Thomas whispered, "stay out of sight." In one motion they all dropped to their knees.

"I know we were ordered not to engage the enemy, but this is a little too easy," Stewart whispered. "We can't very well let these Frogs go."

"Perhaps you're right. Any of you know any French?" Thomas asked of the group.

"I do sir," it was Private Rankin.

"Okay then. Everyone stay under cover. Rankin, wait for my signal and the call to them to stop and surrender," Thomas instructed.

The French soldiers crept along the ground, almost crawling, clearly making their way to the little wood where the grenadiers now remain hidden. Thinking they were making their way to safety, they were unknowingly walking right into a trap.

When they were within 20 yards, Thomas whispered, "now!".

"Arrêter, fixer vos armes!" Rankin shouted.

The French soldiers were caught by surprise. They stood completely frozen not knowing what to do. There was no way they could know how many of the enemy lay in wait in the wood.

"Fixer vos armes!" Rankin shouted again.

After a brief pause, they slowly began to lower their weapons to the ground, one by one, until they were entirely disarmed. Surrender seemed the wise choice, given they had no idea their odds.

"Rankin, Smith, and Lynch, see to their weapons!" Thomas shouted as he and the rest of the grenadiers slowly emerged from the trees. The French soldiers began to grumble something when they realized that they outnumbered their captors. "Rankin, ask them what has happened at the fort."

"The fort has fallen," was uttered by the soldier nearest to Thomas.

"You speak English then?" Thomas asked.

"Yes, Monsieur," the soldier replied.

"Where were you going then?" Thomas asked.

"We were outnumbered, and then then the wall was breached. It didn't seem prudent to remain. We were going to return to the city. There was nothing more we could do here?"

"Unlucky for you that we were here," Stewart chimed in.

"Wi, Monsieur, Bonne chance très pauvres."

It took them a better part of an hour to make their way back down the hill and along the ravine. As they approached the encampment they were confronted by the advance guard. "Halt, who goes there!" a familiar voice shouted.

"Lieutenant, it's us!" Thomas shouted back. "We have returned, and we have a bit of a surprise."

Lieutenant Simcoe stepped from behind the defensive barricade. "I see you've been busy, Corporal Rea. If I remember right, the Colonel gave you expressed orders not to engage the enemy."

"Sorry, Sir. It couldn't be helped. It seems the fort has fallen to Colonel Kempt, and these French fellows just sort of fell in our lap."

"I think you had better follow me to the Colonel," Simcoe returned. "You can explain it all to him."

*****

Over the next several days, the 3rd established a battery at the captured fort. At the same time the 4th, no longer hindered by the French inhabitants of the fort, was able to extend its reach up the ravine, establishing a second battery that could reach the southern battlements of the city. To the north of the city the 5th Division was in place to prevent any support for the city from San Cristabol. Wellington had everything in place. Badajoz was surrounded by more than 15,000 British troops with additional support from the Portuguese and Spanish.

Badajoz sat on a rise overlooking the Guadiana River, which provided a natural defensive barrier on the north. In the first attempt to capture the city, the British had tried cross the river, but the fort at San Cristobal along with the river provided to great a barrier. The south wall had seemed impenetrable with the high escarpments and the six heavily armed bastions. Between the two most easterly bastions, Trinidad and Santa Maria, was where Wellington believed the wall could be breached. Cannon perched at the captured fort, would be able to reach these bastions and create the breach necessary for the storming of the city.

With no French reinforcements insight, Wellington new he had but a small window of time if they were to be successful.

The Colonel

He decided to have the assault commence on April 6th, the day after Easter. If all went well, Badajoz would finally be in the hands of the allies. Preparations continued as weapons were inspected, clean and repaired. Additional cannon arrived and were placed in position.

The 4th Division would be given the difficult task of leaving the trenches and approaching along the Rivillas creed, and breaching the southern wall. The 3rd Division would proceed north along the ridge from the fort and then cross the river and attempt to take the castle that sat on the northeast corner of the city. The 5th Division would attempt to cross the river and create a breach on the northwest wall of the city.

On Easter morning, Thomas sat by himself gazing at the bastions that protected the city of Badajoz. They looked formidable even from this distance. He was not naïve concerning what was in store for the soldiers of the 4th the following day. Many would not survive. He felt an uneasiness growing in his heart. He had always felt a certain confidence on the field of battle, but he didn't like going up against an enemy who hid behind walls. There was too great a disadvantage for the attacker. The sheer weight of numbers might bring victory, but it would not prevent the death of many good and brave soldiers. He felt a vulnerability; perhaps more than at any other time. Would he survive? Could he survive? He would have to. He must survive, not for himself, but for Alice and for the children. It couldn't end here. And yet, it was not up to him, it was God who determined the outcome, life and death.

The paper in front of him was still blank. He didn't want to write it down, but he had to. He had to leave something behind. He had to let them know how he felt. He may never have another chance. But how was he to begin?

April 5, 1812

Dear Alice,

It is Easter morn, the day we celebrate the new life promised by our Lord and Savior. I am reminded once again that this life is frail, but our eternal hope is not in this world. It is in the world to come.

Tomorrow we undertake what some might think to be a forlorn hope. However, I do not agree, for this would imply that it is in fact hopeless. To believe that it is hopeless, would deny that we are subject to the fate of Him who determines all. It is true that tomorrow brings danger and uncertainty, but not hopelessness. It would be inconsiderate to face such uncertainty and fail to take the opportunity to convey to you my heart.

From the first moment I first saw you sitting on the bench of your father's wagon, my heart was yours. There was a voice, crying in a loud voice, "this is the one, she is for you," and so it was to be. But if in that moment my heart became enslaved, it was not until much later that my soul became joined to yours, and my person is now only half of the whole, a whole that was far more than the sum of the parts. When we are apart, I am empty, incomplete, a mere shadow.

It is true that I left you of my own free will, to find honor and adventure. I confess this was because of my own pride. I was a fool, not realizing that anything I might gain could never be the measure of what I already had obtained. Forgive me for the sins of my youth. The passage of time has brought me to the realization that nothing is more important to me than the love we share for each other.

If we are not to see each other again in this world, know that I love you with all my heart and soul. Tell our children that they are my greatest joy

147

*and there has never been a day in which I have not
thought about each one, wishing even now that I
could be with them. Greet them with a kiss, and tell
them for me how much their father loves them, and
how proud he is of them.*

*If you must mourn, then do so remembering,
the pain you now feel is a nothing, and the joy we
had together is the everything.*

Remember me.

Your loving husband,
Thomas

Thomas folded the letter carefully, and then placed it in
pocket on the inside of his coat.

The next morning the grenadiers worked silently,
cleaning their bayonets, inspecting their flints, and making an
inventory of the ammunition. No one spoke, it was unnecessary.
Each man was engaged with his own thoughts, as if alone. By
midmorning the British batteries began their relentless barrage
of cannon fire directed at the bastions of Trinidad and Santa
Maria. By afternoon the affects began to show. The wall between
the bastions had begun to crumble. The French attempted to
rebuild the damaged wall, but the constant battering kept them
at bay, not allowing any significant reparation.

Wellington had intended that the assault would begin at
half past seven, just as dusk approached. The cover of darkness
would provide some degree of advantage to the assault force,
although it was unknown to what degree. The French inside the
city would have a decided advantage having the higher ground.

The 4th Division was 3,500 strong as it made its way up
the ravine toward the city-fortress. A brigade of 500 men would
form the first assault, followed by lights and the bulk of the
Inniskillings. Unfortunately, the recent rains had swollen what
was a minor creek into a swampy bog. This made it difficult for

the attacking force to move with any speed and left them completely exposed to French volleys from above. Nearly a hundred of the advance force were cut down before they had exited the ravine beneath breach. As the grenadiers led the 27th into the water, they now had to contend with bodies of their fallen comrades all around. When they regrouped on the other side their numbers had already declined by a tenth. The debris that had been thrown down as an impediment now provided some level of cover from the French guns.

Thomas and Stewart knelt behind a large boulder with Privates Dolmage and Smith to either side. Just ten yards ahead Lieutentant Simcoe crouched surveying the situation. Up further ahead, Thomas thought he caught a glimpse of Seargent-Major McHugh, who was part of the advanced assault. The space was so cramped that it was difficult to distinguish the different companies. The advanced assault was supposed to hit the breach at its weakest point and try and push its way into the city. The Lights were to attack at the same moment from the west side, provided support and cover fire. The 27th lead by the grenadiers would follow the first assault. Unfortunately there was not enough room to maneuver, making it difficult for the lights to get in position, and allow for the battalions that followed to get through the swamp to dry ground.

"What a bloody mess!" Stewart yelled above the shouting and continual musket fire.

"We can't stay here, were sitting ducks," Thomas returned. "What are they waiting for, why haven't they started the assault? They can't wait for the lights, it has to happen now."

What was unknown to the rest of the division, the captain leading the front assault had been wounded seriously. They were without their leader. The wisened veteran, McHugh was quick to realize their predicament. If they didn't proceed with the assault, the support coming up from behind would be cut down where they stood. It was now or never.

The charge was sounded and the assault began. There was a large breach in the wall created by the pounding from the

British batteries, which had now stopped in anticipation. There was a steep incline leading to the breach and the assault force was completely exposed. Without the cover fire provided by the lights, they would be exposed and vulnerable. Despite insurmountable odds they made it to the breach, but by now their numbers had been cut in half. They attempted to climb through the breach, but the French were waiting.

From his position, Thomas could see the brandishing of bayonet and saber, reflecting the firelight from the top of the wall. There was fierce fighting for a moment as the British soldiers tried to push through the breach, but it was to no avail. Their numbers had been decimated and the French were too strong. All of a sudden the retreat was sounded and those who were still standing retreated from the breach and back down the hill. The French started to give chase, but by this time the lights were in position and despite the darkness, their marksmanship was not to be underestimated. They were able to provide cover fire for those who were in retreat, and the French soon gave up the chase.

The Seargent-major was one of those in the company of those who survived, but more than 80% of the first assault force had been wounded or killed. The first attempt was a terrible failure. The lights had gained an offensive position in which they could provide cover fire, and two additional battalions had now joined the Inniskillings. It was decided that a second assault should commence before the French could entirely regroup.

Lieutenant Simcoe signaled to the grenadiers to get ready. They would lead the Inniskillings into the breach. They obeyed by affixing their bayonets to the end of their muskets. If they were to push through the defenders into the city, it would be at close quarters.

The attack was sounded. The lights began pounding the opening of the breach and the battlements above with musket fire. Then, without hesitation, more than a thousand soldiers began streaming up the hillside toward the breach. The darkness provided just enough cover to create a deception, not allowing the French to know the actual numbers they were now facing.

Right in the middle of the attacking force were Thomas and Stewart, close on the heels of young Lieutenant Simcoe. When they were within fifty yards of the wall a loud "Faugh" went up from the Inniskillings. Musket fire began to rain down on them from all directions.

Thomas felt someone fall beside him, but there was no time to look and see who it was. There would be less than half a minute between volleys and those at the front would have to pass through the breach before the reload. He could see the light glistening of Simcoe just ahead, and he knew that Stewart was close at hand, but other than that it was chaos. The grenadiers led the way into the breach. The Frenchies who were two slow in reloading had to take on the full force of the attack with bayonet. They had put up some minor defensives just inside the wall, but the mass of soldiers coming through the wall crushed everything in its path. It was the job of the grenadiers to push through the French with brute force allowing those were trailing to finish the job.

Just inside the wall the space opened up to a street that ran along the inside of the wall. The French were trying to hold their ground, but it appeared that the British had suddenly gained an advantage. There were not enough French soldiers in defense and for each British soldier that fell, two more took his place as the members of the 4th Division continued to pour through the breach.

Thomas was growing weary with exertion. He had lost count of how many French he had already dispatched. Stewart and Dolmage were battling at his side and together there were cutting a path right through the French defenders. He looked up momentarily to measure their progress when he noticed that Simcoe had become separated from the group. He was fighting for his life, with three of his fallen comrades at his feet.

"Stew!" Thomas shouted, pointing in the direction of their leader.

The Colonel

Without hesitation the three of them moved in the direction of the Lieutenant who it seemed had already been wounded. They threw themselves into the fray, knocking aside two French soldiers with little effort and taking a position between the now failing Simcoe and his attackers. There was a major struggle that ensued. From out of nowhere, other French soldiers joined in. They were suddenly outnumbered three to one. In the dark and chaos, there was no way for the rest of their company to realize their danger. The three friends fought with un-abandoned fervor.

Just as it appeared they had the upper hand, Simcoe was struck in the chest by the saber of the French officer he had engaged. Thomas tried to come to is aid. He knocked the French soldier off his feet with a blow from the butt of his musket, but in so doing he let down his own defense. There was a searing pain in his side, causing him to wince and fall to his knees. Before his attacker could finish the job, Thomas turned and from his knees struck home a fatal blow to midsection of the surprised combatant. Even in the dim light, he could see the eyes of his attacker roll back, as he fell down dead. Then there was musket fire, then again, and everything went black.

*****

It was as if he were floating in mid-air, suspended, with no connection to the world around him. He couldn't feel anything. Nothing seemed real. Somewhere in the fog he could hear voices, not able to make out what they were saying. They were muffled, confused. What were they saying?

Then gradually it all changed again. He was not floating. He was laying on something. He touched it with his hand, trying to recognize the texture. It was cloth, some sort of blanket. He was on a bed. There were the voices again, a little clearer now.

"How is he doing?"

"Lost a lot of blood, but I think he'll live. A bit lucky, I'd say. A little higher and it would have pierced his heart."

He tried to open his eyes. It was too bright at first, but then he tried again. Slowly, he let the light come through a narrow opening. Everything seemed blurry. A little more and things started to become clear. Someone was leaning over him, very close. He recognized the person. It was Stewart.

"Look, I think he's coming awake. Hey, Thomas, how are you feeling," Stewart said softly. "You gave us quite a scare."

"I'll say," another familiar voice came from his left. He turned his head slightly to see Dolmage lying on a cot next to him.

"Where... where am I?" Thomas could feel a throbbing in his head. As he reached to touch it with his hands he felt a bandage across his forehead. "What happened?"

"A musket ball creased your temple, but it is just a scratch. However, you took a bayonet to the back, pretty nasty wound, but it looks like you're going to be okay."

"What about you Adam? What happened to you?"

"Took a musket ball in the leg," Dolmage answered. "Not too bad. I'll be laid up a while, but I'll survive."

"What about the Lieutenant?" Thomas asked. "Is he okay?"

Stewart's continence soured. He lowered his eyes slightly, "He didn't make it Thomas. Sorry, we did all we could. We all liked the chap, he was good sort, and a pleasure to serve with."

"Yes, he was," Thomas agreed, closing his eyes again. Poor Simcoe, he had really grown to like the young officer. It was hard to believe he was gone. He opened his eyes again. "Where are we?"

"It's sort of a makeshift hospital in one of the local churches," Stewart explained.

"Then we were successful, we have taken the city."

"We sure did, but enough about that. I can tell you the whole story later. You need to get your rest. I need to report back to the grenadiers. You get some sleep now. I'll check back later," Stewart stood up and walked out of the room.

The Colonel

"Yeah, you need to some sleep," Dolmage said. "You look horrible." And then he chuckled, his way of letting Thomas know that everything would be alright.

Thomas closed his eyes and soon drifted off to sleep.

Chapter Twelve

What does man gain from all his labor
at which he toils under the sun?

(April, 1812)

Thomas could not be sure how long he was asleep. He had a vague memory of young woman sitting at his bedside and feeding him some sort of broth. She had a dark complexion and coal black hair that hung down around her shoulders. She was Spanish, but there was something strange about her. Her eyes were a brilliant blue almost iridescent. Even when he closed his eyes, he could see her face. He fell back asleep.

The next time he opened his eyes he found Stewart sitting by his bedside. Everything still seemed to be in a bit of a haze. At the foot of his bed there was another familiar face. It was Seargent-Major McHugh. Thomas smiled a bit feeling a bit relieved to know his old friend had survived the assault.

"Ah, I think he's coming awake," Stewart said softly. "Look here Roger, his eyes are beginning to open...Thomas, can you hear me? Come on man, open your eyes. Look here, I've brought you a visitor."

"Easy Stewart," McHugh cautioned. "He's had a rough time of it. If he wants to, let him sleep."

Thomas was trying to clear the cobwebs from his mind, but he felt pretty weak. The pain in his head was still there, although not as bad as before. Now he could feel the pain his chest. It was difficult to breath, even more difficult to talk. "Hello...Mc...Hugh. Sorry...I can't get up."

"Relax Thomas, you take it easy. You don't have to talk if you don't want to. You just lay there and get your rest. You'll see, you'll be up in no time," McHugh tried to sound encouraging, but there was a twinge of concern in his voice.

"Wha...what happened? Simcoe...how'd he die? He was ... so damn young."

"There wasn't anything we could do, Thomas. We got there too late. His wounds were too severe. Fortunately for us McHugh and Dunlop happened along or we would have all met our maker. There was musket fire, but from where, I'm not exactly sure, perhaps from the battlements above. The first shot caught Dolmage here in the leg and he went down in a heap. The second one put a crease in your forehead a moment after you had gotten your revenge on that Frog that had stabbed you in the back. By that time Simcoe had already gone down. I was left alone, standing against four Frenchies who were about to finish the job. Then out of nowhere, McHugh, and Private Dunlop threw themselves into the whole lot. They never knew what hit them. It was over in a manner of seconds. They saved our lives, that's what, yourself, me and Dolmage over there," as he pointed to Dolmage on the neighboring bed.

"It was nothing, really," McHugh stated. "You'd have done the same for us. Besides we couldn't let you have all the fun. Once we saw the rest of the Inniskillings pour through that breach, we just knew we had to follow."

"And follow you did," Stewart continued, "just in the nick of time. In any case, it wasn't over at that point. The Frenchies continued to put up a horrible fight. We had to turn our backs on you, leave you there lying on the street. Fortunately for us, just as we broke through the breach, the 3rd had managed to break through to the castle. A portion of those French soldiers defending the breach had been recalled to support those at the castle, a poor mistake. This allowed us to gain the advantage. Before long we had completely taken control of the streets and by the time we reached the castle the French had surrendered, the city was ours.

By the time we returned to where we had left you, Simcoe had already passed. Dolmage had summoned the help of Assistant Surgeon Franklin and he was busy dressing your wound. We were greatly concerned for your well-being, given the amount of blood lost, but God had his hand on you and it was not your time. Once the city was safely in British hands, we were able to move you here, the rest you know."

"How long have I been here?" Thomas asked.

"You've been sleeping on and off for a couple of days," Stewart answered.

"Just waking long enough to take some sustenance from that dark little *chica*," Dolmage added. "It seems she is the only one who can get you to eat anything."

At that moment, one of the surgeons approached. "How are you doing today, Corporal?" he asked.

"He seems to be a lot better today, William (Surgeon William Galbraith Wray)," Stewart said. "What do you think? Is he going to be okay? How soon will he be up and around?"

"One step at a time gentlemen, the corporal here has had a pretty serious injury. The bayonet nicked his lung. We will have to keep a close eye on him, the danger of infection you know. For now the best we can do is get some food in him and leave him to get plenty of rest. I suggest you leave him for now. We'll keep you informed."

Stewart and McHugh left begrudgingly. Thomas closed his eyes. He could hear the surgeon talking to Dolmage, but he didn't follow the conversation for very long. His head was still a little fuzzy and before long he fell back to sleep.

He dreamt of home, of Alice and his children. He could see their faces through the fog. He longed to be with them, to hold Alice in his arms again. The more he struggled to reach them, the more they faded into the distance. He cried out the name of his beloved, but it was as if she were deaf to his cries.

William Wray was somewhat prophetic. Over the next couples of weeks Thomas struggled against an infection that brought with it a fever that caused him to fade in and out of delirium. The caring hands of his Spanish nurse continue to bathe him with compresses soaked in cool water in an attempt to keep the fever at bay. He tossed and turned in his bed, his breathing was labored and occasionally he could be heard speaking the name "Alice", as he writhed in pain. His condition began to worsen and his friends began to fear for his life. When all seemed lost, as if by miracle, his fever broke and his condition improved.

By the first of May, Thomas was back on the mend. He could now sit up in bed, and he no longer had difficulty breathing. He was still in a weakened state, but it was clear now that he would recover and the worst was over. Private Dolmage did not have the full use of his leg, as of yet, but with the aid of a crutch he was able to take walks outside. Thomas was envious of his friend's freedom, but he was also grateful for the little bit of news Dolmage would bring back after his afternoon strolls.

"There are rumors that Wellington is about to go on the move again," Dolmage reported. "It seems the French army is in a little disarray because of our victory here. Wellington wants to keep the advantage. He is afraid that if he waits much longer, the French will have time to regroup. It seems he plans to leave a skeleton regiment here, while marching the bulk of the 3rd, 4th, and 5th Divisions to join up with the 1st and 6th and retake Madrid, pushing the French from Spain."

"I don't think I'm quite ready to rejoin our regiment," Thomas said in reply.

"Nor I," Dolmage replied.

"What's to become of us?" Thomas asked. "Are we to remain here at Badajoz?"

"No, it seems we are to be sent home. I suppose we're no longer needed here, at least not in our present condition."

Although surprised to hear this news, Thomas was not disappointed. The fight had gone out of him. He was anxious to return home. There was nothing left for him to do. He had served the Inniskillings for nine years. He had planned to leave the service the following year anyway. He had been fortunate to survive his wounds, he knew that now. He would put in a request for discharge. He would not be returning to Spain.

On May 12th, Thomas was able to get out of bed for the first time in a month. Stewart came for his daily visit and found his friend sunning himself on a small bench in the cemetery adjacent to the church. "You're beginning to look like your old self," he said as he sat down on the bench.

Thomas, in fact, had lost quite a bit of weight and it would be several months before he was fully himself again. "You're a terrible liar," Thomas said. "I know I must look like something just this side of death, but thanks the same. Perhaps the sun will put a little color back in my cheeks."

"I've come to tell you that we will be leaving soon," Stewart said, his head hanging low. "It seems we are about to march toward Madrid, to finish the job. There is a rumor going around the grenadiers that you have put in for a discharge. Is it true?"

"It is," Thomas answered. "I was going to tell you Stewart, but I wasn't sure what to say. We started in this thing together and I thought we would finish it together. But, it just wasn't to be. I'm not sure how long it will be before I am fully recovered, and it didn't make sense to wait around here to find out. This whole thing could be over before I'm ready to rejoin our regiment. I hope you're not upset with me?"

"No, not really," Stewart answered. "I'm just grateful that you're alright. If anything had happened to you, Alice would have never forgiven me." He smiled. "You're probably right. This thing will probably be over before we know it and then I will be on my way home as well." He paused for a moment. "It's just that it won't be the same without you Thomas. You're the best friend I've ever known. I've had your back, and you have had mine...It just won't be the same."

"I'm sorry, Stewart. I wish you could return home as well. I think I will catch hell from Bella. I don't like the thought of you going on without me. If anything were to happen to you, I could never forgive myself."

"Oh go on, will ya," Stewart said. "What could happen to me? Besides, I still have the Seargent-Major to look out for me."

"How soon do you leave?" Thomas asked.

"The word is, we start out in three days," Stewart replied. "But don't worry about us, Thomas. You just make sure you get well again. Don't worry about me. You'll see me walking down the lane a year from now."

*****

Three days later, just as Stewart had said, the 4th Division began their march to Madrid. Thomas was able to rise from bed and watch the Inniskillings pass by in the street from the doorway of the church. Stewart shouted to him as he passed, "be sure to say hello to Bella for me. Tell her I miss her."

Thomas returned, "Farewell my friend, take care of yourself!" Dolmage joined him in the doorway and together they gave a faint "Faugh!" as their comrades disappeared in the distance.

Two days after saying goodbye to Stewart, Thomas found himself sitting in the back of a wagon headed for Lisbon. It would take a couple days to reach Lisbon and from there, he and Dolmage would catch a ship for home. It was an uncomfortable journey. The wagon jostled him about, continually irritating his wounds. It seemed as if he could feel every little bump and rut in the road. For the first time, he was looking forward to being on board ship again. The gently sway of a ship in the rolling waves would be a welcome relief to this constant bouncing and banging.

It was hard for him to believe he was actually returning home, and this time for good. He could barely remember the day he had told Alice he was joining the army. It was as if it were a lifetime ago. In the nine years he had served the regiment, he had only been home for a little more than two. James was now twelve, which meant Thomas had been home for less than half of his entire life, and for the younger children, even less. He felt guilty. How would he ever be able to make it up to them? As much as he wanted to return home, he was also afraid. His own children hardly knew him. Would they allow him back into their lives?

160

"Thinking about home, sir," Dolmage interrupted his thoughts. Thomas just nodded his head. "It must be nice, sir…I mean having a family to go home to, someone waiting for you."

"Don't you have anybody at home, Dolmage, er, Adam?" Thomas had grown so use to referring to the rank and file by their surname, that he had almost forgotten that Dolmage had a Christian name.

"Oh, sure," Adam answered, "my parents and my syblings. I simply meant it must be nice to have a wife and kids, you know a family you can call your own."

"Don't you have a girl waiting for you? A nice strapping lad like yourself, I would imagine they were lining up to get at you."

"Well not exactly lining up," Adam blushed. "There was one, Katie Owens, a real beauty. But alas, I'm sure she has forgotten all about me by now."

"I wouldn't be too sure. I once knew a gal who waited more than two years for her beau to come home from the war. Love will always find away."

"You really think so, sir?" Adam seemed to be genuinely cheered by the thought.

Thomas smiled. He was glad that Dolmage's wounds had not been too serious. He had liked him from the start and he would have hated for him to have died at such a young age. He was a delightful young man, full of youth and promise, much like Simcoe. It was a horrible tragedy, the death of the lieutenant. He had tried to save him, but it seemed God had other plans. It was so senseless, a waste.

When they arrived in Lisbon, they had to wait a week before they were able to gain passage on a frigate headed for Portsmouth. The voyage was smooth, much to the delight of Thomas. He was actually beginning to feel at home on the sea, a thing he had once thought impossible.

After arriving in Portsmouth, it was only a few days before they found a ship headed for Cork. By the seventh of June, they were once again on Irish soil, traveling my mail coach northward. Adam was from Limerick County, near the town of Adare. From there, it would be another two days journey before Thomas reached Enniskillen.

"Adam, I have been meaning to ask you about your accent," Thomas started to inquire. "If you don't mind me saying so, it doesn't quite seem Irish."

"No, it isn't. My ancestors immigrated to Ireland from Palatine in Germany, part of a large group of refugees. They were given land to farm in and around Castlematrix, and for the most part these families remained together in close community. As a result, they continued to speak German, and still do today."

"I see. Are you close to your family?" Thomas asked.

"Yes, well it is a very large family, lots of uncles and aunts and cousins and all. We get along, the whole lot. I do miss them, and I am looking forward to returning home."

Thomas allowed the conversation to wane, lost in his own thoughts of home he gazed through the window of the coach, out into the darkness beyond. There was a steady rain falling and the visibility was poor. He didn't really mind, he would not have seen anything anyway. He was deep in thought, thinking about Stewart, praying he was safe. They had been friends for as long as he could remember, it didn't seem right that he was now on his way home, while his friend was still in harms way.

All of a sudden, without warning, the coach gave a lurch, nearly toppling over and then coming to a stop, leaning uncomfortably to one side. Thomas was thrown against the door and Adam against the seat across from him. "What has happened?"Adam shouted in irritation.

"I'm not sure, seems we might have hit something," Thomas said has he tried to right himself.

"Hey there, man, what is the trouble," Adam yelled to the coachman, peering out the window.

"Hit a bad rut in the road...broke an axel, I'm afraid," was the response back.

IGHTGHT

Adam and Thomas gingerly climbed from the coach into the pouring rain, the one favoring his leg, the other holding his side. It was very dark and difficult to see much of anything, but it was clear that the one wheel had come completely off, impossible to repair in the present circumstances. As Thomas tried to gain cover from a nearby tree, Adam walked thirty yards or so up the road, staring into the darkness ahead.

He returned a few moments later and there was excitement in his voice, "I know this place. My cousin lives just a mile up the road. Hey you there, coachman!" he shouted turning back to the coach. "You're not going to be able to make any repairs tonight. Send your man there, down the road to the first house on the right. Tell them that their cousin, Adam Dolmage, is stranded here in the rain and is in need of assistance."

The coachman had already disconnected the horses from coach. His fellow driver proceeded to climb onto one of the animals, and then took off down the road, into the darkness.

Thomas and Adam climbed back into the carriage. It was still leaning, but it was dry inside and this was preferable to the constant dripping of the rain beneath the tree. "It won't be long," Adam offered. "I'm sure they'll waste no time."

Less than an hour had passed before they heard the arrival of a wagon. Adam jumped out of the coach, followed by Thomas. By this time, the rain had slowed to a drizzle. There was just a peak of moonlight passing through a small opening in the clouds above. "Adam!" a voice shouted from the bench seat of the wagon.

"James!" Adam shouted back as he walked toward the wagon. "Good to see ya. Thanks for coming to get us." The two shook hands. "This here is Corporal Thomas Rea, of the Inniskillings. Thomas, this is my mother's cousin, by marriage, James Cunningham."

The two shook hands. Thomas could barely see him in the dark, but he was clearly a man of stature, and his hand was strong and sure, indicative of a man of labor. "Nice to meet you, James," Thomas greeted. "And please, call me Thomas. It seems I am no longer in His Majesties Service. Thanks for coming. We do appreciate your help. I'm afraid we would have been stranded here without you coming to our rescue."

"Glad to be of assistance," Cunningham said. "Now go ahead and climb up. There are some blankets here to keep the moisture off. We need to get you out of this rain, and in front of a warm fire. I think repairs to the coach will have to wait until tomorrow."

"Agreed. Do you think Cousin Anne would mind putting us up for the night?"Adam asked.

"Sure, she'll love to see you Adam. She'll be most happy to see that you are home safe. There is no need for you to go on to Adare tonight, especially in this weather. The coachman and his driver can go on into the village and find the smithy. I am sure they can get the coach repaired come morning."

Thomas and Adam made themselves comfortable in the back of the wagon. After tying the coach horses off to the back of the wagon, the coachman and driver joined them. As they traveled to the Cunningham farm, Adam took the opportunity to explain his relations.

"James here is married to my mother's cousin Anne," he explained. "The two share the same grandfather, Johannes Adam Dolmage, my namesake. My mother's mother and Anne's father, were brother and sister."

Thomas listened intently, even though the details were not really important to him. It was enough to know that James and Anne were Adam's cousins, although once removed, they were hospitable, and they were going to provide them with a warm bed for the night.

Upon entering the Cunningham home, Thomas was immediately struck by the pleasant aroma of something cooking on the stove. Standing just inside the door was a very attractive woman waiting to greet them. She had blond hair tied in a neat bun and deep blue eyes. Her smile was bright and welcoming. "Adam," she greeted. "Gott ist groß. Willkommen Zuhause. Ich bin so froh, dass Sie sicher sind."

"Gott ist groß, Cousine Anne. Es ist gut, Sie zu sehen. Danke, dass Sie uns hier heute Nacht schlafen," Adam responded in kind. "This is my friend Thomas Rea."

"Very pleased to meet you, Thomas," Anne held her hand out to his.

He held her hand gently, it was soft and feminine, something he had almost forgotten. "Thank you, the pleasure is mine, Mrs. Cunningham. Thank you for your kindness."

"Please, call me Anne, and please come in and sit down. I have some stew on the fire. We were just about to sit down to dinner." She said pointing to the table. Thomas had noticed that there were seven children sitting around the family table, the youngest sitting in the lap of the oldest, and only one girl among them, who appeared to be somewhere in the middle by age.

"Hello, Adam," the oldest greeted.

"Hello cousins," Adam returned. "How are all of you? And who is this newcomer?" He was referring to the baby, who looked to be about 18 months old.

"This is Joseph," again the oldest one answered for the rest.

"Thomas, these are my cousins. Let me see here, I will try and remember all their names," Adam said with a smirk. "The oldest here is John, then Robert, that one is William, and there are Thomas and James," he said as he pointed to each. "And this little princess," he said bending down to pick up the girl who appeared to be about five years of age, "this one is Martha, my favorite." The little girl giggled as Adam squeezed her ribs gently.

"I hate to interrupt this reunion with your cousins," James interjected, "but I think I should see that the coachman and driver get to the village safely. I will return as soon as I can, Anne. Don't hold dinner for me. Get something hot into these two. They look like they could use it."

Thomas turned and looked at James, then reached out his hand. "Thanks again, James, I appreciate your help," he said as they shook hands. It was the first time he had got a good look at

165

their rescuer. He was about the same age as Thomas, tall, with dark hair and chiseled features. When they shook hands, Thomas could feel that he was man of great strength and confidence. When he spoke his voice was calm and melodic, and it did not carry the German accent of his wife and cousin, indicating he was of different heritage, fully Irish.

"Don't mention it. I'm pleased to be of service. It is the least I can do for the man who brought our Adam home to us safe." He disappeared through the front door, out into the dark, before Thomas could say anything more.

As they all sat down to the table, Anne asked her oldest son to the say the blessing. They all joined hands as John prayed, "Our heavenly Father, bless us for what we are about to partake. May we ever be grateful for your bountiful provision, and thank you for the safe return of our cousin Adam and his friend Mr. Rea. Bless them both. In the name of our Lord and Savior, Jesus Christ, Amen."

"Thank you John," Anne said to her oldest son, who appeared to be not much older than ten. "Adam, I couldn't help but notice that you were limping. What happened to you, are you in pain?"

"A little, Anne, but don't worry yourself none. I was wounded in battle, a musket ball struck my leg, but it has been nearly a month and I am much recovered. The pain seems a little less each day and I'm sure I will be back to full health before too long. Besides, if you wish to the play the nurse, you must keep a close eye on this one," pointing to Thomas. "His wounds were far more severe than mine, and he was near death just a few weeks ago. He's a hero you know, having saved many a British soldier's life, while dispatching countless of the enemy."

"A hero, really, I had no idea. Are you in fact a hero, Thomas?" the way she asked it, it was hard to tell if she was being skeptical or just inquisitive.

"Your cousin exaggerates, Mrs. Cunning..., Anne. My most recent wounds are only a testament to the failed attempts to save our commanding officer."

166

"Failed, do you mean he died?"

"Sadly, yes. He was a fine young soldier and it grieves me deeply that he is no longer with us. As God is my witness, I did all I could, but it was not enough."

"Oh Thomas, you are too modest, you threw yourself into the defense of our Lieutenant against overwhelming odds, for I should know, I had no small part in it. However, the French are no match for your strength and courage in battle, and you would have succeeded in saving him had it not been for the errant musket ball from out of nowhere that creased your forehead."

"And you as well my young friend," Thomas returned.

"And you were wounded severely?" Anne asked somewhat concerned.

"He took a bayonet in the back, nearly piercing his heart, and yet that did not stop him, as he continued to fight, despite a wound that was nearly fatal," Adam answered on his behalf.

"And are you in pain now?" Anne asked further.

"Somewhat, when cold and wet I find it a bit difficult to breath. But I must say that pain is minor when compared to the homesickness I now feel for my wife and family."

"So you are married, and children as well I presume?"

"Yes, I married before I joined the service. James my oldest has just turned twelve, and William I think must be just the same age as your son John there. Little Thomas is six, Janey is three and Maggie our youngest has not reached her first birthday, and as of yet has never met her father."

"It has been some time, then, since you have been home?"

"Eighteen months ago, was the last time, a very short leave. And now...now I return home for good, never to leave again, if God wills it."

"Tell me about your wife, what is she like? It must have been hard for her, to have you gone from home this long."

"Her name is Alice, about your age I think. It was only when I was so near death, that I realized just how much I love her and just how much I miss her. You are not mistaken. I think it has been very hard on her. She has had to be both mother and

167

father to our children and although she has friends and family around her, I am sure there have been times she a felt alone in her labors. She doesn't say it, she would never complain. However, through the years I have noticed a change in the manner I which she writes to me. There is something hidden, something between the lines. I think she has been afraid. And perhaps for good reason, for I almost did not come home at all. It's only by God's grace that I sit here before you."

"And I," Adam chimed in.

"She must be a woman of great strength, to be able to love you and yet be able to let you go. I think if we were to meet, I would like to know her better. Perhaps we would be friends."

"I'm sure you would be," Thomas smiled.

"Adam," John interrupted. "Tell us some more stories, about Spain, what was it like?"

"Sure thing, John."

Adam proceeded to tell the children a story, while Thomas helped Anne clear off the table and clean the dishes. The youngest two fell asleep in the laps of their oldest syblings, almost as soon as he began. By the time Adam had finished his story, all but the oldest two were sleeping. Together they carried the children to their beds. John and Robert gave up their room and beds to the two guests.

As Thomas lay back in bed, he winced slightly from the pain in his side. He wondered if it would ever go away. It was nice to be in a bed in a warm house again, he had missed it. It was comfortable. He couldn't wait to get home. He heard the front door open and close as James arrived home. He remembered nothing else as he drifted off to sleep.

Chapter Thirteen

[11] He has made everything beautiful in its time.
He has also set eternity in the hearts of man; yet they cannot
fathom what God has done from beginning to end.

(June 8, 1812)

After a month of marches, the 4th Division was nearing Salamanca, Spain, just 150 miles north of Badajoz. It had been slow going, with constant changes in orders from the top, as Wellington tried to locate the main forces of the French army in Spain. If the British army were to push the French out of Spain, they would have to regain Madrid, but Wellington wanted to be sure that his army would not be threatened from the rear, he needed to keep the enemy before them. There were reports that Marmont and his army were near Salamanca, and so the British forces would gather there to push the French east.

The days grew tedious for Stewart. The constant tearing down camp, forced march and then reestablishing a new camp became routine and monotonous. On several occasions the Division had to retrace its steps as Wellington continued to change his plans. At other times the camp would remain in place, but they would be forced to march anyway, will full packs, just to make sure that everyone was at the ready.

Although the advanced assault had taken the brunt of it when the 4th Division laid siege at Badajoz, the Inniskillings had suffered their fair share of losses. Besides Lieutenant Simcoe, there had been a number of grenadiers who had been injured or worse, killed. As a result they would have to rebuild their ranks. With Simcoe dead, and there being a shortage of captains, the chore of commanding the grenadiers fell to, recently promoted, Lieutenant Carlile Pollock. Lieutenant Pollock had been wounded slightly at Badajoz, but had made a complete recovery

169

and welcomed his new command enthusiastically. Pollock was supported by his friend Second Lieutenant William Weir.

Stewart found his new company commander to be a pleasant and respectable sort and was not disappointed by this promotion. Pollock was educated and deeply spiritual, and was eloquent in sometimes entertaining the company at the officer's mess.

Stewart kept busy, once again engaged in training the green recruits as they arrived daily. It wasn't the same without Thomas. His whole military experience had been with Thomas at his side. It felt strange, as if he were all alone. Of course, he was not alone. He was surrounded by several thousand of his fellow soldiers, but it was now strange to him, almost foreign. He no longer felt connected to those around him. He still felt an allegiance to the Inniskillings, but it was different somehow. It was as if he no longer belonged.

*****

Thomas woke to the sunlight filtering in through the window next to his bed. He rolled out of bed, grimacing because of a little pain still lingering in his side, and then he walked over to the window. He looked out onto a beautiful sunny morning, made more beautiful by the previous day's rain. Sunny days were not particularly frequent in Ireland, but when they came, it was a little like heaven on earth. He looked over at the neighboring bed, Adam had already risen.

At breakfast, the conversation was dominated by Anne relating the most recent news concerning her family, all for Adam's sake. This left Thomas to his own thoughts, which was perfectly fine with him, since he really didn't have any desire to enter into any kind of dialogue so early in the morning. He remained content to sit and listen, occupying himself with his food, while trying to appear interested in the conversation.

Later in the morning, he decided to take a walk taking advantage of the sunshine and the opportunity to be alone. As he rounded a bend in the road, he discovered James sitting under a large sycamore tree, reading a book. His first inclination was to turn and go in the other direction, but the other had already looked up and he knew he was trapped.

"Hello, Thomas," James greeted. "Out for a walk I see. I trust you are feeling well, this beautiful day."

"Yes, very well thank you. It is indeed a beautiful day and walking seems to ease my discomfort."

"You are still in pain then, from your wounds?"

"Yes, mostly from the cold and moisture. The warmth and exercise bring me relief, however."

"Were your wounds severe?"

"Do you mean... was I near death? I'm not sure, but I'm told that those close to me were afraid for my life. As for me, I was quite delirious and nearly out of my mind. I can remember none of it. If death's dark angel were knocking at my door, it appears God had other plans...I noticed that you were reading something. Are you a learned man?"

"I'm not sure what you mean. I am just a humble farmer, who enjoys reading. This is a book that was given to me by my Anne's father, *Sermons on Several Occasions* by John Wesley. When I was ten years old my father took me to hear Reverend Wesley speak, an experience I will never forget. He stayed in the home of Anne's grandparents while visiting here in Adare. He captured the hearts of all who heard him speak."

"Are you a Wesleyan then?" Thomas asked.

"Perhaps, but I don't think of myself as such. I've read many sermons by Reverend Wesley, and I'm not sure he would have approved of the term Wesleyan."

"What do you mean?"

"Well, for example, I have just been reading *The Almost Christian*. Reverend Wesley speaks of the importance of what it means to be an altogether Christian. He felt strongly that observing the rituals, the practices of the faith, are not nearly as important as what it means to fully embrace the lordship of

Christ. To be fully Christian in the heart was his primary motivation."

"It sounds as if your faith is very important to you," Thomas said.

"Shouldn't it be, important that is? Shouldn't the things we believe, be the most important thing about us. If they're not, could it be said that we don't really believe them at all. What about you, is faith important to you?"

"I suppose I always thought so in the past...," Thomas paused reflecting. "But I think I have come to realize that I didn't think it important at all, that is until now. Men who have been to war, who have seen the things of which we must not speak of, are confronted with the significance of faith or perhaps I should say, hope. As young men we think we are invulnerable, or perhaps indestructible, but then we come face to face with death and it changes us, changes us forever. It is impossible to walk away from the battlefield and not be reminded of one's own mortality, to realize how we are subject to fate, that which has been determined by the one who determines all."

"Determined, yes," James interjected, "but despite what has been determined, we act by our own will, our human will. How this works is the great mystery."

"It is true, it is a mystery, but when I was near death's door, it was not my human will I was concerned about, but instead I had to trust and hope in the will of Him who knows all. It was His will that determined whether I should live or die. Then there is that other thing, that thing which no soldier ever talks about. That moment, when on the battlefield one holds in their hands the life of another. Even then one does not feel empowered. Even then one knows that there is someone else in control. This too is the hope. To know, that life and death never come as a result one man's will. If I take the life of my enemy, to save the life of my friend, that too is the will of the creator, and none other."

"And yet," James began, "it was your choice to save your friend; a choice that put you in harm's way, going against your

172

instinct to survive. This was both your will and the will of God. Just because God willed it, does not change the fact that you made a choice."

"Is that how Reverend Wesley would have put it?" Thomas asked.

"I would not presume to speak on his behalf, but if I understand his teaching, it seems he would have said *the Author of all will choose to save who He will, but it is still left to each to choose to believe, to choose to love, to choose to be the altogether Christian.* If how God's will and man's will can coexist is difficult to comprehend, it is not due to any limitation of the Creator, but merely a limitation of the created."

"I think that I might also have enjoyed hearing Mr. Wesley speak."

At that moment, James looked past Thomas, over his shoulder and down the road. "Look here, I think that is the coachman on a horse, coming in this direction. Perhaps he has some news."

Thomas stood to his feet just as the rider approached. "Sir, do you bring us good news, has the coach been repaired, will we soon be on our way?" he asked.

"I am afraid the axel was badly damaged," came the reply. "The blacksmith has said that it will take him the better part of the day to make a new one. It appears we will not be able to get underway again until tomorrow morning. I'm sorry for the delay, but nothing can be done. There is not another coach expected by here until the day after. I'm afraid you will have to wait, there is no other choice."

"No apology necessary," Thomas assured. "It can't be helped. It has been some time since I was home, but another day added to my journey is of little consequence. Tomorrow it is."

"Fine then, we will be by here first thing tomorrow and then we shall be on our way to Adare," the coachman instructed.

Despite the delay, Thomas found it restful in the Cunningham home. It was nice to get a break from the pain caused by the constant jarring of the coach as it bounced along the road. Meanwhile, Adam was thoroughly enjoying the company of his younger cousins. Thomas now realized why his young friend had been so at home playing with the young boys in Portugal.

The next morning they rose early. The coach had been repaired and would meet them on the main road. They said their goodbyes to their host and hostess. As James took Thomas' hand he handed him a package, "take this, I want you to have it. It has been a source of wisdom and comfort for me. I hope that it provides you the same."

Thomas realized it was the book that James had been reading the day before. "I can't take this, it is far too generous. This was a gift from your father. It wouldn't be right."

"Go ahead, I want you to have it. I'm sure my father would be pleased to know that it had been passed on. When you're done with it, you can return it."

"Very well, then, if you insist, I look forward to the time that I will be able to return to you in person."

Thomas and Adam walked to the road, none too soon, as the coach arrived moments later. Adam only had a short journey remaining, leaving the coach at Adare. They said their goodbyes and promised to keep in touch. Thomas continued on the coach to Limerick. Here he had to wait for a coach headed north to Galway where he would spend the night. Early the next morning, he was again on the road. It was June 10th. On the next eve he would be in Sligo, and then the next in Enniskillen. He would soon be home.

*****

The sun had just descended beneath the horizon as he walked up the lane to his home. The sky was a brilliant crimson, and the shadows had long since swallowed the landscape, making it difficult to see the details of his surroundings. There was a soft light emanating from the front window, flickering ever so slightly, evidence of the source. The children would soon be going to bed. He stopped for just a moment, staring at the front door. He was home, for good this time. There would be no more going off to war, or adventure seeking. He couldn't subject his family to his absence again. Still, he wondered what it would be like, giving himself to his role as husband and father. He had missed Alice and the children, so much that it hurt, but would he be content to stay at home? Would he grow restless again?

His thoughts were interrupted by someone singing; a female voice, soft and melodic. It was Alice. She was singing an old Celtic lullaby to the children. His heart swelled as he listened. He had long thought that he would never hear her voice again. He turned the doorknob and pushed the front door open, stepping across the threshold, looking upon the startled faces of his family.

"Thomas?" was all that Alice could utter, in her surprise.

"Yes, it is I, returned home."

Alice sat motionless, staring as if she were looking at a ghost. Thomas, for his own part, remained standing at the door, as if frozen in time. He couldn't take his eyes from Alice. It was as if in that moment, time stood still, and they were the only two in the room. For just a moment he thought he could see her sitting on the bench seat of the wagon, that first moment they had met.

"Hello, Father."

Thomas was aroused from his imaginings by a young man standing in front of him with his hand extended in greeting. His mind raced for just a moment before he realized that he was face to face with his oldest son. James was now twelve years of age and had already grown taller than his mother. His hair was the same color as his father's, and anyone who had known Thomas in his youth would have told you that this young man was the spitting image of his father.

"James?" Thomas stammered a little surprise.

"Yes, Father."

"I can hardly believe it," Thomas said. "When I left, you were just a boy, and now you are a man." He shook his son's hand, and then pulled him close, giving him a hug. As he did, Willie and Thomas Jr. embraced their father in greeting. Janey, now three years of age, and Maggie, barely one, sat on the floor at the feet of their mother, not sure what to make of this scene. Janey could not have remembered her father, and Maggie had never met him.

Alice remained calmly sitting in her rocking chair, not having moved an inch. "God be praised, it's really you."

"It's me, Alice," Thomas knelt down and laid his head in her lap. "Your husband has come home, never to leave again."

Alice stroked her husband's hair, tears trickling down her cheeks. "Look Janey, look Maggie, it is your Father. He has come home to you. God has answered our prayers."

*****

It's a strange thing when a man goes to war and then returns home. There is a sense of not belonging. It is unsettling and even disheartening. Thomas knew he shouldn't have these feelings, but they were there just the same, not always out in the open, but hidden deep down, only occasionally rising to the surface. It made him feel uneasy. When he looked at his children, he couldn't help think of how little he knew them, and they him. It was as if he had to discover who they were all over again. The older two boys looked all grown. He had missed so much time with them, something he would never be able to get back. As for the girls, he didn't really know them at all. Janey could not even speak when he had left, and was seeing Maggie for the first time. Even so, he found some comfort in realizing that for them there was much time ahead and he would be able to see them grow into young ladies.

As he sat and watched them play, he wondered what they must think of him. Would they accept him back into the family or would he always remain on the fringe. He so longed to tell them how much he loved them, how much he wished he would have been there for them. How could he begin, what would he say?

There was one person who knew him, who understood what he thought, how he felt. He was so grateful for Alice. She brought sunshine to every moment of his day. She had not changed. Even as the mother of his five children, she was beautiful and full of life as the first day he had met her. When she looked at him, it was as if she saw right through him, right to his heart. She knew and understood him, she had always known.

He had told her of his wounds, he knew he would not be able to keep a secret for long. The pain was still there and he would not have been able to hide it from her. However, he would not tell her of how close to death he had come, he could not. Even so, when she looked at him, it was as if she knew already, as if she had always known.

The days of summer passed quickly and, slowly but surely, Thomas felt the strength return his body. He was truly on the mend, and little by little he was able to return to helping his father-in-law with the farm. James and Willie had grown strong, and with the able mentorship of their grandfather, had grown to be able farm hands. Thomas enjoyed working with his sons at his side. It gave them the needed time to reconnect, to discover one another.

Truth be known, James was too much like his father. At times it was though he was looking into a mirror. It soon became clear to him that James admired him; saw him as some sort of hero. He was humbled by it. He wanted so much for James to know who he was and he wanted to know who his son was, but neither was prone to conversation. They could spend much of the day, working side by side, with barely a dozen words spoken between them.

It was a completely different story for Willie. He was much more like his mother. He wore his emotions on his sleeve, and if prodded the least little bit, would fly into a rage or a river of tears. He was the talkative one, rambling on about this or that, all day long, regardless of whether anyone was listening to him or not. Thomas would just smile shake his head yes or no at the appropriate time, even when he wasn't always sure what Willie was talking about.

Despite their different temperaments, Thomas took comfort in seeing that the two brothers got along, and had a mutual respect, even affection for each other. As for their younger brother Thomas, they seemed to merely put up with his constant questions, and tagging along. They were never cruel to him, but they were not opposed to ignoring him, if given the opportunity.

Thomas was amused, watching his sons. It reminded him so much growing up with his own brothers. He had many fond memories of his youth, many of them which included his best friend, Stewart.

Chapter Fourteen

15 Whatever is has already been,
And what will be has been before;

August 1, 1812

Thomas,

I trust by this time your wounds are fully healed and you are in good health. I must confess that for some time I was concerned about your well-being, and I am thankful that God has deemed it best that you should not have left the world at Badajoz. It is good that you were allowed to return to your family, even though I would much prefer that you were here at my side. It is a strange thing, to continue this venture without my friend and companion.

Once again, God has protected me allowed me to escape harm in the most difficult of circumstances. On the 22nd of July, the 4th Division was committed to one of the largest battles of the war thus far, taking place near the town of Salamanca. The two armies had 50,000 soldiers each and the cost was great on both sides. I almost hesitate in informing you that the 4th Division suffered greatly, having the largest number of casualties. General Cole was wounded in action, although it is believed he will recover. You will be pleased to know that the Inniskillings proved their worth, suffering only minor losses. The battle was determined to be a major victory, even though the bulk of the French army was able to retreat. We now push on to Madrid, in an attempt to push French out of Spain.

I have grown to admire the new commander of the Grenadiers, Lieutenant Pollock. You may remember him as an Ensign, but he was promoted after Badajoz, and has taken naturally to his new role. He is a man of integrity and honor, and demonstrated great courage in the heat of battle at Salamanca.

179

The Colonel

You might remember, the irritant Ensign Weir. His character seems to be absent of any virtue and he continues to make enemies of his comrades in arms, a very dangerous endeavor indeed. It seems he is not content to take his wrath upon the Frogs, but instead he is entirely indiscriminate in his choice of enemies. There does not seem to be a day that passes in which he does not engage in some sort of conflict with his fellow soldiers, the most recent one resulting in a duel with a fellow officer. Even in a duel, it seems he has no honor, for he discharged his pistol before the appointed moment, grazing the left arm of the one who stood at twenty paces. His opponent, having the opportunity to calmly dispatch the young rascal and send him from this world, chose instead to raise his pistol and fired it harmlessly into the air. He offered a warning to Ensign Weir, but I fear the cad is unlikely to learn from such a gracious act. I wish you could have been here to witness the event.

McHugh sends his best wishes. I am confident that you would understand that it is best not to share the details of my recent adventures with Bella, thus causing her unnecessary anxiety. Whereas, you have need of such news, having served with these brave men, for her, it is enough to know that I am well and good. Give her my love.

If God wills it, we will continue to push the French from Spain, putting an end to the war, and we will soon be reunited.

Your Friend,

Stewart Pogue

Thomas folded the letter up and laid it on the table in front of him. As pleased as he was to be at home with his family, he couldn't let go of the uneasiness he felt having left Stewart behind. His friend was still in harm's way. They had always fought together, side by side, watching out for each other, and Stewart had saved his life more than once. Who would his friend rely on now?

*****

Stewart's hope that the war was nearly over, would not come to fruition. The Anglo-Portuguese forces engaged the French and entered Madrid on August 6th. After laying siege for more than a month, they were forced to return to Portugal in early autumn, as the French forces regrouped. It would be another long winter on the Peninsula. There was no indication that the war was coming to an end anytime soon.

Meanwhile, at home, Bella was pregnant and expecting their third child. Bella had chosen to keep it from her husband, not wanting him to worry on her behalf. On September 20th she gave birth to a son, David.

Two weeks later, Stewart received a letter from Bella announcing the good news. It agitated him to think that Bella would keep such a secret from him. He didn't want her to feel as if she needed to bare her burdens alone, even if they were separated by hundreds of miles. This agitation soon turned to delight as he contemplated his good fortune. It was his family that filled him with the determination to survive. Each and every tedious moment of each and every day, was filled with the solace of knowing that his family was well and safe, and that he would soon be with them. He would not let Bella down, he would endure and he would return home.

*****

The days became shorter as autumn slowly ebbed into winter. The trees had lost their leaves and nights were interminably long. Despite the cold and dreary landscape, Thomas' spirits were bright. With each passing day he grew stronger, and before he had come to realize it, the pain in his chest and side had subsided. He was again beginning to feel like his old self. To occupy his days, he reopened the blacksmith shop in the village.

181

James worked in the shop alongside his father. He had a natural aptitude for the trade and it wasn't long before he was as skilled as his father. Thomas enjoyed watching his son learn and grow. He was proud of James-he was a hard working lad, with an even temperament-looking more and more a young man each day.

Smithing was hard honest work and Thomas relished it. It was good to feel the weight of the hammer once again. It was natural, not like the sword. The one was used to create and shape; the other to tear down and destroy. It was as if every blow of the hammer against the iron freed him from a little piece of the memory and pain of war. With each horseshoe and harness constructed, he moved closer to being the husband and father he was intended to be-much less the soldier he had been.

Christmas came and went with no sign of Stewart. Thomas has heard reports that the British remained bivouacked in Portugal. From what he could gather there was very little contact between the two opposing forces as the French continued to remain encamped near Madrid. This at least brought some comfort to Bella, who was most times in a fit of anxiety for her beloved husband. It was a terrible thing, believing that Stewart could return home at any time, while at the same time knowing he might not be long for this world. Thomas tried to give Bella the reassurance that Stewart was a part of the bravest and noblest fighting unit in the entire British army and that his friends and comrades would see him through. He might have been a little more convincing had he not also felt the fear of losing his friend.

(1813)

In early January, Thomas and Alice were surprised to receive an invitation to make a visit to Belle Isle. It seemed the Baron of Erne, and his wife, were making a sojourn north to pay their respects to the Hardinge family. As a result a reception was being held in their honor. It was presumed to mean that there would soon be an announcement of the forthcoming marriage of Ann Hardinge to Robert Crichton. Bella was beside herself with excitement, which provided her at least some diversion concerning her missing husband. Although Alice was agreeable to participate in this venture, Thomas was not so cooperative. It took the combined will of the ladies to convince him that it would be highly improper for them to accept the invitation without proper escort. Appealing to his honor and chivalry, they finally convinced him to go.

Although Thomas had been on the Isle of Cleenish on several occasions, he had only seen the Belle Isle from a distance, never imagining that he would one day be invited to enter through the front door. The entrance was crowned by a beautiful double vaulted ceiling. Thomas had never seen the like of it before. He stood in awe, not really knowing how to proceed. He remained frozen as Bella and Alice followed the butler to the drawing room. Alice turned to him and motioned with a gentle wave, indicating that he should follow as well. The look in her eyes was one of assurance-relax, everything will be alright. Although still hesitant, he followed. He couldn't help the feeling that he didn't belong here.

As he entered the drawing room he immediately felt all eyes drawn to him. It was all he could do to keep from turning around and walking right back out of the room and out of the great house, never to return. Seated at one end of the room was an old but distinguished gentleman. At his side there was a young woman, perhaps just slightly older than Alice. She seemed to be particularly attentive to the older gentleman. Seated on a couch to their right, was an elderly woman, her white hair most distinctive; and next to her a young and quite attractive girl who could not yet have reached her twentieth year. To the left, standing near the fire place, almost turned away, as if he cared not for any of the people in the room and would have preferred to be somewhere else entirely, was a man, not any older than Thomas, with strawberry blonde hair and blue eyes. He was holding a brandy snifter, and was making this the object his attentions. Opposite the fire place, near the window was a small gaming table, which for the present was occupied by two men and two ladies-one whom he immediately recognized to be Bella's father, Reverend Howard-who were playing some sort of game he did not recognize. Behind them, sitting so the light of the window shone upon the book she was reading was a young girl, perhaps fourteen years of age. She looked up momentarily to acknowledge the newcomers, but then immediately returned to her book. At the end of the room nearest him was a piano forte, with two girls-younger than the one at the window, but equals with respect to each other-seated, attempting to play the piano, and giggling with each missed note. They stopped when they realized there were new guests.

"Welcome, welcome," the elderly woman greeted. "We are so glad you have come. Welcome Alice, welcome Bella, and who is this?" She was indicating Thomas.

"Thank you, Lady Hardinge, for your kind invitation. We are pleased to have come," Bella, as was her habit, took the lead in the introductions, as Alice simply followed along. "This is Thomas Rea, Alice's husband, who is so pleased to have joined us." With this last phrase she turned and gave a sly wink in Thomas' direction. "Thomas," she continued, "this is Lady Hardinge dowager Baroness of Belle Isle and her granddaughter, Anne Hardinge."

Thomas took their extended hands gently in his own, "Lady Hardinge, Miss Hardinge,"

"And this here," moving toward the seated man, "this is Lord Crichton, 2nd Earl of Erne, and his wife Lady Crichton."

At this introduction, Lady Mary stepped forward and extended her hand to Thomas in greeting, "Please, call me Mary," she said. "I'm so pleased to meet you, Thomas. I have heard so much about you, from your lovely wife."

Thomas shook the hand of Lady Mary and then stepped toward the Baron with hand extended.

"You'll have to excuse by husband, for not standing, Thomas. He has recently experienced a loss of vision, and he is more comfortable remaining seated. Sir, this is Thomas Rea, husband of Alice Rea," she said, leaning down to speak into her husband's ear.

The Baron raised his hand and took hold of Thomas'. "Nice to meet you young man."

"And this," Lady Mary continued, "is my husband's son, Robert," saying it, as if she made no claim of her own on the young man.

Thomas started to step toward the young Mr. Crichton, but the other turned away as if completely unaware that his stepmother had just introduced him. Thomas made no further advance.

"And over here," Mary continued the introductions moving to the other side of the room, "is John Henry Frith, warden of Enniskillen, and his wife, Mrs. Frith," pointing to those sitting across from one another at the table, "and Mrs. John Crichton (sitting across from Reverend Howard) daughter-in-law of the Baron. There, next to the window, is her oldest daughter, Jane, and over there her sister Catherine, with her friend, Caroline Frith."

Thomas didn't know what to do at this point. He was not one to make small talk, especially with people he had very little in common with. He stood to the side, as Bella, Alice and Lady Mary began conversing, catching up on the latest bit of news. Thankfully, he didn't have to endure this for long, as the butler entered and announced that lunch was served.

The entire group moved from the drawing room into the great hall where there was a long table opulently set. The Lord of Belle Isle had passed the previous year and so the Earl of Erne was given the honor of being seated at the head of the table, with his son at the opposite end. Lady Mary was seated to the right of her husband, with Mrs. John Crichton to her right. Bella was seated to the left of the Earl, with Alice and Thomas to her left respectively. To Thomas' left were Reverend Howard, and then Mr. and Mrs. Frith. To the left of Robert Crichton were

Anne Hardinge, Jane, Catherine, Caroline and finally Lady Hardinge.

Thomas watched Alice to get his cues in etiquette. The ladies carried most of the table conversation, much to his pleasure.

"I understand you are a soldier," Mrs. John Crichton said, "I don't suppose you know my husband?"

"Yes, I am, or I should say was," he stumbled a bit in response, not having been prepared for the question. "I have resigned. What regiment does your husband serve in?"

"He is in the Scot Greys," she answered.

"I don't believe they have been called to the Peninsula, then," he said.

"No, they remain in Scotland, and have been for some time."

"Then I'm sorry to say that I have not had the pleasure of meeting your husband."

"Mary tells me that you were wounded. It must have been horrible."

Thomas paused a moment before responding, trying to find the words. "Yes, I was. It happened so quickly, I had little time to think, but my friends tell me I was near deaths door. Even so, God chose to preserve my life, not so for many of those who fell beside me." He was thinking of Simcoe and O'Neil.

"Did you kill many French soldiers?" The question was posed by one of the young girls; at first, he wasn't sure which.

"Catherine! What a horrible question for a young lady. I'm sure Mr. Rea does not want such questions posed to him," Mrs. Crichton intervened.

"It's alright Mrs. Crichton. It is an important question, and one that needs to be answered, although perhaps now is not the time. Let's just say that I acted my part as the best soldier I knew how to be, but it was not I who determined the fate of my enemy, only God has the power over life and death."

He could see by the reaction on the face of Mrs. Crichton that he had handled the delicate moment appropriately. Out of the corner of his eyes he noticed that the young ladies opposite him were smiling at him as if in admiration. He felt his face growing warm. Lady Mary, always full of grace, was able to divert the conversation by asking Bella how her new baby, David was doing, adding that she was disappointed that she had not brought the baby along. Bella explained that Maggie, Alice's sister, had volunteered to look after the children.

Thomas said very little through the remainder of the meal. There were no more questions, and he was glad for it. He felt more at ease facing the danger of battle, than he did participating in society.

As the luncheon drew to a close, the Earl rose from his seat, holding his glass aloft. Everyone stopped whatever they were doing and it became silent.

"Friends, old and new," he began, "we are pleased that you have graced us with your presence on this occasion. For some time now, we have been living in anticipation of this moment. It is with great pleasure that I announce the engagement of my son Robert to the lovely Miss Hardinge, making the way for these two great houses to be joined. We are deeply saddened by the loss of Miss Hardinge's grandfather this past year, having been preceded in death by his son, her father, and it is my hope that I may carry on as the father of both of these young people as they begin their life together."

Everyone raised their glasses in salute. There was a clinking of glass, then words of congratulations offered to the couple. Thomas watched the two in earnest. Robert Crichton appeared to be amiable in that moment, but there was something in his eyes that indicated that he was less than enthused over this anticipated union. Anne for her part was smiling, and very polite in responding to the words of praise, but she too seemed a bit apprehensive. She was so young. Thomas felt a little sorry for them. When he placed his own glass back on the table, he felt Alice's hand grasp his beneath the table and give a slight squeeze. He turned and looked at her. She too had concern etched in her eyes. She smiled at him. In one brief look she was expressing how much she loved him.

"I have one more announcement as well," the Earl continued after the congratulations were completed. "As much as I am pleased to receive Anne into my family, I am afraid it will have to wait a little longer. I have put forth a request for a Lieutenant's commission in the 27th Regiment on behalf of young Robert, and this past week I received word that this application has been received and accepted and as soon as there is an opening, he shall receive his appointment."

Everyone applauded the news, that is, all except Robert. Even Anne seemed genuinely pleased about this turn of events, even though, it would delay their upcoming nuptials. Thomas was the only one in the room who fully understood the implication of this announcement. The commission could only be purchased for someone not already serving in the army as an ensign and the only way an opening would occur, is if a Lieutenant currently serving, was wounded or worse, killed. He chose not to volunteer this information.

Lunch came to an end, and the men excused themselves to the library as the ladies took a stroll in the garden. This seemed a strange tradition to Thomas, but he was not about to question it openly. Alice gave him a cautious look as they went their separate ways, as if to say, be cordial.

Once in the library, Reverend Howard took the lead in the conversation, realizing Thomas' insecurity. "Are you familiar with the Frith family, Thomas?" making reference to Mr. John Henry Frith, now present. Thomas just shook his head no. "The Frith family is one of the oldest in Enniskillen. Members of the family fought alongside William of Orange at the Battle of Boyne. Most notable, John Frith was one of the early Protestant reformers. He helped Tynedale translate the New Testament and supported Bishops Cranmer and Ridley. In 1553, he was burned at the stake. He was only thirty years of age at the time. John Henry here is a direct descendent."

Thomas pretended to listen intently to his friend's father-in-law, but he had little interest in the history of the Protestant Reformation or the Frith family. He tried to remain polite and give the impression that he cared. When the narrative began to change to a discussion between Mr. Frith and Rev. Howard on the advantages of Protestant theology, he decided to excuse himself.

The Earl and his son were sitting quietly at the other end of the library, neither wishing to disturb the silence. "I suppose congratulations are in order," Thomas directed at the son, not knowing how else to begin a conversation. "You are a very fortunate man, Anne is quite beautiful and amiable, and I think will make a fine wife."

"Here, here." The Earl agreed.

"I suppose you're right." Robert Crichton responded with little emotion.

"You seem rather melancholy, for a man who is about to enter into marital bliss," Thomas was trying to keep it light, but he wasn't sure he was succeeding. It seemed the young Crichton was not in the mood to discuss it.

"It is what it is, and not of my doing," Robert replied.

"You can see by his continence, that my son is less than pleased with this arrangement," the Earl chimed in. "It seems he does not understand his responsibility to the family, and to his own estate."

"Responsibility to the family?" Thomas was not sure what was meant.

"This is an opportunity to join these two great houses, the importance of which can't be underestimated. We are not all masters of our own fate," the Earl said. There was determination in his voice. "The fact is, that the young Miss Hardinge is of an amiable sort, and quite pleasant in all decorum is merely an added blessing."

"Then you are not in love with her?" Thomas directed his question to the son.

"I know nothing of love, sir. Where there is no will, or as my father says, where fate rules, there can be no love. Should her name be Helen and mine Paris, it would be no different. As I said, it is what it is, and it can be nothing else."

Thomas knew nothing of the Greeks and therefore the literary allusion was lost on him. What was not lost on him, was that Robert was choleric and wishing nothing more to do with this conversation.

The Earl discerned the same and tried to change the subject. "So you have been to war on the Peninsula. I imagine you have many exploits to share?"

Thomas didn't really want to talk about the war, but he wanted to remain courteous to the Earl. He began sharing some the history of the involvement of the Inniskillings in the present war, sharing what personal anecdotes he thought Lord Crichton would enjoy hearing. Robert remained penchant, sitting quietly, pretending to listen, but clearly disinterested, lost in his own thought.

*****

"It seems the wedding will have to wait," Bella said, as she walked arm in arm with Alice and Lady Mary through the rose garden. Anne and Jane were walking together at a distance to far away to hear the conversation between the three friends.

"It did not appear that either the bride or groom-to-be were disappointed at this news," Alice said.

"It is true," Lady Mary affirmed. "I can't speak for Anne, but Robert is not agreeable to the union. He feels he is being manipulated by his father. From the time he was a child he has resisted his life of privilege and responsibility. He is not a happy man."

"I feel a little sorry for Anne, though," Alice reflected. "She is a promising young lady, not deserving of a loveless marriage of convenience."

"I share your concern, Alice," Lady Mary offered. "I tried to dissuade my husband, but I'm afraid his mind is made up. As for Robert, I fear he does not have the courage to go against his father with the threat of the loss of his inheritance hanging over his head."

"I wonder if he will find the courage he needs as a soldier." Bella questioned.

"I am afraid this is also not of his own doing. He has squandered his youth in aimless and frivolous ventures. I think his father hopes that soldiering will change his character, but I do not share this confidence," Lady Mary spoke as if she were hesitant to bring criticism on her stepson.

"Enough of this, let's talk of something else. I must say I am quite taken with your Thomas, Alice. He is everything you have described and more, although I must admit that he shows some resemblance to Robert. I imagine that beneath that beard is someone who could pass for my stepson's brother."

"I must admit I have thought the same. Thomas came home from the war with the beard. I do not care for it myself, but I have not had the courage to tell him so. I keep hoping he will remove it of his own volition," Alice said.

"If you wish, I could put it to him," Bella volunteered smiling. "Then you would be off the hook."

Alice smiled back, but said nothing.

"It must have been hard, having him away for so long, and to find he had been wounded so severely," Lady Mary stated.

Alice hesitated before responding, looking at the continence of her friend. "Yes, it was hard, much as it still is for Bella. At some point, I am not sure when, I came to the realization that there was little I could do. He was in God's hands, and it would do little good to fret. I had to wait and hope."

Lady Mary caught Alice's meaning and realized she may have caused discomfort to Bella. "Of course, *God* is in control and we can trust in this. We will continue to keep Stewart in our prayers, knowing that God can and will bring him home safe."

The Colonel

She squeezed Bella's arm as she said it. "And how is Thomas doing, has he fully recovered from his wounds?"

"Physically, he is back to good health. However, I sense there is still some pain. He occasionally wakes in the night with bad dreams. He never talks about it, but I know that he continues to be burdened by the experience. I wonder if he will ever be done with it."

Chapter Fifteen

[7] Since no man knows the future,
Who can tell him what is to come?
(1813)

May 22, 1813

Dear Bella,

It seems an eternity since I last held you in my arms. How do I express the longing I have for my home, for my wife and children. May God grant me grace that I may soon return to you.

Three days past it was announced that we would be given back pay to the 24th of December. I have instructed the paymaster to send this sum to you, for I have no need of it in my present circumstance. Make good use of it as you deem best.

General Cole arrived today to inspect the Division. He was generous in his praise, and offered a word of encouragement to all. He conveyed his fortune in having the privilege of commanding 7,000 of the finest soldiers the British army has to offer.

It is hard to imagine that I have a new son who is now seven months old, and I have yet to lay eyes on him. How I wish could be there, to watch my children grow. Please express my love to them.

Time is short, we are breaking camp again.

Take care, my love.
Stewart

The 4th Division was part of a larger army that began to move across the Peninsula toward Madrid. Wellington had determined that the allied forces would attempt to push the French out of Spain, taking advantage of the enemy's depleted forces. For ten days, the British army swept across the land, marching nearly every day, halting only to guard against exhaustion and maintain equipment. On the 30th of May, they were instructed that all should rest, for they were to resume the march at two in the morning. This implied that something significant was about to unfold.

May 30, 1813

Thomas,

It has been eight days since I last wrote Bella. She should have received my correspondence before this, however, the mail, in time of war, is not a thing to rely upon. If she has not yet received my letter, please communicate to her my love for her and the children.

We are encamped in Carbajales, having crossed into Spain a day ago. We have been instructed to get as much rest as we can, for we break camp at 2 AM. I am afraid that something is amiss, the enemy is at hand. Everything seems to indicate that Wellington will not rest until the French are pushed from Spain. I have no special knowledge of our orders, but my intuition suggests that a great battle is about to ensue.

It is impossible for me to hide my own anxiety in this matter. I am a soldier, and therefore subject to the fate of war, I accept this. However, my family has not chosen this course, and should not be made to suffer, should I not return.

From the time of our youth, we have been as close as brothers. I confess that I must now rely on you in the matter of my family, should God chose to take me home. I entrust to you their welfare. I have complete confidence in your integrity in this circumstance. This and this alone, allows me to go boldly into the field of battle, confidently, with all fortitude.

God Bless you,

Your Friend,
Stewart

Stewart and the rest of the grenadiers were awakened to the sound of the bugle at half past one o'clock in the morning. They had been given standing orders to be ready to march at a moment's notice. As they dismantled camp, word began to circulate that the orders to march had been delayed until 4:30 the next afternoon. This was quite disconcerting since they had been roused from the warmth and comfort of their tents to a rather chilly night. Stewart joined ensign's Drew and Radliffe who had managed to gather some coals from one of the lookout fires and had built a handsome fire of their own to wait out the remainder of the night. It provided some relief as they sat huddled in silence.

In the end, they were able to begin their march at 3:00 PM, crossing over the Esla River on pontoon bridges that had been constructed by the engineers the day before. Once across the bridge, the lead guard consisting of Hussars (Austro-Hungarian horse soldiers) met with light resistance. By 7:00 PM they had made camp again near the town of Almendra. At 4:30, on the morning of the 1st of June, they continued their march throughout the day. In the evening, just after they had made camp, the skies let loose with a terrible torrent of rain that drenched the entire camp. By morning, every member of the regiment was in a sour mood, but it would not deter their leaders and they spent the next day sloshing through the mud left by the previous night's flood.

On the 3rd of June, the regiment remained at arms, not moving from their posts the entire day. It was believed that the enemy was very near. The next day they marched past small villages that had been burned to the ground in the wake of the retreating French army. Stewart was dismayed at such senseless destruction. Hundreds of innocents had been left without shelter.

The next several days were much the same, marching, standing ready, dealing with elements, passing burned out villages. It seemed as if it would never end. There were minor skirmishes, but the bulk of the French army remained at arm's length. By the 19th of June, the resistance had become firm and the Light's from several regiments, numbering about 300, were sent ahead to engage the French. As night fell, so again did the rain.

The Inniskillings were encamped on a bit of rise overlooking the enemy encampment. As the rain began to lighten, Stewart peered through the flaps of the tent. In the distance he could see the many fires warming the enemy in the valley beyond. It was clear they had finally caught up with their prey. It would be here that the French would make their stand.

The next day remained calm, a gentle, but steady rain still falling. The regiment was to remain ready, but there was no announcement of advance forthcoming. They would bed down in the same place. As darkness began to fall, General Cole made a visit to the Inniskillings. Stewart was pleased to serve under so brave and respected a leader. General Cole was a fellow Ulsterman, the son of the 1st Earl of Enniskillen. On this night, it was clear that he was making his last inspection of his troops before the big day.

(June 21st, 1813)

Stewart woke at sunrise in anticipation of the bugler's call. Emerging from his tent, he built a small fire and prepared his morning meal. As he sat musing about the forthcoming battle, he was joined by his old friend Roger McHugh.

"Good morning Sergeant-Major, you seem to have lost your company, (McHugh was a part of the 4th company, while Stewart was still assigned to the grenadiers)," Stewart said mockingly.

"I roused them earlier, they will be ready. I just thought I would take a morning stroll, a sort of examination of the troops," he returned, half joking. McHugh proceeded to sit near the fire and poured himself some tea from the beat up kettle that

Stewart had left at its edge. "Here we are again, old friend, soon to meet the enemy."

"I think this may come to be the end of it, McHugh," Stewart said, not looking up from the fire. "One way or another, I believe it is the end of it for me."

"Now don't get all melancholy on me, Stew. There is no need for that kind of talk. You have come through some harrowing moments with ni'ther a scratch or cut. I tend to think the Maker has always had his hand on you, and I can't think why he would remove it now."

"That is not what I mean. God determines who will live or die, I rest in this. I simply mean I am done with it. I have no more stomach for the battle. I have served King and country for going on ten years, I think it is enough. It no longer holds any adventure for me. Let the young men dream of fame and success, it means nothing to me. It is time for me to go home, to return to my family, and to give them the devotion I have given these years to the Inniskillings. It is something I have thought long and hard on, ever since Thomas was wounded at Bardajoz. It is no longer the same without him here. My mind is determined in this. I have decided to ask the Colonel for a discharge, once this battle is over."

"Aye, I do not begrudge you this decision. Even though I will miss you, I understand your desire to return home. I have always envied you and Thomas your beautiful wives, and wondered how you could remain so long separated from their comforting embrace. Alas, if there was some woman at home who could settle on this old battle worn scoundrel, I think, I too would retire my musket. In any case, I think we may all be returning home before too long. Wellington seems to be determined to push the French out of Spain, and everything suggests that things are about to come to a head."

"I agree," Stewart said reflecting. "I don't believe that the Duke has any wish to spend another winter on the Peninsula. King Joseph and the bulk of the French army lay yonder there and we are positioned to put an end to this campaign, once and for all."

Stewart was referring to Joseph Bonaparte, brother of the emperor, and self-proclaimed king of Spain, a position in much dispute. The French army of 8,000 had spread itself along the Camino Real (royal road), extending southwest from the town of Vittoria. Wellington, whose command numbered nearly 10,000, had split his forces with the Lights and 2nd Division making a frontal assault parallel to the road, with support from the 4th Division. Meanwhile, the 1st, 3rd, 5th, and 7th Division had outflanked the enemy from the north. The French had made a miscalculation, having left several bridges strung across the Zadorro River intact, allowing the allied forces access to cross.

While it was still early in the morning, the 4th division was roused from its leisurely breakfast with the rumble of the passing Lights Division. The Inniskillings quickly broke camp, packed baggage and proceeded to fall in line behind the Lights as they moved toward the impending battle. By midmorning the entire division found itself perched on a rise overlooking the Royal Road, pausing, anticipating their orders. From this position they could observe the movements of both the Lights and the 2rd Division. The summer sun beat down on them as they were entirely exposed, and as the noon hour approached, many found themselves parched and in need of refreshment. As they stood and waited, they could hear their fellow soldiers engage the enemy in the distance. The rank and file began to grow anxious, not fearful, but there was a quickening of the heart in anticipation of the battle. To stand, waiting, unable to act as the adrenaline built, caused a sort of nervous tension throughout the division. Only the officers remained calm, awaiting their orders.

Stewart spoke calmly to the young soldiers in his charge. Whatever was to happen, the grenadiers would more than likely lead the battalion into the fray, and would see their share of action.

They had watched the advance of the 2nd Division for more than an hour when the order came for them to move from their position. They were to cross over a small bridge to join the 2nd on the south side of river. The 2nd had met with stiff resistance and had suffered many casualties, it was now up to the 4th to hold the line and if possible push the French back toward Vittoria where allied forces were descending from the North. It took some time for the 4th to gain the other side of the river, which created a delay in their advance. The Inniskillings were to provide support on the right flank.

The grenadiers led the way, pushing through right to the front of the conflict. Stewart noticed the dead and wounded as they passed those who had fallen earlier, but there could be no delay, they were there to support those of the 2nd who were still standing. The square had been broken and the two adversaries were engaged at bayonet range. The bugler sounded an advance and the Inniskillings let out a loud "faugh" in unison as they charged into the midst of the battle, the grenadiers in the lead.

Stewart could smell the burnt powder in the air as he rushed forward with the company of grenadiers. It was clear that they had arrived none too soon as the enemy seemed to have a slight upper hand. Nearest him there was a British officer who was about to succumb to an adversary. Stewart threw himself at the French soldier with such force that it knocked him flat on his back with the first blow. In the same motion, Stewart engaged a second Frenchman who tried to support the first, however, he was no match for Stewart's strength and prowess and was soon dispatched.

As the Inniskillings had reached the center of the battle, the entire battalion threw themselves into the conflict with such vigor that it completely caught the French division by surprise. Most of those who were still standing were by this time growing faint from the exertion they expended with their encounter with the 2nd. They would prove to be no match for this fresh opponent. Within minutes, the French were sounding retreat, and those soldiers still standing were making haste back up the Royal Road.

Stewart stood in dumb silence as he saw the enemy retreat. He had not expected it to be so easy. He looked around at his fellow Inniskillings and saw the same level of surprise in their eyes as he felt in his heart. They had barely broken a sweat and just like that it was over, with hardly a scratch between them. The 2nd had not been so fortunate, there were dead and wounded strewn across the field. As a portion of the 4th followed the French division to be sure they were still in retreat, others remained to tend to their wounded friends.

It turned out, that Wellington's plan had worked perfectly. At every turn the allied forces had had resounding victories over their French counterparts. The Battle of Vittoria had been a resounding victory for the allies and the French were once and for all pushed out of Spain. The Peninsular War was over. In a few short months Napolean would be deposed and imprisoned on the island of Elba.

*****

(August 2, 1813)

Stewart paused on the road as he reached the top of the rise overlooking Lough Erne. To the north he imagined he could just make out the tower of the castle barracks at Enniskillen. This, of course, was impossible from this distance, but the image was there in his mind just the same. Below him was the Isle of Cleenish, his home. He smiled as he thought of what Bella's reaction would be as he waltzed through the door. The day after the Battle of Vittoria he had gone to Colonel Maclean to request his discharge papers. The Colonel had consented, with very little opposition to his request. He had immediately written to Bella to announce his homecoming, but he was confident that his letter would not have arrived yet, given the inefficiency of the post.

It was no longer difficult for him to remember what Bella looked like. Her image was emblazoned in his mind. The months of separation no longer had any lasting impact on his memory. It was still difficult for him to imagine why Bella had every chosen to marry him. In so many ways, he was below her station.

During the months they spent on the island of Sicily, Thomas had kept badgering him to propose to Bella. He had hesitated, not because he didn't want to marry her, but because he couldn't believe that she would ever accept him. Despite his friend's assurances, he had convinced himself that he had no chance with her. When he was finally able to muster the courage to ask for her hand, he nearly fell over when she accepted.

Time and distance had only served to grow his love for her. He hoped she felt the same. Even now he feared that she had forgotten her love for him, that she no longer needed him. Perhaps she had been hardened by his absence. No it could not be true, not Bella, who was all grace and benevolence. She couln't think ill of him for leaving her, for she was incapable of thinking ill of anyone. She had no enemies, only friends, evidence of her propensity for kindness and charity at every turn. It was what he loved most about her. He was now home. He had come home to her, and he would do all in his power to afford her the happiness that was due her loving spirit and good nature.

Chapter Sixteen

8 No man has power over the wind to contain it;
So no one has power over the day of his death.

Following the battle of Vittoria, the allied armies
continued to press the French army back to Paris. On the eastern
front Napolean had other concerns, as the Austrians and
Russians were beginning to gain the advantage. By the spring of
1814, the allied forces had taken Paris and had entrapped the
French armies. The French generals turned on their emperor
and Napolean was forced to abdicate his throne on April 11,
1814. He was then exiled to the island of Elba, a small, sparsely
populated island in the Mediterranean, just off the Tuscan coast.
The Peninsular War had come to a close and the 3/27th would
return home to Enniskillen. In August of 1814, the 3/27th was
consolidated with their brothers in 1/27th and sent to the
Maritime Provinces in Canada, not to return to Ireland early in
1815.

(May 22, 1814)

It was a bright and sunny morning, the meadowlarks
were whistling in the glen as the wagon made its way down the
lane toward Cleenish Parish Church. James Rea was at the reins,
carefully coaxing the pair of Cobs that pulled the wagon. James
had grown into a strapping lad, nearly a grown man at only
fourteen years of age. Thomas watched him from the rear of the
wagon, admiring his son, seeing a little of himself reflected. Alice
sat next to James on the bench seat, holding their youngest son,
the newest member of the family who was now almost a year
old. Sitting in the back of the wagon were the remaining
children; William, who was now twelve and had already caught
up to his mother in height; Thomas who had just turned eight;
Janey, five and Maggie, three. They were all dressed in their
202

Sunday best. It was a day of celebration, as they were on their way to the christening of little Mary Pogue, who had been born six days before.

Thomas had been home for more than two years, and was settled back into his life as a farmer and blacksmith. There was no yearning to return to the life of the soldier. It seemed all in the distant past, the memories were still there, even worse the dreams, but, slowly but surely, even those seem to be fading. This was his life now, and it was fraught with adventures all its own. Every day his children provided him with new challenges, stretching him in ways he could have never imagined. It had taken a few months for Janey and Maggie to accept him; he had been nothing more than a stranger to them, but now he was their father. It filled him with such pride, watching them grow, each day a new adventure, each day a new joy. It was a reminder to him of how much he'd missed with James and William. Despite his absence, they had both grown into fine young men, and he felt a slight remorse for having left their rearing to their mother. The two boys were especially close to their mother. They watched out for her, as if they were her protectors.

As he sat musing, Janey crawled on hands and knees, trying to maintain her balance in the rocking of the wagon. She looked up at him, "How much farther, Father?"

To hear her call him father made his heart swell. No matter how many times he heard it, the effect was always the same. "Not far, Janey," he replied. "See, just there, through the trees, you can just see the steeple of the church. We'll be there in no time."

"Good!" she exclaimed. "I'm tired of this old wagon. What will we do when we get there? Will we be able to play?"

"Don't be silly Janey," Thomas Jr. interrupted. "We are going to church. We are going to see the christ'ning of little baby Mary. Why do you think we got all dressed up, and came all this way? Do you think we were just coming to play?"

"But, won't there be time to play?" Janey pleaded.

"Hush, child," Alice said, looking over her shoulder. "Don't start whining. I'm sure there will be time enough for you to play with Annie, if that's what you mean. But, before that happens, you need to be on your best behavior. After all, we are here to celebrate the birth of her little baby sister."

Thomas pulled his daughter close and gave her a little hug, as he whispered in her ear. "Don't worry Janey, we're almost there, and I don't think the church service will be very long. It will all be over before you know it." He smiled and Janey smiled back.

As they approached the church, they were greeted by Stewart waiting at the front. He had been home for nearly a year. It had been a great relief to Thomas to see his friend home safe from the war and now they had received word that their old regiment was home from the Peninsula, as well. Sergeant Major McHugh had paid them a visit a week ago. He was on leave and was headed home to Sligo, the neighboring county to Fermanagh, on the west. He had reported that "Boney had finally given up", and was now imprisoned on some island off the coast of Italy. James and Willie and been particularly enthralled by the Sergeant-Major. They sat for hours listening to the old soldier's stories.

Stewart helped Alice and Isaac down from the wagon, as Thomas lifted the younger children and set them down gently to the ground. "Hello, everyone. Thank you for coming. Bella will be so pleased that you are here."

"Don't be silly, Stewart," Alice responded. "We wouldn't have missed it. How is Bella, is she doing well?"

"She's fine, Alice. She came through it without any difficulty, up and around the very next day, as if nothing had happened. And Mary is a beautiful little girl, although she has lungs that would make any bugler envious; hollered like a banshee when she entered the world. Com'on now, they're waiting for us in the church."

The christening was lightly attended, a few members of the Parish, the Reas, and Ann Hardinge. Thomas had been right,

204

it was a short service, and before long Janey got her wish. The adults gathered in the sitting room of rector's home, while the children played outside.

"Mary is a beautiful baby, Bella, I'm so happy for you," Ann said as the ladies were all seated, the gentlemen remained standing.

"Thank you, Anne, would you like to hold her?" Bella said as she stood and carried the baby over to where the young lady was sitting.

"I would love to, thank you," as Bella gently laid Mary in her arms.

"I understand you have still not married, Anne?" Alice questioned. "It has been nearly two years since you announced your engagement, if I'm not mistaken."

"You're not mistaken. Shortly after my engagement, the Earl was able to secure a captaincy for Mr. Crichton, or should I say Captain Crichton. He has been serving in the Canadas. I believe a wedding will take place when he returns, when that will be I'm not sure."

"It must be frustrating to have to wait so long," Bella said. "I don't know why we should have to wait around for men to come home from war, before we can have the security of having said our vows. What are we to do, sit and pine for them? Of all the gall," she then looked in the direction of Stewart, who had not really been paying attention to the entire conversation, but was wise enough to know that this last comment was directed at him.

"Now Bella, I didn't intend to make you wait," he tried to defend himself. "Truth be known I was a little afraid you wouldn't have anything to do with me...that is once I had lived the life of the soldier."

"Do you think me so fickle that my love would wane just because of the distance that separated us?" At this point it was becoming clear that Bella was laying it on a little thick at Stewart's expense.

"Well...uh no, I don't mean to say that you were fickle...I...I just meant," Stewart was trying to recover, but was about to dig the whole deeper when Thomas came to the rescue.

"Easy Stewart, I think you might want quit while you're ahead. It will do you no good to try and defend your actions of the past. It would only serve to bury you deeper in the mire. Just say you're sorry and move on."

"Oh, I see, Thomas," Alice entered the fray. "Just say you're sorry, and move on, is that your philosophy?"

"Now Alice, don't drag me into this, I was only trying to help out a friend. You know that I have never been anything other than completely devoted to you and desire nothing more than for you to be happy."

Bella was laughing by this time, realizing that her attempts to rattle Stewart had only served to stir up her friends. "Let's not quibble, Alice and Thomas, I am afraid we might give poor Ann here the wrong impression about marriage."

"Oh, no, you needn't worry about me," Anne stated emphatically. "I have no romantic ideas about marriage, especially my own."

"No romantic ideas about marriage? Why Anne, what could you ever mean?" asked Bella.

"Well...what I meant to say, was I have no unreasonable expectations," the color in Anne's cheeks began to darken. "It's just...well my marriage to Robert Crichton, will be one of ...well of practical circumstance."

"Practical circumstance, really, don't you love him?" Bella already knew the answer to this in her heart, but it still required asking.

"I'm sure I will grow to love him, in time," Anne replied. "And I hope that he will grow to love me as well. Anyway, we hardly know each other." The others sat silently, each contemplating the implications of Anne's words. "Have you always loved Stewart, Bella? I mean, have you always known that you loved him?"

Bella turned and looked at Stewart and then smiled. "Almost from the very start, Anne, although I think it may have been different for Stewart."

"Nonsense, Bella, I think I fell in love with you the first moment I saw you. If it took me a little longer to profess my love, it was more a lack of courage than any lack of conviction."

"And what about you Alice, was it the same for you?" Ann asked.

"I think I can answer for both of us," Thomas interjected. "It is true that I loved Alice from the first, but it is not exactly the same as the love we have now. When we first met I could only hope that I would spend our lives together. Now, I can't imagine my life without Alice. The love has changed from wishful, to becoming something that is essential, life giving."

"I would like to know this love," Anne said so softly that only Alice, sitting nearest to her could hear. Alice reached out her hand and touched Ann gently on the arm, as if to say she understood. The others remained silent, not knowing exactly what to say. As if on cue, Mary began to cry, breaking the uncomfortable silence.

"I am afraid she might be hungry, you better give her to me," Bella instructed. Anne obeyed, handing the baby back to her mother. She then walked to the window, gazing out to the open spaces beyond, lost in thought, isolated from those in room.

Thomas felt a sort of sadness on behalf of Anne. She had grown into a beautiful young woman, full of life and grace. Robert Crichton was not deserving of her. Although, he had only met Captain Crichton the one time, he had formed an early opinion of him. He was self-absorbed; no doubt a product of his upbringing, having lived a life of privilege without an understanding of the responsibility and integrity that is required of such privilege. Ann, on the other hand, understood everything about privilege and responsibility. She was all caring and kindness, unlikely to be concerned for her own needs, having a deep appreciation for life's blessings and a strength and fortitude well suited to facing life's difficulties. She deserved better. It was wrong for her to be enslaved in an arranged marriage of convenience. She should know what it meant to love and be loved. She deserved to be happy.

(August 28, 1814)

Enniskillen had become a thriving community, and the summer months brought a flurry of activity as people from all around converged on the market town to buy and sell their wares. As Thomas and James crossed over the draw bridge on the south of the village, Thomas encouraged his son, who had the reins in his hand, to go easy, for they did not want to trample any of the pedestrians walking in the street. James followed his father's instructions and carefully guided the wagon until he brought it to a stop in front of Mr. Kennedy's. The two had come into town to sell some produce from the farm and to get a few supplies.

"I want to stop here just a moment, to say hello to Mr. Kennedy. You may wait here if you like, James," Thomas said, as he jumped down from the bench seat of the wagon.

"Father, I was wondering...would you mind if I went up to the Castle? John Boyle has enlisted in the Inniskillings, and I thought I would pay him a visit."

"Alright, you may go, but don't be getting in the way of the soldiers, mind yourself." John Boyle, although two years James' senior, had been a boyhood friend of James for as long as Thomas could remember. The Boyle's had originally been from Donegal, but John's grandparents had been able to secure a plot of land that bordered the Copeland farm. They had been good neighbors and John was a good boy. Even so, Thomas was none too pleased to have James hanging around the castle barracks. "I will meet you at the front of the castle in two hours.

"Thank you father, I will be there." James hopped down from the wagon and was off in a blink, running up the main street toward the Castle.

208

"Hello, Thomas, what brings you to town?" An old familiar voice sang out from somewhere behind Thomas.

Thomas turned to see the chiseled frame of John Kennedy, his former mentor and employer. He hadn't changed much through the years, with the exception of a few gray hairs that were beginning to show on his temple. "Just here for some supplies, but thought I would stop and see an old friend." The two shook each other's hand and then walked into the shop together. Thomas was flooded with memories as he smelled the hot iron and burning coals. A young man was hard at work shaping an iron rod. Thomas saw a little of himself in the young man, remembering back to his time as an apprentice in the shop. Fifteen years had passed, but he could remember it as if it were yesterday.

"I see you have a new apprentice, John," Thomas said with a wry smile.

"That I do. That I do. Nothing like you, but given time I may be able to make something of him," Mr. Kennedy chuckled as he said it.

"You let me know how he works out, Mr. Kennedy. If smithing is not to be his vocation, I have a young man, who may be able to take his place a year from now." Thomas said half in jest.

"Why Mr. Rea, I may take you up on it, if young Johnson here doesn't work out." With this the young apprentice looked up from his work.

"But whatever do you mean, Mr. Kennedy," the young man said with anxiety. "Are you unhappy with my work? Don't I do everything you ask of me? If you are dissatisfied, all you have to do is tell me. Please don't give up on me. I'm trying the best I can!" The young man's voice cracked slightly with this last utterance.

"Relax, George, I have no intention of 'giving up on you'. Now, don't you pay no mind to our conversation, and get back to work." He smiled at Thomas as he said it.

The Colonel

It had been all in jest, but Thomas was almost serious in suggesting that James come and apprentice in the shop. He had tried to teach the boy the trade, but his son would have none of it. He was too distracted, always day dreaming of other things. Thomas hoped that Mr. Kennedy might bring some focus to the young man. They talked for a little while longer. Enniskillen had grown so large and work for the blacksmith shop had increased enough that Mr. Kennedy thought he might be able to use a second apprentice a year hence.

After visiting his friend, Thomas unloaded his produce at the market and then purchased the list of supplies Alice had asked for. He then drove the wagon to the north end of town toward the Castle. As he approached, he began to muse. This was where he had first met young Simcoe; it seemed a hundred years ago. He could still see the young lieutenant barking orders at the new recruits. He was haunted by the memory of Badajoz, and the young officer struggling against insurmountable odds, courageous to the end.

As he entered the barracks yard, he was surprised to be met by Roger McHugh. "Hello Thomas, what brings you to the Castle; come to check on the troops." McHugh said with a smile.

"Hello McHugh, I didn't expect to see you here. No, I just came to retrieve my son James. He has been visiting one of your new recruits."

"Ah, yes, I thought I noticed the resemblance. He's over there next to the horse post, watching the afternoon drills. A fine measure of a man, nearly fit for duty I think."

"Now don't you going trying to recruit that child," Thomas warned. "He has not yet reached his fifteenth birthday."

"Don't get your ire up, Thomas, I was only making jest." I'm sure when he's ready, you will be the first to direct him to the enlistment office."

Thomas wasn't sure this was true, but he didn't let on. "Last time I saw you, you were headed home to Sligo. I thought you had given up the life of the soldier."

"No, not yet. I did go home to Sligo, even found myself a wife of all things. But I couldn't give the life up altogether. After just a few months, I was going crazy. In fact, it was my new bride who insisted I return to the regiment. And so here I am. Of course, now there is no war to fight, and so I am stuck here training up new recruits. A remnant of the 3rd was sent to the Canadas, but rumor has it that they will not be there for very long. It seems unlikely that they will send these new recruits on ahead, when they can simply wait here for the regiment to return."

"I don't understand, why would they return? Are they not needed in the Canadas? Thomas asked.

"They may be needed there, but perhaps they will be need here more. Old Boney has been exiled to Elba for nearly four months now, but already there are rumors circulating that the French are trying to rebuild their army, and that there is an underground movement to help the Emperor regain his throne. It seems this battle over the Peninsula has not found its final conclusion."

"I understand that the son of the Earl of Erne has gained himself a captaincy in the Inniskillings and is even now in the Canadas."

"It's true," McHugh confirmed. "I met the man just before the 3rd departed. If you don't mind my saying so, he is a poor excuse for an officer. He is quick of temper, and a little full of himself. This combined with his lack of military protocol, will make it a hardship for those who must serve under his command."

"I have met him as well, and I am of the same opinion. You will need to keep an eye on that one. It occurs to me that he will be of little value in battle. Leadership is not one of his natural qualities, self-preservation might be."

It was one of the misfortunes of the British army that men could be promoted to positions of leadership merely due to station. Wealth and privilege was not always a recipe for

211

leadership, and rarely had anything to do with the prudence or fortitude needed for command.

Thomas found James just where McHugh had said he would be. The new recruits were in the middle of drills, rehearsing the square. Thomas recognized John Boyle on the edge of the square. He was a strong, rugged young man, quick witted and well suited to soldiering. He was no doubt aware of his friends presence, as James watched from a distance, but he gave no indication, remaining focused and disciplined, obeying every order that was shouted by the ensign in charge, with promptness and precision.

"Your friend, seems to have adjusted well," Thomas said to James, as he stood beside his son watching the drill. "I imagine he will make a fine soldier."

"And what about me, Father," James said in a somewhat somber voice. "Do you think that I will make a fine soldier as well?"

"So you want to be a solider," Thomas said, trying to gather is thoughts, wanting to be careful with how he responded. "It is not quite as adventurous and romantic as it may seem. Always having to obey the orders of others, never able to make your own decisions, sleeping beneath canvas in all sorts of foul weather, is this the life you want?"

"What's the matter? Don't you want me to join the Inniskillings?" James asked, with a note of concern in his voice. "After all, you were a soldier."

"Your still very young, James. When the time comes it will be your decision, I just want you to be sure you know what you're getting into. It's not all glory and adventure. The soldier's life is a hard one and not to be entered into lightly."

"I'm almost fifteen, nearly full grown. John is barely two years older than I am. Look at some of those recruits there. I'm sure I could best most them in a fight, if it came right down to it." There was a little irritation growing in Jame's voice. He had always been a little rash and his temper could get the best of him. Thomas attributed this to the boy's mother.

"Now don't get your ire up, son," Thomas tried to sound calm. "I was just saying you're a bit too young. Your time will surely come, and if you decide to enlist, I will support you in it. There is no need to fret about it now. We are no longer at war with the French, and it seems the Inniskillings will soon be returning from America. You are a strapping lad, and I'm sure when the time comes, there won't be a soldier who could stand against you in battle. We will talk about it again, when you reach your seventeenth birthday."

James seemed to calm slightly, but Thomas gathered from his son's silence that he was still thinking about it. He understood a young man's ambitions, in this way James was very much like himself. It would be difficult to deter his son from wanting to join the Inniskillings, and in some ways he was proud that he would want to follow in the footsteps of his father. The best he could hope for was to encourage him to wait. This would be no easy task. Young men have a difficult time distinguishing past, present and future; everything must happen now. Fortunately, the British army was not in the habit of enlisting fourteen year old boys. In any case, Thomas was already dreading the moment Alice caught wind of this conversation. He couldn't keep it from her entirely, and he already knew her opinion on the matter. The news that her oldest son wanted to be a soldier would not be received with favor.

(1815)

Roger McHugh had been correct in predicting the return of the 27th to Ireland. Early in the year, the first and third battalions returned to Enniskillen, where they were promptly consolidated into one battalion. The regiment numbered just under 800 and was now in need of a new commander. Major John Hare was acting commander, but the regiment was typically commanded by someone of the rank of Lt. Colonel or higher. The Earl of Erne took this as opportunity, purchasing the commission for his son Robert at a healthy sum of £5,000. The

213

price implied that there may have been some bartering employed, no doubt because Captain Crichton had limited experience and was not well suited to the task. The fact that Britain was currently at peace, may have also had some influence in the matter.

It was a mild winter, and spring brought with it hope. James celebrated his fifteenth birthday, while Alice anticipated the birth of her seventh child, due sometime in May. It had been months since James had said anything about wanting to join the Inniskillings. Alice had erupted when Thomas told her, as he had expected, and showered James with lamentations about a mother's love for her son, and how cruel for him to even consider leaving home at so young an age. This had been enough of a rebuke for James to refrain from speaking about it aloud again, but Thomas new his son well enough to know that he still kept it alive in his heart.

Early in March, rumors began circulating that Napolean had escaped from the island of Elba and would soon be rejoining his army. This brought grave concern, and anticipation that Britain would soon be at war with France, once again and this brought noticeable activity at the Castle barracks.

*****

In point of fact, Napolean had escaped from Elba and landed near Cannes with 600 guardsmen. He began to move on Grenoble where he was met by the 5th regiment of the French army who were now under the command of the Bourbon King Louis XVIII. When confronted by soldiers who had once been in service to him, Napolean boldy walked to meet them alone, leaving his loyal guardsmen to watch. He uttered the now famous words, "Soldiers of the 5th, you may shoot your emperor if you dare", none did. By March 19th, Napolean had reached Paris and regained control of the government, the Bourbons, meanwhile, had fled to Belgium. Within two months the emperor had rebuilt his army to more than a quarter of a million soldiers.

*****

(April 16th, 1815)

Thomas found himself stumbling around the kitchen trying to be of help in making preparations for the evening meal. Alice was now eight months pregnant, and was experiencing a great deal of discomfort. Despite her strong constitution and determined spirit, it was difficult to continue to provide the necessary care for her family. Margaret, her youngest sister, was still unmarried, and would stop by on occasion to lend a hand with children, but on this particular night, Thomas was left with the domestic duties.

As the family gathered around the table, James was inconspicuously absent. "Where's James," Alice asked, as Thomas was about to say grace.

"I have no idea," Thomas replied. "Come to think of it, I haven't seen him all afternoon. Willie, do you know where your brother is?"

William always knew where his brother was. In fact, it was strange that he would be at the table and his brother absent. He was known to follow his brother around twenty fours hours a day. "Ah...not exactly, I'm sure he will be home soon."

Thomas could sense a little deception in his son's voice. William was not adept at telling lies and it seemed clear that he was at least omitting the truth in this instance. "Willie, where is your brother?" He said a little more sternly.

"Sorry, Father, I promised I wouldn't tell."

"Promised you wouldn't tell us what?" Alice rang in, clearly growing anxious.

"William, spit it out! Where is James?" Thomas let is voice raise in crescendo.

The Colonel

"He...he has gone to join up...to join the Inniskillings. He left first thing this morning."

Thomas jumped up from the table, nearly upsetting the entire dinner. He made straight for the door.

"You bring him home, Thomas. You hear me! You don't come back without him!" He could hear Alice shouting as he left the house. He went into the barn and threw a saddle on one of the horses. Within minutes he was off down the road toward Enniskillen. A thousand thoughts raced through his mind as he rode the eight miles to town. Memories came flooding back of the Battles at Maida, Busaco and Badajoz, only now he had the vision of his young son in the midst of the fray, battling for his life. It was unthinkable, he was just a boy.

As he entered Enniskillen, he didn't slow the gallop of his mount. He nearly toppled a man who was carrying a crate across the main street. At he arrived at the Castle, he leapt from the horse and tied him to the nearest post, barely noticing the lather that had gathered on the horse's coat from the hard ride. As he approached the front guard, he shouted, take me to your commander young man, I must have words with him. The guard was so shocked by the force of this command that without thinking he signaled for one of the soldiers just inside the gate to come forward. He then instructed the private to take Thomas to the Colonel's office.

As Thomas and his young guide entered the Commander's Office, they found themselves interrupting the Colonel taking his evening meal. "What is the meaning of this?" The colonel shouted as the two came barging into the room. "What is so pressing that I must me interrupted during my supper? Explain yourself, private."

"Excuse, me sir...this man here...well I mean to say..."

"Sorry, Colonel Crichton," Thomas interrupted. "I'm afraid it is my fault. I insisted upon seeing you immediately. I'm afraid I came with such enthusiasm, that the private here had little choice."

"I see...I suppose I can deal with you later, private. Leave us." The private backed out of the room, half saluting as he did so.

"Thomas, isn't it", Robert Crichton, said in a somewhat civil tone. "What can I do for you? Would you please take a seat? Perhaps you would take some refreshment," he signaled for his assistant to make a place at the table.

"No, no thank you Colonel Crichton. I'm here about my son. I just received word that he has enlisted with the 27th, this very day."

"Let's see, oh yes, James Rea. Your son is he, I had no idea." The colonel seemed to be genuine in his surprise, but Thomas was not so sure. "Fine young man, quite stout, I am sure he will make a fine soldier, one you can surely be proud of. What seems to be the problem?"

"Begging your pardon Colonel, but he is just a boy, in a man's body perhaps, but just a boy just the same. He just recently passed his fifteenth birthday. I'm sure you can see this is much too young an age to be entering into the army."

"I see, this is a predicament. I have the enlistment roster right here. He signed it and indicated that he is seventeen. I see no reason why I shouldn't have trusted him. I'm not sure what you think can be done about it now. He has enlisted, signed his own name. What's done is done?"

"But Colonel, surely you can understand the romantic ambitions of a young boy, realizing that he does not have the prudence to make such an important decision without the input of his parents." Thomas was pleading at this point.

"I know no such thing. He seemed to me to be of clear mind and heart. No one was forcing him to do anything he had not already made up his mind to do. Besides, it is not up to me to suffer him a discharge once he has enlisted. It is up to the Adjutant's Office in London."

"What do you mean?" Thomas was beginning to lose his patience. "Surely you could find it in your heart to strike his name from the role, and allow him to return home with me.

The Colonel

When the time comes for him to be of age, he can return of his own will."

"I am afraid not," the Colonel was also showing signs of irritation. "It is out of my hands. I suggest you write to the Adjutant's office and if they consent to the discharge I will grant it. Until then, the young man in question will remain in my charge."

"But surely you realize this could take weeks. You have to believe your superiors would not question your discernment in such a matter. You have the power before you to change the events which only took place hours before."

"I'm afraid it is impossible. I must insist you abide by my decision, it's final. If you wish to change this matter, you will have to make your plea to London."

Thomas realized he was getting nowhere. The longer the conversation went the more heated it grew. He was going to have to relent. "May I at least have a word with my son?"

"Yes, of course." The Colonel snapped his finger and his assistant came running, as if he were a trained hound. "Ensign, take Mr. Rea here to see his son in the mess. I'm sure the rank and file have not completed their evening meal, as of yet."

Thomas followed the ensign to the door. "Obstinate fool," he whispered to himself as he left the office. 'It seems he has no real mind of his own, or at least no heart,' he thought.

Thomas waited outside the mess, as the ensign went inside to get James. A few moments later his son emerged, his eyes showing his apprehension of his Father's reproach. "Hello, Father."

"James, I thought we had made it clear that you would wait until you have come of age. To do such an impulsive thing, without consulting with me or your mother...your mother, can you imagine the grief you have caused her."

"But father, I am of age. I am certainly not the first fifteen year old to enlist in the British army and I doubt I will be the last. I was ready, even if you and mother were not. I want to be a soldier. Besides, this way I will be able to serve alongside John

Boyle. We can serve together, sort of watch out for each other, like you and Uncle Stewart." (Stewart was not actually an uncle, but it was what Willie and James had always called him.)

"So that is it. You want to be like Stewart and myself. I can't say I am not proud of you wanting to follow in our footsteps, but I'm afraid you have made this decision rashly. Your Colonel seems unwilling to reverse this decision, but I'm going to make my appeal to the adjutant and get you discharged."

"Father, no! It will do no good. I'll just up and enlist again."

"Never the less, it will be done. As soon as I have the paper work, I will return. You can count on it. In the meantime you keep your nose dry. You listen to everything the Sergeant-Major says, and you should be alright."

Thomas reached out his hand and his son obliged him by shaking it. James smiled slightly, then turned and returned to the mess. Thomas then set about finding Roger McHugh. He would have to rely on his old friend to keep an eye on James, until he could resolve the situation.

The ride home was nothing like the one coming. Thomas kept the reins and only allowed the horse to proceed at a slow walk. He had no desire to face Alice that night. There would be hell to pay, and he would face the brunt of it. He had no idea what he was going to say to her. Despite the hope of appealing to the Adjutant, he was afraid that Alice would not be satisfied with anything short of a forced desertion on the part of her son.

Chapter Seventeen

[11] Wisdom, like an inheritance, is a good thing
And benefits those who see the sun.

(June 3rd, 1815)

There was a gathering storm on the Peninsula, nothing to do with climate, but everything to due to the reemergence of the Emperor and his army. In March, the members of the 7th Coalition had agreed to each contribute 150,000 troops to the cause of defeating the French once and for all, which amounted to an army totaling nearly a million; four time that of Napolean's forces. The Coalition had set a date of July 1st to invade France, much to the disappointment of the Duke of Wellington, who in early June was already transporting troops across the Channel to Brussels. The Prussians likewise were gathering in Belgium and ready to strike.

Thomas had been making weekly visits to the Castle Barracks to visit James and to check on the progress of his correspondence with London. Today he was not alone. Stewart had joined him to keep him company on the road. As they approached the Castle, he could sense there was something wrong. There was a soldier at the gate, but there was less activity than he would have expected.

The two friends approached the guard and Thomas gave greeting, "Hello, there young fellow, I don't believe we've met. I'm Thomas Rea, here to see my son James."

"Yes sir...I mean no sir, I am afraid you are too late. The regiment has left, all that remains is Lieutenant Johnson, myself and a few green recruits."

"Left, what do you mean left? Left where? Where did they go?" Thomas was shouting.

"Sorry sir, but the regiment received orders to report to Cork, to find transport to Belgium. They are going to meet the French."

"When...when did they leave?" Thomas could hardly believe his ears.

"Four days ago, sir; in the middle of the night, less than 24 hours after receiving their orders. I guess Colonel Crichton was anxious to please his superiors and wasted no time."

"Four days ago! They could be nearly to Cork by this time. Quick man, take us to the Lieutenant."

The soldier obeyed without question. Given Thomas' demeanor, the young soldier didn't seem prepared to put up an opposition even though Thomas was a civilian. As they entered the office of the Lieutenant-the office of the commander of the barracks-Thomas didn't even wait for the young officer to stand. "Lieutenant Johnson I presume."

"Yes, and who might you be," he was now standing.

"Thomas Rea, Corporal Rea, now retired and this is Sergeant Pogue, also now retired, both of the Inniskillings. I hear the regiment has left town."

"That's right, four days ago." The Lieutenant was trying to behave quite professional, even though he didn't look as if he had reached his twentieth birthday.

"Did my son, that is to say Private James Rea, go with them?"

"Yes, he was on the roll. Is there some problem?"

"Then there has been no correspondence from London on the enlistment status of my son."

"Not that I know of," the lieutenant began rummaging through some papers on the desk. "Wait, here, there is a communication from London, just arrived yesterday. It hasn't been opened. It is addressed to Colonel Crichton. I was going to send it on with the post."

"May I see it," Thomas asked.

Without thinking the lieutenant obliged and handed it to Thomas, who, without hesitation, tore it open and began

221

reading. "See here!" the lieutenant shouted. "You have no call to do that."

"Relax, son," Stewart intervened, "the Colonel won't mind. If it's what we think it is, we will hand deliver it to him ourselves."

> *May 21, 1815*
>
> *To Colonel Robert Crichton*
> *Commander of the 1/27th of foot*
> *Enniskillen Castle Barracks, Northern Ireland*
>
> *Dear Sir,*
>
> *As per the request of Corporal Thomas Rea, and as born witness to by Sergeant Stewart Pogue, the office of the Adjutant shall grant Private James Rea, discharge from his duties in the 1/27th of Foot of the British Army, given that all evidence supplied to us demonstrates to this office that he is of too young an age to be enlisted in His Majesties Service at this time. The Private in question shall be discharged without recompense, to be in effect upon the receipt of this letter by the Commander of the 1/27th regiment of foot.*
>
> *Sincerely,*
>
> *William Barlow*
> *Acting Adjutant*
> *H.M.S*

"Here it is, Stewart," Thomas exclaimed. "The letter we have waiting for, having arrived three days too late."

"Nonsense, Thomas, it's not too late. There's still time. We will just have to deliver the letter to Colonel Crichton ourselves." Stewart was trying to console his friend, recognizing Thomas' obvious disappointment.

"What do you mean, *we*?" Thomas asked, looking at his friend in surprise.

"You don't think I'm going to let you go chasing down the regiment on your own. I'm going with you."

Thomas grabbed his friend's hand. "Thank you, Stewart. I was hoping you would say that." He then turned back to the lieutenant. "I'm afraid there is no time to lose. You will excuse me if I take this letter with me, but I assure you, we will not rest until it is placed in the hands of the Colonel. If you have no objection, we must say our goodbyes, and be off, for there is not a moment to lose."

The lieutenant just sat dumbfounded at his desk, not sure how to respond. Without waiting for a reply Thomas dashed out the door of the office with Stewart close behind. "I will have to return home to say my goodbyes to Bella, I'm sure she will understand. Gather whatever supplies you can, and we will meet up at Innismore Hall," Stewart shouted as the two made for the horses.

"Agreed!" was all that Thomas uttered as he jumped into the saddle, wheeled his mount around and headed for home at a gallop. "Tell Alice not to worry. We will bring him back..." Stewart's voiced trailed off.

Thomas was not at home for long before he was back on the road again, headed toward the meeting place suggested by Stewart. He felt a little guilty leaving Alice, just when she was so near the birth of their child. Margaret was there to help with the younger children, and Willie and Thomas would lend a hand. Alice was beside herself with grief when she heard that James had left with the regiment. It was all Thomas could do to console her. He kept trying to assure her that everything was going to be alright, he would bring James home safe. She was crying as he gave her a hug and kissed her upon the lips as they said their goodbyes. He was determined to not let her down.

"Don't worry," he shouted over his shoulder as he started down the lane. "We'll be back before you know it." He turned and looked back as he rounded the bend, just long enough to see Alice waving to him from the front porch.

He met up with Stewart at Innismore Hall has predetermined. They sat for a moment planning their route. They would take the same path as the mail post, but they would have to rest the horses frequently. The Irish Cob was a draught horse and not accustomed to long journeys. It would take them at least three days to reach Cork, maybe four. Although they were on foot, the Inniskillings had a four day head start. They could only hope that the transport ships at Cork were delayed if they were to catch the regiment before it sailed. They had little time to waste.

Much of the first day had already passed before Thomas and Stewart had even begun their journey. They spent the first night camped beneath an old oak tree overlooking Lough Gowna, and the second night in the tiny village of Shannon Bridge. On the third night, Thomas decided to take advantage of the hospitality of an old friend, and they stayed in the home of Adam Dolmage. Their young friend was delighted to see them, especially Stewart, since he had not heard that Stewart had returned home safe. The three friends visited into the evening, before Thomas put a stop to it and insisted that they go to bed. As much as he enjoyed reminiscing, his son was still on his mind and he would not be able to rest until James was home safe again.

It had taken two and a half days to reach Adare and they were still a good full day's ride from Cork. By the time they reach the port city, the 27th would have been gone from Enniskillen for more than a week. The next morning they rose early and set off, riding as fast as they could, and for as long as their mounts would allow. It was Stewart who kept insisting that they take moments to rest. He knew that it would do them no good to drives their horses into the ground. The only way they would complete the journey was to provide the horse with enough rest and refreshment. If the horses gave out, they would be stuck.

It was very late on the evening of June 6th when they finally reached Cork. The two made straight for the harbor to see if they could gain any news about the Inniskillings. Much to Thomas' disappointment, the transport ships had already left. They were one day too late. They would have to make the channel crossing as well. Unfortunately, every sea worthy ship had been used to transport the British troops, and as a result they would have to wait for an available merchant ship to take them across.

It was difficult just sitting around waiting for a ship, but wait they did. Finally, after three days, they found the captain of a small schooner who was willing to take them on as passengers. He could take them to Ostend, Belgium where they would have to travel overland to Brussels, the intended destination of the Inniskillings.

British troops had been sailing across the channel for several weeks. With the addition of the Irish regiments, Wellington had assembled an army of nearly 100,000.

The journey to Ostend took a week. Stewart and Thomas stepped onto Belgium soil the morning of June 16th. They immediately set off for Brussels. If all went well they would meet up with the Inniskillings by the next morning. Thomas grew anxious as they passed through villages that were in a state of upheaval. Word had already reach the people of Belgium that a confrontation between the French and the Allies was about to commence and that it would be happening at their doorsteps. By midday they had reached Ghent. Thomas inquired after the 1/27th, but the only news he was able to obtain was that British soldiers had been marching through to Brussels for the past several days. There was no way of knowing how recently the Inniskillings had passed.

That night they slept in a barn on the southern outskirts of Brussels. They had been able to learn that the British Army was actually encamped further to the south of Brussels near the village of Waterloo. They had also learned that the French had arrived and the fighting had already begun. Stewart didn't think

225

it wise to try and locate the Inniskillings in the dark. There was no telling who they would stumble into with the enemy so close at hand. Although reluctant, Thomas finally consented to spend the night in the hay loft, but they would resume their journey at first light. It was a restless night for Thomas, he kept dreaming that James was already engaged in the battle, and that he had come too late.

When Stewart opened his eyes to the new dawn, Thomas was already awake, standing at an open window that faced the southeastern horizon. There were occasional flashes of light against the gray sky, indicating that a battle was already underway. They made haste, only taking a brief moment to purchase some bread and cheese for breakfast from a local farmer and to gather their belongings, before heading off in the direction of Waterloo. As they approached the village, they began to encounter small companies of British soldiers. After questioning one of the rear guards, they were able to determine the exact location of the 1/27th, just a mile south of Waterloo. Evidently the cannon fire they had witnessed in the morning was the initial stages of the attack by the French on the Prussian Army to the east. Thomas felt some relief in this. It was still possible that the Inniskillings had not yet met the enemy.

Just before midday, they came upon the perimeter guards of the Inniskillings encampment. As they approached, an all too familiar voice rang out, "Halt! Who goes there?" Both Thomas and Stewart were dumbfounded, as they both recognized the voice, even though they didn't immediately recognize the soldier it emanated from.

"John...John Cullen is that you," Stewart finally blurted out, just before Thomas was about to utter the same response.

"That would be Sergeant Cullen, if you please," The guard replied. "And I don't believe you have told me your names, now have ya."

"John, it's us, Thomas and Stewart, your old comrades in arms. Surely you remember us." Stewart shouted.

"By golly, it is you, come to me right out o' the past. I can hardly believe my eyes and ears. What brings you here, just when we are about to put Boney in his place, once and for all."

The three friends embraced. "John Cullen," Thomas finally was able to speak, "what a sight for sore eyes. How long has it been, perhaps ten years?" Thomas stepped back admiring his friend. John Cullen was still a giant of a man, although seasoned a bit with age. "And look here," Thomas said pointing to his old friend's arm, you have earned your sergeant stripes; good for you old friend, good for you."

"It has been a very long time, friend. I have been nearly half way around the world and back since I last saw you. Now tell me, what in the world are you doing here in the middle of Belgium. I suppose you have decided to reenlist and you have come to rejoin your friends in the Inniskillings."

"Not exactly, John. I'm here to retrieve my son James. Seems he has gone and enlisted behind my back, and he only a boy of fifteen. I have the discharge papers here, if you could just direct me to Colonel Crichton."

"Sure, I will take you to him myself...hey you there, private, take over for me here," Cullen shouted to one of the soldiers standing nearby.

As they walked through the camp, Thomas proceeded to explain the entire circumstances which had brought Stewart and himself to this moment. Cullen listened intently, without interruption, merely smiling and nodding his head to indicate that he was in fact paying attention. He was clearly overjoyed at seeing his old friends.

"Perhaps you would like to see your son, before you meet with the Colonel," Cullen offered. "I believe our friend the Sergeant-Major has been keeping an eye on him," he then proceeded to lead them through the camp.

They found McHugh, sitting near a campfire and enjoying a leisurely luncheon. "Hello, McHugh, how is James getting on," Thomas said as he greeted the Sergeant-Major.

"Hello, Thomas, Stewart," he nodded to both, "I was wondering when the two of you might show up. The minute we left Enniskillen, I was sure you would follow us. Your son is doing fine, Thomas. He will make a fine soldier, although I believe you have other intentions."

"I have here the letter of discharge from London," Thomas patted his chest where he had placed the letter inside his jacket. "I mean to take him home with me, today if possible. Can I see him?"

"Sure, sure, but I think he will be less than happy to see you. He is quite determined to make his own way. Come with me," he proceeded to take them to James' tent. "You have come just in the nick of time. I believe we are soon to engage the enemy. Orders have already been circulating the camp to make ready. I believe we go to battle in the morning."

"Aye, that is what I have heard as well," Cullen affirmed.

The camp was a flurry of activity, as if in anticipation of the upcoming conflict. When they found James, he was sitting with his friend John and a several other soldiers of the rank and file. They were talking and joking as if they didn't have a care in the world. Although James was only fifteen, given his stature, he could have almost passed for the oldest in the group. He stood up in surprise when he recognized his father amidst the men walking toward them.

"Hello James, may I see you a moment, alone," he said in greeting.

"Hello Father, I don't understand, what are you doing here?"

"Come with me, we need to talk." Thomas said it firmly enough so that James knew not to argue. The two walked into a small birch grove at the edge of the camp.

"I have come to take you home, James," Thomas finally said, as they stood face to face. "I have here a letter of discharge issued by the adjutant office in London. I wrote them several weeks ago about your age, and they have complied, agreeing that you were too young to enlist in the first place and that you

228

should be relieved of duty, with no suggestion of consequence. All that is left is to present the papers to the Colonel, and then it will be done. He will have to comply with the orders."

"But Father, don't I have a say this? Surely you can't expect me to up and leave the regiment on the eve of battle. Can't you see how this will look to the other members of my company, my friends?" James was pleading.

"I do understand, and I empathize, however, you must understand that I am quite determined in the matter, and the decision has been made. You shall return home with me, this very day."

"But Father..." James tried to make another plea, but it was no use.

"There is nothing more to be said. You will follow me to the Colonel's tent at once. We will say no more of this." Thomas didn't allow his son to argue the point, and James new enough to know that his Father would not bend.

Together they walked to the Colonel's tent, in complete silence. McHugh led the way, while Stewart and John Cullen trailed behind, chattering the whole way, reminiscing of the old days. Behind them, was James' friend John Boyle, trailing behind at a distance.

There was no guard at the entrance of Colonel Crichton's tent, and so McHugh, Thomas and James entered without announcement. To their surprise they found the Colonel was not present. Sitting over in the corner with his head in his hands was a young lieutenant, the assistant to the Commander, the same young man Thomas had encountered in the Colonel's office back in Enniskillen. As they looked around the tent, Thomas noticed that the Colonel's cot was neatly made and a dress uniform was carefully laid upon it, as if waiting for the owner to don it.

"What goes on here?" McHugh finally broke the silence. "What are you doing there young man, where is Colonel Crichton?"

"I tried to persuade him, but he wouldn't listen to me. What are we going to do? I don't know what to do?"

The Colonel

The young lieutenant was clearly not in control of his senses. "What do you mean, what are we going to do? What is the matter young man? Out with it," McHugh was a little more forceful, trying to get the lieutenant to give some sort of explanation.

Without looking up the lieutenant simply pointed to the desk sitting to one side of the tent. On the desk, clear and simple, was a letter. McHugh went to the desk, held the letter in his hand for a few moments as he read it and then, without hesitation, handed the letter to Thomas. He then went through the door of the tent. "You there," Thomas could hear McHugh's booming voice. "You, Private Boyle, do you know where Captain Hare is? Then go to him at once. Tell him to come to Colonel Crichton's tent immediately. Tell him it is of extreme importance."

Thomas read the letter while all this was going on:

June 16th, 1815

To the reader, I, Colonel Robert Crichton, have this night, determined that I shall relinquish my commission in the British Army; a commission of which I never aspired to, but was thrust upon me by wealth and privilege and the stubborn predisposition of my father. In so doing, I understand that I have abandoned my service to my King and Country, toward neither of which have I ever felt any sense of loyalty or duty, and therefore neither do I feel any obligation or debt.

I came to this decision briefly after realizing that the regiment under my command would be placed at great risk by being placed in the center of the line, meeting head on the frontal attack of the enemy. I think this a foolhardy venture, that I neither support, or wish to be a part of as a soldier and certainly not as a commander leading his troops to certain failure.

I do not enter into this decision lightly, realizing that I have brought shame on my glorious family and that I now relinquish all connections to said family, and country. It is said that it is better

230

to die a hero than to live a coward, however, I find myself in the position of having to choose the latter. Time will test the truth of this proverb, and I shall be living proof.

Regrettably,

Robert Crichton, esq.
Formerly Lieutenant-Colonel of H.M.S.

Thomas could not believe his eyes. In the entire history of the British army, nothing of this sort had ever happened before. There had been desertions, of course, hundreds, but never by a regimental commander. The embarrassment to the crown, not to mention the effects on the morale of the rank and file, was unfathomable. He had known Robert Crichton to be a man lacking in honor and integrity, but he could have never imagined such a brash decision. It was unthinkable.

The whole time he was reading, James stood quietly watching the reaction of his father. "What is it, Father? What has happened?"

"Be still James, I must not speak of it. Wait outside, I will speak with you later." James did as his father instructed.

After James had left the tent, John Cullen and Stewart entered, with McHugh a moment behind, showing a solemn mood. "What has happened, Thomas?" Stewart asked. Thomas proceeded to show the letter to Stewart, who then passed it on to Cullen. Just as Cullen had finished, Captain Ware entered the tent.

"What has happened here?" The Captain shouted. Sergeant-Major, explain yourself. Who are these men and what are they doing in the Colonel's tent?" referring to Thomas and Stewart.

"Captain Hare, let me introduce you to Sergeant Stewart Pogue and Corporal Thomas Rea, both retired from the 1/27th. They arrived here on business with Colonel Crichton when we were all surprised to stumble on some very disconcerting news.

Show him the letter, Sergeant Cullen." John proceeded to hand the letter to the Captain.

Captain John Hare was an experienced officer, and second in command of the 1/27th. He was a capable leader and respected by those who served under him. As he read the letter is continence turned sour.

After pausing for a moment, reflecting on the problem, "I don't think there are words that can describe how contemptible an act we are witness to. Desertion of an officer, no less a regimental commander, is nothing short of diabolical; even more so, given that it comes on the eve of battle. I suppose there are two questions that must be answered and promptly: Who else knows about this? And what are we going to do about it?" Captain Hare was calm, even to the point of being stoic.

"In response to the first, only we here in this tent, including that sniveling lieutenant over there, know at this point, and perhaps the two privates just outside." McHugh answered for the entire group.

"The effect on the morale of the regiment could be devastating," Captain Hare said aloud for all to hear, given it was what everyone was thinking. "If word gets out, it could cause a massive desertion. I certainly don't want to be the one to tell General Wellesley."

"Perhaps we could just say the Colonel was taken ill, and is unable to resume command until he is fully recovered," Cullen offered.

"A reasonable idea, Sergeant, however, all it would take was for one junior officer to stumble into the Colonel's office and realize that he was gone. Within minutes the whole camp would know, a good idea, but risky..." Captain Hare paused again, searching for an answer to their predicament. Silence reigned as all present remained contemplative.

"I have an idea," McHugh finally broke the silence. "What if we were able to replace the Colonel...well, I mean just for the moment. Suppose we could substitute a look alike, someone who was close enough in appearance that he could fool those at a distance. Only the senior officers would know. I'm sure they would understand the need, and would not betray the confidence."

"Interesting idea," Captain Hare interjected. "It will be dark when we begin tomorrow's campaign. We are expected to take position before dawn. By the time it is fully light, the battle would have commenced, and everyone will be too distracted by the conflict to pay any real attention to the imposter. It is possible, it might work. Do you have someone in mind?"

As if on cue, everyone present turned and looked at Thomas, and for the first time he realized where this going. "Oh no, I know what you're all thinking and it is not going to happen."

"But Thomas, you have to admit there is a strong resemblance between you and Colonel Crichton, same build, same hair color and very similar features. In fact, I think if we trim that beard off of you and shape your mustached and side burns to match the grooming of the Colonel, I imagine you could be his twin." As McHugh said it, John Cullen and Stewart nodded their head in agreement.

"But impersonating an officer, I could get shot," Thomas pleaded.

"I highly doubt it," Ware interjected. "Impersonating an officer is a court martial offense, but since you are no longer in the army, it would hardly be worth the army's time. As far as getting shot, keep in mind that this is a conspiracy that we are all a part of, and I think Wellington himself would support us, given the circumstances. I think you are more likely to get shot in battle, than you are of having to face a firing squad. The question is, will you come to the aid of your former regiment. You have to understand the importance of what we are asking. At the same time, know that we understand the sacrifice you would be making."

"I came here for one reason, to retrieve my son and take him home. I left the Inniskillings behind more than two years ago and I have no desire to return," Thomas continued to protest.

"What you do mean, retrieve your son?" Hare asked. Thomas handed him the letter, the captain read it over quietly. "It seems this letter is addressed to Colonel Crichton, and he is no longer here. He is the only one who can release your son. Of course, if you were to perform this favor, I suppose Wellington himself would grant your son an honorable discharge."

"What? That's blackmail!" Thomas was nearly shouting.

"Perhaps, but I am left without little choice," Hare said calmly.

Thomas looked around the tent, he could sense that everyone was in agreement; there was only one course of action. He turned to Stewart, "what do you think?"

"It seems you may have little choice," Stewart offered.

"That settles it then," Captain Hare did not even give Thomas a chance to respond. "Lieutenant!" he shouted. "Get up out that chair." The Lieutenant obeyed, although hesitantly. "I need you to find Captains Tucker, Smith, and Jones and have them report here immediately. Tell them the Colonel is in need of them, nothing more. And let me make myself perfectly clear, if you breathe a word of this to anyone, I will see to it that you face a firing squad, do you understand me?"

"Yes sir, Captain," the lieutenant left to find the senior officers.

"Now, McHugh and Cullen, I will leave it to you to transform Mr. Rea here into the perfect replica of a British officer. Once the other officers have arrived, I will go over tomorrow's orders or battle plan. Fortunately, I was with the Colonel when he was briefed at headquarters. One other thing, Thomas, despite your military experience, I hardly think you are prepared to step into a command position over night. You will only be a figurehead, a facsimile. I will be at your side the whole way. I will be in command."

"I understand," Thomas agreed. "Captain, if I might ask, what are we to do about the two young men outside?"

"One of which is your son, I presume?"

"Yes, sir."

"They will have to be told. Can we trust them to remain in confidence?"

"Yes, sir, I believe we can."

"Then so be it." With this, Captain Hare stepped outside.

"Well this is a fine mess you have gotten me into, Sergeant-Major," Thomas said, turning toward McHugh.

"Ah, stop your belly aching Thomas. It will be alright, you wait and see." Thomas was not so sure.

The rest of the afternoon was spent in grooming and dressing Thomas to make him look as much like the Colonel as was possible. When the other officer's entered the tent, there was a ride range of shock and dismay, but not one resisted the plan; each understanding the implication and importance of its success. Together they outlined the plan of attack for the next day, although it was clear that Thomas would not really be giving any orders, and that the real leadership fell to Captain Ware.

Chapter Eighteen

[14] *When times are good be happy;*
But when time are bad, consider:
God has made the one as well as the other.

(June 17, 1815)

As the sun descended beneath the horizon, rain began to fall, first a drizzle, then a gentle pitter patter, and finally a torrent. The three friends sat huddled together in the Colonel's tent, Thomas, Stewart and John Cullen. They remained silent. The only sound was the rhythmic pattern of the rain drops beating against the roof of the tent. Their meditations were interrupted when the Colonel's assistant broke opened the flap of the tent and entered. "I have a dispatch from Wellington," he said, as he handed it to Thomas.

Thomas thought it kind of strange, he wasn't really in command, but the lieutenant treated him as if he were. Not thinking, Thomas opened the dispatched and began reading. It confirmed that the Prussians were offering three corps in support of their position, and therefore the British Army would stand and hold its position at Waterloo. This meant that they would engage the army tomorrow as first anticipated.

"Have you shown this to Captain Hare?" Thomas asked.

"Yes sir, just a moment ago. He simply said to get some sleep. The 27th will rise at 4:00 sharp."

"Very well, lieutenant, you better get to bed," Thomas instructed. The lieutenant left without comment. "I suppose the same is true for the three of us." Cullen got up to leave. "John before you go, I wonder if you might do me a favor."

"Sure Thomas, anything."

"There is no telling how things will go tomorrow. I was wondering if you would keep an eye on James, sort of keep him under your wing, if you know what I mean."

236

"Sure thing, Thomas. You can count on me. I won't let any of those Frenchies get anywhere near him. You have my word on it."

"Thanks, John. I knew I could count on you." Sergeant Cullen step through the tent door and Thomas and Stewart were left alone.

"Stewart, things could go badly tomorrow. I think I can rely on you to convey my love to Alice, if I am unable to. Tell her I did everything I could."

"Don't worry Thomas, you'll be alright. I will make sure of it. There is no way that I am going back home only to deliver bad news to Alice. She would have my head."

"What do you mean?" Thomas was a bit bewildered.

"I mean that I will be standing right next to you tomorrow, when the fighting commences. You don't think I would let you and James go into battle without me. I would never here the end of it. I have had your back many times before, and I will again tomorrow."

Four o'clock came early. The rain had stopped, but had left a lasting impact. The entire region was a soggy mess. While it was still dark, the Inniskillings assembled and began their march through mud and water to the field of battle. Thomas was on horseback, removed some distance from the closest foot soldier, so that in the dim light it would have been impossible to distinguish him from the actual Colonel Cricthon. He pulled the lapel of his coat up around his neck, partly due to the cold, and partly because he was still self-conscious and afraid that all eyes were on him.

Daylight began to strike before they had reached their destination, although the sky was still overcast and kept the conditions gray. As visibility grew, Thomas found himself looking around at the soldiers nearest him, but it appeared that no one paid any attention to him or to the rather haggard looking soldier walking next to his horse. Stewart had managed to borrow an old uniform of Sergeant-Major McHugh, but it was badly in need of repair, and ill-suited to the corp.

The Colonel

The intended battlefield was actually a good mile south of the village of Waterloo. The Duke of Wellington had positioned his army on the higher ground, as was his habit. The previous day had seen a confrontation between the French and Prussians to the east. The French had won the day, but instead of retreating, the Prussians had managed to circle back to the Northwest and were now moving to support the British and the Dutch, who were now face to face with the main forces of Napolean. Wellington was depending on the Prussians to support his left flank; the French were believing they would be too late.

At mid-morning, the 1/27th was held at Mont Saint-Jean Farm, awaiting orders. To the southwest, Wellington's right flank had already been engaged by the French at Hougomount. This was Napolean's first attempt to break the British line. The conflict was fierce and went back and forth as neither side could take advantage.

As the Inniskillings sat in wait at Mont Saint-Jean, Thomas tried to remain as inconspicuous as possible, staying detached from the main body of the regiment, only having contact with his assistant, Stewart and Captain Hare. From a distance, he kept an eye on James, who was always in the shadow of John Cullen. At noon came the order to deploy. The regiment was to take position at the crossroads at La Haie Sainte. This was right in the center of the British line, not more than 400 meters in front of Wellington's command post.

Once in position, the lines of the Inniskillings remained spread to minimize the target for the French artillery. Thomas remained on horseback, riding back and forth behind the lines of soldiers, shouting words of encouragement. Shortly after noon, it all began. In the distance he could see the smoke emanate from the French guns. Before the sound reached their ears, the ground erupted violently with the impact of cannon ball. Dirt and debris and were thrown into the air in such volumes, that visibility became impaired. With the first impact, Thomas' horsed reared and he was thrown backward to the ground. As he regained his senses, he reached up and touched his forehead where a trickle of blood had formed. He regained the horse's reins and jumped back into the saddle. Everything around him was in chaos, the wounded crying out in anguish, the dead lay silent. They were being torn apart and the battle had barely begun. Thomas was able to locate Captain Hare in the melee.

"We are being decimated!" Hare shouted above the roar of the cannon. "We must take a different position, or we will soon be lost." He turned to the bugler, "sound a withdraw! We will reform line 50 yards up the slope, and force the French guns to recalibrate. With all this smoke and debris, it will be awhile before they will have noticed our change in position."

Thomas rode up and down the line, shouting, "Withdraw, 50 yards!"

Captain Hare's quick decisiveness may have saved the day. The French guns continued to pound the field in front of them, unaware that they had moved to a position behind. The smoke and debris continued to block the Inniskillings from view. As it was, the regiment had already been reduced in number by one fifth. The guns eventually went silent. All up and down the line, those who were still standing tried to care for the fallen. The initial battering of the French artillery had taken its toll.

Thomas could sense that they had not heard the last of the guns. The artillery commander was merely allowing the smoke to clear and recalibrating the distance. "I think we need to be prepared to move again," he said to Captain Hare. "I believe those French guns will not be silent for long."

"You may be right, but we have orders to hold the line. We can't give up any more ground. We must stand and fight."

"Might I suggest, we move forward, slightly in front of our original position."

"I see what you mean," Captain Hare acknowledged. They were counting on the French having recalibrated, if so the cannons would be too long. "Give the order, at the first sign of the resumption of the guns, we move forward and form line 50 yards in front of our original position."

The Colonel

Moments later the ground erupted again, and more soldiers lay wounded and dying. Without hesitation the company commanders ordered their troops forward. It meant having to pass through the barrage of cannon fire, but as they reached their original position, they found the reprieve they were looking for as the artillery was now passing over head and exploding behind them. Unfortunately, Captain Hare was struck by shrapnel in the leg, leaving him incapacitated. A private who was standing nearby, was able to drag him to safety, but he could no longer stand and was not fit to command.

Thomas dismounted and knelt beside the Captain. "It seems I have taken a slight wound…" Hare said between grimaces. "I'm afraid I will be of no use to you now, it seems you will have to take over."

"But…" Thomas started to resist, but thought better of it. "Don't worry Captain Hare, you will be alright. We will have to carry on without you. Private, find the surgeon and have him brought to Captain Ware!" He shouted above the din of the incessant cannon explosions.

"Colonel!" A lieutenant nearby shouted, pointing to the south. Across the field, French cavalry had emerged and were heading straight for their present position. Through the haze of the cannon fire, the eagle emblazoned on a flag could be seen leading the fast approaching cuirassiers. They were trapped, cavalry in front and cannon balls exploding behind. They would have to stand and fight.

"Form square!" Thomas shouted at the top of his lungs. "Wounded to the center of the square, prepare for cavalry!"

Without hesitation, the entire regiment moved as one forming a square, four lines deep on each side. Bayonets had been affixed to the ends of their muskets, which were then pointed outward from the square, forming a nearly impenetrable defense. The outside line was on their knees, the second line bent, and the third and fourth standing erect. Thomas regained his mount and sat in the middle of the square, inspecting each side. They were ready.

To his left, standing in the middle of the square, Stewart remained, as if a bastion of defense, prepared to take on anyone who got too close to the commander. In the middle of the right side of the square, stood John Cullen, with James standing at his side, miraculously both were unscathed. Sergeant-Major McHugh was in front.

As the French cavalry drew within 50 yards, McHugh could be heard above everyone, "fire!" Those in the regiment who were standing let go a volley, horse and men fell to the ground, but the bulk of the cavalry came on. There was a horrible clash as horse and soldier came together, the front of the square taking the brunt of the charge. As those in front fell beneath the carnage, others moved forward to take their place. At first it seemed that the square would break beneath the assault. There was a small breech that allowed a couple horses to pass into the square. Thomas knocked the first from the saddle with one blow from his sword. Stewart dislodge the second with the butt of his musket. The breech closed and the square reformed, standing firm. At every turn, there was a fierce struggle to gain an advantage. The French cuirassiers had the upper hand, being on horse, but the Inniskillings fought bravely, failing to give an inch.

Time seemed to stand still. As Thomas looked around the square, it was as if everything had slowed down enough for him to see every movement, every clash of weapons, and every cry of anguish. The Inniskillings were fighting with a sense of urgency, defending the square at every station; as if every soldier knew that if he fell, the entire square would collapse. Each time a soldier fell, another took his place.

The French cavalry remained engaged until it was clear that they were not making any headway. The signal came for them to withdraw. The momentary pause, allowed the Inniskillings to assess the damage. The wounded were pulled back into the center of the square, where the surgeon was busy attending to their wounds. Although they had been able to hold their line, those who were still fit for battle, had been reduced to half in numbers. Captain Hare had been attended to, but he was unable to resume command. Captain Tucker had been wounded severely defending against the charge of the cavalry. Captains Smith and Holmes had both been killed by cannon fire, as had Lieutenant Fortescue. All told, every senior officer and been wounded or killed, but one. The only remaining officers were Thomas and one lieutenant. The companies were now left under the commands of sergeants, of whom McHugh and Cullen were still standing.

The cannon had stopped and the French cavalry remained at a distance. They would not remain there long. For the time being, they had managed to hold their ground, but he was certain the worst was yet to come. A quick assessment of supplies indicated they still had plenty of ammunition. The French would attack again and it would be prudent to give them a different target. Without hesitation, he shouted to those still standing to form line, two deep. He would trust the marksmanship of the fusiliers, while at the same time hope that the French cannon would remain silent. He rode up and down the line, shouting encouragement, reminding them to wait until they were given the order to fire. This time they would not wait for the French cavalry to draw close before offering some resistance. Those kneeling would fire first, followed by a second volley before the order would be given to reform square. All the training would now have to pay off. The range of the musket was limited to about 100 yards. This would leave them less than ten seconds to reform the square, and if they failed to do so, they would be cut to ribbons.

They stood waiting, Thomas' stallion prancing back and forth. "Steady men, they will come, but don't fire until ordered to do so. Be prepared to form square." The square was particularly affective in defending against the charge of a cavalry, but it limited the musket battery. Thomas was trying to take advantage of both. Fortunately, the cannon remained quiet.

Without warning, the French made another assault, this time in two waves. When the first wave reached one hundred yards, "Fire!" rang out up and down the line. This was followed almost immediately by, "form square!" The precision with which the Inniskillings made this maneuver, probably saved the battalion from being completely overrun. The first wave of the French cavalry was struck head on by the musket volley. The marksmanship of the Inniskillings was telling as the majority of the first wave of the assault were struck, horse and ride falling to earth. The square was formed just as the second wave of the cavalry attacked. Thomas shouted encouragement to the soldiers around him, "Stand Firm! All of England shall know of your courage today, and all of Ireland will sing ballads in your honor."

The Inniskillings were ready. Again there was a huge clash as the two combatants were thrust together. The fighting continued on for what seemed an eternity. At some point, Thomas was knocked from his mount and found himself back to back with Stewart, engaged in hand to hand combat with French soldiers who had broken through. He had lost awareness of what was going on around him. For the moment, he only had one thought, *survive!*

McHugh was given charge of the company of grenadiers at the front of the square. They were the strongest and best trained of the regiment. He continued to shout exhortations, reminding them who they were, and that they could stand against any foe. It seemed the French had gained a foothold when McHugh was struck in the shoulder by a lance. He fell to the ground, and was nearly trampled by a horse. Rolling beneath the horse, he stood up on the other side, pulled the lance from his shoulder and proceeded to launch it at the French soldier atop the horse. The cuirassiers was struck in the chest and fell back off the horse dead. McHugh gave a cry, "Faugh!" which seemed to invigorate the grenadiers, he began to fight with a new fury, driving the French back.

X.
"On! On!" was still his stern exclaim;

"Confront the battery's jaws of flame!
Rush on the leveled gun!
My steel-clad cuirassiers, advance!
Each Hulan forward with his lance,
My Guard--my Chosen--charge for France,
France and Napoleon!"
Loud answered their acclaiming shout,
Greeting the mandate which sent out
Their bravest and their best to dare
The fate their leader shunned to share.
But HE, his country's sword and shield,
Still in the battle-front revealed,
Where danger fiercest swept the field,
Came like a beam of light,
In action prompt, in sentence brief –
"Soldiers, stand firm!" exclaimed the Chief,
"England shall tell the fight!"

XI.
On came the whirlwind--like the last
But fiercest sweep of tempest-blast –
On came the whirlwind--steel-gleams broke
Like lightning through the rolling smoke;
The war was waked anew,
Three hundred cannon-mouths roared loud,
And from their throats, with flash and cloud,
Their showers of iron threw.
Beneath their fire, in full career,
Rushed on the ponderous cuirassier,
The lancer couched his ruthless spear,
And hurrying as to havoc near,
The cohorts' eagles flew.
In one dark torrent, broad and strong,
The advancing onset rolled along,
Forth harbingered by fierce acclaim,
That, from the shroud of smoke and flame,

Pealed wildly the imperial name.

XII.

But on the British heart were lost
The terrors of the charging host;
For not an eye the storm that viewed
Changed its proud glance of fortitude,
Nor was one forward footstep stayed,
As dropped the dying and the dead.
Fast as their ranks the thunders tear,
Fast they renewed each serried square;
And on the wounded and the slain
Closed their diminished files again,
Till from their line scarce spears'-lengths three,
Emerging from the smoke they see
Helmet, and plume, and panoply, -
Then waked their fire at once!
Each musketeer's revolving knell,
As fast, as regularly fell,
As when they practice to display
Their discipline on festal day.
Then down went helm and lance,
Down were the eagle banners sent,
Down reeling steeds and riders went,
Corslets were pierced, and pennons rent;
And, to augment the fray,
Wheeled full against their staggering flanks,
The English horsemen's foaming ranks
Forced their resistless way.
Then to the musket-knell succeeds
The clash of swords--the neigh of steeds –
As plies the smith his clanging trade,
Against the cuirass rang the blade;
And while amid their close array
The well-served cannon rent their way,
And while amid their scattered band

The Colonel

Raged the fierce rider's bloody brand,
Recoiled in common rout and fear,
Lancer and guard and cuirassier,
Horsemen and foot,--a mingled host
Their leaders fall'n, their standards lost.
The Fields of Waterloo
By Sir Walter Scott

John Cullen fought without abandon. His giant stature was unmatched by any member of the Inniskillings. One by one he was knocking Frenchmen from there mounts, and finishing the job when they hit the ground. One of the cuirassiers, rode at him from behind with a lance aimed at the middle of his back. Just before the sergeant met his doom, musket fire was heard, and he turned to see the cuirassiers fall from his horse, the lance falling harmlessly to the ground. Looking to his left, he saw the smiling face of James, "someone has to protect your back," the young man said, with a wry smile.

There was no telling how long it was before the French withdrew, leaving the Inniskillings standing on the very ground that they had occupied earlier in the day. They had failed to yield an inch. The cost was great.

Of the 750 soldiers who had entered the battle, 500 had been casualties, dead or wounded. Out of fifteen officers, only one had gone unblemished. Miraculously, Thomas, James, Stewart and John Cullen had all come through unharmed. Captain Hare, would survive, but was unconscious due to loss of blood. Roger McHugh, although wounded badly, would survive. Sadly, James best friend, John Boyle had been killed in the second cavalry assault.

Thomas stood silently gazing up and down the battle line to the east and then to the west. Across the field, lay the dead and wounded, some still struggling for life. His emotions were torn, he was relieved that his son had come through unharmed, no doubt to the heroics of John Cullen. He felt pride in the Inniskillings. To a man, they had fought with courage and

246

fortitude in the most difficult of circumstances. They had been unyielding, resolute in their duty. He was also distraught. There was such great loss. Many of the men who died this day were husbands and fathers, whose families would soon hear of their loss, never to see their loved one return from the war, and all because one man, in his pride and vanity, and sought to increase his power, and extend it beyond the limits of which any one man should aspire.

In the end, Wellington and the allied forces had won the day and brought to an end, once and for all, the rule of the emperor, Napolean. The center of Wellington's line would not yield and would not allow the French to pass, despite one assault after another. This defense was due in part to the unwavering fortitude of the 27th. Although the cost had been great, the entire battle may have turned on the valiant efforts of the Irish foot soldiers.

Not far away, Thomas noticed his son kneeling on the ground over a soldier, his friend, John Boyle. He walked over and gently put his hand on his son's shoulder. "He was a good soldier and a good friend, I am sorry for your loss," He said trying to offer some comfort to his son.

"He was the best of friends, and I will miss him," James looked up at his father, there were tears forming in the corner of his eyes. "Father, I didn't know it would be like this. I guess I never really understood what you had been through as a soldier. Your stories always seemed so exciting. I never understood that there was also pain in those experiences. Now I understand."

"A soldier carries many burdens, son. Not all of them are things he can share with others. You were young, too young to know the pain I had experienced. Your mother knows and that is enough. One thing I have learned is that you can't blame yourself. There was nothing you could do to save John. It is God who determines who should live or die, not the will of man. Look around, two thirds of the Inniskillings were casualties this day, and yet you and I stand here unharmed. This was not because we were the better soldier, it was merely the grace of God, nothing else."

"I understand…but I'm not sure this will bring comfort to John's mother," James bowed his head, looking at the ground. "What will I say to her?"

"There is nothing you can say to ease the pain a mother experiences at the loss of a child. Do you remember when young Alice died? Your mother was inconsolable. This is the nature of it. What you can tell her is how much you loved him, and how you grieve his loss. If she can't be consoled, she can at least find comfort in knowing that her son was a good man and a good friend. The memory of this is something she can hold in her heart, and someday it may even replace the pain. Come now, there are still others here who are living and in need of our aid. We can mourn the dead later, but for now let's try and bring comfort to the wounded."

The survivors of the 27th saw to their wounded and returned to their encampment. Thomas, Stewart, and John Cullen gathered at the Colonel's tent to discuss what would be done next, while James remained at the door as a guard. Captain Hare would survive, but his present condition would not allow him to resume command of the regiment anytime soon. In fact there, was no one prepared to take the responsibility. More problematic, was the fact that all who had been privileged to this conspiracy were either wounded, dead, or now sitting together in the tent. They were all at a loss. What were they supposed to do? Surely, Thomas could not continue with this ruse.

James entered, "There is someone coming, an officer I think," he said, rather nervously.

"Return to your post and announce the visitor properly," Thomas instructed. "And whatever you do, stay calm."

"Who do you think this is?" Cullen asked.

"I'm not sure, but we are about to find out," Thomas said, trying to act calm.

James returned, "Colonel Fremantle to see you sir," James announced as officially as he could. Thomas rose. Lieutenant

Colonel Fremantle was an Aid-de-Camp to General Wellington, and had been watching the battle from the command post.

Thomas stepped forward and shook the Colonel's hand, "Colonel, nice to see you. This is Sergeant Cullen and Sergeant Pogue, what can I do for you?"

"Gentleman," Colonel Fremantle gave a cursory bow to the other two. "Colonel Crichton, the Duke of Wellington has asked me to come to you directly, to convey his gratitude and pride for how your men handled themselves in the field today. He understands that your success came with great cost, but he also wants you to know that your efforts may in fact have been instrumental in saving the day. As a result, he would like the privilege of meeting you, and should you be available, he would like you to dine with him tomorrow night, at which time he will be able to personally convey his gratitude in this matter."

"That is very kind of the General, and I must say very generous..." It was at this moment Thomas paused and looked at both Stewart and John to see if there was any indication in their eyes concerning how he should respond.

"Very generous indeed, but I think ...that is I mean to say Colonel... that there is something you need to know." At this point John Cullen's shook his head slightly back and forth, suggesting that it was a bad idea to reveal anything, but Thomas had already begun, and there was no going back now. "Sir, I am not Colonel Crichton."

"What do you mean you're not Colonel Crichton? You are wearing the uniform and you are in his tent. Who in God's name are you then?" Colonel Fremantle was confused and growing irritated.

"My name is Thomas Rea, Corporal Thomas Rea, retired, sir. As to how I have come to be wearing this uniform, I think I would have to start by having you read this." He handed the letter to Fremantle that only twenty four hours earlier he had read for the first time.

The Colonel read, half grunting every few lines. "This is quite unbelievable, a Colonel in his majesty's army, deserting. It is unheard of, preposterous. You expect me to believe this," he said throwing the letter down onto the desk he now stood in front of.

"Preposterous to us as well, but just the same it did happen," Thomas explained. "And what's more, we became aware of it only yesterday. Rather than submit the regiment to the embarrassment of having their commander desert on the eve of battle, it was determined that we would proceed with the deception you now see before you. Please understand, that in no way was this deception for selfish gain, but was merely an attempt to preserve the morale and prestige of both the regiment and His Majesty's army."

"And who was aware of this deception...this impersonation?" Colonel Fremantle said with a scowl.

"Captain Hare, second in command, now lying in a bed in the hospital; Captain Tucker, Captain Smith, Sergeant-Major Roger McHugh all wounded in today's action and currently recovering; Captain Fortescue and Private John Boyle, both dead, and those you see present here. To be honest, we were just discussing what we are to do next. Clearly we had no intention of maintaining this ruse beyond this moment."

"I see. This is a bit of predicament. Impersonating an officer in the British army is still a criminal offense, but given the circumstances and those who were part of this confidence, it is clear that the intentions were at least honorable...I would agree that what to do now, is a most curious problem. For the moment, I imagine you can understand that it would be inappropriate for you to attend dinner with the Duke tomorrow night. However, leaving the regiment without a leader, at a time when they have suffered such loss would seem imprudent..." The Colonel paused for a moment in thought.

After this brief pause, gathering his thoughts, he continued, "If I may make the following suggestion or perhaps I should say request. Can I ask you to maintain this deception for a little while longer? At least until I have an opportunity to discuss it with the Duke. Sit tight and remain as the acting commander of the 27th, until you hear back from me. Do you think you could do this?"

Thomas was quite dumbfounded. This was not the response he had expected. He hesitated for a moment, but there was clearly no alternative. He would have to stay with the Inniskillings a while longer, at least until they could figure out how to reestablish leadership for the regiment. "I will do it," he said, after his momentary reflection. "But please understand, I have no motivation here, other than to protect the integrity and reputation of the Inniskillings. As soon as this situation can be resolved, I will gladly step out of this role. Might I suggest, as soon as Captain Hare is well, that he should be given command of the regiment."

"This sounds reasonable, but as I have said, I must confer with the Duke. It seems we have here a very unusual set of circumstances. You shall hear from me shortly with further instructions. In the meantime, I will stop by and check on Captain's Hare progress and inform him of my confidence in this matter. Thank you for a very interesting visit, gentlemen." Colonel Fremantle rose and left the tent, leaving Thomas Stewart and John, each of them deep in thought, trying to come to grips with what had just been said.

"Well I guess that's that," Cullen said rather nonchalantly. "It seems we must continue to refer to you as Colonel Cricthton, at least for the moment."

"It seems so." Thomas said. He was deep in thought, wondering how he was ever going to explain this all to Alice.

Chapter Nineteen

[11] The race is not to the swift or the battle to the strong,
Nor does food come to the wise or wealth to the brilliant or favor
to the learned; but time and chance happen to them all.

(June 19, 1815)

The following afternoon, Thomas and Stewart visited the makeshift hospital to check on the wounded soldiers. McHugh had taken a lance in the shoulder, but was recovering nicely. Captain Hare had been wounded in the leg, and had lost a lot of blood, but was now awake and sitting up in bed, although in a weakened state he was well on his way to mending.

"Hello gentleman, it is good see you are still standing," Captain Ware greeted. "I don't suppose you would be able to give a report, that is, if you wouldn't mind."

Thomas knew exactly what he meant, "We were able to hold our line, but at great cost, 105 dead, including Captain Fortescue, and 373 wounded, including Captain's Smith and Tucker and every lieutenant, but one. There remain 220 who are fit for service."

"And it seems, this number includes you as well. I must say that I had imagined the two of you would have been long gone by now."

"Beggin' your pardon Captain Hare, but given the circumstances it seemed proper that we should stay, at least until you were able to resume command, or until some other arrangements could be made. We couldn't very well abandon the Inniskillings, especially with all the officers here in bed, recovering."

"And your son, is he well?" Captain Hare asked.

"Yes, sir, thanks to the efforts of Sergeant Cullen, he came through without a scratch."

"Or perhaps, thanks be to God, since anything could have happened in that chaos," Hare offered.

"Yes, sir," Thomas replied.

"Well gentleman, I suppose it is up to us to decide what to do now, or should I say, it is up to you. I was paid a visit by Colonel Fremantle this morning. He informed me that he had already spoken with you and that you managed to spill the beans." Thomas was about to offer up an apology, but the Captain waved him off. "No, no, don't worry. It had to come out in the end. He further informed me that the General is desirous of keeping this thing quiet for the time being. It seems he knows Colonel Crichton's father, and would like to find a way to tell him the news himself. Given the losses suffered by the 27th, the General has ordered the regiment to return to Ireland. He is asking that you remain in command, that is to continue this deception, at least until the Inniskillings are back home, at which time command will be transferred into my hands, assuming I'm recovered by then. In any case, we are to report back to Enniskillen and await further orders."

"But surely once we return to Enniskillen, we shall be found out. Someone is sure to recognize that I am not Colonel Crichton," Thomas suggested.

"Don't be so sure. Crichton was not a very public figure, and I think that we can keep you out of sight long enough to accomplish the task. I'm sure it will only be for a few days, or at the most a few weeks. I don't think there is anyone who could tell the difference between the two of you, especially at a distance."

"I can think of one," Stewart whispered in Thomas' ear.

"What about my wife? I'm quite sure she'll notice, when I don't return home." Thomas asked.

"Of course, she will have to be brought in on it. We couldn't very well expect you to deceive your own wife. I'm sure she will be able to keep a secret, once she understands the importance of it."

The Colonel

There was no getting around it. The decision had already been made. Thomas would have to return to Enniskillen playing the role of the Colonel. It seemed unlikely that they would be successful in keeping up this deception, but there seemed to be little other choice. No one was about to reveal the truth, especially at the moment the British army was celebrating so momentous a victory.

"Don't look so disheartened, Thomas, or should I say Colonel Crichton. After all, in the end you will have accomplished your objective, you will have returned home safely with your son. I'm sure, once it is all over, this will be the only thing that really matters," Stewart said as they were leaving the hospital.

"I suppose you're right, Stew, but it is not exactly how I had envisioned it. I had hoped to spare Alice the knowledge that her son had actually been involved in any kind of fighting, but I am afraid it is unavoidable now."

The next few days were spent tending to the wounded and packing up the camp for transport. Given the number who had been injured, Colonel Fremantle had made provision for wagons that would help provide transport to the coast where they would find ships to take them home to Ireland. Even with the wagons the journey was slow going. Many of the wounds were severe enough, that there was a fear of losing soldiers in transport. Thomas made it very clear that the wounded would be given every privilege and no man would be left behind. It was two weeks before they reached the port of Cork.

They remained barracked in Cork for another two weeks. The ocean voyage had taken its toll on those who were in a weakened state. Thomas would not allow the regiment to continue its journey until all were fit for travel. Given a moments rest, he decided to send a letter off to Alice. It was difficult to find the words to express what had happened.

August 4, 1815

Dear Alice,

254

It has been more than a month since I left you to find James. Know that both of us are safe and are now on our way home. We are traveling home with the 27th. Expect us soon. It is all I can write for now.

I love you, and James sends his love as well.

Thomas

It was short and to the point, and would calm her fears. He wanted to write more, but he just didn't know where to begin. It would be better to share everything in person.

The Inniskillings would remain in Cork for another two weeks. By the time they were ready to travel north to Enniskillen, news had already begun to circulate that they had been heroic at Waterloo, saving the center of Wellington's line and saving the day. As they passed from village to village on their way home, onlookers would take to the streets and cheer them on. It was becoming clear, it would be difficult for the Inniskillings to enter Enniskillen discretely and therefore have Thomas escape detection.

On the final leg of their journey, Thomas pushed them on to arrive at night, hoping that the darkness would provide him with some cover. As they arrive in Enniskillen, lights came on in the shops as they moved through the main street, and the citizens came out to see the heroes returned home. They passed through town and made their way straight to the Castle barracks. Thomas and Stewart were alone in the Colonel's office, the rest of the regiment settled in, when a knock came at the door.

Stewart rose and opened the door. To his surprise, he found John Trimble (Alice's brother-in-law) standing at the door. "Stewart, good to see you, I'm wondering if you could direct me to Thomas, no one seems to know where he is and I have a matter most urgent."

Stewart, stepped aside and allowed John to enter the office. Thomas rose, "John, what are you doing here?"

John Trimble looked at Thomas with confusion written across his face. He hadn't expected to find him in the Colonel's office, and certainly not in the Colonel's uniform. "I...I don't quite understand... the uniform..."

"It's a long story, John. I'll tell you in good time. Why have you come? Is there something wrong?"

Regaining his composure, a solemn look came across his face. "I have been sent here to fetch you home. I'm afraid I bring you sad news, horrible news..." He could barely continue. "Alice, your wife, she's dead. She died of an infection after giving birth to your son, eight days ago. We have been trying to contact you, but had no way of knowing exactly where you were. I'm so sorry, Thomas."

Thomas fell back into the nearest chair, placing his face in his hands. "How can this be? My Alice, is she really gone?"

Stewart walked over to his friend and placed his hand on his friend's shoulders. "I'm so sorry, my friend. This is a horrible tragedy and quite unexpected." Tears were forming at the edges of his eyes. "We all loved her."

"I am sorry, Thomas, that I had to be the bearer of such news, but I have come to bring you home. Your children need their father," John said.

"Of course...you're right," Thomas said, tears streaming down his cheeks. "I must go home. Stewart, would you fetch James, he must be made aware. We shall leave at once."

It was night and so no one saw the four men leave on horseback. Once they crossed the south bridge out of town, Thomas kicked his mount into a gallop, the others followed. They rode hard and fast through the night, everything passing in a blur. As they arrived at the Rea home, Thomas jumped from his mount and in one bound was on the porch and then through the front door. Next to the fire sat Maggie, gently rocking a baby in her arms.

"Hello Thomas, welcome home," she rose and stepped toward him. "This is John, your new son," she held the baby out to him.

Thomas took the baby in his arms, tears welling in eyes again. "Thank you Maggie for being here. Tell me, what happened."

"Of course," Maggie said, "please sit down and I will tell you everything." Stewart and John Trimble sat down as well. "Your son was born on the 5th of August. It was a difficult birth, Alice was in great pain, and when it was over she had lost a lot of blood. Right from the start, the doctor was concerned. The birth had left her in a highly weakened state. A day later she developed a very bad fever. She had an infection, and she was in a very bad way. For three more days she fought with all she had, but she did not have the strength. In the end she succumbed and the Lord took her home from this place. The day before she expired she received you're note from Cork. For the moment it seemed to give her strength. She so much wanted to see you again. But it was not to be, he spirit was willing to live on, but in the end the strain on her body had been too great. Here was her reply to your letter. We had no idea where to send it." She handed him a letter.

August 7th, 1815

Dearest Thomas,

I have received your news and my heart is overjoyed that you and James are safe. I knew that you would not fail me. I have given birth to another son, I named him John. I hope you will like this name. It seems the birth was too much for me, and I am now not long for this world. It grieves me that I will not be able to see you again before I leave, but I rest in knowing that you are safe and will return home to care for our children. It saddens me that I will not be there to watch them all grow, but I count my blessings, for God has blessed me greatly with the days he has granted.

Know that I love you beyond measure, and I do not regret one moment of our life together. Take care of our children in my absence. They need you now more than ever.

Say goodbye to James for me, and let him know how proud I am of him.

Goodbye my love,

Alice

Thomas could barely read the lines as tears filled his eyes. Over and over he read, as if reading it again, might change the outcome. How could Alice be gone? It was unthinkable. All the years he had served as a soldier, it had never once occurred to him that Alice might not be there when he returned. He was the one at risk, not her. How would he go on? How could he be both father and mother to his children? What would he do without her at his side? What dreams could he now dream?

"The children?" He finally asked, in a soft voice.

"They're all asleep, Thomas, but they will be overjoyed to see you. They have missed you so much," Maggie said.

Thomas rose and handed Maggie the baby. He then walked out of the room and into the night. He wanted to be alone. He needed to sort out how he was feeling and what he was thinking. He looked down at the uniform he was wearing, reminded of his predicament. Stewart walked up behind him.

"I'm deeply saddened for you, Thomas. I wish I knew what to say, what to do," Stewart tried to console his friend.

"I know Stewart. There is really nothing that can be said. We all loved her. She was a beacon of light in our world. We will all miss her...You must go home, Bella will be grieving as well, she loved her so. She will need you now, more than ever. Go to her, and kiss for me. Go friend, it is time for me to be alone."

Tears had now formed in Stewart's eyes as well, remembering the friendship shared by Alice and his wife. He embraced his friend and then left him alone. Thomas remained on the porch, reflecting, wondering what he must do next.

Thomas rose early the next morning, just as the sun was emerging from the hills to the east. Not far from the house, in the corner of the field he found the cross that marked Alice's grave. As he stood over the grave, he remembered the first moment he had met her, that summer afternoon, as she sat on the seat of her father's farm wagon, the sun glistening off her red trusses. He couldn't take his eyes off of her, she was captivating. What was more amazing, even as he had caught himself staring, he found that she had been staring right back at him.

"Alice, my love, why did you have to go?" he said softly as he looked down at the cross. "I'm so sorry I was not here, I do miss you so. How do I walk through life, without you at my side? How can I be both Father and Mother to our children? I know I must let you go, but I'm afraid. For the first time in my life, I am really afraid. Goodbye, sweet Alice. I will hold you in my heart."

James found his father standing over the grave. "Aunt Margaret says that it's time breakfast, Father. She was wondering if you were joining us."

"I will be along, I was saying goodbye to your mother," he turned and looked at his son. "How are doing, son?"

"I do not know what to say or think. She was so young, I never expected that she would not be here when I came home...I'm so sorry Father," James began to cry. "It's all my fault...if I had not left, you would not have had to follow...you should have been here, she shouldn't have died alone."

"Ease yourself son. It isn't your fault any more than it is mine. You were chasing your dreams, no one can fault you for that. We do not understand these things, only God does. He has his own timing. It is not for us to understand it. It is what it is. Now come, let's go and bring comfort to your siblings. They will have missed us."

One by one the children came to embrace their father as they arrived for breakfast. Janey and little Maggie held on to him for the longest time, not wanting to let go, almost as if they were afraid he would leave again and never come back. "Now, now Janey and Maggie, your father has come home, ne'er to leave again. Don't fret now."

Turning to Alice's sister, "Margaret, I can't thank you enough for caring for the children in my absence. It gives me great peace to know they have been well looked after."

"It has been my pleasure. They are my sister's children and I will not abandon them to others."

Thomas had always been curious as to why Margaret had never married. She was attractive enough, and a pleasant sort. There had been suitors, of course, but evidently none had been the right one. "I wonder if I can bother you to watch them for a while longer?" he asked.

"I was wondering about the uniform. What have you gone and done?"

Thomas went on to explain all that had happened, how he had been talked into impersonating Colonel Crichton and what had happened at Waterloo and how the Inniskillings had been heroic, but at a great cost. "So you see, I must stay with the Inniskillings a little while longer. At least until Captain Hare can resume command. Even now I have been gone for too long. It would be important to keep up appearances, so that no one becomes suspicious."

"I can watch the children, of course, but do you really think you can keep up this pretense. After all, someone is sure to recognize you."

"It is true, but we must at least try. It will be alright," he tried to be reassuring even though he was not so sure himself."

Chapter Twenty

⁵ As you do not know the path of the wind,
or how the body is formed in a mother's womb,
so you cannot understand the work of God,
the Maker of all things.

It had been two weeks since the Inniskillings had returned to Enniskillen. Thus far, none had questioned the identity of the Colonel. Captain Hare was mending nicely and would soon be able to return to duty. A letter had arrived from London indicating that they would be visited by Colonel Fremantle, as soon as he was able. Thomas was beginning to feel a sense of relief. It would soon all be over. Then one morning, he was surprised by an unexpected visitor.

Thomas could hear shouting from outside the office. "I insist on seeing Colonel Cricthon, this very moment," it was a woman's voice. "I have an important matter to discuss with him."

"But miss, the Colonel has asked not to be disturbed."

"I hardly think such an order applies to me, I insist you let me see him this very moment," at this the door flung open and Miss Ann Hardinge burst through.

"I'm sorry Sir, this young lady has insisted upon seeing you," the young corporal who was attending the door was red faced.

"It's alright Corporal. She is here now. You may leave," Thomas tried to sound calm, but his heart was racing. He had almost forgotten that Colonel Crichton was engaged, and that his fiancée was sure to call on him at some point.

"Mr. Crichton, or should I say Colonel Crichton, I find it difficult to understand how you could have returned more than a fortnight past, and yet you have not tried to contact me, nor made any attempt to visit me." Amazingly, she didn't seem to realize that she was not talking to the real Robert Crichton.

"Miss Hardinge," he was searching for the words, "I'm sure you can appreciate the responsibility of a commander so soon returned from war. I'm sorry if my business as a soldier has inconvenienced you." He tried to put a little sting into the last few words, as he thought Robert Crichton would have done.

"Am I to understand that we are engaged, and that our marriage is forthcoming," she was getting right to the point. "Or have you reconsidered. If so, I wish to hear it now."

"I gather from your forthrightness, that you still have every intention to marry me. Is this your desire, after all?" He tried to sound distant and cold.

"It matters not what I desire, but only what has been promised. A promise I expect you shall want to keep. It is desired by your father and by my grandmother. As for me, it matters little what I want, only that I should not have to face the ridicule of being embarrassed publically by the announcement of a promise that was never intended to be kept." Thomas was beginning to wonder if she was arguing for or against the marriage; it was becoming difficult to tell. She continued, "I have come here to ask that you settle on a date, so that our families might finally be at peace."

"I see..." Thomas hesitated. He wasn't sure what to do. He couldn't very well break off the engagement without giving some sort of reason. He couldn't suggest a date, only causing the young girl more pain. She deserved better than that. "Perhaps you could give me some time to think about it." It seemed a curious response, but it was the best he could do. The reality was, he needed some time to think. Should he tell her who he really was? Should she be brought into his confidence? He wasn't sure.

"Very well, as long as I have your assurance," she said. "I will return here one week from today to receive your answer. Good day." With that she turned around and marched right out of the office the same way she had marched in.

Thomas fell back into his chair. He could hardly believe what just happened. He couldn't wait to tell Stewart. He was sure his friend would find the whole thing quite amusing. How was it that she didn't recognize him? Did she know her fiancée so little that she could not tell the difference? He was in shock.

That afternoon he went to visit Captain Hare. "This is an unfortunate turn of events," were the first words out of the Captain's mouth. "We can't very well tell her the truth without the Earl finding out, and I don't think Wellington would want any of this to get out until they have had the opportunity to inform the Earl themselves. We have to wait until Fremantle arrives. Do you think you can put off this Miss Hardinge until then?"

"I'm not sure; she seems quite determined. I will try of course, but I may have to bring her into our confidence. It may be the only way. In any case it seems strange that she didn't recognize me, even though we had only met briefly, twice before. Even more, I'm wondering what happened to the real Robert Crichton. Did he return home? Perhaps his father already knows the truth."

"I doubt very much if he returned home. He would know that prison, or even worse, would be in his future if he were ever caught. I don't think the Earl would harbor him in any case. He would understand the implications. If he were aware of his son's actions, he would distance himself. No, I think we can assume that Crichton fled the continent. Perhaps went to Africa, or maybe the Americas. There is nothing left for him here."

"I suppose you're right," Thomas said. "It just seems a strange thing. We haven't heard anything of him. As for Miss Hardinge, I may be able to put her off, but I must admit, that I'm uncomfortable deceiving her. She was a friend of my wife, and is still a friend to Bella Pogue. I'm sorry she has to be involved in all of this."

The week passed, but Ann Hardinge did not show. Instead a footman from Belle Isle arrived with a note addressed to Colonel Crichton. Thomas opened it and red it as the footman remained.

The Colonel

Sir,

When last we spoke, we had come to an agreement that a date should be settled upon for our upcoming marriage. An unfortunate circumstance has not allowed for me to visit you on this day. Please accept my humble apology. As a way of making recompense, I invite you to Belle Isle two days hence, so that we can settle this matter amicably. I will expect you around 2:00 PM.

You may send your return answer with Mr. Jones.

Your servant,

Ann Hardinge

Thomas didn't know what to think, let alone how to respond. He read the note again. It was a strange correspondence, so cold and distant. Nothing like one would expect between two who were engaged to be married. It was almost as if Ann was hoping that Robert Crichton would reject her. He looked up at the footman, and realized he had to give an answer.

"Tell Miss Hardinge, that I will be happy to accept her invitation and I will be there on time, two days from now." Thomas didn't feel he could refuse. He would have to face the music.

"Very well, Colonel Crichton, I will give her your message." Mr. Jones promptly turned and left without another word.

The day came. Thomas saddled his horse himself and slipped away. Only Captain Hare and his assistant were aware of his absence. He rather enjoyed the ride to Belle Isle. He kept his horse at a leisurely walk. It was only a five mile journey, and he enjoyed the solitude, being alone with his thoughts. He still was not sure what he was going to do or say. He thought he could suggest a date, but make it far enough in the future, allowing plenty of time to cancel when it seemed prudent. If only he could think of a good reason for breaking off the engagement, it would be much simpler. He could tell Ann the truth, if only he were sure that Colonel Fremantle would agree that this was the right course of action. Unfortunately he had promised to continue the deception, until such a time that Fremantle released him from his promise and as of yet he had not heard from him.

When he arrived at Belle Isle, Jones greeted him at the door and then led him into the drawing room. "Miss Hardinge shall join you shortly, Sir." He was left alone.

A few moments later, Jones reentered the room, followed by Bella, Stewart and Ann Hardinge. Thomas was in shock, what were Bella and Stewart doing here? The two of them seemed just as surprised, as they looked at Thomas, then at each other, and then back at Thomas. "Well, Colonel Crichton, what a surprise. We did not expect to see you here," Stewart said.

"Mr. and Mrs. Pogue, isn't it," Thomas tried to sound composed, although even his greeting, his tone of voice, was too personal to sound anything like Robert Crichton.

Before any of them could say anything else, Ann interjected, "I think it's about time for someone to tell me what is going on here."

"Why Ann, whatever do you mean?" Bella tried to sound convincing.

"What do I mean? I think you know what I mean. Ten days ago I make a visit to see the man I believe I am going to marry, and who should I find, but Thomas Rea sitting where Colonel Crichton should have been, in the Colonel's uniform no less."

"Then you knew the whole time," Thomas said, embarrassment written all over his face. "I thought it strange that you didn't recognize me."

"Of course, I knew," Ann continued, showing her contempt. "Do you take me for a fool? Of course, I couldn't let on, only because I couldn't imagine what would have prompted you to impersonate the Colonel. What has happened? Is he dead or something?"

"No one would ever take you for a fool, Ann. Please don't think that we would ever willingly deceive you, but we were left no choice. Please let Thomas and Stewart explain," Bella was apologetic for the group.

"It's true, Ann, we didn't want to hurt you, or deceive you. It was an unfortunate circumstance that brought us to this place. A circumstance that was the direct result of a decision made by Robert Crichton," Thomas began. "Now please sit down, so I can explain what has happened, and please know that none of us wish to cause you any more pain." Ann relented and took a seat, Bella sat next to her as a symbol of support.

Thomas related the entire story, how Robert Crichton had deserted on the eve of battle and how a conspiracy was formed to protect the morale and integrity of the regiment. Then, how Wellington himself insisted that the deception be maintained until such a time Captain Hare could take command of the regiment. "So you see, Ann, it was never intended that you should be deceived in this matter, in fact it was an oversight on our part, forgetting of the marriage contract that had been made between Colonel Crichton and yourself. For this, we are most profoundly sorry."

Ann stayed silent, pondering all that she had heard. "And what of Robert Crichton, do we know what has become of him?"

"No, Ann. That remains a mystery. It appears he has fled the continent. It's likely that we shall never see him again."

"I take this to mean that I have been released from my promise of marriage," she said rather stoically.

"Sadly, this is true," Thomas said. "I am sorry to be the bearer of this news."

"Oh Ann," Bella interrupted, "I can't believe that you ever had any real feelings for Robert. You can't be saddened by this news."

"It's true, Bella. It's no secret that I wasn't in love with Mr. Crichton. However, I had resigned myself to the fate, and now I find myself wondering what is to become of me. I found some satisfaction in knowing my future, even if it included a marriage of convenience. I would have been content, raising my children in the security of Belle Isle. Joining our house with the Earl of Erne would insure the future of the Belle Isle. Now this future is uncertain."

Thomas interjected, "If I may suggest, Miss Hardinge, you are an intelligent and attractive young woman. I would not give up Belle Isle anytime soon. It seems to me that you shall attract other opportunities, if you so desire. Given that the true character of Mr. Crichton has now been revealed, I think you should consider yourself fortunate that you weren't bound to this man."

Bella placed her hand on Ann's shoulders, "this is true Ann. Don't be discouraged, this should be seen as a blessing in disguise."

Ann smiled, "I will try to see it this way, Bella. In any case, and now that I understand the circumstances, I am pleased to discover that you would not have willingly deceived me. It would have been a far greater pain should I lose you as a friend...As for you, Thomas Rea, I was almost determined to carry out this deception and trap you into marrying me, just out of spite. I certainly would have it had not been for my respect for your dearly departed Alice...Please accept my deepest sympathies. She was a kind spirit, and we shall all miss her. Merely out of my fondness for her, I will accept your apology and forgive you this one time."

"Thank you on both counts, Miss Hardinge. Alice was fond of you as well, and confided in me on more than one occasion that she was distressed that you were marrying Robert Crichton. I'm afraid she didn't like him at all. I can't help but think that she would be embarrassed to know that I have been forced to impersonate the man."

"Well I think we are all agreed, none of us liked the man," Stewart spoke for the first time. "Now, is anyone else hungry?"

"Stewart!" Bella scolded.

The Colonel

"No, Bella, he is quite right. I think it is time to eat." Ann then rang the bell for Jones.

*****

Two weeks later, Colonel Fremantle arrived. Thomas, Stewart, John Cullen, Roger McHugh and Captain John Hare were all assembled, each having knowledge of the incident, and each having his part to play. Much to everyone's surprise, Colonel Fremantle didn't come alone, but instead was accompanied by Lady Mary Crichton.

"Good afternoon gentleman, thank you for seeing me. I am sure you weren't expecting Lady Crichton, however, I have just come from Castle Crom, and as I am sure you will understand, she has an interest in this matter," Fremantle explained.

"Then you have met with the Earl and explained to him the situation?" Captain Hare asked.

"No, not exactly. Lady Mary has been brought into our confidence, however, due to circumstances which shall soon become more clear, we have refrained from telling the Earl anything."

"I trust that we have come to some sort of resolution, and that he will have to be told. I can't see carrying on this charade for much longer," Thomas insisted.

"A resolution has been suggested, but there are some particulars, that must be worked out, assuredly. Please let me explain...I am sure that everyone assembled here can understand the delicate nature of this situation. It is unprecedented that a senior officer in the British Military would desert his post in wartime, let alone on the eve of battle. It poses a serious embarrassment, at a time when we have just celebrated a most important victory over the French and their supposed emperor. I hope that you can all understand the importance of keeping this matter quiet, especially given that we

268

have been able to restrict the knowledge of this event to those few assembled here and General Wellington, himself."

Everyone in the room nodded in agreement as Fremantle continued. "The General has instructed me to offer the following resolution, in hopes that everyone here would be in agreement, and support it without question. First of all, it is suggested that the event in question never happened. The roll call for the Battle at Waterloo shall be altered such that Captain John Hare shall be listed as the commander in charge of the 1/27th of Foot, and any record of a Lieutenant Colonel Robert Crichton shall be stricken from the military record. This is easily accomplished, since Colonel Crichton had, shall we say, a very brief military record. The record shall also show, due to his heroic action at Waterloo and the courageous defense of the center of the line by the 27th, Captain John Hare shall be promoted to Lieutenant Colonel and shall be given command of the regiment, to take place immediately. I have a letter to such effect in my possession even now, signed by the General and the Adjutant."

"Thank you sir, that is most generous, but what of Thomas?" Captain Hare asked.

"Of course, please let me finish. I will get to Mr. Rea in due time. The record shall show that the actions of the 27th were both courageous and heroic and as per your recommendations, medals shall be given to several of its members. As to Mr. Rea, or should I say, Corporal Rea, it can't be overlooked the level of sacrifice you have made in the most difficult of circumstances, especially at a time in which you were mourning the loss of your wife, a fact of which I have only recently become aware. Although we can't officially grant you an officer's commission in the British army, since you are no longer enlisted, we can offer you the same privileges granted to such a commission and a promise from the Crown to provide you with a reward which has yet to be determined. I in fact, have a letter stating this very thing in my possession as well."

"Now we come to a matter, I find a little more delicate, one in which I think I will have Lady Mary speak, if she would be so kind. It is important, Corporal Rea, that you understand this comes in the form of a request, and should not be taken to be a manipulation of any kind. Admittedly, it is a most unusual request. Lady Mary, would you please explain?"

"Of course, thank you Colonel Fremantle, and thank you gentleman for allowing me to be here," Lady Mary began. She continued, "I am sure you are all aware of how damaging this incident is to the Crichton family and how devastating the news would be to my husband, the Earl. What you may not know is that the Earl is in very poor health, he has lost his eyesight entirely and age is catching up with his body. The Colonel, at my request, chose not to tell the Earl of the betrayal of his youngest son, knowing that it would serve to create distress, and perhaps negatively impact his already declining health. For this I am very grateful, for Robert has proven to be a source of great pain for my husband and it would be my desire to see him spared any further pain, if at all possible. This is where we come to a special request of you, Thomas. It seems, we would have no difficulty keeping the Earl from knowledge of this circumstance, but for one simple thing. You see, the Earl and his son were quite distant from each other, and it was not uncommon for them to remain apart for months, even years at a time. However, there is the matter of the promised marriage of Robert Crichton to Ann Hardinge. The Earl has been anticipating this wedding and would certainly attend."

Thomas didn't like where this was going. He was beginning to grow uneasy and nearly interrupted.

Lady Mary continued, "It is proposed that the marriage continue as planned, if Thomas would be willing to stand in for Robert Crichton. You see, the Earl is completely blind, and the guests list could be rather limited, and it would not be difficult to maintain the deception a while longer, for I fear the Earl is not long for this world. It should also be understood, that this marriage is a marriage of convenience, and no other expectation comes with it. However, this suggestion is not made lightly, realizing that both parties have to be agreed. But let me suggest, that such an arrangement would not only protect the Earl, but would prove to also be highly beneficial to both Mr. Rea and Miss Hardinge."

"I think I must stop you there," Thomas could not remain silent any longer. "With all due respect, Lady Mary, I understand your desire to protect the welfare of your husband and the Crichton name, however, I can't imagine how this is beneficial either to myself or Ann Hardinge. For that matter, what makes you think the girl in question would ever agree to such an arrangement. I mean, what do you think she is going to say to all of this? It's preposterous!"

"I suppose we should ask her this very thing. The lady in question, at our request, is waiting just outside. We can bring her in and you can put the question to her directly," Lady Mary was quite calm, and too confident for Thomas' liking.

Colonel Fremantle rose from his seat and opened the door, inviting Miss Hardinge to enter. The others in the room remained quiet, each grappling with what they had just heard in their own way. Stewart had a wry smile on his face, almost as if he was enjoying seeing his friend placed in such a precarious position.

Ann Hardinge took a seat, Lady Mary addressed her, "Ann, Thomas here wants to know what you think about all this, the proposed marriage and any benefits that you might find in such an arrangement."

Ann hesitated, looking as if she were a little frightened of the large group that was gathered. She turned and faced Thomas directly. "I'm sorry to have placed you in such an embarrassing situation Mr. Rea, but Lady Mary and myself have discussed this arrangement in detail, and it is important that you know up front that I am fully supportive, however, at the same time I have had great doubts that you would ever submit to such an arrangement."

"You would agree to maintain such a deception, agree to marry a man you hardly know, but why? I don't understand this, what could possibly be gained?" Thomas' head was spinning by this time. He just wanted to run from the room and never look back.

"You forget, Mr. Rea, I had already resigned myself to marry a man I did not know, a marriage of convenience, not of love. If you look at it from my position, very little has changed, only, if you don't mind my saying so, I would have much less to fear in this proposal, since you are clearly a man of greater integrity and virtue, than Mr. Crichton. In that sense, my position has improved. Lady Mary as assured me, and I trust her word in this matter, that the Earl will remain committed to preserving Belle Isle as long as I consent to marry his son, and in his eyes or shall we say heart, this is what will be so."

Thomas looked at Ann and could see in her eyes that she was completely at peace with her decision, even hopeful, a hope that was hanging on his decision. Before he could say anything, she continued, "As for you, Thomas, if you don't mind me calling you by your Christian name, I believe there might be some benefits to you as well. First of all, please know that I have no expectation beyond the legal nature of this arrangement. I do not expect you to love me or that our marriage will be complete. However, consider the benefits for your family, for your children. After we are married, I would expect that your children would come and reside with us at Belle Isle. Besides the change in station, they would also gain the benefits of education and position. Imagine the possibilities. And although I could never replace their mother, who I consider my friend, I would care for them as my own, and they would enjoy all the prosperity that Belle Isle can offer. Please consider this."

Thomas was thinking about it. It was almost beginning to make sense, but in the back of his mind, he couldn't let go of how crazy it all seemed. What would Alice have thought of all this. Of course, if she had not died, none of this would even have been possible. The whole thing seemed ridiculous. What was he going to do? "I don't even know what to say. This whole thing still seems quite preposterous. I mean really a marriage of convenience. I don't even know what to think."

"It does seem a strange circumstance, Mr. Rea, I agree," Colonel Fremantle interjected. "Although a very amicable arrangement, it is difficult to get past the unconventionality. I don't think we could expect you to absorb all of this in one sitting. Perhaps you need some time with it. Go home and spend time with your family. I'm sure that Lady Mary and Miss Hardinge would expect no less."

"Of course, the Colonel is right," Lady Mary agreed. "This is not a simple request, and we would not insult you by forcing you to make a rash decision. Take your time. Only, I must return to Castle Crom ten days from now, I will be staying at Belle Isle. It would be most gracious of you if you could have a decision by then. Please know, Thomas, I would be deeply in your debt. To spare my husband this pain, would be a great service, one I could never repay."

"Then that settles, it," Colonel Fremantle concluded the meeting. "Colonel Hare is now in command of the 27th, Thomas Rea, you are relieved of any further duty, and free to return to your family. Lady Mary will await your decision, not more than ten days from now, and I will await her communication until then. I am afraid I must return to London, and so I will say my goodbyes to you all. Let me remind you all, this meeting has never taken place, and I am counting on all of you to never speak of it again."

Chapter Twenty One

*[16] No one can comprehend what goes on under the sun.
Despite all his efforts to search it out,
Man cannot discover its meaning. Even if a wise man
claims he knows, He cannot really comprehend it.*

Thomas was sitting on the porch in front of his home, watching his two girls playing in the grass, not far away. John was sleeping in a cradle next to him. He used his foot to gently rock the cradle. Isaac was inside, no doubt tormenting his aunt. James had taken his two younger brothers fishing. James had been more attentive to his siblings since returning home, perhaps a carryover from the guilt he felt over leaving. He was a good son, and would grow into a fine man; he had the right kind of heart. The battle at Waterloo had changed, made him grow up a little faster than he should.

It was good to be home, but Thomas missed Alice greatly. It was not the same without her. She had been his companion and friend, his soul mate. It was nice that Margaret was willing to help out from time to time, but she was not someone he could talk to. She was reserved, not prone to emotional transparency, nothing like her sister.

Tomorrow he would have to go to Belle Isle. He still didn't know what he was going to do. He could see the benefit to his children, but would they accept his decision? Would they want to live at Belle Isle? The two girls would go, they were too young to know any different, as for Isaac and John it was the same. But what about James and Willie, would they go willingly? What would they think of their father remarrying after so short a time? Would they understand?

As he sat musing, he noticed a carriage coming down the lane toward the house. It was Stewart and Bella, come to pay a visit. He stood as they arrived, not leaving the porch, not wanting to disturb the baby at his feet. Bella stepped down from the carriage holding Mary, who was now one year old. Stewart followed and lifted David to the ground, Annie and James followed. The children greeted Janey and Maggie and remained with them in the yard. Thomas offered his seat to Bella.

"Well what brings you two here?" Thomas asked.

"We came to see how you are getting on, and to see the children," Bella returned.

"What Bella means, is that we came to see if you have come to a decision," Stewart corrected.

"Oh Stewart, you didn't have to tell him that," Bella chided. "Don't listen to him Thomas, we came to see you, and nothing more. It is true we are curious, but we know you will tell us in your own time."

"Well, truth be told I am just as curious," Thomas said. "I have not come to a decision, and quite frankly I don't know what to do...It is the damnedest thing. I can't seem to make up my mind. I suppose what concerns me the most, is that I am actually considering it, that is, I might actually go through with it. I just don't know. What do you think I should do?"

"Well, Thomas, if you must know..." Bella tried to offer an opinion, but Stewart interrupted.

"What Bella was about to say, is that as your friends, we don't really think we should steer you one way or the other. This has to be your decision. And whatever you decide, you can always count on us to support you and the children."

"I was just going to suggest, that it is not all that difficult a situation. Ann is a perfectly amiable young woman, and I am sure she would accommodate your wishes, not wanting to put you in an uncomfortable position. I'm sure if you married her she would do right by you and your children, regardless of the conditions."

"Sounds a little like you're in favor of it, Bella," Thomas said.

"I'm not saying one way or the other, like Stewart said, we will support you no matter what." She was trying to be diplomatic, but Thomas wasn't sure her heart was in it.

"What do you think Alice would have said, I mean after all, she hasn't even been gone two months, and the two of you were best friends?" He asked.

"That's just it, Thomas, I was her best friend, and perhaps I knew her best. As much as she loved you, and you her, she wouldn't have wanted you to continue to pine for her after she had gone. It was not her way. She would be content with knowing you did what you believed was right in your heart.

She trusted you. It's not about what she would think, the decision is yours, and she would tell you so, if she were here now. Whichever decision you come to, you won't be dishonoring her memory, as long as you do it honestly."

Thomas knew Bella was right. His decision had nothing to do with Alice, she would have understood. This decision was about his future and future of his children. He couldn't make it about anything else. "And what about you Stewart, you mean to tell me that you have no opinion about this matter," he said to his friend.

"Oh I have opinions, but I'm afraid I can't offer them. We have been friends for a good many years, and we have often relied on one another's advice, but I can't risk you making this decision just because of my counsel. Our friendship is too important to me. I trust your judgment and whatever you decide I will stand behind you, regardless of my opinions." Stewart was not going to yield in this.

"You're right, you both are. It's my decision to make, and if Alice were here, she would say the same without any judgment. It falls on me, but as of this moment I am still undecided."

"Don't worry, Thomas," Bella said softly. "When the time comes, you'll do the right thing."

*****

Early the next day, Thomas rose and set out for Belle Isle. It was a beautiful morning, the air was fresh and the larks were singing. It was if all was right in the world, and yet Thomas felt this heavy burden weighing him down as he rode toward his destination. As he came within view of the castle he stopped momentarily, admiring the setting. It was a grand place, nestled amongst the trees, a beautiful garden, full of bloom sat in the foreground. It wasn't difficult to see why Ann loved it so and why she would do almost anything to keep it.

Jones met Thomas at the door and showed him to the drawing room, where both Lady Mary and Miss Hardinge were seated.

"Welcome Thomas, we are glad that you have come, and within the time appointed. We trust you have come to tell us your decision," Lady Mary took the lead, even though she was not exactly the host.

"Thank you, Lady Mary, yes I have come to tell you my decision, but before I do, I wonder if you would allow me the privilege of speaking to Miss Hardinge alone for a moment. I'm sure you can understand that words must be said between us, for this decision concerns the two of us more than any other."

"Why of course, Thomas, I completely understand," Lady Mary said.

"If I might suggest," Ann said, "it's a beautiful day, perhaps you would like to take a turn in the garden?"

"That would be fine, thank you," Thomas replied. "If you will please excuse us, Lady Mary."

Thomas and Ann stepped through the glass doors leading out onto a veranda that opened into the garden. Ann led the way, walking just in front, not exactly sure what the etiquette was.

"Before we go any further, I must apologize to you," Ann said. "I know that this entire proposal was a bit presumptuous and placed you in a most awkward of positions. I find it somewhat unfair that you should be forced to make such a decision in so short a time, but Lady Mary was insistent. Either the decision must be to move forward with a wedding, or we must find another course of action."

"Please be at peace, Miss Hardinge, I understand the circumstances fully and if I have been inconvenienced, it is not been of your doing and I do not hold you responsible. Quite the opposite, I find that you have behaved most respectfully and with proper decorum and grace. If someone should apologize, it should be me, for it was I who first tried to deceive you."

"I have already accepted your apology in this matter, and I think it would be appropriate for you to call me Ann, since a proposal of marriage has passed between us."

"You're quite right, Ann, I'm sorry. Before I announce my decision, there was something that still bothered me. If it's not too forward, I want to know your heart in this matter. It still seems an unfortunate set of circumstances that so promising a young woman would have to resort to committing to a marriage that would be, let's say, distant and superficial. Certainly, someone like yourself would have dreams of a romantic inclination. Would you or could you be fully content in this arrangement?"

"I think you will find my contentment doesn't come from feelings of romance as much as the reasonableness of my circumstance by comparison. Although we only met the one time, I learned of you for the first time from your wife. What I now know is that you are a man of courage and of integrity. You are kind and loving to your family and treat everyone with fairness and justice. If I don't know you well enough to love you, I do respect you and this is has much as I can hope for in any prospect.

Can I be content in living my life with a man who I respect? I think it is easy for me to answer, yes, since this is much more than I had previously hoped. What is more, if you agree to this proposal, it means you will trust me to be a mother to your children, and I consider this both a blessing and a complement that I will endeavor to live up to. As far as romantic inclination, I surely have dreams like any young woman, I will not deny it. However, I have remained reserved, not wanting to give in to the inclinations of the heart. I have no expectations and of course it would be unreasonable to think that you would be able to give your heart to another, so soon after the passing of your dear Alice. Don't forget, I saw the two of you together, and I observed the depth of the love you had for each other. I must admit I admired you both for it. I could never give my heart to a man with no hope of his love in return. I will not expect more from you, than you can give, this I promise."

Thomas hardly knew what to say. Ann was a strange girl, strange in the way that she could keep her emotions buried so deep. He could sense that she had depth of feeling, but she kept it hidden. She was so calm in her speech, with no hint of how she really felt. Everything was carefully thought out, but not always convincing, as if she was holding something back. He would prefer that she let it out, to say everything, but he knew it was not her way. He liked what she said about respecting him. He respected her as well. They were both placed in an impossible predicament, and she was handling it with as much grace and dignity has could be expected. He had always known what his choice would be, but now he was confident that it was the right thing to do.

"Ann, thank you for being so candid, it would do no good that we should start by being dishonest with one another. I have come to my decision, and I think you have already guessed. I will agree to this marriage, but I must ask you to consider my conditions. First, we will settle on a date, not less than three months from today. I think that Lady Mary will agree to this. During this period of engagement, I will make regular visits to Belle Isle to make calls on you, sometimes alone, at other times with my children. This is solely for us to get to know each other, and for my children to have the opportunity to know you as well. Secondly and most importantly I ask that you continue to be honest with me. If at any time during this period of time you come to a place where you can't continue in this proposal that you will acknowledge it to me at once, without any regard to the opinions of Lady Mary or concern for her husband. This I must insist upon. If we are to marry, it will be because we have decided it and none other. If this inconveniences others, so be it. Thirdly, if my children are unable to accept this set of circumstances, then we shall not marry. Their happiness will come before my own and therefore before any others."

Anne didn't hesitate in response, "I accept all of these conditions, they are most reasonable, and I will suggest one other. If at any time you change your mind within the next three months, you will tell me so, and the proposal will be dissolved without question and without ill will. I promise."

"Well, it is settled then," Thomas said. "Shall we return and give Lady Mary the news?"

"Yes we shall. Thank you, Thomas." As Ann said this, Thomas noticed something in the way she looked at him, something in her eyes. It was sincerity, or perhaps a hint of emotion.

*****

The wedding date was set for October 25th, at Belle Isle. Lady Mary had consented to all conditions of the engagement, having little choice. It was decided that the Earl would be told that Ann and her grandmother had adopted the children of a dear friend who had died in childbirth and who's husband had tragically died at Waterloo. It seemed a fitting half-truth given the circumstance.

It was difficult at first for Thomas to explain to the children that he would marry again, so soon. Surprisingly, James was more than helpful in calming the fears of his siblings, having been part of the original conspiracy and understanding the conditions of the arranged marriage. This support was more than Thomas could have hoped for.

Two weeks after the agreement between Thomas and Ann, the entire Rea family was invited to be guests at Belle Isle. Margaret attended as well, serving as nanny for the children. Ann was delighted to see the children, being especially attentive to the little ones, showing them the nursery and introducing them to some of her childhood toys. James, Willie and Thomas Jr. found themselves a little out their element until Ann suggested they make a tour of the stables. The groom helped them to each saddle a horse of their choosing and they spent the remainder of the day riding.

The next morning they went for a picnic down by the lough. The boys spent the day fishing, while the girls picked wild flowers and made wreaths. Thomas sat with his back against an old willow tree, watching as his children played in the sun. It was a peaceful place, Belle Isle, different than their home on the farm. Here time seemed to stand still. He felt at ease, and at rest.

The children had warmed to Ann, she was more than comfortable with them and he found himself admiring her for the effort she made with them. She had an easy way about her, a pleasantness that was natural, not put on. They were from different worlds, but it was as if she would be comfortable in either. There was no pretense with her, she saw him and his children as her equals, with no thought of distinction of class or rank. The children enjoyed spending time with her, especially Janey and Maggie. Belle Isle had clearly made a big impression on everyone.

A week before the wedding, Bella made a visit to Belle Isle. She found Ann sitting alone in the garden. When she approached, Ann noticed her coming and turn and looked away. Bella greeted her, "Hello Ann, am I intruding."

"No, I have just been spending some time alone, thinking," as Ann turned to face her, Bella could see tears in her eyes.

"Why Ann, you've been crying. Whatever is the matter? What has happened?" Bella asked, empathy in her voice.

"Oh nothing, I'm just being silly really. It's nothing. I can't imagine why I'm being so emotional." She tried to smile, but her heart was not in it.

Bella sat down next to Ann, "Now come on Ann, we are friends, you can tell me. What is bothering you? Is it the wedding?"

"No, not exactly. It's just that…well, I hardly know where to begin…It's just that I have lied to Thomas and I don't know what to do." Ann began to cry all over again.

"Lied? What do you mean? How have you lied? What did you say?" Bella was confused.

"When we first agreed to marry, that is, when he agreed to the wedding, I assured him that I had no expectations, that this was a marriage of convenience only, beneficial to both parties and that he should not feel any obligation. And now…and now," between sobs, "I have found that I have fallen in love with him…" more sobs. "And I don't know what to do. It's not fair, not fair for him. I know that he can't love me as I do him, not when Alice has only been gone these four months. And yet I love him…It's horrible, Bella, to love someone, when you know they cannot love you back. Oh, what am I to do."

"Tell him, Ann. You must tell him. You don't know that he can't love you as you hope. It's true that his love for Alice was deep and true, but it does not mean that he cannot love another. Alice is gone and she would not hold him to it. It might be too soon, but it might not, you will never know until you tell him."

"But, what if he can't love me back? To tell him and to find he does not love me, I would rather die. How could I live with him day in and day out, loving him, but not being loved in return, and what's worse, knowing that he knows, and that he would pity me for it."

Bella paused before responding. She put her arm around Ann and held her close. "Ann this is the way things are. We love and we hope to be loved. Each time it is a gamble, but unless you are willing to let your heart go, you will never know what love is. Alice and Thomas took this risk, as did Stewart and I. You must tell him, what happens after that is not in your control. If in the end you cannot marry. Then so be it. Marriage should never be a matter of convenience, regardless of circumstance. It must be a shared life, a life of love, of trust and of covenant. Anything less is a travesty…Ann, I knew Alice my whole life, Thomas too. When she died, it was like losing a part of myself, and knowing her the way I do, she would want us to go forward without her. She would not want Thomas to remain alone. I think she would be pleased that he has found someone like you and I think you would be happy for you as well. Now, no more of this crying. You must pick yourself up, and go see him. Go tell him how you feel."

The next morning, Thomas was gathered with his children at breakfast. He was slowly growing accustomed to the routine of being both father and mother. Margaret would still check in from time to time to lend a hand, as well as Alice's parents, and John and Mary Trimble, Alice's sister and brother-in-law. Just as everyone was sitting down at the table, James came in from having tended to the animals. "Father, I think we have a visitor. There is someone standing down by the old oak tree, I think it might be Miss Hardinge. What is she doing here, and why hasn't she come up to the house?"

Thomas looked out the front window. James was right, it was Ann. "You take care of your brothers and sisters, James, I will be back in a moment."

Ann stood looking down at the cross where Alice was buried. She had admired Alice. It was difficult to imagine her gone. She had been so full of life. "What do you think I should do, Alice? ...If only you **could** speak to me, to let me know that all is right."

"Hello, Ann," Thomas said, trying not to startle her. "What are you doing here? Is there something wrong?"

"No, not wrong exactly..." Ann was trying to find the words. "I wanted to see you. I've never been here before. I had to ask for directions in the village. When I saw the cross, it just sort of beckoned me. I don't know why I am here exactly...I just had to talk to you, before the wedding."

"What's the matter?" Thomas was trying not to press. He could tell that Ann was anxious. "Are you having second thoughts? You have always been candid with me. It's alright, whatever it is you need to say. I will understand."

The Colonel

"Not second thoughts, exactly...You see, the problem is...I don't think I have been totally honest with you, and I want to make it right. If we are going to go forward in this, no matter what happens, I must at least be honest with you," she was still fumbling for the words.

"What do you mean? In what way have you not been honest with me?"

"I know that you think I have been very reasonable, and that I have made no demands on you...you know expectations of romance."

"Yes, you have been quite reasonable, and quite fair. Beyond that you have been very kind, and quite pleasant to both me and the children, we could expect no more. Why has something changed?"

"Yes, it has. Changed in way that I never expected or could have imagined...I, well,.... I have fallen in love with you. I know that I said that I wouldn't, and that I had no expectation of romance, especially given that your loss was so recent. I didn't plan on falling in love with you. I didn't even think it possible. I was perfectly content with an amiable relationship built on respect and kindness. It served a good purpose. I didn't think I needed anything else. It was more than I had hoped for. And then all of a sudden, I don't know exactly when, I found myself falling in love with you. And now I'm afraid, for the first time, really afraid. I'm afraid that you won't love me back. What I mean is, you can't love me back. It's not possible, is it? Could you love me?"

"So you think you have been dishonest with me, and now you want to make it right. You think that if I can't love you, then you can't marry me, is that it?"

"Yes, I made you a promise and I am bound to it. I told you that there would be no expectations. You have been a perfect gentleman, and I have put you in a terrible predicament, asking you impersonate another, just for the sake of saving my Belle Isle. And now I no longer care about Belle Isle. I would give it all up, if only I knew that you loved me. I would come live with

284

you here, if only you would ask me to. Only, please tell me now, don't let me suffer any longer not knowing. If you love me or even if you think you could learn to love me, tell me now, but do not tarry, and do not play with my affections, if you cannot love me, then say it now and I will turn and leave and there will be no more talk of a wedding. For I cannot bear the thought of living with you daily and loving you-for I will not be able to help myself-and not knowing your love in return. Don't ask me to do this?"

"My dear Ann," Thomas said. "From the start, this entire plan was fraught with pitfalls, not the least of these being the complete lack of consideration given to romance. It was not fair to you, not really. I can only think of one way to remedy the situation. I think it is time for us to start afresh, to begin anew."

Thomas knelt down on one knee and took Ann by the hand. "Ann, will you do me the honor of becoming my wife. I promise to love and cherish you all of my days."

"But can you love me?" she replied, tears forming at the edge of her eyes. "Do you love me?"

"Yes, Ann, I do love you, and have for some time now. I'm not sure when I knew this, but it's true, I know it now."

"And Alice?" Ann said, still in disbelief.

Thomas turned and looked at Alice's grave, his hand still holding Anne's. "I loved Alice with all by heart and soul. She was life itself to me. I shall never forget her, but her memory will not come between us. You will have all of my heart, and nothing less. It does not mean that I loved Alice less, she would understand this, and I think in time you will understand it as well. What is more, I think that she would be pleased to know that you were caring for me and for our children. She loved you, she told me so herself."

"Then yes, I will marry you."

Thomas stood to his feet and they embraced, and kissed for the first time.

"As for Belle Isle," he said, still holding Ann in his arms. "I will not make you give it up. I know how much you love it. It will

285

be an adjustment, one I think the children will adapt to much quicker than I, but it's not without its merit, and I am sure you will help me find my way."

"Thank you, it is my home, and I will endeavor to make it yours, but it is no longer the object of my affection."

"I think we have tarried here long enough," he said, brushing the tears from Ann's cheeks with his hand. "I believe the children will be wondering what has become of us. Come, shall we join them for breakfast."

As they walked hand in hand, Ann was overwhelmed with emotion. Never in her whole life had she known such joy.

The End

If you enjoyed The Colonel, then read the following excerpt from the sequel, coming soon.

Ontario
Sequel to *The Colonel*

Most of the guests had gone, only Stewart and Bella remained in the library with Thomas and Ann. The children had gone to bed.

"Well it's done," Stewart said.

"Really, Stewart, sometimes you say the strangest things," Bella responded. "You make it sound as if the wedding were an ordeal, how romantic of you."

"I think he was referring to the deception of the Earl," Thomas suggested.

"Exactly," Stewart affirmed. "I don't think the old guy had any idea what was happening."

"I don't think you should make light of it, Stewart," Thomas said. "As much as Lady Mary thought it was the right thing to do, I still feel a little guilty about the whole thing."

"What, you're feeling guilty about marrying me?" Ann chided. "I think you should have said something before now."

"That's not exactly what I meant. It's just that I would have liked to use my own name."

"Well regardless of what name you used, I am happy for the both of you," Bella said.

"Here, here," Stewart raised his glass, "to the bride and groom."

"To the bride and groom," Bella said in kind.

"To friends," Thomas returned.

"To friends," they all toasted together.

For the first time in her life, Ann felt genuinely contented, almost blissful. She had only known a life of privilege, but it was not a life of her own choosing. There had always been the expectation of how she would live, determined by the choices of others, not her own. She had been promised in marriage to Robert Crichton, before she was even old enough to understand what had happened. He was not a man of her choosing, but when she came of age, she consented, not because she was agreeable to the arrangement, but because she knew nothing else. It was impossible for her to imagine any other life.

She met her intended for the first time when she was only sixteen. She was only a girl, and he was man. At first, she admired him, he seemed so debonair, but this lasted only a short time. It didn't take long for her to realize that he was troubled and self-absorbed. He was bitter and resentful of his father and of his heritage. It was clear that he didn't want to marry her, but would do so only to insure his father's favor, and to secure his inheritance. She knew that he would never love her and she had resigned herself to knowing that their marriage would be empty. It wasn't a strange idea to her, she had known others who had entered into marriage out of convenience, and she had been willing to make the best of it.

She could hardly believe her eyes when she saw Thomas in the office of Colonel Crichton, wearing his uniform no less. She had not let on initially, because she couldn't imagine the circumstances which would have prompted such a deception. When the truth was finally revealed to her, that fateful afternoon when she had invited the three friends to Belle Isle, instead of being angry, she found herself relieved. For the first time, she could imagine a life of her own choosing, one that didn't include the rogue she had been promised to. She had always admired both Thomas and Alice, and although at the time she could not have imagined that he could love her, she saw in Thomas the prospects of a husband who would at least respect her and treat her with kindness, it was his way. It was curious, her relationship with the three individuals who sat before her. In station, she was their superior, and yet, she had never felt their equals. This was in part, because they were older and removed from her by ten years, but it was also because of their heart and character. Thomas and Stewart were the sons of freeholders, not peasants exactly, but not gentleman in the strictest sense of the word. However, she saw in them strength of character and integrity that made them more gentlemen than anyone she had ever known. She was blessed to know them, and found herself aspiring to measure up to them.

Bella was like no one else she had ever known. She was full of compassion and grace. Although born of the privileged class, she considered everyone her equal, showing kindness and respect to all regardless of station. Ann admired this quality in Bella and esteemed her highly. She was grateful that Bella had accepted her as a friend from the start, and she wanted to be deserving of this friendship.

She loved Thomas, more than she could express in words. He was her savior, she knew that now. Had she been bound to a life with Robert Crichton, it would have destroyed her in the end. She needed Thomas. She needed to be loved and to love. Tears began to well up in her eyes as she realized her good fortune, a fortune that had come as a result of the tragic loss of Alice. How strange it was the workings of the hand of God. Why was it that she now found herself in this place? What could she have done, to deserve such favor in His eyes? Who could understand it? She could not.

Thomas had been reminiscing with Stewart and Bella when he noticed that Ann had grown quiet. He could see the tears gathering at the edges of her eyes. One let loose, and trickled gently down her cheek. "What's this? Ann, are you crying? What is wrong? Are you unhappy?"

"No, Thomas, not unhappy. These are not tears of sorrow, but tears of joy. Today, you have made me the happiest of women." Ann then put her arms around Thomas' neck and they kissed.

"Bella, I think that is our cue to retire. It is time we leave these two alone," Stewart said. The two of them stood.

"I'm sorry, you two, I didn't mean to drive you away." Ann apologized.

"Nonsense, Ann, we know when we aren't wanted," Bella said. "We are going to say are goodnight's now."

The friends parted. Ann looked back at Thomas, "Do you really love me Thomas?"

"Yes, I really love you Ann," Thomas replied and they kissed once more.

*****

(1817)

It was an adjustment for Thomas as the new master of Belle Isle. He was not accustomed to living a life of leisure. He barely knew what to do with himself. If he had not been preoccupied with his children, he may have grown discontented in a very short time.

James had grown independent and often remained to himself. His short stint in the army had changed him. He now had a quiet maturity, lending a hand to his stepmother when needed, spending long hours reading and studying, making improvements to his limited education. He no longer dreamed of being a soldier, the events of Waterloo had destroyed any romantic aspirations he felt about war.

Willie and Thomas Junior enjoyed spending time with their father. Thomas would take them hunting or fishing, or they would just go to the stables where he would show them how to repair the tack, or how to care for the horses. Ann would often find him working the bellows and shaping a new shoe for one of the horses, while the boys looked on. It seemed, he couldn't leave his old life as a smithy entirely behind.

Ann was fond of Janey and Maggie, and it wasn't long before they returned this affection. They were old enough to remember their mother, but not so old that they would hold on to her memory and resist the attentions of their new stepmother. Ann showered them with love and affection and they flourished in her care.

Ann also gave plenty of attention to the two youngest boys as well, Isaac and John, although she had plenty of help

290

from their nanny in caring for them. All in all, it wasn't long before they were all comfortable in their new home. It took some prodding to get the children to remember that they were now the adopted children of Robert and Ann Crichton. Of course, when they made the mistake of using their actual surname of Rea, strangers would attribute to it a child's absentmindedness, not thinking there was anything to it. It was actually more difficult for Ann to remember to refer to Thomas as Robert in public, since she always called him Thomas at home.

Thomas grew more and more uncomfortable with the deception. It wasn't in his nature to lie, and it continued to bother him that he was pretending to be something he was not. He kept hoping that the Earl of Erne would somehow stumble upon the truth, regardless of what the outcome would be. He would be willing to give up Belle Isle entirely just to regain his identity, but he could not force the issue, he could not and would not hurt Ann in this way.

The real Robert Crichton had completely disappeared. There was no indication that he was anywhere in Ireland or England. He had completely given up his old life, and there was nothing to suggest that he would every return to claim it. For all they knew, he could be dead. It was likely he had fled to the colonies, North America, the West Indies, or perhaps even Australia. As time passed, it became more evident, that he was unlikely to ever return.

In December, Ann gave birth to her first child, a girl. Thomas held the baby close against his chest as he sat on Anne's bed, "She is a beautiful little girl, Ann," he said. "I think she has your eyes. What do you think we should name her?"

"I was thinking...would it be alright if we named her Alice," Ann said, a slightly nervous smile across her lips.

"Of course, that's perfect. Thank you. I think Alice is a just perfect," he looked down at his new baby girl. "What do you think? Do you like the name Alice?" He was not really expecting any kind of response, for she was asleep.

Alice Rea, he thought to himself, not Alice Crichton. Reverend Howard would perform the christening and he would get it right. Still, it bothered him that he had brought another child into the world, and this time under false pretenses. He was her father, and Ann was her mother, but she had arrived in a world in which her father had taken another man's name. It had now been more than a year, and each and every day, he regretted having ever agreed to continue the deception. He was not sorry that he had stepped in to lead the Inniskillings at Waterloo and he was certainly not sorry for having married Ann. But, it should have ended there. To continue in this lie, just for the purposes of preserving a father's faith in his son, a son who clearly was not deserving of such faith, was a foolish endeavor. It was vanity, nothing more.

It couldn't continue. He knew that in his heart. He could not stand before his children, knowing that he had sacrificed his integrity. He could not have little Alice grow up believing he was a liar. It would have to end.

Two weeks later, it was time for Alice to be christened. Not surprisingly, Lady Crichton arrived at Belle Isle to pay her respects. Thomas saw it as an opportunity to make things right. That evening he found her sitting alone in the library. "Lady Mary, may I have a word," he said politely, but with a serious tone.

"Why, of course, Thomas. What is it? What can I do for you?" She was always amiable.

"Well, I suppose, I wanted to talk to you about the Earl. Well indirectly, anyway," he was finding it difficult to know how to begin.

"Don't you mean Robert? Or should I say, don't you mean you. Have you come to speak to me about our secret?"

"Yes...but how did you know?" Thomas was becoming anxious. He needed to get it off his chest. Now that he was so close, he found it unbearable to endure it another minute. He wanted so much to leave the lies behind and to become himself once more. He was just about to shout it.

"It's not surprising. I rather wondered how long it would be before, you came to me. You want to stop the deception, to allow the truth of who you are to come out? Is that it?"

"Yes, I thought I could do it, maintain the lie and all, but now I find I cannot. I cannot allow my children to grow up knowing their father has pretended to be something he is not. I am asking your permission to stop this deception, once and for all."

"Do you need my permission?"

"Perhaps not, but I am asking just the same. I know of your affection for the Earl and your desire to keep him from the pain of knowing his son is a scoundrel, but I wonder if you have fully calculated the cost."

"You mean the cost to your family."

"Well, yes, but maybe to yours as well. Is it right, regardless of your motives, for you to withhold the truth from your husband? Surely, a lie is still a lie, regardless of how pure the motive. Is it right for you to keep your husband in the dark about the criminal actions of his son? Even if he is so near the grave that even now one foot stands alone in the realm of this life, is it the right thing for you to lie to a man whom you love? Don't you owe him the truth, regardless of how painful?

Lady Mary paused before answering. "I cannot defend my actions against such argument. I would be lying to you, if I didn't admit to having these same feelings these past several months. So you believe I should tell him the truth?"

"I believe he deserves the truth. He is an honorable man, and expects the same from those closest to him, including you. He is much stronger that you realize. He has met with disappointment in the past, no doubt even disappointment brought about by the one in question. He has dealt with each of these moments with grace and dignity. There is nothing to suggest he will not do the same this time. It dishonors the man to suggest that he is too vain to accept the truth. I'm not telling you what to do, but I am pleading for myself, for Ann and for my children, to release me from this promise."

"It might mean losing Belle Isle. As Thomas Rea, you have no right to it. What does Ann think?"

"I will speak to her first, but I believe she will agree with me. She would give up Belle Isle, if she needs to."

"What about Colonel Fremantle? Would he agree to this?"

"I can't be sure." Thomas knew that this was a potential stumbling block.

"Then I will tell you what I will do. If you go to Fremantle and if he releases you from your promise, then I shall follow and do the same. Go to London, seek him out, and when you return, if the Colonel agrees, I will tell the Earl the truth."

About the Author

Michael Rea was born in Eugene, Oregon and spent his entire youth living in the Pacific Northwest, where he enjoyed many moments camping, hiking and fishing in the Cascade Mountains of Washington and Oregon. He attended Westmont College in Santa Barbara, CA where he earned a B.A. in Chemistry and upon graduation, enrolled in a graduate program in Chemistry at the University of Illinois. Although expecting to complete his Ph.D. and begin a career as a research scientist, he unexpectedly fell in love with teaching, completed a M.S. in Teaching Chemistry and embarked on a career in secondary education.

Aside from his love for science, and his newly discovered passion for writing, Michael is also an artist, specializing in landscape and wildlife paintings in oil. He and his wife, Janet, love to travel and they make an effort to visit at least one national park every summer. These trips have greatly contributed many of the subjects for his paintings, while at the same time providing him with a time to get away to write. Together, he and his wife share a love for literature. A list of his favorite authors suggests a diverse influence on his writing: Isaac Asimov, C.S. Lewis, J.R.R Tolkien, Sir Walter Scott, Alexander Dumas and Charles Dickens.

With over thirty years of experience in education, he has taught courses in all levels of mathematics and science, art, philosophy and religious studies. Science and the arts don't always mix well, but Michael's proficiency in both makes for an interesting combination, as does his eclectic background in coaching, teaching, and high school administration. He currently divides his time between his love of teaching chemistry and physics to his students and his love of oil painting and writing.

Today, Michael and his wife live in Temecula, CA. They have three children and three grandchildren.

The Colonel

www.ingramcontent.com/pod-product-compliance
Lightning Source LLC
Chambersburg PA
CBHW070309260626
47160CB00003B/783